LI QUID GEOMETRY

A NOVEL BY

CYNTHIA LASKY

S·T·A·R·PUDDING·PRESS

VERMONT CROSSROADS PRESS

Portions of this work have appeared in *Mulch* and *Lillabulero*. The author wishes to thank Princeton University Press for permission to reprint excerpts from *The I Ching or Book of Changes*. The Richard Wilhelm translation rendered into English by Cary F. Baynes. Bollingen Series XIX. Copyright © 1950, © 1967 by Princeton University Press. Copyright © renewed 1977 by Princeton University Press.

Printed in the United States of America

ISBN 0-915248-26-3 (paper)
    0-915248-28-X (cloth)

Library of Congress Catalog Number: 79-64250

Cover photographs by Cynthia Lasky and Marsha E. Gold

for m.e.g. and d.b., who both lived through it

ACKNOWLEDGMENTS

This book exists outside my study only by the grace and hard work of several people: Carolyn Stoloff, who started it all; Carolyn Bilderback, who helped; Marsha Eva Gold, who designed the book; Sara E. Pyle, who edited; Jo Moskowitz, who proofread; Stan Moskowitz, who more than helped with paste-up; and Paul Pines, who arranged distribution. To them and to the others who contributed in many different ways, my love and deep gratitude.

I would like to express my special thanks to the Wurlitzer Foundation of Taos, New Mexico, for extending to me the two residence grants during which a large part of the book was written, and to Henry A. Sauerwein, Jr., its director, for his unfailing helpfulness and kindness.

Most of the journal entries and the poem on page 88 were written by Marsha Eva Gold who with great generosity allowed me to select and use portions of her notebooks.

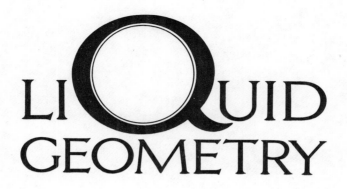

prologue
June, 1969

The gypsy moth is a native of eastern Asia. It was introduced into Massachusetts in 1869 by an amateur entymologist who was doing research on silkworms. Through his carelessness, it escaped and became a pest in the forests of the entire East Coast area.

In the absence of natural predators, the moth has reproduced enormously. The eggs live through the winter, then hatch in late spring. The larvae, small black-and-orange caterpillars, feed on the leaves of deciduous woods. They prefer oak and birch, but will also attack maple, ash, beech, and even, occasionally, pine.

In midsummer, metamorphosis occurs. White-winged moths emerge, leaving their hard, dark, scaly cases clustered in the hollows of trees.

Whole forests in New England, New York, Pennsylvania and New Jersey have been defoliated by gypsy moth larvae. If one region is infested for more than three years, the trees die. Before that, however, measures are usually taken to drive the moth from the area. It then migrates to other regions; but always returns, in time.

maggie
carried a fur purse that summer. then she slept twenty hours a day. sometimes she woke when the sheets were very hot, very creased, and, naked amid the cracker crumbs, knew she'd eaten some.

mama would be pleased, she thought, smiling inside herself; and, after a few brushes with her palm, again passed out.

maggie—marguerite starski, but always and indelibly lower case—: all shades of gold, rust, copper threads weave the tapestry through which she stumbles, square-cut eyes closed, victim of the mythic; her ribs show.

hand between her legs, her own wet warmth half-conscious pleasure muffled peak—drop. she pulled the knees up, small cropped head fell forward. let the hand nestle.

maggie are you there are you alive maggie where are you?
hm. should. answer her, her, i should
maggie? will you open the door? at least let me—
n-no.

there had been yellow pills, and a joint, fifty cigarettes smoked in dim five-minute wakeups for that purpose since this morning. now, she gulped the rest of the muscatel and staggered into the kitchen.

it. . .reeled.

on the ledge, three antique bottles sparkled, deep green and amber. the colors danced dissolved became a pulsing funnel then which merged with the edges of her-self, that is, the edges of a panic that had become almost synonymous with: maggie.

maggie. maggie.

small marble and crystal eggs there. tall mottled feathers. virgil i never asked for, but, a rabbit? surely i have the right to one white rabbit. and, seizing that tremulous coherence, she clamped herself into a fist for a minute and got up onto the ledge and out through the window.

five stories down, through black iron bars, the street loomed. maggie crouched in a corner, in brawling sunlight. uncoagulated fragments came crawling. they were there, they were gone, in a shudder of radiant dread that filled her skull with the force of a soft explosion; pressed against her eyes, ears, nostrils; sealed up every pore. then the voices started.

little saw-toothed voices, wheels cutting through the fog. they made sounds that were not quite words, and bled. they were predictable and implacable. once she had danced for them. she gripped the bars as hard as she could and screamed SHUTUP-SHUTUP until her chest rattled and ripped into one of those spasms of coughing she always thought would be endless.

huddled on flaking iron, knees up; humble in the pitch of need that yapped like a hound, maggie wrapped thin arms around a small, racked frame; as though to keep her lungs from bursting through their envelope of skin and spilling down through the air, onto the pavement, SPLAT on the heads of passersby. . . .

can you *see* their expressions (she thought to her-self; in a flipness of tone that approximated the impulse to slip through the bars and plummet to a death she didn't believe in) as the lungs of maggie starski spill like hot bloody birdshit right down on them? and would have giggled had she not been strangling. but:

the coughing began to subside. the voices were fading. the flipness, potentially lethal, was also her passport to momentary respite; and the world, it turned out again, was bright and very noisy—an assault to which she responded with almost-routine panic. now she could put a name, a frame, to: someone below playing bach and simultaneously howling; a naked blackbearded man on a roof; a blonde in tight pants, white cat slung across her shoulder; a painted pelican named richard passing forgodsake now of all times with his goddamn camera under her fire escape; shouting and pounding.

maggie listen i'll call the police if you don't—

they were so worried. they called each other up, she knew, she could see them, each on her end of the line: dark and silver rebecca, and long, blonde susan.

> *have you heard from maggie,* they'd say.
> > *when did you talk to maggie?*
> > *is she still not answering the phone, do you think she*
> > > *would*
> > *reading all the time now is that like maggie?*
> > *how she really, do you think*
> > *did she seem....*

and besides, there are better ways, maggie mused; dreamily watching, with pain that was almost pity, her ex-lover snap a picture of an old man sprawled on the pavement near the park, then move away; even a razor blade....

a current of air moved, and she cringed, shivering in the hot june day, sniffing, wondering, how can there be a scent of lemon blossoms on a breeze on avenue b?

maggiemaggiemaggiemaggie—

all right. i give up. okay.
and scrambled in the window over the ledge past the bottles not even brushing the eggs the feathers across the kitchen and opened the door just as susan was turning away.

*

> *susan*
said, "no. maggie's not here, who's this?"

7

the thoughtful light-blue eyes, usually averted (when a door opened to susan she would be looking over her shoulder; in photos —even as a child surrounded by buoyant blond brothers and cousins, a lawnful of them, all beaming straight into the camera— susan would always be caught at the exact moment the shutter clicked, gazing vaguely off somewhere to the side and downward), now fixed on

maggie: across the kitchen on the floor shivering propped against the stove tiny pale with eyes like holes blasted into her skull and hair like a copper cowl.

"yes hello richard, this is susan. susan mather, yes. . . ." the head across the room swiveled, "no. no i don't know when, she's out of town. connecticut. no. yes, i'll tell her. okay, bye," and slammed down the receiver, stood up, stretched the long, muscled body, wrinkled the rabbit nose, and said, "you don't need that guy."

"what's he want?"

"his photos."

"he wants his *photos*? he *has*. . . ."

"he said. he wants to see you, that's all."

"yes. oh, susan, he's so. . . if i could keep contact with. . . his photos are really, you don't know"

"of course i know, i've seen them, i'm not blind. only myopic."

"hey. . . ."

"all right. but he's even crazier than you are. he's dangerous."

"no. crazy yes, dangerous no."

"he is. rebecca thinks so, too. she said he was."

"rebecca has been watching too many owls and drying too many snake skins out there in the wilderness. she's scaring herself to death. it's one of the things she likes to do, you know that. susan. . . ."

"*contorted*, that's it. she said there was something contorted about him."

"oh, richard's too stiff to bend over, let alone contort."

"maggie. . . ."

"well, i'm trying. don't you want me to try?"

8

and susan (vague and solid; a long saxon skull, wispy blond brows but something very fleshy, very mortal) tried to decide if she did; saw her confusion mirrored in a mischievous urchin smile; and felt the edges of her own mouth quiver against her will.

"that's it. *you'll* be all right," maggie said, laughing, thinking that, for a descendant of cotton mather, susan did very well; was, indeed, delightful—rosy as a milkmaid now, the heavy folds of her face transformed and glowing with health-sun-life as she, maggie (wedded to darkness), never would be. and, trembling, felt the laughter change; tears begin to well; the sense of precariousness, of teetering that made her consciousness a path along precipices of hysteria.

"maggie...."

"the goatherd's dead."

"maggie."

"no, i'm okay, i'm okay."

"sure?"

"yes, really."

"okay, then, let's go somewhere."

"where?"

"i'll tell you when we get there."

"i don't know."

"come on. comb your hair and come on."

"susan, i really don't know."

"all right, don't comb your hair, then."

"i mean.....i told rebecca i might come...."

"good. i'll ride to the station with you. *come on.*"

*

"miss starski, hey."

"mmmyes, mrs. latz."

"that young man was here again the skinny englishman. sitting on the stoop, looking for you to come out. i told him he could go on up or go away but

9

sitting around like that you know...."

"yes, mrs. latz, i know."

"you're a nice girl, miss starski, i always said, what you doing with trash like that, huh? mrs. pepper, she complained...."

"mrs. pepper?"

"you know, the blonde woman, hefty, lives across the street. she has a white cat and three kids...."

"o yes, i've seen her. what'd she complain about?"

"well she said...well, people doing it in your apartment, right in front of the window you know, and the kids, but i told her, not you. maybe that guy he copied your key and got in when you weren't there, i wouldn't put it past him to...."

"no, mrs. latz, that was me. on the floor with three guys you mean, right?"

"ha-ha, miss starski, very funny. now when you gonna settle down and get married like your girl friend here?"

"susan? susan's not married. are you, susan?"

"why, i...."

"don't tell me, girls, don't try to fool mrs. latz. all i want is you should be happy. you just tell that skinny guy...."

"all right, mrs. latz, i will. bye bye, now."

"okay, miss starski, take it easy, bye...."

and they stepped out into the hot clashing colors, the riotous smells, of avenue b in june. a thin film of grime dulled it all. summer grime, maggie thought, don't confuse it with cold weather grime. what a connoisseur, my my. and which do you feel is superior? in what sense superior? as it pertains to the eyes, the throat, or perhaps you mean its insulating propensities? yes, indeed—richard-talk. what a chameleon i am, a white sheet, i take on the color of anyone, SPLAT from a bladder of paint and i'm black richard, blue susan, silver rebecca with green edges....

she said, "i hope she's there. i said i'd call first."

"i'll call," susan said, "when you're on the train."

"you really want me to go."

"yes. country. air. food. health, remember? how much do you weigh these days, by the way? around ninety?" susan said, fending a brown hand away without breaking her stride, as though a stray piece of paper had blown up agianst against her.

"i weigh a lot more than ninety."

"you don't look it. there's a bus, come on, run," and they pounded over the curb, up the steps, laughing, laughing, the bus driver grinning, New York faces weary, wry, knowing, as they lurched back and collapsed on the hard, blue-green plastic seats, maggie coughed, choking; susan pounded her back, snarling, "three packs a day, how can, how," as the bus glided by con edison's three tall red-white-and-blue striped smokestacks spitting spume into the sky is our sewer, maggie thought; shaking; watching the smog rise above birds clouds and arch, a soft shell pillowed over the pores of the city, the planet a poisoned chick birth is explosion is fragments shoot out into space where

"it's okay," she gasped. "i don't want i can't"

"here," susan said, "let's get off. you need something to drink."

"no, i'm okay. i'll miss the train if we.... here's union square already, anyhow...."

"where's the bmt?"

"no, not there. that's the lex. i always get mixed up if"

"wait now, is this uptown?"

"yes. but that's"

"but this is"

station change

this is a

station change

hey.

the bmt's this way.

no baby,

that's grand
central.

11

it can't be grand central..

why?

because we're at *times square*!

are we going ar
o
u
n
d
i
n
a

circle

?

w
e
l
l

i don't exactly . . .

hey!

susan?

come here a . ·.·

SUSAN!

no
no
it's this

SU . .

way .

yes, i'm
maggie, i'm over here WHERE???

?

??
?
?

HERE!

here,

?
? ???
?

?

h
e
r
e

.

. .

.

.

ii.

These constants: a reservoir, forest, a house, and the Lower East Side of New York—teeming life forms that loom and then flatten. A bridge painted orange. A bungalow. Roses. A tenement. Animals. Then there's the box of round-headed map tacks I've spilled on my desk, years later, I pick them up and try to pierce fluttering wings, a vain effort to stop them, to make shadows into coordinates. Numbers sweep by and recur—'69, '38, '34, '70— they pulsate then fade then return as, deep in the seams of June, an old man squares a sun with cupped hands; tracing a four-cornered secret

> maggie/knew.

But it is Rebecca
who comes back to seasons as though she and not they have left: spun one cycle, and now—tasting intimate flavors, sounds, smells—she remembers: I live here one fourth of my life. This is also home. . . .

We're not in New York, now. It's sixty-odd miles to Avenue B. This is Westchester—moist woods where little worms dangle, curling, in leaves whirling white by a trail, past a maple they call the devil-god, up, past a gesturing dinosaur, up, up, but just as the water appears the path turns down: the wall of the dam rising, top a long line drawn across the sky, changing with every step. We see it now through the eyes of a woman with dark/silver hair, who woke early, stepped out in the dawn, clear, singing, she thought,
There it is again: life again—and she began to walk.

Always as she approached
the reservoir, there was a sound like a motor; a blue glint. Then she was below the wall. The pressure of water had cracked the stone etched with streaks of ivy. The path curved up, past purple swamp flowers, soft roar of narrow falls, then opened out
She lay on a flat, almost vertical rock.

13

Its roughness scraped her skin. A plane swooped. The hot gold disc climbed a few feet into the sky.

Above the water
a bird, that morning, was almost part of a twig; until it hunched its wings, turned, and then was still again.

in late June
Rebecca
swam nosing around the rock shelf: the world of the reservoir so clear she could watch small bullet-shaped fish in schools. One big green loner swam by, chirping at her. A piece of driftwood looked like a buffalo head: foreshortened skull, snub-snout. Man's voice, child's voice, where are they? Moss spurted out of underwater rocks in delicate, pubic tufts. A caterpillar shimmied through the water. *Buzz-crunch*: something was eating soft wood. They were on the island, too close.

Braced, palms pressed against two trunks, eyes closed
(listen. listen
A tree's skin wrinkles at the armpit, just below the branching out
(*listen*
Warm, dim. The day misting down....

I am thirty-four years old.
I am thirty-four years old.
I am thirty-four years old.

So many times I've seen the trail like this gray like this. That sun turned white, stayed up for half an hour. The forest has cancer. Caterpillars dangle from the trees, suspended, larvae of the gypsy moth, they feed and grow fat. They're on the oak I loved; the devil-god, encrusted; then the young aspens, birches, stripped to rags.

"Why don't you get a gun?" the water inspector said, "if you're gonna trek around here at all hours? There's a wild dog pack around, they're worse than wolves. Get a gun permit, get a little something like this," and patted his own pearl-handled virility; and I, I-Rebecca, laughed, and turned up onto the trail above the stream quick-flashing patches of silver I walked back down through the woods and up the drive to my house, a shambling gingerbread house I'd thought when I saw it first: so different from any other, so lopsided-lovely. Later, I'd built on the big, jutting wood deck, *on stilts*, the workmen had laughed, and where, now, a small figure sat.

"I hitched in from town," she said. "Did Susan call you?"

"She might have. How long have you been here?"

"Oh, I don't know." maggie smiled, stretched: in jeans, a work shirt, the cigarette pointing upwards—a wise, tough, delicate slum kid she looked today; but always those dark, square-cut eyes were ancient. "It's great to be here. Can I take off my shirt?"

"Sure. There's nothing around but wild dogs and the mailman," *Rebecca* said; and lay back; and *maggie* said,

"You should be made love to . . . . . . "

watching the big woman, wanting to touch her. A spray of dark and silver hair mixed with gray paint peeling up from the deck boards. The hazy light shadowed her jutting cheeks, hawk nose, her eyes hidden under translucent lids

    (evergreen forests slope down in fog .   the sea .
chilly tide pools . thin strips of sand . rivers .
falls   the chiseled crags . fir, spruce . .
the small coastal towns . cannon beach . gold beach .
   foam silver . dark green . a northwest landscape
      of: Rebecca: who opened her eyes, then

rringgg . . . rrringg . . .

Through the screen door, maggie saw her kneel down by the phone. She talked. Then she came out and walked down the steps, slowly, slowly, the drive, the little mowed path, and around her grasshoppers were leaping in every direction. Something had happened. A frog squatted near the top step: its amber eyes jutted up, dull gleam bisected by a horizontal slit—it looked

15

drunk. For the fourth day straight the sun was a white splotch through haze. The air seemed composed of fine, white sediment. Something had happened. Rebecca walked down by the pond now the white cat in maggie's lap tensed, the red cat crouched up on the railing, one moment the world was completely still— then the frog sprang leaping down the steps, they scrambled after it, maggie ran indoors she couldn't stand, that jutting deck commanding a view of, all of, she didn't know what but knew, something, while,

Rebecca Stark sat kicking her feet in a pond in Westchester, N. Y.

Kay Stark lay out on a highway, torn almost in three;

Adam Stark muttered, "the only hill in forty miles, the only three cars, the *only*,"

blood cascading down his left leg. His spine was twisted, peculiarly. A man in white put his hands on him. . . .

Adam

is strapped down. Bumping along, he can see the sun, orange splotch turning a deeper and deeper cerise, it's an eye, no, a pupil of fire that glares from behind blue and silver bars opening closing squeezing wringing burning the sirens are screaming

painpainpainpainpain

iii.

The leg isn't too bad. It's as though they move splinters of glass around inside the tendons, but he can take that if he knows when they're going to touch him. She won't let them take off his leg, he knows that. It's in her own interest, after all, she is a version of him. But the back—that is something else. Hell when he lies still, unspeakable when they are turning him. They say he has to be turned at least four times a day.

Some part of him says they are torturers, and he is in their

16

hands, literally, but he can't yet feel frightened or angry. He is submerged. Since they cut down the shots he spends four hours out of each six drowned in pain and heat, somehow July is inside his leg, inside his spine, and the fluid runs out of him, soaking the sheets within ten minutes after they're changed. He lies, passive, clinging to thoughts of the needle that changes him into a lilypad floating along the pain's surface.

His stepmother's head appeared, making a gap in the curtain. For five seconds, she was a flat portrait: sinister Beatrice-head, swathed in stripes.

"No peeking, please," the Thai nurse said. "I'm giving the patient therapy."

"Peeking! Why...."

"Please," the nurse said again.

"What do you mean, telling me...."

"Beatrice, go away. Go aWAY," he yelled.

Her face flickered a moment, then disappeared. The nurse put a cigarette between his lips and lit it for him.

"Don't let anyone tell you you're weak," she said, carefully. "Do you understand? You'll get well. You can do anything you want."

"Okay," he said. "Yes. I know what you're saying. Now, is my wife dead, will you tell me?"

And Adam Stark wants to know: what was your sin, Father? Walter? visited on me—to change your name? leave the Faith? something before that, or after, or some evil on-the-road, were you on that road? You must have been, some time in those years you wandered the West.

I can see you there. But can I be you?

So long ago. Thirty-one years ago. All those men. From up here where my spine is fused to a bent rib of sky, I can see the roads leading west, swarming with men who wear knickers, their cap brims pulled over their eyes. They meet, talk, drink, laugh, argue, hitch, hop the trains headed for towns like Durango, Fort Wayne, Platte, Laramie—names resonating romance, adventure; and it *was* adventure, he told me....

On leisurely Sunday mornings, he'd told them those stories. The West was still there in the thirties, he said; the Space. Capital W, capital S in the way he said those two words: West, Space. They sat looking out of their huge picture window. The bridge glittered, orange paint on a blue page. "Yes, if you go away, you can take that one with you," he'd laughed; sometimes they all laughed, there in that Nob Hill penthouse. But mostly his father talked, happily, seriously, about: knocking on farmhouse doors, getting work out in the fields, riding box cars with fugitives, drunks, hobos, rich kids, and anarchists—everyone did it who wanted to get there or get away.

Near Adam's bed a book waits for him: essays by his father's idol, H. L. Mencken. Adam can't read yet, can't focus. He's doped, they tell him. A breeze blows in here from the river, they tell him. They tell him they'll have to operate several times if he wants his leg.

(His father's cool moist hand, blunt fingers, a strong smell of sweat, *is that mine? his?* a voice telling stories, now Adam's a kid again through a moist beaded screen he sees the hot fields; sees his father work, hurt his back, sees him go to the bonfires out by the tracks, sees him talk, hitch, read, then a man in L. A. said, "You *can* understand, damn it, Starski," and now he has to read his inscription aloud:

"Adam: don't forget I paid 69¢ for this book. Dad."

In Adam's clear moments, this frightens him. All the few letters his father ever had written him had been signed, *yours truly, Walt Stark.*

"Dad, Kay is dead, isn't she."

Bea was talking. His father had disappeared, suddenly. Bea talked talked words running into each other the nurse said and she said and

"If she's not dead, where is she," Adam said very coherently. cluck-twitter. She, whom he'd always called Bea, signed her letters *love, Mom.*

"You're lying," he told her, quite lucidly.

18

"Jews," his stepmother said, "do not lie. Jews have never been criminals, migrants, or drunks. Never."

"Bea."

"Liberals, yes. Social Democrats. In Russia all of the Jews," she said, "were for Kerensky."

He told her that you had to have the red card if you rode the trains in the north, but if they caught you with one in the south they would kill you.

"Because Jews," she said, hardly breaking pace, "don't drink. Of course, an occasion. But Jews," she chanted, "do not get drunk."

He was trying to blink the sweat out of his eyes. The white walls steamed. Her figure swelled, rippled, the air wavered, all their gills pumped away. Sound did not carry. Then someone came in, loomed, a shiny tray, dope peddlar, *jab*—he felt nothing. The walls changed to blue to green veils shifting, billowing. Beatrice, his father, the nurse, were bright, runny stains. As he floated off downstream, one petal, he thought of how they'd indecently married in June. Were they covered with roses, he wondered.

They'd come on a hot, grubby day to the tenement where he and his sister were staying with Jake and Bella. All the windows were open, and soot blowing in from the airshaft, and Becky and him in the bathtub, keeping cool; splashing. They'd come and ripped them away.

They had been so shocked. Then came Uncle Jake Starski, whimsical drunk, once a prodigy, now a hack pianist, and his insane Bella. Highly improbable poultice they were, but they soothed the stunned children. Less than a year: and then they— *not we*, Adam thought flatly—had to be ripped away. We had no chance after that, he thought. We festered.

The stream filled with colorful, cancerous entrails and lobsters and crayfish contorting and mingling one moment they melted the banks sprouted trees and he saw an elf, gnome-face above him, and his sister, too, and he asked, again, and she told him, and everything went away.

19

I.
THE ROSES
(1970: SUMMER)

1.

I once knew a girl in Paris who looked like maggie. One morning I found her sprawled, face down on her bed, still dressed in last night's print silk, and a bunch of red roses stuck into a vase on her dresser: the ten o'clock sun on them.

Outside my window, in dry country, hummingbirds whirr near red hollyhocks. The blossoms are facing away from the house. When the afternoon sun glows through them, I see roses in clusters on high, thornless vines: I see maggie—who never has been to Paris, nor seen earth so cracked as this, sky so huge, sage. Her country exists in a mind, or a city; and she wears interior colors—night-golds; purples.

What can she have to do with my mythical roses?

Stuck in a quicksand of memory always, immersed in past— sometimes I scare myself out of it. Sometimes, just here in the garden, I meet it: the present, the moment, *now*, weeding, *now* sifting loose dirt through my fingers, the odor of marigold sharp in my nostrils, but this time a ghost of my father stands up on the deck: that one visit he made here, last summer, when Adam was finally moved here: a cripple. Behind the closed door of the sunroom he lay, doped, out of consciousness; Beatrice attacked the red rug with a broom, beat it, flayed it; and Poppa stood watching me, wondering at me, his blue eyes confused, as I came up the steps, my arms full of tomatoes.

"Your mother did that."

The eternal cigar in the side of his mouth, the white shirt, the tie, they all look so peculiar out here: yet, I know from the way he lounges there by the railing—he loves it. I think of the months he spent hoboing through the West, just after my mother,

"Your mother did all those things. But you...how can you? You were only a baby," he said, "when," and stopped. . . .

but, already, it's wound back: to June or July, '38, and that curly-haired child on the step with Jake—that's me, that's Becky at three years old. Smell the sea, taste salt, sweat. Adam is off with his friends, and the ladybug came tottering up the step.

I shrieked and shrank away. Jake picked it up. He said words but I heard only sounds at first, light tenor voice rising, falling, the delicate, shining thing held out to me on his palm. *ladybug, ladybug.* Tiny intricate markings, dark red in a big brown hand, *fly away*, see, there she goes, *home.*

He reached over then, picked me up, cradled me. My face nestled into the curling black thicket inside his shirt. He told me that in June roses grew there.

Every summer I order a couple of pintfuls of ladybug beetles to keep down the bugs in the garden. Good bugs eat the bad bugs. Mosquitoes eat me, now, in late afternoon, time for tea—time for dinner, birds. Hurry, they're plump with my blood. Yet, I lie back; I press my bare arms, my bare legs to the soil. I am part of this, earth, staring up, I am part of that, sky, trees, here, *now*, try to find it: but there's only blurting green, dumb green on vacant blue, green massed and mocking my effort to keep it between me and step, sea, a haunted street, leading to that vision lurched into focus so suddenly, now, that I, the child at the beach, am hurtling down, through a whistling, a roaring succession of selves, *I am, he is she is we they are*—vast, translucent stretched layered over the Past, back, back, when did they start? When did he no she no I start, split?

Cinders bit into my face. Turning, I saw a blue roof; round border of lips moving, mute. Grass, then bleached voices, calling, *where are you*, and chasing me over a hill to a haze with white shutters containing, pain, *where*, my voice, lost, running, *are you*, then scrambling then falling then someone died.

Some body is gone.

This face, this scraped skin, these fingers—may I keep them? I? My? round body; a smell that is summer and water, my wet sandy trunks, burning sand, burning hot sidewalk yes: in summer caterpillars fell out of the trees. I ran down the sidewalk as fast as I dared, hopping to skirt the ones already squirming along the ground, terrified some would fall on my head into my hair. In the bungalow, my warm dark mother laughed nervously. There was a vase of long-stemmed dark red roses, and blood cascaded down her hands, over her long fingers.

Wedged on a wooden board, bumping along through the hot night, I'm thrilled that all those red and white lights move out of our way. Her eyes, dark, confused, watch me, now, from behind a screen; and the hysterical sirens scream. Is she excited, too? thrilled? happy?

A man in white puts his hands on me. My father's pale blue eyes watch me: cold; vague. My pale, heavy father—what does he see?

Matte brown, with two friends, he frowns : he was thin, he wore knickers; a cap with a brim shaded him from the sun of 1938. When he got to the Coast, a man said to him, 'But you *can* understand, goddamn you, Starski, *you can.*" He shook his big head there as here, after thirty-one years, fifty pounds, his name streamlined and how many thousands of dollars, he shakes his head at me, his child; and I say,

"But, Dad, you *can* understand..."

"You know, Becky, a guy said that to me in 1938 in L. A...."

"No, but *now*. Listen. Listen, *you can....*"

"I guess what you mean is you want to *marry* a sculptor," he tells me. He heaves himself up, again shaking his head, the cigar in his teeth, he walks away.

I spring to my feet in one long, dizzy motion; reel out of the garden and cross the lawn, clutching a trowel, clutching balance, as I did last summer after the phone rang, *where's maggie?* A breeze turns the big metal sculpture I carved when I still when I

25

still hear my father's voice up on the deck I pass now, calling, "Adam," and "maggie," then into the kitchen containing food food for the mouth not the stomach or not even, I do not taste the cold chicken encased in congealed sauce the black bread the ice cream I'm stuffing inside myself now I can't stop it, *must, stop it, before*, but I can't: I'm at that other window.

It's... any hot, bleak day in summer; but there must be cornflowers, blue in a vase near a photo of Jake seated at a piano: tuxedoed, smiling, his hair slick, black, a white line down the middle. His tenor voice lilts, *I met her in Venezuela*. Dust scallops the pane through which I look, see his silhouette moving, behind me, superimposed on a wave of birds circling a water tank, *don't turn*, across Second Avenue wing tips are glinting in late sun, then, he put his hand on my breast.

Call it two years ago. Now I stand watching a face wobbling wet in a toothpaste-flecked mirror; yet also back there in a room with green walls, I am backing away from, Jake, his big hands, his voice breaking, it's sliding around now I can't stop it, STOP— then we stand in a limbo of silence.

"Why me?" I said finally. "And why tell me?"

"Ah, Becky. You look so much like your mother...."

I dry my face; try to imagine them as they were. On the Lower East Side, in 1919, their parents speak no English. They're hopeful; they're poor. The oldest son, Walter, at nineteen, is starting a junk shop. Jake, seventeen, plays music, parties, he quarrels, violently, with his father, and leaves for three years he wanders, no word, not even a card to his sweetheart, like in the old movies, the girl next door was: my mother. The celluloid cracks, for a moment, their outlines blur. Then my mother has married Walter; Adam is born; Jake returns, he leaves, Becky born, and the junk shop is now an antique store. Walter can send his wife and kids to the seashore, the bungalow, where all these lines converge in a ring, enclosing: roses; a ladybug; Jake announcing his marriage, my mother screaming, their bodies colliding, but, what did I see? crouched under a step, outside—Jake emerges, unsteadily, he fades down the street; then my mother is falling, a milk bottle smashing under her arm, one jagged finger of glass, piercing, clear as my own flesh.

"But why tell? and why did you tell *him*?"

"Well, Becky. We knew it wasn't quite an accident. And he blamed himself, he was holding on to it, you know the way he does. It was a year already, you got to let go of the past if you're going to live, I believe that. We were drinking, besides, and I— I thought if I told him it wasn't his fault, then he could let go of"

Momma? *Momma?*

She lies in her coffin, the color of putty where she isn't rouged. All the lines of her face have been smoothed out. She looks like a wax doll.

"Oh, she looks just like she's sleeping," her brothers and sisters squeal. They lie around like fat white slugs. Sometimes one of them lifts up a head and wails. Then Beatrice comes picking her way through the clutter of prone flesh, loose-jointed and delicate, she slams the lid of the coffin down, places a big tray on top, and sinks into a chair next to it.

The box squats with its crown of food, polished, dark: wood? A substance containing—flesh? Can you still call it that? or is it meat, really, now—like the corned beef, salami, the tongue,

"Well, you don't have to eat that," a thick voice told me. There's bread. There's cheese. Or, just take a danish, then all will be well. Go ahead, grab it, it's going by, quick, quick, ahhhh. Delicious. Try some more, more, go ahead, there's lots to eat on that elegant coffin. Cram some Velveeta between your teeth, look, there's a smooth kind of gook, creamy, mmmm, more, have more, eat, you got room, kid, more, MORE....

I am throwing an egg across the room. Somebody says take care of the kid. Get that kid out of here, quick now, who's gonna do something about that goddamn kid?

Cold water works best on the wrists and the back of the neck. And the face, of course. Water, then out the glass door for some air, turning bluer, the greens turning deeper as dark comes on. Bailey is trying to climb my left leg, hissing, puffed up to twice his usual size because maggie's dog, Cairo, is hurtling up the steps. Now I see maggie and Adam come up the drive; and behind them the evening star: brightness that pierces me, always. Their voices, their laughter, the dog barking, wildly excited whenever he goes down the steps up the steps down the steps I can't face them now.

So it has come to the madness of fleeing my brother, my cousin, my two best friends, as they approach I run back inside, out the back door, then, up the slope, under the worm-laden trees all alone now across a yard this is the end of June this is a day when red roses came, was that today? or four days ago? One dozen long-stemmed American Beauty, the blood running down Mother's hands today last week or, thirty-two years ago,

BUN-galow, Becky sang into the shiny blue curtain; bu-BUNGA-low, sand streaming down her skin, all her round body hot, steamy and wet, bunga-

"Come on out, Becky," her father said, "while there's some hot water left. The rest of us want to shower, too."

"But I'm not finished yet."

"Do you know you've been in there for half an hour? Do you want help with something? Becky?"

"No, *thank you*. I'll come out myself."

"Next week?" Adam's voice sneered; then her father said,

"Becky, you have to get out of there. Jake is waiting down-town. We have to get dressed to go to the"

"Becky"

"Becky"

"Becky, *Becky*"

is   running

running

the softening sidewalk the trees black iron spikes gaping gate open then the white haze and a word that went with her mother, *sanitarium*,

("It's not a hospital, dear," said her aunt, "it's a")

slope turning black flaking under my feet and I stumble and cinders.

A voice, calling.
Light, changing.

Becky rolled over and lay on her back on grass. Sounds rose up out of her chest and then crashed and receded on impact with the seawall in her throat. Shadows crept over her. Then the wall melted, she heard her own voice, but nobody came.

From somewhere high up I can see my own body. I feel myself feel cinders, hear the dim voice calling *Becky*, or is that *Rebecca?* Dispassionately, I'm recording a snuffling, as though my thoughts have become, since that day and forever, quite separate from the life of my nose and throat. . . .

The voice got louder.
A beetle runs over my face.

The world was bright black screaming I scrambled up and my father was hugging me dragging me over the cinders with one hand the other hand spanking me it doesn't hurt I am sobbing but
that other one sits up there . coolly . wondering,
what has got into him? what thing that's trying to shake us both to pieces?

sing/thinking

ladybugladybug
fly away home
your house is on fire
your children are
gone

2.

maggie had a white, long-haired cat named The Roses.

She could not find a name for the kitten, until one day it leapt on her father's old upright piano, its beautiful tail just grazing the vase as maggie walked in, saw it, saw Adam there near it, completely oblivious, and shouted, "THE ROSES!"

He'd brought her some.

That was the first time he went to see her—the summer after his accident. She was spending most days at her parents' place on Second Avenue. A man was lying across the doorstep. His eyes seemed curdled yellow and blue and looked like they might drip out of their sockets. He was soaked in vomit. A young cop came by and poked at him with his stick, "aaaah, he's all right," and the man toppled onto the sidewalk, limp as a stuffed puppet.

Adam stepped over him, walked past a row of broken mailboxes, up a spiral of steps and across more bodies sprawled on the landings, five flights, to where a door stood half open. An old woman sat facing it: small, in an overstuffed chair, in a stained, pink housedress, with very bright eyes and a wispy white pigtail that lay on one shoulder.

"Aunt Bella?"

Her eyes focused on him. Her plump-shrunken body thrust forward. A spate of sound, flowing—Yiddish. He shook his head, trying to mime incomprehension. She spoke again. A higher voice came, then, from some hidden room. The old woman's hand signaled: wait. He nodded, and, feeling absurd, he held out the bunch of crimson roses.

She stared a moment, then pointed to the piano: the same piano, squatting still in the same place, Adam realized with wonder. Half of its keys were gone now—it had aged, slowly, slowly, as she had aged. Everything's weathered down to its roots, he thought, somewhere hard sharp crackling shapes spatter quick-change, but, not really; that can't exist and this also; not in one universe.

He took three steps, thrust the bouquet in an empty vase on the piano top. Bella smiled, nodding; her yellow old-woman's-flesh spreading, falling in thick wrinkles. He thought of chicken fat. Fat, fleshy warmth. Fish and Yiddish. . . .

There was so much red plush here; such dark corners—like puddles of time, Adam thought, and felt the skin in the naked space between his nostrils and upper lip start to tingle. All the furniture seemed dark, heavy, cushioned and covered with smooth stuff that somehow absorbed all the light coming in with street noises and soot through two open windows. The roses glowed, a cluster of jewels in this musty museum, as alien as Adam himself standing, staring, half-cringing, mute, until maggie came in: a pair of glasses perched on her nose, a purple scarf wound around her head, and, in her hand, a bowl she nearly dropped when she saw him.

He said, "Hello, maggie." She screamed, "THE ROSES." He dove, caught the vase, the white kitten leapt over his hands, and, laughing, "Good work," maggie said; then, "Mommala. . . ."

Mucous and soft fat: maggie's voice in Yiddish—the language they'd used when they didn't want him to know something. They —Bea and Walter. At home in a penthouse that can't exist, or one day in a big, rented hall as he sat next to Bea, Bea superimposed on a girl in a purple scarf handing a bowl to an old woman, both of them mumbling the same liquid-gutteral sounds that had issued from Bea's narrow lips, and his father, now, laughing, laughing. His father is drunk on a couple of shots of champagne, drunk because Walter Stark drinks only four times a year; still, he hasn't forgotten his days in the road: drunk or sober, the clerks

31

from his store are always invited. *And they're not even Jews*, Bea
spits out in English; her lips disappearing, her cheekbones protruding farther and farther out. Now Rebecca is taking another
big slice of cheesecake. Adam has somehow turned over his chair,
jumping up, he grabs a girl in blue organdy, pulls her against
him, a hard wad of primroses wedged in his ribs as they dance,
they dance, but...

The music is charmless; raucous. There's nobody at the
piano. We're three thousand miles from New York, and besides,
the brothers Stark-Starski don't speak—haven't spoken for years:
since the day Walter came with a new wife a new life and carried
his children away in the beige and brown Packard, remember,
remember, Becky? And won't speak, Adam thought, till they die.
The word 'grudge' was invented by Walter Stark. Keep your
mouth shut, he tells Bea, back there at the table; and here in the
foreground come back into focus, *come back*, there's an old
woman, burbling, now a few drops dribble out of her bowl onto
faded pink cotton.

He reached out a hand to steady her. She smiled, spoke
again. maggie said, "She wants to give you some soup."

"Oh no thanks not now," he said quickly. The old woman
nodded, braced the bowl on her lap, and began, again, to eat.

There was something about that. *Creaturely*, Adam thought,
repelled and touched in the same instant. *Can she have mothered
me?* He said,

"Where's your father?"

"Sleeping." maggie sat down, lit a cigarette. "Look, I don't
know what you know. Has Rebecca told you...?"

"Not much. We've talked a little, but—she says she doesn't
come down here much."

"She doesn't come down at all, now. She used to until about
two years ago, then...oh, I understand. It's pretty depressing,
really."

"I wanted to come before. When we left, I mean after, when
I was a kid, I used to make plans to run away and get back, I
tried a few times, but, then when I could I didn't, I don't know

32

why, it, just didn't seem possible then, and after...."

"It's all right," she said.

"It's not all right." Anger snapped through him. "It may be all right for us. But they're old. How can they"

"Hey." She touched his wrist, lightly. "They do. Lots of people do."

"I'll write my father."

"No. Rebecca already spoke to him. I think he really...oh, I don't know. She wouldn't tell me what happened. But anyway. ...Welfare gives them enough for food and rent. They wouldn't leave this place if you gave them a mansion. It's mostly medication is a problem, and doctors. At the clinic he always has to wait, and...."

"What clinic? What's the matter with him?"

"Oh, you don't know, then." She sucked her cigarette. "Cancer," she said, and looked—*into* him, Adam thought; yet, it was not an intrusion. Those dark, square-cut eyes were so intimate they seemed to understand all the need, the pain that had ever existed. "It's his lungs," she said. "They're giving him eight months. And I—well, I had cancer four years ago, so I'm sort of...."

"*You* had cancer?"

She nodded. "They took out part of my thyroid. See?" Her forefinger traced a faint band, like the print of a chain, across her throat. "And it's supposed to be hereditary. So when I see Poppa...."

"Listen," he said, "do you have anything to drink here?"

"Sure. There's juice and...oh, you mean liquor? We...I...."

She looked at her mother and stopped. Adam turned from one to the other, in the short, crackling silence, then the old woman burst out laughing: loud, high-pitched cackles that went on and on, that broke over maggie's features like hard waves slapping her,

"Momma, please. Momma...."

A big, black, long-haired shepherd dog rushed in from the kitchen, stopped just in front of maggie and stood, braced on four

33

stiff legs, tiny red eyes looking at her; keening. She bent forward. "No, Cairo, no. You be quiet." The dog sank onto its haunches, its long snout raised, emitting whines, yips, so expressive they sounded like speech. "Quiet," maggie repeated, "ssh," the dog's moans blending into the old woman's cackling then maggie, too, was screaming. "SHUUUUU-EEEeeee," mock-exasperated; clowning, for maybe ten seconds Adam wanted to laugh, but she clutched the dog's long mane with a violence that wasn't comic. She dragged the tense, heavy-boned body across the floor, claws scraping, fighting her all the way out of the room—then a spate of short screams.

She came back and stood in the doorway, her mouth twisted, slightly open, and shivering so hard Adam could almost see soft molded cartilage beating against her bones. A small white bubble of foam had formed at the edge of her mouth. Her mother's laughter had stopped. The room was quiet.

"It's awful, isn't it," maggie said, leaning against the wall: her bitterly thin frame held up, it seemed, by that sickly green plaster surface. The bubble glistened, poised, not dribbling yet from that place where her lips dimpled into a corner. Her voice was so muffled he had to strain to hear the words, blurred, as though coming through on a radio not quite tuned in, "I mean, beating. Sometimes I think he begs me for it. It's awful. That it should take that."

A voice to her left said, "Whatsa matta?"

"It's okay, Momma," maggie muttered. Adam turned sharply.

"But what's wrong?" the old woman asked in almost accent-less English. Her eyes raked Adam's face. "Is maggie upset?" The phrases spattered out of her mouth, staccato, like seizures.

"I, I"

"Who's he, maggie? a frienda yours?"

He said, "I'm Adam Stark, Tante Bella. I lived here for almost a year when I was a kid. With my sister, after my mother died. You took care of us. Adam," he told the old face, attentive, interested, absolutely impervious, "Adam and Becky. . . ."

"Oh, oh, yeah. Yeah. You look lika nice friend."

maggie said, "Momma, it's okay. I'm sorry. It's time for your nap, now, come on," then she slid into Yiddish again. Her mother whined an answer, voice like the dog's, Adam thought, but she got up, finally, shuffled past him, her head down, stockings flopping over her scuffs, she left the room.

maggie fell into the overstuffed chair, rubbed her hands quickly over her face, then lay back, looking half wild, half humorous.

"I thought she didn't speak English," Adam said.

"Yeah, well, she likes to pretend she doesn't."

"She had me fooled."

"She's very good at it. Even I forget sometimes, I act like she doesn't know what I'm saying, and then—well, you saw."

"But why? What set her off?"

"Oh, you don't know. I thought Rebecca. . . okay. My father's alcoholic, see, so we never keep any liquor in the house. Except that I hide a bottle of wine for myself. She knows, I'm sure, but we both pretend she doesn't. So when you asked for a drink, and I almost let it out in front of her. . . ." She lit another cigarette. "She's very smart, but she's nuts. And it's worse now my father's drinking is worse. He's in pain, all the time, and he—well, like, he'll drink up the Welfare money if we don't hide it. For a while we had a deal with the bar down the street, to give him just so much and we paid by the week. It wasn't a bad arrangement, but now he's too sick to go out. It was kind of like the electric bill. . . ."

She cocked her head to one side and beamed. Her whole face shone: so radiant that it should have been joy—and it was utterly sad. A mask, he thought, containing the almost irresistible plea to be mirrored in some other flesh.

He'd never felt less like smiling. He squatted in front of her, arms on the arms of her chair, and took her shoulders in his hands. Her face lost its smile: looked desolate, Adam thought, as though she had just seen a field of corpses.

He blurted, "You're too young to be so old."

"Oh. . . ." She smiled slightly. "Do you want some wine now? She's gone to sleep. . . ."

"No, what I need is some air. Why don't you come out with me? We could have dinner."

"I can't," she murmured, "really. I have some things I have to do. But I'd like to...I mean, could I see you later?"

"Sure you can see me later. When, later?"

"Call me, okay?" She coughed.

"Yes. Why don't you put that thing out?"

"Hmm." She looked at the cigarette. "Once I had a fantasy...."

"Tell me."

"It's silly." She puffed again. There was a whistling sound as the smoke traveled down to her chest. She met his eyes finally. "That I'd meet someone who, when I wanted a cigarette, would kiss me instead."

He took the hot white cylinder out of her fingers and crushed it. A smile formed under his lips, felt, the stillness and something jetted up inside him, yet stillness contained it; contained them, he thought, the walls might shatter. Trucks. Voices. maggie—a magic he'd thought was gone with Kay, mad Kay and now maggie, mad, *no*, something said, *get out*, now, he was standing swaying holding a hard little bundle of bones but such vivid life. Barking then, somewhere, below them, her arms wrapped around him, words swirled bubbles inside his head there's a water ballet syncopated with barking, louder, the palms of her hands (*psalms of hands*, he thought) pressing, two circles of heat on his back and her ribs pressing fingers, lips, opening, howling, then, teeth in his leg.

Black numb white and a thread of red.

Cairo lay on his side, one back leg lifted. Adam looked down at his own knuckles. maggie, a shuddering gargoyle a few feet away, said,

"I'm sorry. He...."

"I'll call you later."

"Are you okay?" she called after him and he tossed a word back up at her like a coin, and ran: dodging bums bottles voices a clatter of life bursting out through the half-open doors, the aroma of stews, of whiskey, and small grimy faces, his fingers bumping on hard wads of gum stuck under the, dodging, down, clutching the, bannister—

(*Lifeline: Lead me, O bannister, back. . . .*)

But his hand remembers, and won't let him laugh. Hurtling head-long, abandoned by all his fine irony, even by numbness now, he is defenseless against this long coil of wood he used to slide down. The old super's voice yelled after him. Jake yelled. Bella yelled, sometimes, and sometimes Rebecca would slide down, too.

Not often. Mostly she sat in the kitchen and gorged on slices of bread heaped with mayonnaise. Bella stood back of her and with a comb painstakingly fashioned the long, corkscrew curls that hung down past her waist. Through the building, the school, the whole neighborhood, those curls were magnets for ink, scissors, paint, and whatever else came to the hands of his enemies, friends. . . .

Becky: *doesn't come down here much.* Sister, enemy: *doesn't come down at all now, why?* Adam wondered, bracing himself in the doorway near a shoe, leg, bottle, *it can't be, no, not because it's pretty depressing, really.*

Walking down Fourth Street, he'd seen her come out of a doorway. She'd been to a party, she was all decked out, feathers and pink, but the dress had so far to go over her stomach, it pulled up in front, so short you could see the white panties bunched around small, chunky hams. He'd started across the street. She called out. He walked faster. One of his friends said "Your sister," then looked at his face.

When he watched her now, rattling around in that beautiful body, as though it were armor, he thought she must still expect ridicule, even attack, quite gratuitously. Gum and coffee and elegant food prepared lovingly, later those spasms of shame—yet, he knew just as truly someday the mark had to be him. It was his mother, too. He had been there. He'd seen it. It may have shaken him more. He was six that week. Black iron bars and a white place and their father's cold, pale blue eyes—they'd watched the back of him, leaning a bit to one side, walk away.

(*Later...later....*

She was still busy at eight. *Later.* Sixth Street, Eleventh Street, next mirror, next drink, *later*, dark, neon green over the next bar next telephone, *later*, *later*, nine-thirty, ten, *later*, ten-thirty, eleven, *no answer.* Cold black air splashed his face. He walked uptown, wobbling, suspicious of everyone in these crushed, desolate streets, *des-o-late*, *so late*, world spinning, city an airshaft that's tilted at ninety degrees so that Adam can stagger through,

let *her go now*, he thought; *let her go....*
(*click....*

"Oh, oh, Adam, I...is it too late?" Her voice sounded fuzzy. "I fell asleep. Did you call before ... I.... Do you still want to come? I'll meet you...."

and Adam walked back down, down, on the long empty swathe of concrete lined with black shapes immobile yet threatening motion, the night pulsing, endlessly, down, past Fourteenth Street, he crossed to the Bowery again, Second Avenue, down and back, back, to

maggie...it's June; or July; or, whenever he walks east on Tenth Street, Adam will see her thin silhouette drifting towards him, easily, in the warm night; a shadow of shepherd dog running circles around her, clutching the thong of a leash in his teeth.

"I'm so glad you waited...so sorry...when sleep takes me I...."

Black slacks. A black jersey. That desperate smile. Her father had been in two nursing homes, she said, but no more: he got too unhappy. The problem at home is with her mother, so hard to deal with,

"and I get crazy. But my therapist helps with that."

38

"What kind of therapist?"

"Psycho. Ann, her name is. I see her once a week and I'll pay when I can. She's kept me going so far. But, sometimes, when the traffic light is red, I, I . . . see green."

"Really? See with your eyes?"

"It seems. I've been in the nut house a couple times—didn't Rebecca tell you?"

Four paws pad, their two sets of footsteps, at three in the morning the small yellow lights from an all-night fruit stand glitter; three-thirty, *laaaast, call,* and out again, four. . . .

"My hour. Isn't it funny," she said, "it's now, always, I—find myself."

"Want to come to the country with me?"

"Tonight?"

"Why not? It's beautiful now. Wild strawberries by the creek. And the whole place reeks of roses."

"Roses," she murmured, her face smiling-sad. "So lovely of you to . . . hmm. I have to fight with a doctor, things like that, for the next few days, but then. . . ." She looked up at the sky a moment: dawn, slow and delicate through the New York haze. "Then—I think I'd like to."

3.

The little cat prowled the car; the dog stuck his long snout out
the window; as Adam and maggie came down the slope into
mist, all the trees blurred, as though under still water. Stillwater
Valley, I've called it: a red mailbox labeled STARK/WOOLF, a
pond, Rebecca's house above the lawn and the larger house at the
foot of the drive where a fat little boy knelt in gravel. Adam
waved as he moved to let them pass, "Charlie Woolf," he said,
"lives in that house. They're good people."

He swerved the car up the hill and stopped and they got out.
On the deck, two cats crouched—red and white molded figurines,
flashing to life as Cairo rushed up, plumed tail wagging.

"Let's go inside a while," maggie said. "Okay? Do you mind?"

"I guess not. But you wanted to swim." He followed her into
the sunroom. "What's wrong."

"Nothing." She sat down, seemed to fold in on herself. Adam
sat beside her.

"maggie. . . . What's wrong?"

"I don't know." She huddled against him, suddenly, meager
body tense, "Maybe. . . maybe I'm afraid of what's happening
between us. . . ."

The sun colored her legs, rose. Her gnome face, the pain in her
laugh. He wanted to say, "My love, my quietness;" but he'd left
Kay's wild smile pinned up, caught in fine granules of silver it
beamed down on his hand moving over her throat, a brown
nipple, a scar on her shoulder, scars on her right thigh and across
her hip. He thought of claws.

"My body's a bruise," she said.

She looked up at Kay, then, and Adam felt her cut off: this half-sex they had.

"I'm sorry. Later. . . ?"

"Sure." He stood up. "We just got here. Want some"

"Coffee? Is there any?"

"Okay. I'll make it. You stay there," Adam said.

He stood looking out the glass doors as he waited for water to boil. Birds said sky said rain soon rain. He heard it before he could see it cut through the air, spray on windows, the lamp swinging, big drops. Outside the short-haired white cat, Tonta, sat crouched, dripping. All of her muscles showed. A butterfly in her mouth twitched, tiny, pale yellow shred—tissue. She put it under two paws and sat blinking. Would she forget it? he wondered. He carried the two cups back to the sunroom where maggie still sat.

"Here," he said, "we'll be okay. It'll be all right, okay," he crooned, holding her fluttering ribs knees hands belly her whole small body of cluster of birds, but she said,

"I have to go."

"Are you crazy?"

"You mean you haven't noticed yet?"

"You can't go," he told her, "not this way."

"But I, i," *careful. don't let the sounds fly. be careful, slow, careful,* "i came here to see you and—be with you. not to. . . ."

"But it's okay. It's my fault, really. I want you to say," he said, "I mean stay. Look. . .on that branch, there's a cardinal. Look. On the cherry tree."

"Adam. . . ."

"There, look, there he goes. Baby, baby, it's really okay. Really."

And all the walls echoed, *okay.* The windows, the ceiling, the whole house in chorus, *okay,* the world's full of *okays,* and she almost laughed, *but,*

"Oh, I'm so ashamed. . . ."

"Of what?"

41

(the rain slanting, cooling; the muted light spilling around them through two walls of windows)

"Just—don't let me have anything sharp," maggie said.

The speed of it always amazed him: how her eyes welled up suddenly, summoning something deep in him, yet—he doesn't want grief. He wants to bubble and play. He knows under these windows, just hidden by that cherry tree, Kay cavorts, wild and happy. She rolls, soaking, down the hill, drunk on the smell of wet grass, Kay is naked, dancing, white skin gleaming, black hair, Kay is pale; Kay's long fingers are clutching a shotgun, Kay's fingers are gripping a wheel as tarantulas flip, spinning over the softening concrete in front of them hot air in waves, "I'm all right, I can drive," Kay mutters through rigid jaws, rigid eyes straight ahead, rigid hands pull the car left, an explosion of light, glass, and metal, a year: the loneliness like a clamp—hazy, biting. But, what am I doing here now, Adam thought; with this crippled bird?

"Listen," he said, "let's go away somewhere. For a few days, a week. I don't want Rebecca involved in this."

"Where is she, anyway?"

"In the city. She'll be back tomorrow though, early. We can leave the kitten. I'll leave a note for her, she'll understand, Okay?"

"I don't know. I...can't think right now." She drew away from him, got up, her eyes not quite focused. The dog nudged her. "Go on out, Cairo," she said, but he nudged again. "You can go....Isn't it awful?" she said. "He thinks he's still in the city. I'll just go down on the lawn with him...."

After she left, the scent of the roses he'd picked for her followed him from room to room: everywhere in the house, roses—early July, early evening. Adam saw lightning over the hills, but there was no thunder. He saw maggie pause near his sister's mobile sculpture, the black shepherd running circles around her, she watched the metal arms for a while and walked back, slowly, up the porch steps. He thought she would come in, then, but she turned, lit a cigarette; leaned on the railing.

"maggie: " Hands press on her shoulders. Her skin coils away. She doesn't turn.

"I thought I might sleep on that couch," she says. "Okay?"

"O-o-okay." Hands seem to recede without leaving her shoulders. "It's not very comfortable."

"Don't worry. I'm fine. It's all fine, really. I'd just like to be alone with the country tonight."

His hands lifted, this time. "Sure."

"We'll go, okay? I think it's a good idea...wherever...."

"Okay."

Steps, receding. The door closes. She can breathe easy again, in the warm air, *eeaasy*, she thought, *it can't work. i can't be with any one, two, three....*

She lay down on the musty pillows, and felt herself rocked by the huge summer night, a sea, and this porch a deck. Cloud-fingers were sculpting the moon, pied and ruffled, two days from the full; the earth one month past solstice, brimmed, sounds and smells maggie could not identify, yet she knew them as well as she knew—*myself*, she thought: *completely, and not at all*. Lights from small boats in the sky, as sleep took her, blinked, *soft, breathe...now, then, see*, she thought, *despite: sometimes it all—vibrates.*

*

Birds woke her early, that morning; the next; and the next. Birds scuttled in front of the waves as she wandered, collecting shells, staring at foam, then she came back to where Adam lay, lazy, happy for one or two days. On the third he turned: *taciturn*, maggie thought, trying to feel whatever was held back, so tightly, because it was: *vicious*, Adam knew—*why am I vicious when I love?*

43

DANGER, a sign said, EROSION.
DO NOT GO BEYOND THIS POINT.

"But that's where we could see both sunrise and sunset over water," maggie said. "Oh, let's go down."

"We'll have to be careful. Wait here, and I'll drive the stuff around and drop it. You hide it in the bushes while I park. If we go down that slope, no one will see us. We'll just get buried in a slide."

"Oh no we won't."

A carlift, he thought, his mood lightening; and later, whenever he thought of that trip, he saw maggie dance-clowning, spinning their gear down the pocked, eroded slope as the sun set. Halfway down they saw the lighthouse: its bright eye sweeping across them as they climbed through vines, set up camp on the beach. They stood close, then, looking out at the waves; the sky fading.

"We mustn't forget this," he said. "I mean, no matter how bad it gets, we should be able to think of this. It might keep us alive."

"Yes."

"What's that?" he said, looking over her head. She followed his glance around the bend of the cliff to a barracks-like structure: huge, studded with windows and windows, all black.

"Oh let's go look...."

"In the dark?"

"Sure."

Skeleton walls, floor, ceiling, windows like eyes gashed out—it must have been scavenged: there was nothing inside but dust and a few spiders, no sign of human life ever lived in the sagging, symmetrical hulk. maggie said, *what's that?* She took the flashlight and moved off down the hall. He heard it, then; followed the light and the dog through labyrinthine corridors, then her croon came from inside a room.

He said, "It could be sick."

"I'll check." Her face turned up to him, humorous, pleading. "Don't look at me like that. I'll keep it, not you. Cairo, go away."

44

"That means we'll keep it. You're moving in, aren't you? And Rebecca will be...."

"Oh, Adam, I don't know if"

"I do. You are." He crouched beside her. "Is it a male?"

"Female. All calico cats are female."

"That means kittens, too. maggie...."

"But she could die here...."

She brought it into the sleeping bag with them. The dog crouched nearby on the sand, grumbling. All night they bumped against each other. Something was biting him. He looked down at her, curled around the cat, a sleeping child, as a late quarter moon rose he finally slept a little and woke to a hard-edged red sun, rising.

She was sitting up. She smiled, blurry. He snarled something, struggled up, forced himself into the ocean. Cairo lunged after him. The cold water took his breath, and after a minute he hurtled back to the beach where maggie sat, the cat in her arms. Cairo shook himself, looking half his size with the bushy fur wet; and maggie dodged, laughing, she wrapped the towel around, Adam, wrapped his body around hers, almost mechanically—the love abstract; far removed from his tingling skin, his foul humor.

"Let's go," he muttered.

They climbed the slope, put the cat and dog in the car, then came back to pick some blackberries—*propitiation*, Adam said, *for Rebecca*. They drove west slowly along the north shore, maggie hunched on the far right side of the right seat, the cat in her lap.

"Colette?" she said. "Theodora?" He gave her a brief, sour look. "Let's stop a while," she said. He pulled the car off to the side of the road and leaned forward, forehead pressing the steering wheel.

"Does your back hurt, Adam?"

"No. Come on, let's go out if we're going."

They walked to a small inlet beach and sat down near the bay shore; not touching. It was very quiet. Cairo inched his head and big shoulders between them.

"It hurts like hell," Adam said.

"Oh, love.... I knew...that climb...."

He looked at her grave small face. Sea sounds, rushing, a few salt drops. Their hands touched across black fur. She said,

"I'd like to live by the ocean sometime."

"Maybe we could."

In the beginning light rain they skipped back to the car. She curled close to him, hand on his knee, as they drove through a welter of billboards, hot dog stands, cars, then turned onto back roads lined with lopsided houses, red barns, the sweet, wet, grain smell. Harvest. The little cat had settled pillowed in Cairo's fur.

"Gelsemina?" maggie said.

"Let's wait and ask Rebecca."

"She'll be upset."

"Ve-e-ry."

"We should have called her. Why didn't we?"

The sun was making rainbows on wet concrete as they turned onto Hollowbrook Road, wound down past the ramshackle barn and turned in at the mailbox. A rope was hanging half off the deck,

"Like a noose," maggie said.

"Stop that, baby."

"Okay." She picked up the cat. "Just bring the blackberries. I'll get the rest in a minute. Don't be proud."

All the curtains were drawn in the sunroom. Rebecca, half-dressed, lay on her bed amid pillows and books. She waved, list-lessly, as they came in. Adam put down the blackberries. "I'll get the rest of the stuff," he said, and walked out.

"Hey...wait...."

"Why? Let him cripple himself if he wants to," Rebecca said tartly.

"Oh, Rebecca...I don't know what to say...."

"Can't tell you."

"Did you see what we found?"

"Oh, yes." The tousled figure hoisted itself to a sitting position, "Why did you even come back?"

"Why? I . . . we wanted to."

"Really? Oh, I meant, I guess you don't want company."

"We missed you."

"Oh, stop it. Why didn't you call?"

"I don't know."

"You know how much I hate to wait."

"Yes. I asked Adam why we, I mean . . . Rebecca, I'm sorry."

"I just don't understand *why*. . ."

"Why what?" Adam said, coming in with the sleeping bags.

"Why we didn't call her."

"We tried a couple of times, but"

"The hell you did, dear brother." She stood up. "I hardly went out this week. I hate feeling this way."

"We're sorry."

"So you're sorry. But you bring back a cat, for God's sake— yours just came out from under the couch yesterday," she told maggie, "and"

"We can give this one away," maggie said.

"We will not. What the fuck," Adam said, "we were on vacation, we weren't thinking about the time, I'm sorry we didn't call but"

She never could find that place again.

Adam tried to come with her. "No, please," maggie had said, and so he had watched from the deck as she climbed the slope. Cairo followed her, then ran back down to him, ran up to her, circling, she is receding, or, Adam wondered, is that me? There, in the upper left corner, a seam opens, briefly, and maggie steps through: into flickering darkness. The seam knits behind her; and all that space she has never believed is sealed off, a clever trompe l'oeil, all those colors, that manshape—just paint on one side of a screen turning opaque now figured with trees

(And darkening. . . .

worms, leaves, so many greens. how these fingers glow, maggie thought, pink, green. woman, man. could i be only a—creature? this skin, muscle, bone, she thought, they are:

47

in-car-nation: the human dimension: a handbook of earth i can barely read. flesh against bark, that's rough, worms are smooth, don't crush it, *feel it.* this spot is an eye, that split trunk is a headless girl upside down, uh-oh, watch it she thought as she crossed a rise and the reservoir gleamed below her; *i need a mind to draw lines for me. . . .*

She climbed on a rock, looked across at the far shore, absently. Torso of hill and reflection: no seam between water and shore, one continuous form, and the lower half bulged as palpably into the lake as the upper half into the sky. Something said to her, *don't go down to the reservoir. Don't go down to the path*; and she turned away, back, over crumbling stone fences, she waded, and through a field of white lacy flowers as high as her shoulders, and down to the creek.

Wild raspberry vines ran beside the bank: tiny red sparks, here and there. Something incredibly bright orange flashed, just above the trees. Cairo was crashing through brush, snap-crackle, but no—that's not Cairo, she realized: *that must be someone behind me.*

Down through a swathe they had cut for telephone poles, she could see the house, dwarfed by ash, maple, and pine. A shape was climbing towards her. A man's shape, she thought, *Adam: call him, go on, call;* but she grasped a vine, silently. Thorns bit her palm as she wrenched at them. Very deliberately, maggie dragged them along the inside of her arm, *this is pain*, she thought coolly; the soft spot inverse to the elbow and down to the wrist, *this is real*, and back up, slowly, skin turning pink and a few scarlet threads, *but not deep enough*, dropping them quickly she held the hand closed, the arm hidden, hot, against her side; then, as his arms came around her, she turned him a shining face.

"Guess what," she said. "A butterfly ran into me!"

4.

It's when I sleep on my left side that I slide so easily into that seat: engulfed, alone, in spite of Adam's hand on mine, eyes wide to: Sunday, 1939, late August: their two heads in front of me.

I roll back—to darkness. Tiny invisible bugs are biting me. Time looms: the colors in that fabric glow, so richly, just before they turn transparent.

All I know now
is rain. Always walking through rain to the mailbox, I put things there, take them away. Yellow rivulets cut through soft mud, gravel, where the car lurches sometimes if it hits a big stone in the drive that leads Past—dark gold surface, stretched, constantly turning to mottled, dark purple, a bruise: August. Fungi like testicles. Rain pocks the face of the pond—tiny circle-worlds merging, emerging, fading, then bubbles come up

(*Go home. . . .*

Mushrooms. Black flowers. Small oriental umbrellas. Red phallic ones, big ugly orange ones growing up into each other, go home. Where: the clock, the refrigerator, the insects, *tick-click-buzz*, a march; or a muted polka. I laugh aloud, and Sossa comes running, barking, as though an intruder has come to the house. One pink rubber sandal lies, bruised, on its side. A blue candle. The furniture is just there, an assemblage of dusty surfaces, this world I'm in, worlds I am: just concentric circles of surface, no matter how deep I cut.

I flex my hand; watch how the skin moves over the vein. It's not lovely or unlovely: it's just flesh. Tendons bulge under knuckles, hollows, and delicate small bags of skin, oh, I am suffused with a sense of blemish—of how my life's leaking away.

But, enough of all this artificial routine, I decided; and sat down to eat with everyone else, in the kitchen. The cat eats her Friskies. And Sossa eats kibble. And I eat raw vegetables out of the colander, squatting against the wall—each cherry tomato a small, cold explosion of sun in my mouth. But the cat left too soon and I followed her, found her curled, elegant, white, on the red rug: she blinked at me. I lay down beside her and buried my face in her soft, purring belly and almost slept.

Inside my head spinning vagueness touches a sharp edge: *recoil; cut;* an old man's voice says: *What are you doing, Rebecca?*

"Who are you?" I said, my voice bringing me up, back. An indigo river, streaked surface of glass with black branches beneath it, still, leafless in August, in August the worms are all gone and white moths float around in this room full of absence. The air starts to shimmer like water. The streaks on the pane change to flakes, spinning white like moths white like the one cat who made it through winter, snow, white like the color of maggots of death of eternity. White powder feathers the ice-coated boughs. And on lower Second Avenue, whitish-gray crystals clog curbs, drift and pile on the window sill where I perch, peering through soot-streaked glass.

Focus on green walls; a bed; then an old man's features, sharpening, white hair, a white mustache, face tilted up to the left.....

maggie's father sits under a blanket, his thin palsied hands out in front of him, dry beech leaves rattling over a lake frozen white like the ice crawling over the pane. Musing? Listening as she bends over him, purple scarf wound round her head, wisps of hair in her eyes, talking to him. Or maybe she's holding a steaming bowl under his chin, her thin hands shaking, spilling the broth on gray wool on white bones the black caverns of eyes the lips dribbling as ice seals the glass, hides the scene from me, as it hid water that mocked her eyes, one day in August when she and I went left at the fork, just above the creek; passed the striped maple, the beech grove; a huge fallen birch to climb over; then, down to the reservoir.

I'd almost reached shore when I heard her cough. She was far back, about midway between the two points of a crescent of land that reached into the lake. On the rim of its thickest part, far to our left, ran a dirt road. Cars came there sometimes, the water inspector's red truck, and in winter the snowmobiles. But on its tapering arms there were only trees, shrubbery, and on the side we'd just come from a path no one used but Adam and me. She coughed again. I turned. She seemed suspended there, vertical, hovering in the same spot, her arms floating, eyes intent, staring at water a couple of inches below her face.

I called, "Are you okay?"

"Yes. *No*," she choked. Her head bobbed down, up, down, up. Urgency flooded my legs, my arms. I swam back. "I can't breathe," she gasped.

"Grab my ankle."

Late afternoon sun streaked water warm blue under blue sky enormous blue bowl of day late August. What she would call with distaste a "red-white-and-blue day." She loved fog, rain, darkness. Not far ahead the mud beach was already in shadow. Her fingers, her hand, clutched my ankle, her coughing vibrated up through my leg into my own lungs, my arms pumping endlessly there between point and point. Rocks jutted up. I put one arm around her ribs bulging against a cold layer of skin and levered us both past the stones and driftwood that littered the shallows, the mud melting under my feet, then a firm, muddy shore.

"I know one thing," she said. We both looked at the far shore, where Cairo lay quiet in full sun, his furry black shape in a bush near two small heaps: our clothes. "I'm not swimming back there."

"Right. No one can see you. Just don't move. I'll walk around."

And out here alone in this soft, moving element: past the rocks now, past the driftwood, past shallows and shadow, back under the sun: in that short stretch I've done fifty times, where I couldn't touch bottom, where maggie had foundered, I knew I could founder, too. Nothing moved over the road to my right, and off to the left, past the two points of land, nothing—blue vacant lakewater; home to me, alien too blue lethal womb, and awareness of that could tie knots in my muscles, could cramp my breath coming in spurts now as I changed from sidestroke to crawl and then back, trying hard to blot all thought of distance out, all judgment, all computation of how far how near the voluptuous birch tree that grew on the edge of a small blob of island near shore, crawl again, sidestroke, crawl, float, and...

Rock. From here I can half-wade, half-float, fingers, feet scraped as I clamber out the air raises small hairs all over my skin. Cairo's tongue licks my legs, weightless, rubbery. I throw on my clothes. I roll up her shirt, scarf, sandals, and jeans that seem small as a child's, and wave back to her, still where I left her: a brown girl-shape, huddled on mud.

On that trip, as I traced the long, rounded inside of the crescent—a scramble, at first, through thick shrubbery, and then faster where woods have been pushed to one side by whatever machine gouged a road through here, bordering water stained pink as the sun slides behind the curved torso of hills; behind maggie; who makes her way slowly across the mudflats, so naked, so clearly in sight that I'm shouting, GET BACK. GET BEHIND THE TREES. She doesn't hear, or she pays no attention, she straggles on towards me as I start imagining cars, bikes, trucks, planes, the air bursting with voices, the water inspector, the Woolfs, oh, the whole population of Stillwater Valley there, staring and snickering; staring and shocked. . . .

On that trip, as interminable as the swim had been, my greatest fear was of Cairo: the half-insane animal I knew I couldn't control, that nobody controlled; who could scream people out of a room, who got so frenzied going down steps, any steps, New York City steps or the eleven steps down from the house that he bit the flesh nearest him—my leg, for instance.

("That's not a bite," maggie said. "It's a nip."

"Nip, shit. It HURTS."

"It's that he gets so excited. He doesn't mean. . . ."

"I don't CARE what he means. Besides, he doesn't bite Adam."

"That's special."

"Why? Because Adam's a man?"

"No, he used to bite Richard. I don't know, he loves Adam, or . . . well, he's scared of him. Adam's . . . Cairo's, you know, just a dog to him."

"Cairo's a dog to me, too, for God's sake."

"Not in the same way."

"Okay. You're right. *I'm* scared of *him*," I said furiously.

"Well. . . ."

"WELL. . . ."

"Slug him. Beat the shit out of him next time he tries it."

"I don't WANT TO slug him. It's crazy. HE's crazy. Why should. . . ."

"I understand," maggie said; thinking, okay: i'll take my crazy dog and move back to the city.

We sat near the pond, not speaking. A speck of hot orange, her cigarette, moved back and forth. Smoke. Stars in the water. I thought, it won't work. Cairo nudged my hand with a stick.

"He brought that for you," she said.)

The next day, I'd balled up my fist and punched him square in the muzzle, as I'd seen her do. He'd rolled to his side, and lifted one back leg, the long black fur falling away to expose a soft, gray, quivering belly; and I'd thought, well, maybe it will work. It. Something. She'd only been there a week. She'd only been there ten days when I finally met her, near the place where the road bends up to the left and the spur of land forming the crescent bends right. And the dog had been docile. And no one had come.

She pulled on her clothes, lit a cigarette, sucked, squatted, shivering in the warm dusk, and stared at the water, a dark blue now; stared at the short, straight, invisible line I had swum, a taut string to the bent bow of land.

"You know," she said, "I really might have...really...."

I squatted down next to her. Somehow, my body felt loose, in tune with itself as it was almost never. At the extremities, something breaks down and it feels like relief. But how long can we live here, I wondered, as dark came down slowly; and can we live only here? Why must we teeter on some kind of cliff, flirt with drowning, rage, play out some version of Russian roulette before we are free to sit quietly here in the huge, cooling night, by a reservoir?

With maggie, you couldn't forget death, pain, need—not for long. She would laugh, play, create that delectable zzzzing of excitement, of joy, about nothing-at-all—a stray phrase, maybe, slipped from your mouth and she tossed it up, bounced it high off her left heel, caught it, then flipped it back at you, sparkling, transformed, the whole world turned to festival suddenly you would be turning a somersault; dancing; humming a song that you've never heard, noticing how soft that corner of Cairo's mouth, reading her poems, playing music, and you've never known how much you love to read, play, how much you love—yourself; her; the shining, ridiculous world, this big, funky house, that so absurdly shaped bowl and that silly fork, but, it's shaped like a claw.

And the carnival music continues to play. The confetti is tumbling around your head. All the festivities whirl on, but now you are standing still, in the midst of it; not speaking, looking at maggie, who doesn't move; doesn't speak. Eyes like dark pools welling, not overflowing, quite.

She told us about how the water had changed to veils that beckoned, seductive—the coughing had saved her. I don't know when she began to see flesh dripping off our faces, lips melting down over our teeth, like grease, she said, and our eyes dropping

54

out of their sockets—all that. For hours she'd sit in her room, a maggie-interior, cluttered with amber and green bottles, clothes thrown in corners, layers of smoke, her drawing table under a window muffled in African cotton, and Georgia O'Keeffe's flower-genitals low on a wall just above a blue candle. Outside the rain fell. The leaves turned yellow, red, the few leaves that the worms had left fell, mushrooms, everywhere. Three cats died. The fish in my tank died. "I'm okay," she said, "when I'm watching the candle." A slow, slow crescendo of creaking. A chamber of whispered screams. Outside the squash ripened. Corn ripened. It was in May that they gave Jake eight months. maggie moved here in August.

II.
NIGHT SPASMS
(THE MOLE)

5.

*The jeep came round a bend in the hill's shoulder. He
stopped in a shadow and looked, and when he looked
again the weather had changed, it darkened, it was
snowing, he could hardly see but he drove on, he thought
the gate would come soon. Near the bottom there's a
dark shape—short stretch of ice? No, now he sees, it's to
the left, it has bulk, he accelerates, he's speeding, whiz-
zing past, he grazes it, flies out, up, arcs through mist
he's falling threads of fog melt on his face like cobwebs
his blunt fingers smell of childhood music superman is
Adam thudding crash no jolt no sharp he can't speak he*

    ("Mr. Stark? it's time for your, *wakeup,*"

    "Adam? are you okay? Adam?")

He can't hear.

  On this side,
some things changed. Like the skull she found by the side of the
road one day on her way to get cigarettes, deer's skull? dog's
skull? and nailed up by the glass doors. "Our masthead?" Adam
said, but it stayed there: whitish-gray bone traced with zig-zag
patterns an insect's trail had engraved on its forehead and down
the snout. She threaded a piece of wire through its sockets to hold
the thing flush to the wall. A shrew's tiny corpse had nestled into
one of them.

Then there were two big snails to keep down algae in the aquarium; a fire extinguisher; stones shaped like eggs; and dead flowers she left littered on shelves, such beautiful shapes, Adam thought, she taught me to see: so much I hadn't seen before. But mostly, there was a quasi-magical sense of time loss. Poised on the point of a pin, there would be one hour for everything, and nothing, before one or two or all of them had to go to the city.

The city loomed: sixty miles south, and a thousand psychic light years, its suction tugged at them all as they sat talking; leafing through catalogues. Rebecca played Mozart's *Don Giovanni* again and again. She and maggie made lists. . . .

It's evening. Crossing the red rug, from kitchen to staircase, he sees them, in the next room. At the table across from the windows, again and still, he sees them—maggie in the chair that's covered with smooth yellow plastic; Rebecca by the toaster, behind wads of chewed-out sugarless gum she is writing as maggie reads aloud from:

Whole Earth Catalogue: star map; bargain sleeping bags
Edmond Scientific: a gyroscope, a compass, a handsaw
Lakeland Lumber: a new kind of plastic, little gold nails
. . . . .

and it all would end up like the fifty dollars of fabric she'd bought to make curtains: on the floor, full of teeth and claw marks.

"New moon in Scorpio," she said, looking up from the almanac. "A time for new beginnings."

Tiptoeing down the steps, too early, he hears her voice first. She says, "We could lower the ceiling." Their laughter spurts. He crosses the rug as though he is crossing a mine field, he enters the room. Silence follows him with a thud. On the straight, hard chair between them he sips his coffee as each of them tries one limp sentence, he stares at the blue-and-white paisley tablecloth.

There is a coffee stain near the toaster; an overflowing ashtray.

He will turn off side three. The red cat, Bill Bailey, may curl up next to his leg, as Adam plays his guitar, a hot little sandpaper tongue may lick his ankle. He'll watch the air slowly heal where his presence punctured it. Again they'll talk. They'll plan. A haze of projects will bud, grand designs will flower and grow, large, larger, until they seep through the walls and sashes like heat does; and maybe dissolve in cool gray air where the sun is flirting out, in out, from behind a mass of clouds.

The light whitens. Cairo paces. A scuffling sound from the bathroom means one of the cats is stalking some wild creature blundered in for refuge. Adam starts to strum some of the old songs his father knew, long ago, on Sunday excursions they'd harmonize: *Hard Travelin'. Which Side Are You On. Get Thee Behind Me, Satan. The Song of My Hands. . . .*

"That was good, Adam."

"Yeah." Looking down and away, he started to pick out the Bach chaconne.

"Does your back hurt?" Rebecca asked, unsympathetically. "Is that it?"

"No. For Christ's sake, can't you let me forget my back?"

Cairo paces. They look at each other, and nod. Without a word, they get up and go into the kitchen.

rrrrrringgg

    crash

"It's Susan."

"Tell her we'll call her back. We can't stop now."

"Don't burn yourself," maggie shouted.

"I never burn myself," said Rebecca.

She stands at the stove with a slotted spoon, skimming the vat of hot syrup. Drops coat the walls. The windows are steamy. The jars, ladle, tongs have been set out on a towel. maggie sits on the three-step ladder, surrounded by bags and bowls, she is peeling apples.

"Be careful," she told Adam as he came in. "There's broken glass. A jar cracked."

"Susan says she'd be honored to hear from one of you when you feel you can spare five minutes."

"She's hurt," Rebecca said, "Oh God."

60

"I don't blame her. You haven't called her in weeks. Or anyone else, either."

"I know. Other people just seem...ouch. This stuff is spitting."

"What are you making this time?"

"Apple butter."

"Why don't you make apple wine," he said, "while you're at it?"

"Now that's an idea!" Rebecca said. "Apple wine...or cider...."

"No, NO," maggie squealed, "forgodsake, don't start...."

He's not an intruder. She has to move out of the way a little so he can rummage inside the refrigerator, but mostly he just glances off the invisible wall that's grown up around them—a fly, buzzing, sometimes swatting itself, at a window.

The wine is almost gone. The day is trickling by like a shrunken stream in a wide, dry, riverbed.

She ran out after him, shivering on the deck, she said,

"Don't.... You're doing something, you know."

"Am I?" he said. "What?"

"It's...you're pushing us both away. It's not...."

"No? You sure?" Her forehead wrinkled. He let her struggle, enjoying it, as a light rain started to fall. Her eyes begged him, then gave up but still the lower part of her face searched for words that he knew wouldn't come.

"Go back in," he told her, "it's cold."

The hunk of gray-white bone grinned at him with its broken snout. The door closed. As he went down the steps, he heard again Siepi's arrogant baritone, trying to soften itself.

Side five. Mandolin. Another concealed identity, yet another abortive seduction. He'd begun to hate Mozart.

Always at dusk blue deepening earlier each day a school bus wound yellow down the road slick black bordered with dying grass. He had to stop every few yards as its lights flashed and another child got out. The rain was gone. As he carried his gallon

of burgundy to the car, in darkness, the smell of October suddenly streamed up into his nostrils; and for a moment he wondered
what this was all about.

She'd said, "Are you disappointed?"

Driving home, he knew all over the wet roads there were
small frogs. A leaf scuttled in front of the car. He almost ran
over it.

*

*The car just ahead is a pale green limousine, changing, a
gray panel truck, changing, limousine, truck, gray,
green, changing but always crawling, too slow; and
Adam is speeding along the black road, the white line on
his side broken but he can't swerve to the left, hurtling,
can't stop in time time time to* wake up *time* wake up *one second before the collision.*

She said, "I have three hundred dollars. Escape money."

"That should feed you all winter, the way you eat."

"I don't mean that. I have Welfare for that. I mean boots and
socks, that stuff. And we have to weather-strip, don't we?"

"We have most of that stuff already. Don't worry, it's not the
Arctic Circle."

She said, "We could build a telescope. . . ."

Many spiders now—little scurrying black legs. Last night one
had come into bed with him. The lake was low, with jutting
stones and driftwood, and there were new mud beaches where
water had come to his chest in summer. A strip of land led out to
the island where the voluptuous birch leaned over water, its
branches like curls shaken out, its crotches and hollows scarred
with dark brown, transparent pods, slightly ripped. They would
return in June, their new egg cases bulging.

He climbed on a stone, squatted, took the brandy out of his
pocket and gulped. On the far shore, one lemon yellow aspen,

62

escaped from the scourge, fluttered, tremolo, though he felt no wind. The trees near him looked alien. Their bones protruded, sinewy hips, thighs, graceful, but *alien*, he thought; *or I am*.

Always at dusk he had drunk at least a quart.

She'd said, "I can't stand hurting people. I feel their pain."

"*What?*"

"I, i said...are you disappointed?"

The sound of her voice made him shudder. He was repelled by the look of her, flesh, pimples, foam always trickling down from the side of her mouth. She slept downstairs now: on the couch across from Rebecca.

It's morning. Bumping against the basket of wandering Jew, too close to the rail, the shape of the telephone changing as he descends, the aquarium comes into focus, he hears them. Laughing. At night, by the light of a half moon mingled with that green glowing worldful of quick-moving specks and four cats on the dirty red rug, he hears them. Whispering. Once he heard them near dawn. Stumbling down, stumbling up, or hurtling along that endless broken white line, in the space between sleeping and waking, he hears them. He hears them. He keeps a bottle of brandy upstairs: to pass out.

She said, "Feel this. Do you think it's grown?"

"What? What do you mean?"

"Well, it's...been there. The doctor says he thinks it's benign. I should watch it, he says."

(*rrrrrrr*

"What's that sound?" Rebecca said.

Adam put a finger to maggie's throat. "Isn't that right around the thyroid? Where you...?"

"Yes. But the doctor...he thinks it's benign."

(*rrrr...rrrr*

"What's that sound?"

They followed it to the bathroom, where Tonta, the short-haired white killer, had cornered a mole. Rebecca dragged her out and closed the door and all three of them crowded around the sink above a small brown creature cowering back of the pipes. maggie knelt, peering.

"It should have some residual eye—flaps? But I don't see. . . ."

"No," Adam said, squeezing down. He ran his finger along the tiny face. Nothing: featureless fur from the top of the head to the snout. Rebecca's knee pressed his shoulder. "No. There's nothing at all."

"It's scared. I'm going to put it outside," maggie said.

"Be careful. They carry rabies."

"Just keep the cats in for a while." She picked the mole up, gently. "Oh! Oh, look at its hands!"

She carried it out the back door, carefully set it down in the grass, then came back and said, "You know, 'simple' isn't the same as 'easy'. Not always."

"True," Adam said, amused, but she didn't smile.

"I have to think," she said.

She wanders into the small room adjoining the bathroom— her witch's den, with a drawing table pushed off to one side, piled with sketches, abandoned now, she will look at the candle; for hours, the room filled with smoke and Rebecca outside pacing or cooking elaborate food that she will refuse when she comes out, looking dazed. . . .

It's evening. She huddles under the quilt, the shepherd next to her; hugging a pillow printed with brown, white and blue pinwheels. Tonta poses, a white icon carved on the ladder that squats below the pipe that angles up from the potbelly stove across the room and goes out through the wall just above her bed.

"When are we going to take that apart and clean it?"

"mmmm."

A white flash, as Tonta leaps, misses a fly, and, grazing the ladder, barely lands on her feet. Ears flat, she scurries under the bed. Cairo growls. And Rebecca comes in and places black bread and a stew of beef, mushrooms, and carrots on the table.

"Are you asleep?"

"mmmmm."

"Do you want to eat?"

"I, uh, mmm."

"What?"

Her eyes half-open, she tries to speak. The words stick together like glue in her mouth. They eat. Adam drinks. Side seven wears on. Don Giovanni invites the Statue to dinner. Rebecca stops gobbling and says, "That's the thing—he really has guts, the bastard." She looks at the quilt. "You sure you don't want any?"

"N-no. Please. . . ."

"Okay. Sleep," Rebecca spits, and once again falls on her food.

The lumpy pink quilt shifts. The moonlight slants, pale, through the windows. Adam stares at the slowly congealing sauce on his plate, as Rebecca mutters, he leans back, head swirling. That's a devil moon, he thinks—three quarters.

*

It's blue tonight: a bright blue Volkswagen Squareback ahead on the road crawling slowly again the black concrete the white line again broken speeding, but this time he's managed to pull out, left, in, time, and passing, see on its side between the two doors an emblem. Oval. Blurred letters, he knows they contain the clue, that if he could read they would tell him what to avoid, what color what shape of green gray blue crawling, looming, beckoning,
> *just a flick of the wrist,*
Adam thought; as the walls of the attic sharpened around him. Just an incredible minute, then . . . . . .
> *maybe, this time.*

He'd slept only two or three hours. His clock said midnight. From downstairs he heard a clicking. He got up, dressed, and, from the top of the steps he saw maggie, high on a ledge she was kneeling, hemmed between spider plant dripping new shoots and a calla lily, *clickclickclickclick*. She was weather-stripping a window.

"For God's sake."

She turned. "Oh. Am I bothering you?"

"Yes. Why don't you wait till tomorrow?"

"I have to get some work done," *clickclick*, "now. Shit," she said, as another staple fell out, "I need nails."

"Why *now?*"

She looked at him briefly. "I may not be able to later," she said, and turned. Precariously, she began to climb down.

"Wait. I'll get them for you."

"I need the hammer, too."

"Yeah," he told her, "I figured that out already."

"I'm sorry."

Hordes of cockroaches fled as he turned on the light in the kitchen. He rummaged under the sink, screws, nails, and found the hammer wedged between jars labeled applesauce, plum jam, apple butter.

"Where's Rebecca?" he said, handing them up to her.

"I think she went to the reservoir. I was half asleep when she left. Would you...could I have a cigarette, too?"

"Sure. Give me the staple gun."

"Oh, Adam, you don't have to. . . ."

"I know. I don't have to do anything. Can you stand hearing something that's not *Don Giovanni?*"

"Of course." She looked shocked. "Has that been bothering you? I thought you liked it."

"I do. But not five hours a day."

"I'm sorry. You should have said something."

"Well, now I did."

He put on *Sketches of Spain* and started to weather-strip the door.

"You know, we don't have to do such a great job," she said. "This must be the warmest room in the house. Except upstairs."

"It saves on heating bills. The thermostat's here."

"Why do we never use this room?" *clickclickclick.* "Did you, last year?"

"Yes," he said. "I don't know."

"It's strange. It's like an entrance hall."

"Well, the telephone's here. The aquarium. . . ."

"That's it," she laughed, "the aquarium room. We could make my room the cat room, with toy mice and catnip, they'd love it. The sunroom can be for Cairo, with lots of bones. . . ."

"We could move out and leave the house to the animals."

"Right. But then, where would we go?"

He heard her begin to climb down. Then something clinked. As he turned she was grabbing at the lily, teetering, as it fell,

"Oh, SHIT no no no no. . . ."

"Just take it easy."

She knelt by the shattered pot, her glasses awry, as he went to get dustpan and broom. "Is there another pot?" she called.

"We'll find something. Here, you hold the dustpan."

Adam swept up most of the dirt, then squatted to pick up shards of terra cotta. A few shoots had broken off. She held the dustpan in limp fingers; said, "Balance isn't my strong point."

He took off her glasses, placed them on a shelf, and touched her cheek. "Look, it may survive. And Rebecca certainly will."

"She's so proud of that plant."

"That's right. It may do her good."

"Hey. . . ."

"Really," he said, as Miles' trumpet soared to the close of *Solea.* "Don't you think so?"

"I guess. . . ." She smiled reluctantly. "Maybe, a little humility all around would help."

They squatted amid the debris, the big plant between them, its spray of roots exposed, as the record ended, they swayed towards each other. For a second she lost her balance, swayed backwards, and his face changed, then changed back again as she caught herself, swayed back towards him and they kissed, lightly.

Now: does he say, "Let's go upstairs?" Does he take up the

kerosene lamp they used to light their way last summer before she receded and his flesh refused her again, again, which happened first? The dustpan is still in her hand. Cats are scrabbling in dirt. The record scrapes. She ducks her head, quickly, she nips the side of his neck, drops the dustpan and stands up. She mumbles something: "Like...even, love. . . ." and it gathers from deep in his belly, it flows down, it rises. They stumble, holding each other, up fourteen steps; and he's limp before the bed has even been touched.

She said, "If you'd only share it with me. Like last spring, we could at least—touch each other. And we got over it."

"Did we? You never came with me inside you."

"That was—my problem. But now I feel like you hate me." There was a scraping sound. "We don't have to fuck," she said. "Let's just lie here and hold each other."

"Yeah, two cripples. Two eunuchs," he snarled, and tried to caress her breast. Her hips. Scars, scars, the small knobby lump in her throat and the texture of goose flesh. The smell of her is distasteful, yet he probes, groping outward, and she gropes. From inside, from outside, their tentacles soundlessly slide on this extra, transparent skin he's grown, hard as glass. Somewhere there must be a fault, someplace, he thought, to smash it and let the pent-up waters gush. . . .

"Did this happen with Kay?"

The door opened downstairs. Rebecca's voice called, "Madamina...come on, kitty. Come on, Cairo." The door closed. Boots stomped, in counterpoint to that scraping, then the click of the light switch. Inside Adam's eyelids, a thousand cockroaches scuttled to their cracks.

She said, "My God, we just left the plant lying there. On the rug. The dirt. She'll. . . ."

"Look, you can't be with both of us."

"What? I...you mean. . . ."

She sat up abruptly, and reached.

"You left them downstairs," he said, "for once."

"Can't be...who can't... Adam? Who are you really jealous of?"

68

He's tired. Dead tired. The white line is blinding him, now, and the windshield sweating, black tentacles sinking into the road, turning liquid as Kay's voice comes out from between maggie's lips,

"What's the matter with your sister? Why can't she find a man?"

"That's Rebecca's secret."

"Great secret," Kay sneers. "Like your mother's 'accident,' right? Like your father's and uncle's 'secret.'"

"Leave that alone."

"Why? Is screwing your brother's wife sacred? Or your sister?"

"Cut it out, Kay."

"Hmm? Why the fuck did you marry me?"

"Okay, you want me to answer that?"

"Maybe you better not," Kay grit through clenched teeth, staring straight ahead, neck rigid, long fingers rigid stone-white on the wheel, "or sure, yeah. I might as well know the whole ugly saga."

"Pull over."

"I'm okay, I can drive."

He said, "Look, as a matter of fact, we never did. Okay?"

"No, not okay. Why not? You think either one of you really ought to have kids?"

"Pull over."

"Go to hell," Kay said, and flicked the wheel left as his fist exploded against her face the bone crumpled the windshield shattered, a cyclone of flame shot into his back as his hip thudded, knuckles scraped cinder, hot, black, and the flaking white line burning into his forehead behind his eyes—it is all ash.

"White's the Chinese color for death," he muttered.

"What?"

The bed moved. Through narrowed eyes he saw her sitting cross-legged between his knees, her shirt unbuttoned, her hair—not long; not black. He said, "Why don't you go smoke a cigarette?"

Someone was shoveling dirt or gravel. He turned over, stared

69

at the framed collage of dried leaves she'd made for him last week. There was a frond of fern, one oak and two sprays of white blossom on a gray background. The scraping noise stopped, then Don Giovanni was trying to rape Donna Anna, side one. Again the bed shifted with maggie's small weight. Then she stood, looking down at his back, she said,

"I'm sorry. I didn't mean. . . ."

Late in October,

Adam woke to see snow on red leaves; and, echoing off the walls of this attic where she had huddled under him, then beside him, and then moved away as his impotence turned to rage to icy, impersonal calm, three words. They drew him from under the covers. They thudded against the window in big, soft flakes, dissolved at impact, then reformed again: the same pattern.

cure means separation.

A truck, its hood lightly powdered, slid by on the road. A spider's eight legs scuttled down the curtain. Slow flies buzzed, staggering over their brothers' corpses littered in heaps on the sash. *cure means.* . . . The tentative rap of a hammer. A tinkle. The same thoughts, always circling back to the same conclusion. He pulled his clothes on and went out to the landing.

cure means. . . .
I gave myself a brother. Now I take him away.

For the last time from this perspective, above that space between sunroom and kitchen, he looks down: through plants trailing, partly obscuring the windows, crouched by the doors, he sees her removing a shattered pane.

He said, "What the fuck—what time is it?"

"Ten. I'm sorry, did I wake you up?"

"Oh no, of course not. I always sleep best with a chain saw next to my ear."

"I'm sorry. I was trying to be quiet."

"What the fuck are you doing?"

"Putting a cat door in." She held up a wood frame containing a hinged square of metal. "See? Now they can go in and out whenever. . . ."

"Oh, Christ."

Rebecca looked out from the kitchen and said, "Have some fucking coffee. We have to fucking leave in a fucking hour."

"You're so funny."

"Did you happen to notice it's snowing? It will be slow driving down."

"It won't stick," maggie said. "And think—tonight you'll be in San Francisco."

"Where it will be raining." He started downstairs. Cairo reared, his claws scraping the bottom step. maggie leaned back, her eyes on the rug, as Rebecca emerged again to hand him a cup.

"If you're not back in three weeks we'll come get you."

"I hope I can last that long."

"Well, you don't *have* to go."

"Don't I?" Adam said.

*

The back of the pickup bulged with some kind of construction, draped in black. It came up the drive, slowly, followed the curve to the place in front of the house where his car sat, not stopping, and then the car was gone as though an eraser had passed through it, soundlessly, still, but inexorably it continued down to the road, and turned; and faded

6.

(oct. 26, 10 P.M.)

cairo is sleeping in my bed—bailey probably luxuriously
spread out on the bathroom warm rug—i envy them—
their sleep seems so pure. the essence of sleep—terror and
seduction on a seesaw. i shifted down rapidly and the
place that i found myself was curled up on the bathroom
floor under the sink, where that mole was found. mole,
in shock, seemed dead. when i picked him up he was
quite alive and when put outside began digging into the
soil immediately. revived in his own element. mole has
no eyes. wild little creature portruding trunklike flesh
nose claws so huge on turtlelike legs, softest, most sensual
fur. found no trace of where eyes might have been
evolutionary years ago—i wanted to find the eyes. . . .

when i myself seem to have shifted back up it was quite
fast—realized i'd been very depressed in that place—felt
like i was dying, going with it—WHO THE HELL IS
SHIFTING THE GEARS? is it psychic? physical? must
make difference between what's set off by emotional
reaction and independent changes. disturbing in that i
cannot almost always count on myself. my subconscious
leads a life of its own. was this subconscious surfacing at
full force? experience itself not as disturbing as the gear
shifts. . . . . . .

*

It rains. It's warm.

On the other side of the two-day chasm my job in the city gashed into every week, the day I put Adam on the plane, and a long detour home, I ran up the steps, eager, happy, now, I heard Mozart from that magic world on the other side of the glass doors. They opened to lamplight; warmth; and I found she had wired a mirror up over the back-door window.

"Is it okay?" she said, "Is it. . .? I really love it, don't you? You look out and see. . .yourself."

It rains.

The snout leers after me as I go down the steps to the wood-pile, but those big white flakes were only a promise of winter. Already they've melted, and my boots trample piles of damp leaves, as I load my arms with wood, small spiders scatter. My arms full, moccasins slithering over the deck boards and one foot almost plunged through a rotting plank, I lurch back against a rail. From behind the doors, I hear the pound of a hammer. She's in there building a doghouse.

She squats, determined, a cigarette in her teeth, on the rug reddish-brown with sawdust, littered with nails and a saw and five big planks of plywood. Her ribs stick out.

"Why don't you break for lunch? There's stew."

"Okay. No, I'm not that hungry. But I'll have something with you. . . ."

Smoke, smoke at the table, the yellow chair, the ashtray; coffee, The Roses and Madamina stalk nails. Cairo chomps on a stump of old bone as I gobble the stew and she mouths two spoonfuls of yogurt, "I'm full." There's a piss-yellow puddle under the ladder and one in the doorway. I curse, but maggie says,

"I'm worried about him. He's getting emaciated."

"How about *you*?"

73

"Oh, I'm—wiry. I don't have diarrhea, anyhow. I think a rice diet is supposed to be good for that. Or fasting."

"I might try fasting myself. I can't fit into my clothes."

I soak up the rest of the stew with a heel of bread, resisting the urge to lick my plate. I gulp my apple, then stare down. Nothing else. No more to put in my mouth. Looking up, in the silence, I see her compassionate face. She pushes the half-full container of yogurt across the table.

"There," she says, "will that satisfy you?"

It rains.

The saw scrapes. The hammer pounds. Heat fills the room, and a somnolence—a reluctance to step outside, to see the sky gray the grass yellowing and the few shriveled apples dangling, brown, from their boughs. Half past four by the windows: Bailey drowses in my lap, a husky, curled warrior. I watch the other three cats walk down the drive in a neat row, calico, white and white, then scatter as the red fat-assed car Charles Woolf drives turns in and belches to rest by his house.

She said, "It's like having no skin."

In one picture, she kneels on the floor: in her terrycloth bathrobe, chin jutting, her arms around the black shepherd, whose snout almost touches her mouth. It's evening. She had just taken a bath. I lay in my bed near the wall of windows and watched her tongue-kiss him, then she would take him to lie with her under the pink silk and velvet quilt someone had given her. There was a satin pillowcase he'd ripped a hole in; and gnawed her fur purse to shreds.

There was a black hat someone had given her, too. Broad-brimmed, a hole in its crown, it has fallen near me. It's morning. The sparkle of Mozart's overture seems to reflect the cool sunlight cascading in through the windows and bounce it off walls, chairs, a ladder near maggie's bed, and The Roses curled white against Cairo's deep, impenetrable black.

She sits on top of the quilt in her old black polo, no pants; one

74

leg up, the other crossed under her. Little-girl legs. Dark bush, much darker than hair on her head. Simple. She would say "vunable."

"It's vu*lner*able."

"Oh." Softly, "We were on a subway together, we were both going to—the Big Apple; but I got off a stop ahead of you. Then I saw you coming towards me, but still we were going to the same place." Smoke drifts out of her hand. I put another chunk of wood in the potbelly stove, and smoke fumes out of the seams in the pipe that needs cleaning. "I was wearing a cop's gun. I had a white dog on a leash. Then a cop stopped me, gave me a ticket. He told me that it's against the law to frighten people."

She gets up to change the record. Side two. Mellifluous, Don Giovanni tries to seduce Zerlina; and maggie puts on the strangely formal black silk man's dressing gown someone had given her.

Elegant, tawdry, she sits down at the table. The dog lurches after her, carrying a lamb bone, he slumps near her foot. He still shits liquid: sick yellow puddles lying all over the house.

It's noon. The bone has started to splinter. We've reached side six, but the first few bands are chewed into ridges. We start where Donna Elvira proclaims her undying passion despite despite despite and I need to get out.

"Let's take a walk."

"Don't you want to listen through to the end?"

"Yes, but. . .it's the first nice day in a week."

She stretches, lazily. "O-o-okay. Let's go. . . ."

She's walking slower, now. She stops. She runs her hand along pillars of smooth gray skin in the beech grove. She bends: she inspects roots, twigs and stones. She stoops. The wind blusters above our heads, and with every gust, leaves fall. Very carefully, she will select one leaf, or peer at a fungus growing on dead bark—her attention more and more exact as her breath goes.

"I wish you'd be careful," the water inspector said, "now that hunting season's on."

Above the falls, we met a log with a face, and lay next to it. Yellowish foam gushed down over rocks. Floating leaves clogged the pool below.

"Where's Adam now, I wonder."

"He's home, I guess. Funny word for that place. Where are you?"

"Right here," she smiled. "I *think*."

"I mean—what happened last night?"

"Oh." The smile dissolved. "You mean in the bathroom?" She looked down at her hand moving over the log. "I just kind of—passed out."

"I know, but, but, I, didn't know what to do. Should I call your therapist? If it happens again? Should I have her number?"

"No, I don't. . .I don't know. Look, I didn't tell you, but I've been seeing this neurologist in the city. He thinks some cases of *petit mal*, you know, epilepsy, never get diagnosed. It's a special kind, called temporal lobe epilepsy—the spasms don't show up on tests."

"And he thinks you have it?"

"He thinks—maybe. He gave me pills, and Ann says it won't hurt to try. . . . "

"Should I give you one if that happens again?"

"No. They work over the long run. I don't think. . . . Listen, if. . . . "

"What?"

"It's a hard thing to say, but, but, if you're getting tired of this, I could—I could still move back down to the city."

Cool air drifted up from the falls. Yellow leaves, a red bird. Rough texture of bark on my palm as her fingers traced circles, spirals, arabesques around mine in a slow dance: but always we follow the contour; the twist in the hard grain.

I said, "Suppose the positions were reversed. Like, if I got— sick, and I said that to you. How would you feel?"

"I guess I'd be very insulted."

"Yes." I looked up, then quickly away from her eyes welling liquid that seemed to suffuse my own body. "That's all there is,

isn't there? Caring, I mean, really caring about somebody. What
else is it all about?"

We both stared down at the log; inhaled the sharp, sweet
evergreen smell. The sound of the water resonated as our two
hands moved over the smooth, gnarled wood.

*

seem to be writing some kind of journal—
(oct. 28)
because i am so tenuous most of the time it may be a
good idea to keep a sort of record of things. i get so tired,
physically, mentally, like heavy dry heat has been blown
into me—then the winds come—strong, energy, super
wide-awake feeling—alternating very quickly—so that if
my intentions are inclined in a direction i predominantly
now cannot sustain them—i wilt as heavy as elephant
ears dropped around me—happening more and more
frequently, curious because when i am 'awake' the surge
of things happening here—prospective work, reading,
etc.—is very vivid. . . . .

*

and, ran out of cigarettes again and so down the hill to the
house where big steaks sit on the table ready to fry, and big
greased potatoes to roast, for big Charles, his paunch hanging
over his belt; and Charley, too fat to run or play ball already, the
nurse from school said, *that's not healthy*, he's only eleven years
old; and Miss Charlene, big, beefy, blonde; and Carrie—the
mole on one side of her chin with two hairs sticking out of it, tired,
small gray eyes and her hips spreading, bursting the seams of the
cheap green slacks she wears as she carries little Charlotte, who
wails and howls, back and forth, back and forth; those chubby
cheeks still seem healthy, but, two years from now?

77

"No, you take the whole pack, maggie," Carrie says. "When I run out next time I'll come up and ask you." And rocks the baby, kisses it, croons and coos until it is quiet, and lays it down in its crib and pours out two cups of coffee and sits down, heavily.

"*Now*: that child has a good pair of lungs, I'm tellin' you. You sure you don't want to eat somethin', maggie? I have an apple cake here, it's store-bought, but pretty good. I think I'll just have a little, not that I ought to, but. . . . You sure? You're gettin' skin and bones, you know. I wish I could trade some weight with you, or my Charlene could. Ever since she got pregnant, that girl eats. . . . Believe it or not, she was slim a year ago. Well, of course, I was glad to take her in, I mean your child is always your child and I never liked that guy, neither. But maggie, I didn't expect as how I'd be babysitting all day and night and feeding them both and these days Charles keeps gettin' home earlier, people don't want to spend money on vacuum cleaners no more. He hasn't hardly made a sale in the past month, though don't let him know I told you. And prices is goin' up, why those steaks there cost nine dollars down at the corner, that's a lot, you know, maggie, but somehow I just can't bring myself to scrimp on food, no matter how poor we are. That's right. And that cheapskate not givin' in a cent for his kid, let alone for hisself, why he's here for dinner half the time. He's here five nights out of seven, I swear. And takes her out to the movies, now he'll spend money on that or on wherever they go, I have my idea about that, too. And her not doin' a lick of work, inside or out, why, the two of them run around as though they were never married and she a single girl. But when they was livin' together he wouldn't give her a dollar to have lunch out with her friends, maggie, that's how jealous he was of her. Wanted to coop her up in that little apartment like some old-time Italian would. Why, he even objected to her having coffee in her own kitchen with the girl who lived next door, just because she was colored, he said. Come home one day and throwed a scene, right in front of the girl, now I don't like that. Whatever opinions you may have of 'em, I don't hold with hurtin' peoples' feelings if you don't have to. Though of course it's true Charlene never cleaned the house. Not that I'm spick-and-span myself, as is perfectly plain to see, but there are limits. And then she'd be just as likely to spend the grocery money on some of that weird stuff she got into, herbs and stuff. We always give her extra though when she asked. Then he found out and we had our words about it. Uh-huh. Well, that's when it all come out, but there was no love lost for quite a while before that. Well, you tell me, maggie, what does a man expect when he marries a seventeen-year-old girl and then gets her pregnant right away? Sure, he's a lot older. Combs his hair and dresses that way to try to look like a young kid, but he's twenty-eight—so he says. Ten years difference, almost, and that's if he's tellin' the truth. Which I doubt. No, don't go yet, you have time for another cup, don't you? I tell you, every time he calls me 'Mom' it gets my fur up. But I didn't object to the marriage, that was a year and a half ago, maggie, because, well, with her runnin' off the year before that and gettin' involved with all that black magic stuff—oh, all I saw was a bunch of books about witchcraft and a Ouija board, and some herbs and pieces of fabric, I don't know what she used 'em for—not that I believe in it, but there's something just not wholesome, you know what I mean? And I didn't know who she was with nor where, and her only sixteen, after all. Well, the last time was five months. The year before she got married. We had a detective agency, maggie, and the police, and none of them couldn't find her. One day Charles got so desperate he got a fake mustache and dressed up like one of them beatniks, if you can imagine it—would have been a scream if we hadn't been worried to death—and he goes down to Greenwich Village to ask around, see if he could find anyone tell him where she was. No, it didn't. He was down there three days hisself, never did tell me all of it. No, she finally come on home by herself. So, then, when this Jerry come on the scene, and him with a steady job—he's a construction worker, maggie, no great shakes, but I'm not a snob, I was just as glad to see her settled somewhere. I didn't know, of course, what his character was. No, Charles don't like him much, neither, but mostly it's him and me don't get along. I don't want to be like a, you know, mother-in-law, but I tell you, if she follows through on that extension course and gets her high school diploma, she can do a lot better, with someone else or alone. To tell you the truth, my Charley has more sense than either him or her already, and he's not twelve. Speakin' of whom—there goes your dog, maggie, down to the mailbox to wait for the school bus. Now, isn't that a picture. Uh-huh, he's there every afternoon, and if that bus is late, he keeps on waiting until it's come. No, I don't think he'd bite any of us. He's not a bad dog, maggie, we know that. He gets all excited, is all. They don't understand that, across the road, they're scared of him. I tried to tell them, but there it is, some folks really have different ways of lookin' at animals. They don't let 'em in their house or pet 'em or spoil 'em the way we do. Now, here's the bus, and I declare, here's Charles already, too, and it's not three o'clock. They all come up on me at once. Well, Charles will keep them Jehovah's Witness ladies away, anyhow. They was due here at four. No, maggie, you don't have to go just because...oh, all right. You all stocked up with candy for this evenin'? Sure, any time. I told you, the next time I run out I'll come get some off you...."

*

And then there was Joel....
who brightened the halls in the night school where he and Rebecca teach two evenings a week they perform *I am, you are, he is*, for the local Spanish housewives and clerks and delivery boys of the Lower East Side, near where maggie's parents live. Joel lives near there, too: small, sprightly in white wool hat this first cold snap of the winter, his curly hair and a turtleneck and tight pants, striding, briskly, on Second Avenue, I-Rebecca see him, I dash out of Mike's Luncheonette, calling, HELP, Joel, there's a kid ran away from home in there, he is starving....

But Mike is feeding the kid. He feeds Cairo, sometimes, he tries to feed maggie. Every Monday and Tuesday before diving

80

into that world of institutional green and chalk and fear ("no, I, no unnerstan'"), Joel and I sit at Mike's: under plants, by the corner window, the radio blaring, as we prepare classes, prepare reassurance, eat bran muffins, coffee, and talk, Joel, talking now, slowly, kindly, he tells the kid about a place for runaways, he can trust them, they won't rat to his family....

"Come on up and see me."

Joel's penthouse: a shack perched on top of a tenement, Second Avenue. Out on the private, enclosed bit of roof, Joel grows tomatoes in boxes every summer. Inside it's slum-luxury: plants curling everywhere typed sheets of paper scattered and two smelly schnauzers who leap, snuggle, and somersault round the refrigerator containing just wine and pineapple yogurt,

"Yeah, I stopped smoking again. Try Number Thirty-Three," Joel tells me, after the kid has gone. I sit, stiff, on the couch with dusty gray wads of stuffing falling out of it. "You want to be protected," he says.

"Ye-e-es...."

"Don't lose that," he grins. "That's a good one. Keep that one."

Joel—swarthy skin, beard, a long, foxy face with pursed lips so goddamned obstinate, sometimes, snappy sometimes officious, but—beautiful.

That night I drove home at eighty miles an hour, through crackling cold. Frost whitened the deck boards. I crashed in the door, calling, *maggie,*

"My god," she said. "What happened?"

"Nothing. It's really beautiful out, really cold." I couldn't seem to catch my breath. "I may burst."

"What *happened?*"

"I told you, nothing. An afternoon with Joel. That's all."

"I see."

"Stop smiling. It's nothing. I'm fat, and I haven't had a period for three months, and that kind of thing is over for me...."

"Oh, Rebecca...."

"And, let's not talk about it. How are you?"

81

"I'm...okay. I kept waiting for kids to come, and"

"Kids? Oh, I forgot. None came?"

"Uh-uh. I guess around here the parents would have to drive them and it's too much bother. Besides, they might not want to come near us—especially tonight. I mean, we're kooks to them, I bet."

"Do you think so?"

"Sure. The witches on the hill. I've been feeling like one...."

"Well, of course. It's appropriate. Really we ought to celebrate."

"I think so." maggie smiled. "Well, in the absence of broomsticks—how about the swing?"

"Good idea. That should get rid of some of this energy, too."

("Happy Halloweee'eeeen....")

high, swinging, dizzy, above the creek chains hold a small slab of wood to the iron bar wedged in the flesh of two maples,

"push me!"

creak-whoooshhh, up/*splash!*

to a sky black with clouds like spilt milk, then Cairo; surges, dripping out of the ground, an invisible wolf to my red, riding,

"LIE DOWN NO OH NO HE'S"

"I've got him. Jesus."

"Thank youooooo....I'm going right into those clouds zooommm...."

thinking, yes, mother, but...no, but, to hell with you, mother, who looks like everyone's grandmother, witch—i remember: the god drove his milk truck, *rumble*, between the stars, that's thunder. that's wheels *creak* chains and *clank-clank* that's bottles breaking and spilling the wild glowing white as a shadow of moon disc slides behind cloud but her hands glow too, warm on my back . again, pushing me,

push me back again,

maggie...

whispered,

82

swing up. swing down. swwwwinggg,
high to sweet fall but don't cry, don't, crybaby—that's just a
moon and a cloud. that's all. just a big white face in the sky,
won't get *me*, she thought, *i* didn't spill any
> *think, think, thing,*

did i? did i?

> *what was it, then?*

mother of secrets; what?

> it's only...

wet wind in my eyes; an aroma, piercing the night, of apples,
scattered across the creek turning to earth and a sound of chain.
but let's be serious (gripping the cold metal links, bit, into her
palms) she thought, you, hiding there in the leaves—let's be real
for a minute. no milk-spilling nonsense nor chains bottles ohno
ahaha....

"Hey. Are you all right?"

"yeahahadon't stophahaaaaa...."

"Forgodsake. You sound like a maniac," Rebecca said; dark
maroon tone asking,

> *Should I be worried?*

don't tell her, whoooshh

> *bitch*

"aiiyam one. it comes out of, i just assumed that milk comes
out of...bottles...."

"What? I can't understand you."

"neither can aiieee," maggie yodeled
(it's okay, tell her. it-is-fine....)
but the presence behind her had moved; the warmth gone.

"Rebecca? where are you?"

"Over here. My arms are tired."

"Were you breast-fed?"

"What? Did I hear you right?"

"Yeah i said were you breast-fed. Breast-fed. BREAST...."

"Okay okay, no. Why? Were you?"

"YEESAHAHAH...I WAS...."

"Look, I want my turn. Come down. Now."

"But I'm just getting, up...no, listen. Just push me a little more, okay? then I'll stop," she called in her most sober tones; and the hands came back. that's it. just don't go too far out, in, and the hands will come back, maggie thought, i'm a sneak. i-am. rotten? totting, corruption of me, of him—already the maggots are crawling towards, oh no, not yet, please—not every crevice. . . .

She bent her head back, pale fingers were rippling above, that's leaves, and the cloudful of moon, albert ryder saw that way: painted it straight from the literal, i bet—like i—did. was. am, not, an artist, okay. okay, but so much more time and for nothing. for no damn excuse, for this pain: a life with no skin; and that cloud, so compelling, is only

(*swing, high, swwwinggg*)

a puddle of milk-white feathers, or skeins the princess wove to rescue her twelve enchanted brothers,

"Rebecca? Did you read Andersen's fairy tales?"

"What?"

"There's this fairy tale—I think it's called The Wild Swans. There's a princess. . . ."

"That's me."

"No, her name is Elise, not Rebecca. You're from a different. . . ."

but, what's in a name? she thought then; or a fairy tale? maggie elise ariadne rebecca, *she*: sits in the cart, mute, riding away to the stake still her fingers weave shirts with green flax that she made from stinging nettles her bare hands had gathered, not silk, maggie thought, jolting, swerving; not worms. . . .

"Hey, stop it!"

"What? I'm not"

no: nor a fluid secreted from any-body, nor, brown-transparent casings they've left to remind us why there are so few leaves left to turn this, fall was in August; and this month seems like December, and January he's due to

(*where are you?*)

Rebecca

said, "Oh, well, these trivialities. What's in a name?"

a trickle of...laughter. that's me. more and more, dribbling
into that other stream. are we becoming one person? are two of
us even...necessary? the swing dipped; and what's in a myth,
maggie thought, but another lens?

(pale as a cat's third eye. my familiar.

i know you, she told the thing filming across her vision, it:
flipped maggie up, down-in, side, and, let her hands slide; her
back arched, neck and head bent, her eyes wide to the wind from
the arc of the swing was itself a zoom lens focused on one soft
blur. hands: loomed, contacted, poked, ten excla-MA-tion points
into her, back

zoom

(my in-sides are laughing

zoom

make a sound: now; or must it be ice? must the executioner's
hand be on him before i can speak, save myself, save my

zoom

but no shirt. no flax, what's flax? one should have white
hands and long graceful fingers to weave

zoom

shirts? flax? maybe a sheet to wind

timetimetimetimetimetime

echoed out of the sparse leaves shivering, up, or is that maggie,
shivering, down, winding, up

two three four

zoom

the lens pitched her, large-small, far-close, her hands trying to
crawl up the chains and still that staccato collision means: hands
that are pushing her out and yet holding her up into air

(out of water that day was my own hand holding her ankle.
my lungs. my fingers clasped round)

zoom

a witch: in-side, out-side; which? maggie whispered,

six seven eight nine

                                              no
                          time winding ten twelve
                                         stop it

          zoom
ONE . . .
                  to spin. one to weave. one to cut
                         zoom
          zoom
                              pumpkins; broom, -sticks-of-her-fingers
                              (they laughed again, softly,
                              to sweep, in-to, out-of
                              (which? ? ? ? ?

                  zoom
          are you trying to get away?
                              yes yes yes YES!
   "What? I can't hear you," Rebecca said; and maggie tried to
shout, *listen, then! listen to me!* something surging that's different
from all the voices, *it's not okay.* tell her, *time.* shout, *listen.*
shout, *speak, save yourself, save your brother.* . . .
   "What?"
                         LISTEN!   (maggie shouted)
   "WHAT? ? maggie, goddamn it"
                              LIFE!!!
   and after? trailed back on a wisp of sound; but they're gone.
and she's still holding on to the swing, her hands, fingers, the
wine-apple surf, swinging, high to those wavelets of cloud but all
here: maggie: soaring astride the wild, whinnying breakers of
smell, touch, hearing, taste, sight. . . .
   "Yeah, whatever you said. Come down."
   "Okay, okay. I'm coming."
   scrape: earth. that's me. him. shuffle: leaves on the ground.
no flight. no dance but a *danse macabre*, feet caught in a red
mass, and cursed because i'm not there: I'm not taking care of
him, okay, *name it:*
          ("It's about time!"
   "yes i know"

                                 86

"What? Rebecca said. "What's the matter?")

dying.

maggie half stood, swaying; her cheeks wet. "No, nothing. I'm just—dizzy."

"Let's get some coffeee."

"You don't want to swing?"

"No, I'm cold. Aren't you?"

"I guess so. I'm sorry I took so long."

The moon emerged, low, just above the horizon, then sank into mist: yellow: color of squash, of urine, the sun and the school bus yellowing down the road every day now, maggie thought—horror is colored yellow.

"Don't you think it looks like an egg?" she said.

"What?"

"The moon. Sometimes it makes me happy to hold an egg in my hand. Just to hold it. Hey...."

"What?"

"Don't be mad any more. I'm sorry I hogged the swing."

"It's not that. It's, you close me so far out...."

"Yes. But sometimes it isn't possible to...look, it's like a zoom lens. It gets going faster and faster, and then"

"Then?"

"Snap. Void. Except there's a place in it sometimes that dips...."

One hand traced a motion. Her head cocked, dropped: a dove, nesting. They walked up the steps: gray wood, late October already; the swans that she'd never seen, gone. She opened the door. In sudden warm lamplight her face, growing thinner each day, changed.

"What's the matter? maggie...?"

"No, oh, oh, look. They're like rainbows."

"What?"

"The stars. Look, they're really jumping around up there."

Madamina rubbed her leg. Rebecca leaned against the railing, looking up at the sky. Something shivered between her belly and her chest.

"But," she said, "they're so dim. It's almost full moon."
maggie's chin came down. "You don't see a lot of colors?"
"No. It sounds—beautiful."
"It is." She looked up again. "I guess—I shouldn't want to lose
it. No matter what."

*

(nov. 1st)

my father web of death each week has spread coveting
over him...me watching...him being...

the words 'my father' have no meaning for me

but this man's hands, his hands
his eyes, his hands
i live in them
where will they go
papa lead me there

i can remember nothing else

your hands come to me in the veins of fallen leaves
but your eyes. . . .
will a mole inherit them and keep them secret
behind a mask of fur
will i collect moles to find them again

7.

Giant bootprints in mud. Airplane drone. Fall fall fall fall, winter coming—the underbrush trampled and brown as I come down the hill, off the trail, now, I see a different space: winter silhouettes, stark, through the rain falling, dark and warm.

Under the devil-god, a multifaceted beast riddle walked on three legs: the Fox, or the Welsh Mother Goddess who eats men. The bright orange cloth I have tied around Cairo's middle flaps as he lunges, long hair flying, across the path. Through a screen of sudden rage I see his beauty, his liveliness as an impudence I want to beat to bloody pulp. I am afraid of my violence. How when one thread in the net of control snaps it rushes out. . . .

The day I began to fast, I'd put a roll near the toaster. I went to the bathroom to wash, put my breasts in their caskets, my feet in their portable torture chambers, the outer camouflage smoothed down over it all, then the earrings maggie had given me; came back and found—no roll. Cairo lounged on the rug, a few crumbs in front of his narrow snout. I reached. He scrambled under the table, I lunged, stuck my hand in to drag him out and punish him, he, had, taken, my, FOOD. . . .

Teeth sank into my finger.

I pulled my hand out, stared at the ribbon of blood, and then, slowly, stood up. I walked to the kitchen, slowly, the rage turning icy-numb, I found the broom and carried it back, slowly, then it was coming in short, sharp spurts I jabbed with the

89

handle, low—careful, aiming at soft spots in the black pelt, the cornered wild creature cowering, fangs dripping, growling he snapped at the wood as I thrust it, baiting him now and the sweat trickling over my scalp; through my hair; yet my mind is perfectly calm.

Consider Nero, and Henry the Eighth, and all those very fat men so involved with others' blood, I thought, revving the motor up. I coasted downhill and stopped by the mailbox. Nothing— nothing from California. The shepherd's beast-head lifted as I turned onto the highway, "Get down," I snarled, and he cringed back down on the seat. Slopes of twigs gleamed, lacy-naked in dim November sun as we hurtled south. Consider: cruelty is the other side of greed. Now a black line cut through the sky turning gray, just past the tollbooth, tall buildings came into view and a sign said

ENTERING NEW YORK CITY.....

Still, a fountain geysers rainbow-spray out of the river. Flocks of birds wheel over Fourteenth Street, down Second Avenue, as I park near a cluster of shiny bikes, the radio blares Janis Joplin dead of an overdose. Scrawled on the wall:

Q. Mr. Gandhi, what do you think of
   Western Civilization?
G. I think it would be a good idea.

I waited on the corner of Fourth Street for the light to change. Cairo sat by my leg, docile. Across Second Avenue, through Mike's dirty window, I could see maggie at a table with someone I didn't know. Two ten-year-old boys buzzed around me, "Hey, gimme a kiss, gimme," leers not yet quite at home on their grimy faces. I crossed, tied Cairo's leash to a parking meter in front of the window, and went in.

Steamy warmth, an acrid smell. WNEW jiggled and jolted rock, rock-a-bye to the counter full of scarred Lower East Side denizens. Outside, Cairo barked, straining towards the window. towards maggie in shiny black slacks, a work shirt, the purple

90

scarf on her head, hunched over a cup she listens as a big, chubby man with smooth skin the color of coffee and cream talks, talks.

"This is Jesse Clarke," she told me, looking up. "Rebecca."

"Uh-*huh*," the man smiled.

I nodded. "I've heard about you, I think. You're a musician?"

"Uh-huh."

maggie said, "I better go talk to Cairo."

The fan blew trailing leaves around. Mike leaned across his counter and yelled to me, "Coffee?" Jesse stared at me frankly, smiling. I turned to watch maggie kneel outside on the pavement, her hands in Cairo's bushy fur. Mike set a cup in front of me.

"Something to eat?" he twinkled.

"No thanks, Mike. I'm fasting. I need to lose some weight."

"A healthy young girl like you? Don't be silly," Mike said, and patted my shoulder, "you don't need to lose anything. You should be fatter."

"That's right," Jesse said, as maggie came back in, "you don't want to get like *her*."

"Hey, Miguel," a man at the counter called. "Is there a chance of some food around here?"

"Okay, okay, in a minute," Mike yelled, then turned back to us, shaking his gray head. "Too many customers," he grumbled, "too much work. If I win on this next race, I'll retire. I bring you a muffin," he told me, winking at Jesse, and danced back behind the counter.

"Like who—what were you talking about?" maggie said.

"You. You're getting skinny. There was a time, you know, when you had a figure."

"You mean when you kept making remarks about my fat ass?"

"Well, that's true. You did get a little. . . ."

"Hey—did you hear Janis Joplin died?" I blurted.

"Joplin?" Jesse sat straight up. "When? What of?"

"I just heard it on the radio. They said an overdose."

"Overdose, hell," Jesse snorted. "She wasn't taking anything she could overdose *on*."

91

"Then what. . . ?"

"The music. It's really threatening them, more than any political group. You look at it. Hendrix, now Joplin. . . ." He sat back, his deep voice flowing out, as smooth as his skin. "It's changing the way people think, and in a way the power don't understand. They understand just enough to know they don't like it."

"But to the point of. . . ?"

"To the point of, sure, lady. We're talking revolution. You think they'll let that happen if they can stop it?"

Mike came back, twinkling, and put a toasted muffin in front of me. Two young men started in the door. Mike leapt out in front of them, suddenly fierce, he shouted, "NO, no more—I'm CLOSED."

"But it's not even one o'clock. The place is full of people. . . ."

"I'm still closed." He shut the door in their faces, as Jesse chortled, they backed off, and one collided with Cairo. He jumped away as though he had hit a hot poker. Cairo lifted his snout and barked.

"We'd better go," I said. "Before he bites someone."

"Oh, I don't think he'd. . . ."

"No? He bit me this morning."

"He *bit* you?"

"Yes. Bit. Not nip," I enunciated, holding my right hand out to her. "See? Bite. Blood."

"That dog is crazy," Mike said. "He's too skinny, that's his problem. Like you. Here, I give you some hamburger for him."

"Oh, no, don't. . . ."

"Why not?" Mike said over his shoulder. He rummaged in the refrigerator and came back with a wad of meat wrapped in foil. "Here. You give him this. Don't worry, it's good."

"How much do we owe you, Mike?"

"Three coffees, forty-five cents. That's all."

"That's not the way to make money," Jesse said.

"Money—the horses make me money. This place. . . ." He

lifted his eyebrows skyward, then moved way, muttering. maggie turned to me.

"Listen, I don't know what to say."

"Let's just go now."

"What about that muffin?" Jesse said.

"Here, it's yours. Bring it with you."

Then we were walking three abreast, with Cairo licking his chops and straining at the leash maggie held, down Second Avenue, Laundromat, hardware store, *Jesus Saves* in neon across from it, and a *Hare Krishna* chant drifting out of a nearby second-floor window, as we started to cross Third Street, then, in the middle, maggie clutched under her coat.

"Omygod. My slacks are coming down."

"Hold on," I said, "let's get to the curb. I have a safety pin."

She leaned against a wall as I ferreted out the pin and tried to gather the folds of shiny black material into it. Giggling, we huddled close together; and people walked by and a few feet away a tug of war developed as Cairo tried to drag Jesse off the sidewalk. maggie yelled, "NO NO LET HIM HE'S TRYING TO SHIT!" then, a broken whisper, "Oh, God," and covered her mouth. Faces turned. I almost collapsed with laughter. My hands still stuck to the pin in her waistband, I gasped,

"Hold still."

"Goddamn these pants. They're supposed to stay up."

"Well, you know," Jesse called from the curb where he stood with the crouching shepherd, "people who wear pants generally have something to put inside them."

"OH SHUT UP. . . ."

A flock of white birds swirled up, such a motion of joy that I reeled; then her hand was on my arm, her voice throbbing, low with excitement, reassurance: *we're in this together. . . .*

Jesse is gone, now. We've locked Cairo into the car. And we are walking, she and I, on a narrow sidewalk, past open stalls full of fruits and vegetables, under signs in Yiddish.

"He likes you," she said.

"I like him. What does he play?"

"About five instruments. Mostly trumpet."

"He's the one you lived with, right?"

"Yup. Eight months. I really did have a fat ass—we used to make gorgeous dinners every night, the two of us. He's a great cook. Every night he wasn't working or out with somebody else, that is."

"Oh, did he do that?"

"Yes, well—that was part of the program. I'd really convinced myself it was fine, you know—a woman would call and he'd tell me all about how wonderful she was, and I'd be *happy* for him. . . ."

"I couldn't stand that."

"I couldn't either. That's one reason I left him. I didn't know it at the time, but. . . well, now I do. He really likes women, you know, it's never casual and, well, it seems okay with the girl he lives with now. Grace, her name is. She's beautiful. Nuts." She hesitated, then, "Sometimes, maybe twice a year, he comes around and we—for old times sake, kind of. A beautiful lover, really. And smooooth. . . ."

A cluster of women picking out vegetables blocked the sidewalk. We stepped down into the street and immediately were jostled by a man in a black hat and side curls. The smells of Jewish cooking streamed out of the windows. Voices chattered in Yiddish, and maggie, I realized, could understand them. In her scarf, her jacket, she seemed native to this: a sprite, still—yet rooted in such fat soil.

I said, "How's your father?"

"The same, I guess. A little weaker."

"Were you there this morning?"

"Yeah. But—I can't go there alone any more. I get crazy. If someone's with me—Jesse came up today—it's better. Or Susan, yesterday. . . ."

But, it's now: it's *now*, I stand here immobilized by the hard ridge of shame that runs from my belly up to my throat; afraid of her eyes, afraid that I might melt, on this street spitting smells and sounds that batter against this tunnel we've entered, separately, unknowing, until at moments like islands we find ourselves alone together: enclosed in a silence that finally, small and cold, my voice punctures:

"Everybody but me."

"You don't have to. I know—it's pretty depressing. . . ."

"It's not that. You know it's not that. Don't you?"

"Look, you don't have to explain. You can't, that's all."

She touched my arm; an attempt to release me, but something pushed up at the ridge, pressing hard on my chest. maggie linked her arm in mine and pulled me gently along. The ripe kosher smells faded into Italian aromas of garlic, olive oil, as the alphabet changed, *it's okay*; my stomach growling along Canal Street, coffee, coffee, then we turned uptown again, *okay, you can't,* in luncheonettes where the smells blend, the sounds merge, the colors all run together in scattered monochrome pools out of which humor bubbles, the grease that this city runs on, and on, and, on, *you can't, that's all.*

That week I starved myself, to be thin like her; mad like her. With her hand on my arm, I welcomed every tremor of dizziness, each distortion I thought might transform the opaque walls of my consciousness into windows through which I could look, or climb, even, into that other dimension: that glow I've called *maggie. . . .*

It drew us into the streets one whole night—in and out of bars, picking up men, then discarding them. Under a sky stained red, we wandered, past manholes like mouths of hell, the steam spewing up towards the street lights that turned her face purple, and neon, dim green, orange. West of Sheridan Square the streets turned darker: deserted at 4 A.M., except for a few skinny cats and us and Cairo. We climbed on a car in front of a little red door that said #13½ Perry Street. Clouds were gathering, moving swiftly, but it was the stars that seemed to move, advancing, in formation, to some celestial conference; or war.

I said, "Look, there are the Pleiades. And there's Perseus."

"Where?"

"That kind of triangular one, with the line coming up. Just

beyond Casseiopia, there, see?"

"You're really getting good. I've hardly learned any of them." She swiveled her head on the windshield. "I can't, can't, concentrate, hardly at all. I used to be able to. . . ."

"What does the doctor say? What's his name, Cecchetti? The one who gave you the pills, does he still think it's epilepsy?"

"Yes. Cecchetti. Strange man," she said. "I think it's too early to tell."

"Have you noticed any difference?"

"I don't know. I'm nauseous on just two glasses of wine, but. . . ."

"What about that lump?"

"It's the same. We're watching it. Oh, look—the stars are double!"

"*Double?*"

"Yes, don't you see? Almost all of them."

"No." I squinted. "Well, maybe a couple. Not most of them."

"Oh." She shivered. "It's—cold. Don't you think? All of a sudden. That must be true about the hour before dawn."

"There's more than an hour," I said, stretching. I felt perfectly warm. "But let's go. I wanted some coffee, anyway."

"I guess we should. Oh, it's so perfect here." She sat up on the hood, cross-legged. "This was my time, when I lived here—between about three and seven. I used to walk, all over. . . ."

"Alone?"

"With Cairo. Nobody bothered me. I'd talk to people or mostly they'd talk to me, but—I'm not a victim type. You're not, either."

"What's a victim type?"

"Someone who wants it, I guess."

We look up at the sky. I squinted again. With my eyes narrowed, I could see a few more of the stars doubled. Out from under the clouds they moved, still quickly—but now they seemed unmistakably warlike, and implacable. Next to me, maggie breathed deeply: a scraping sound as the air whistled in through her chest and out. I thought of the fifty cigarettes she smoked

96

every day; the scar on her throat and the scars slashed into her arms. And then of the tons of food I stuff into myself, gorging, aching, yet driven until my stomach rebels. And of my brother and cars, in Texas, in California—what is a victim type, maggie? and where, where is Adam now, I wondered—sleeping? Alone, or at home with my father and Bea, or. . . .

"There's a coffee place open just a few blocks away," maggie said, sliding down the fender. "We really should leave a note for the owner of this car. Do you have any paper?"

"I have a check. We could write on the back of it."

"No, your name's on it. This has to be anonymous. How about"

"You're really going to do it?"

"Sure. Gimme."

> *Dear Mr. Car Owner:*
> *Good morning! Ariel-Caliban thanks you for your*
> *hospitality on a trip taken this morning.*

She showed it to me. I took the pen out of her hand, still perched on the hood, I leaned the slip against the windshield and added,

> *The car has not moved, but we have. Again, thank you.*

"Right," she said, grinning. I folded it under the wiper and slid down, slightly dizzy and feeling as though I were really disembarking.

"Who's Caliban in this scene?" I asked suspiciously.

"We're both both, of course. Aren't we?"

I'm far from that now. In time like a sidewalk unrolling, slowly, quickly, I'm carried away from her; in space, far. The voices are different, as I slide past, and the light; yet textures, sounds, colors, and smells still spiral around and back, intersecting this lengthening spine to which my feet are fixed; that moves forward, only. Inexorably, the two motions cross and criss-cross, returning me to: New York: 1970, 5 A.M., mid-November.

The stars blurred. A fuzzy-edged half-moon rose above buildings. Traffic lights clicked in the naked streets and birds were just beginning to wake as we walked the few blocks to Riker's.

There was a stink of stale grease as we entered, sat down at a horseshoe counter. Two young hoods watched us from the other side of it. Beside me, a small, seedy man was reading a paper in Italian. A boy slumped next to maggie; strands of limp blond hair dipping into his cup. The counterman, gaunt and gray-haired, stood in front of us.

maggie said, "Two coffees."

He nodded. Then, "Faaauuuughh. ' Tis an unweeded garden. Things rank and gross possess it.'" he said, raising one hand dramatically, pausing to glance at the hoods, then bringing his fist down hard on the counter, "'MERELY....'" he spat, and opened his eyes wide at maggie.

"Yes," she said, gazing at him solemnly.

"Yes," he repeated, nodded again, looked again at the hoods, and went to get our coffee.

"My God."

"Yes. He always does that. Shakespeare, only Shakespeare." She beamed. "I love him. That's why I thought of Ariel and Caliban back there. I used to come here around this time just to listen to him."

The counterman came back, reserved now, his manner almost elegant despite the stained white apron he wore with his neat shirt and tie. He put a platter of eggs near the seedy man's arm, then, with a flair, he set two chipped cups in front of us. The hoods were staring at maggie.

"What do you think that is? Italian?" one of them said, loud.

maggie looked down. The seedy man folded his newspaper, glanced at us covertly, and started to eat.

"Maybe Sicilian, huh. And Scorpio, I bet. Huh?"

"French," the seedy man whispered to me hoarsely.

I said, "Why don't you leave us alone."

"Who's talking to you, huh," the hood snarled, curling his lip.

I glared at him. maggie shuddered. The blond boy raised his head, fixed red-veined eyes on her, and started to talk. No food, no sleep for days, he muttered. Tomorrow the army physical. If this doesn't work, he said, leaning almost on top of her, there's always Canada. She nodded, with the sympathy she calls up for anyone, *anyone*, I thought, and fought down a spasm that might have been hunger, or jealousy.

"Witch."

The word floated back on a layer of smoke as the hoods swaggered out the door. The boy was mumbling, the paper beside me had been unfolded again, the eggs were gone but still an aroma lingered. The boy mumbled, "Hunger pangs, that's not bad. It's the lack of sleep really drives you crazy." The counterman came back with two checks and the coffee pot.

"Filthy lucre," he told us sternly, pouring.

I dug out some change as maggie smiled at him, but, *you-crazy, drive, me-crazy*, spun round in my head, *she-crazy*, so fast for a moment I almost gagged, yes—we all have our reasons: our secrets that we reveal to her, unsolicited, spreading our arms wide open while she keeps hers wrapped around her own ribs, yet they seem to embrace us with instant incredible warmth that she can exude, even now, staring into her cup, her voice confiding; placating.

"Look, do you see what the milk is doing? It's like a—film."

"It's probably sour."

She dipped her head. "No, it smells okay. It's just lying on top of the coffee, not mixing. Isn't that strange? How's yours?"

I looked. "Same thing. I hadn't noticed."

"Hmm. It looks like there should be—a hole in the film you could drink through." I stared at her. "Yeah, that's not bad," she smiled. "You look tired, hey. How do you feel?"

"A little dizzy." I shook my head. "How are you?"

"O-o-okay. But let's go, before we're too tired to walk across town."

Trash skittered across the sidewalk. The air felt chilly but good as she closed the door, and we walked back out into the streets of Greenwich Village, at dawn, I realized: this was the

99

birthday she'd asked me to ignore. She was twenty-five. We had walked a tacit celebration, a tacit farewell, before the seige that we both knew would begin...soon.

The little seedy Italian followed us out; down Seventh Avenue he leered behind us, murmuring; disappeared; then drove up next to us, in the cool, gritty dawnlight, he called,

"Lesbiannes...." —the way he said it like a name: two girls with the same name, a plural, Mariannes, Lesbiannes— "You are happy?" friendly, almost, curious, cruising along beside us, "You are happy as you are?" then shifting back to, "Lesbiannes! LesbiANNES!"

We walked away from him, arms linked, locked together against his voice, but still it floated all around us; between us. That moment I looked at her, and saw an old woman: muffled and cloaked, a fugitive at a railway depot in Central Europe, the late thirties; on her face a mask of suffering. I saw my own life behind the lines—an occupied country while I was with her. In Washington Square, we lay on our backs on stone slabs, parallel, close, we watched the sun come up. The street filled with trucks and cars, the smell of cinder. My throat felt raw. My muscles ached as though I'd been punched. In that bitter light, I looked at her lying next to me, smudges under her eyes, no longer old, but limp as a rag doll. Her skin seemed smeared across her cheekbones like chalk.

I closed my eyes: saw an ugly, sardonic fantasia made up of fragments of our lives these past months: the trivialities constantly turned catastrophic, the minor accidents we would inflate to high tragedy, she and I. It was absurd—this landscape of coffins studded with double stars that glinted like rainbows promising truth, truth, radiant truth; yet I couldn't give up the hope that it might be real: though the road to it might lead through cancer, or epilepsy; or—schizophrenia.

"Hi."

I opened my eyes. She was sitting up, smiling. She stretched her arms over her head, emitted a long, high yodel, then jumped to her feet and up and down a few times, pointing east. I dragged myself up. We skipped across Fourth Street, half dancing, the city clanking, and clouds obscuring the sun above a busy, business-y world of people scurrying, shoulders hunched, heads down, to work.

I left her in front of that door, then dragged myself through a day like a marathon: errands, classes, the clouds dissolving to dirty rain, and the nerves of the city seemed to clank inside my veins. By the time I came out of class and drove downtown I had reached a frenzy of nervous exasperation.

I sat, dry-mouthed, waiting behind the wheel. She came out running, rain streaming down her face. "What a night," she panted.

"Cairo, get the fuck down," I snarled. "Look, we have to start leaving him up there. He's just too much trouble."

"Okay. Listen, Susan wants to come up for Thanksgiving. Like a communal dinner. What do you think? We could ask Jesse, and Joel. . . ."

"Sure, a party. Just what we need. Why not everyone's sisters and brothers, too?" I said. "Goddamn these wipers!"

"Hey, take it easy."

"Well, fuck it, I can't see."

"Look, we can stay at Susan's tonight. She suggested it."

"No. I want to go home."

"Then let's stop and get something to eat. The rain might let up."

"You know I'm fasting."

"Well, maybe you should stop. How long has it been, three days? And with no sleep. . .you know people fasting don't usually run around. . . ."

"I don't *want* to eat," I snapped, as we turned onto the East Side Drive. Muddy water, spewed up by a passing truck, almost blinded me. "Goddamn sonofabitch," I shrieked.

"Hey, look. . .okay, if you don't want to eat, how about coffee?"

"*We're going up there. Now*. Stop talking, it makes it worse."

"Okay." She folded into herself; and I hunched over the

wheel, in tense silence, I peered straight ahead, ashamed, yet I knew the exasperation was there like a dog, to keep panic, bleating, enough in control so that I could function. We crossed the bridge; passed the tollbooth. The traffic thinned. Even through darkness, I could feel the presence of trees. I looked at her, huddled in shadow, her face pinched,

"I'm sorry," I murmured.

She smiled, wanly. "We'll make it. We always do."

Now in the darkening room, Cairo sleeps, a bison—the strange, soft corner of his mouth. The Roses curls, beautiful, beside me; a strip of Madamina in the chair. There is a dripping sound.

maggie lies in her big blue sleeping bag, muttering far into not-really-sleep; her eyes somewhere troubled.

A cough. Smoke.

On sudden impulse, I got to the kitchen and pick up a knife, without hunger, I cut a segment of apple and bite into it. The juice puckers soft membranes in my mouth. The texture is strange. I am aware of every fraction of throat, of esophagus, as the pulp travels down. I leave the rest of it lying and go back, noisily, I sit down and try to make a list for Thanksgiving—a people-roster I write in a tiny, cramped hand, I can't see well.

She said, "Some things can't be trespassed on."

Five-thirty and dark. Plastic hangs by the window, ready for stretching and stapling, to keep out the cold. The ladder stands under the pipe. Two cats are pregnant. maggie's breath rasps. It rains, it rains, as I light the lamp, my own hand appears, skeletal, on the wall—

hazy flesh; dark bones.

*

there was a scorpion on the ladder.

a concentrated malevolence
          maggie
tried to back away from, but space, changed, every, step
was tiny; infinitesimal. she tried to call, tell rebecca to
get, out, *she was close to the door, she had a chance; but*
the effort of, sound, swelled the membranes inside her,
throat, and stuck, the space-balloon choking her silent
          (can't. . .
               speak, speak
stretching and shrinking her, turning it all, all, all, all,
every thing
          in-side-out

III.
MOLLUSC

8.

17   *Following*

Thunder in the middle of the lake:
The image of FOLLOWING
Thus the superior man at nightfall
Goes indoors for rest and recuperation.

"In the autumn electricity withdraws into the earth and again rests.
Here thunder is in its winter rest, not thunder in motion.
Thunder in the middle of the lake...times of darkness
        and rest."

*

Long threads of rain streaked horizontally backwards outside the
window as Adam's plane came over the hills, then limbo: only
the wing slanting, gray turning reddish and brightening now it
broke through and he saw water, and a white city floating, it
seemed, under heavy clouds: home: San Francisco.

The air still carried that special damp chill. The cable car
clanked round the corner at Jackson and Polk, past that bar into
which Adam walked, had one quick drink, then walked out. The
doorman smiled at him, brightly Californian. Too young, too
new, he thought.

"Well," his father said, "how did the treatment feel?"

"Pretty good." He looked out at the bridge, disappearing in
fog.

"The doctor said five times, right?"

"Six. Look, Dad, I thought I'd take a ride down to Big Sur."

"That's a good idea," Bea said. "Let's all go."

"No, I meant...I thought I'd go with a girl."

"Oh?" Her thin lips narrowed. "Who? Someone you used to know?"

"The physical therapist at the hospital."

"No kidding. Fast work," his father said. "That may do you more good than all the traction machines in the world."

"Is she Jewish?" Bea asked.

"Nope."

"Mmm."

"Oh, Bea, get off his back. He's only taking the girl for a ride."

"One thing leads to another."

"Is she good looking?" his father asked, leering slightly.

"Yeah, she's pretty. Very blonde." He smiled at Bea. "Very waspy. We're getting married next week."

"You may joke. . . ."

The white line is thick and broken with colored studs in California, bright yellow and red tracing south past cluttered houses and shops, then it all widens out: Half Moon Bay; Carmel; the road where he'd camped with Kay one whole week they had listened to Monterey jazz every night they'd come back to eucalyptus, a perfume surrounding their tent,

> *No, keep away from that. Dangerous intersection.*
> *Stay Right. Two Way Traffic, don't, DON'T TURN. . . .*

"Are you all right?" the girl next to him said.

"Sure. I just don't feel like talking. Okay?"

"Okay." Her voice sounded doubtful. She huddled away on the far right side of the right seat, and looked at him. Adam pulled the car over and got out.

He walked to the edge of the cliff. Reddish, clustered bushes covered the ground, the steep slope. Waves gleamed, foaming on a small strip of beach far below. She came to stand beside him. He tried to ignore her, irritated in spite of himself, he moved a few steps away from her. The ground was pebbly. He shot downward, suddenly, almost a vertical plunge, then jolted to a stop, just as suddenly, on a small butte.

She braced herself just above him. "Are you all right?"

"Of course," he snapped. "Stop saying that, will you? We're not at the hospital now, you know, and I'm not a cripple."

"Of course not. I just meant. . . ."

"How does that look to you?" He pointed down at the beach. "Want to camp there?"

"I, I—guess so. I don't have to be back until"

"Good. I brought a sleeping bag and some towels."

"I'll get them," she said. "All right?"

"Sure. If you're feeling that lively."

He watched her slender body disappear over the edge, then reached into his pocket and pulled out the pint of brandy. The sharp draughts warmed him as he squatted, waiting. Pebbles scattered past him, then, his sleeping bag plummeted by, "HEY. . . ." He looked up. She'd crouched at the edge, about to toss a towel, "Hey, you're starting an avalanche. . . ."

"What?"

He jammed the bottle back in his pocket and started after the bag. The gravel seemed looser here—so loose it gave him no purchase at all. Except where a rock or log had fallen across the slope he slid, grabbed at vines, tried to hold on, *hold on*, but his arms weren't strong enough, never had been, *never enough*, "Stop," the girl was calling, "wait," but he'd panicked now: scrabbling he slid, slid, and finally stopped, scraped and battered, against a big exposed root.

"Shit shit shit shit." Pain knifed down his leg. She was climbing down towards him, nimble, he thought, as a goat. "I can't move. Why did you have to throw that stuff down?"

"But that didn't. . . . I just thought it would be easier. Let's get you down to the beach and onto your back. All right?"

"No, not all right. I can't even. . . ."

"Sure you can. Just roll, let me do the rest."

"Wait, let me take a drink first. You want some?"

"That didn't break? Sure, gimme."

"Really? You sound so much like a Sunday school teacher. . . ."

"Oh, no."

The sun had set over small, blue-violet waves by the time they had settled him into the sleeping bag; one orange streak bisecting the sea like a bright equator. Little fishing boats were floating across it. One was anchored right on it. The sky filled with red and blue creatures constantly changing shape; tone.

"How's that?" she said. "Comfortable?"

"Oh, it's fine as long as I don't move."

"Then don't. Ask me if you need anything. All right?"

"I don't seem to have much choice." He looked at her thin face smeared with sand, now, as fog moved in, swiftly obliterating the sky, their hands touched. "Aren't you cold?" he said. "Come on in."

"I'm afraid I'll hurt you."

"Well, you can't spend the night out there."

She smiled and climbed in beside him, carefully, jolting him only a little, she wrapped her arms around him, one palm against his back, flat. The light faded. Sea sounds rushed around them.

"That feels good," he said. "Your hand, there."

"Yes. Warmth always helps."

"You think I'll get up there tomorrow?"

"Or the next day. You can do anything you need to." She moved closer to him. Her fingers probed into the muscles around his spine. The pressure, even the pain of it, eased him. "Do you think you can sleep?"

"After that, sure. Can you?"

"Mmm-hm. 'Night." She turned and seemed asleep in a moment.

Damp seeped into the bag, and cold. Her hip bumped him. She turned, back, forth, back, her light breath warming a patch of his neck, tickling. One pale curl had stuck to the curve of her cheek, just below her lashes. Adam wanted her suddenly, started to reach but pain, pain sharpened the edge of even that slight motion. He tried to shift, fell back, rolled onto his other side with a wrench that left him shaking and finally passed out, much later, then woke in what seemed no time at all. She was lying facing him, eyes wide open.

"How do you feel?" she said.

"I don't know yet. I have to get up anyhow. Some things you can't do for me."

"Wait a second." She unzipped the bag and rolled up to her knees above him. One hand braced his shoulder. "Can you do that? Roll up? Slowly...now try to, that's it," as he got onto his feet, but he crouched back down, quickly.

"Christ," he muttered.

"Listen," she said. "Let's spend the day here. I'll get some food."

"What time do you have to be back?"

"Tomorrow. Eleven. We could wait until morning, but I think you should be in a real bed tonight, and get some heat under you."

"That would be nice. Meanwhile, I'm gonna piss right here."

"Of course," she said, but she turned to look at the ocean, *a nice girl*, he thought, feeling ludicrous. "And," she said, "I was thinking—would you like to come and stay with me in Mill Valley? Until it's better? You won't be trapped in a city apartment then, and I could give you massages and...."

"That's quite an offer." He crawled back towards the sleeping bag. She helped him in and zipped it around him.

"Well, I, I'd, like to."

"Let's see if I can get up there first," he said. "Where are you going to get food?"

"Well, there's a little store I saw up the road. Carmel would take longer."

"That's all right. Why don't you go on into Carmel and pick up a bottle of something, too? I mean," he said, "would you?"

Much later, she said, "See? I knew you could do it."

"It wasn't exactly fun. Pass that whisky back before you start driving. Vicious stuff you drink."

"I didn't know what you like. I'm a wine person. Here, let me help." She crawled in and propped him up on the narrow back seat of the car. "That was really a long haul. You see, when you have to, you can do anything."

"Christ," he said, swallowing, sputtering. "You sound so much like Pollyanna sometimes I can't believe it. Or like some kind of soap opera. . . ."

"What?" She paused on her way back out of the back seat, she half twisted around, her face above him.

"I said. . . ." But he stopped: at that moment he saw the hurt begin in her eyes, bewildered, behind her glasses—a startling, vivid, dark blue.

*

throw once, twice, thrice. . . .

2   The Receptive brings about sublime success,
      Furthering through the perseverance of a mare.

Strange acorns. Strange oaks. A little house that Hansel and Gretel might have found on their way through the forest, but, there were no redwoods in Germany. Red hoods? Wolves? A witch's house? *Are you a blue-eyed witch, Jeannie? warming me, here, there, don't stop, more,* far more than the noisy electric heater against which Adam leans now she's left for work the emptiness comes; after hours of feasting still the despair feels so strong.

"I want a child, Adam."

"Forget that. Really. You know we're just together for a while."

111

Rain. The roof is a sieve and the wood floor soaked, will be wet for days, nothing dries in the redwoods, his back hurts more. The dampness penetrates here as nowhere else. Big black cobwebs hang in the windows. Corpses of beetles float in the dishwater. Now the lights are flickering.

(why do you stay?

"Who? Where?"

you Adam, why do you

"Why do you stay, Jeannie? When I'm a bastard half the time, can't forgive you for not being someone else?"

"I love you."

"You can't. You don't know me. Your love is a misunderstanding."

"Oh—turn over. I'll give you a back rub."

"Damn it, NO,"

and they wrangle all night a storm blowing up outdoors but here there is love love at dawn the animal flow that's *Jeannie*, so earthy, her beauty, so uncomprehending, yet playful, a wisdom: slender loins moving deeply against him encase him in warmth, moist-tender, as gray light seeps through the drapes it's wet again, leaves dripping, pleasure, pleasure, then she is gone; and he falls back, letting sleep take him—another, heavier lover, most of the day, he is drained, *this can't last: it's not real*, this rhythm of mindless loving all night and the days limp dragging about and staring at rain, then rage, then wild desire, that darkness beckoning, overwhelming him, then he hates her; and then he loves her, ten times a day, back and forth, and Jeannie provoking him constantly with her lethal, dumb-animal vulnerability,

"Why do you give me all this power? It's not fair. I can't. . . ."

"Give you? You have it. I don't give it to you," she tells him.

4:15. Brandy. He lets his fingers wander the strings idly, watching the rain make glistening violet-yellow-green gullies, *she's* late. *She's always late.* A pale yellow organ called slug lies stretched on the window beyond the sand dollars, scattered, and Jeannie's *I Ching*, outside, on the ledge, it oozes downward. He sees its horns; sees something dark inside and a thing attached to

112

its tail snaps off the window. It oozes over the ledge, and then there's only the top of the wood box, the smell of bay, and sand under his fingers.

"I treated an interesting guy today, from New York. I think he's Jewish."

"Oh yeah? Did he have horns and a tail?"

"What?"

"Why should I give a shit if some guy you met is Jewish?"

"I don't know, I just happened to think. . . ."

"That he's an exotic like me, huh? Did he turn you on?"

"Oh, Adam, you know. . . ."

"Did he? Did he try to? You know all us darkies like blondes."

"Please stop it. Why, why. . . ."

"Well, why do you take it? All this shit. It makes me even angrier that you put up with it. It's so—abject."

"What can I do?"

"Why the fuck do you ask me? Think for yourself, for once. It's so clear, it's so goddamned clear you should kick me out."

"But how can I? I love you. . . ." so simply; all that warmth, all the time, her pale blonde skin exudes warmth as she sleeps, he turns her over and it rises from her. She murmurs—what? Fine silk texture of flesh, light fuzz, the sheen of her shoulder so white against his brown fingers a shadow where it dips near the pulse in her throat; the inside swell of her thigh belly breast rising, quietly, falling, the nipple hardening under his hand now her eyes open slightly: a blue glint. She turns to him, smiling, sleepy. . . .

A jay screams. The neighbor's rooster crows, it crows all day, *timetimetimetime*, and the space beside Adam is empty; a cup by the bed, Jeannie's lips graze his eyelids and now again he is staring at: speckled trunks not quite oak; green moss; downy birds perched on wet wood, the manzanilla glistening, muscle-red, buff, and everywhere slugs—shapes of slugs in soaked gravel, slugs in pools, even after the rain stops, and spiders, outside, inside, *I miss her. . . .*

He missed her whenever she left. He waited for her, all those hours alone were focused on, four o'clock, 4:15, 4:30,

"Why can't you be on time, damn it, Jeannie."

"I don't know, things always seem to come up."

"Why? I don't make *you* wait."

"Sometimes you do. But I don't mind," she said mildly.

She had a long, slow patience that awed him: like cows when they stand in a blizzard, they wait it through, steadily, calmly, and Jeannie would wait through anything, calmly, even his rages, most of the time she seemed to trust in some essential harmony, but for Adam it's: 4:25. The dog across the road barks. The sound of a car, then a door slams,

"Oh, no, goddamn it. You know I don't like sweet wine."

"Oh—did you tell me that? I'm sorry. . . ."

"Twenty-five million times I've told you. I think your head has as many leaks as the ceiling. Why, *why*. . . ."

"I'll go back and get some dry stuff. Burgundy?"

"No. Christ, no. Can't you see it's not just the wine? It won't work, it can't, the only decent thing is to end it completely."

"Are you tired of me? Of making love?" She kneels above him, takes off the glasses that shield her eyes so absolutely direct, those huge pupils, that must be some part of their power, he thinks, but she smiles, and, "Hmm?" she murmurs. "Are you tired of my body?"

57 *The Gentle (The Penetrating, Wind)*

Success through what is small.

("The Gentle means going into. . . .
The Gentle means crouching"

Colored lights have appeared up and down the road. Supermarkets are giving out raffle tickets for turkey. A warm, green holiday season is beginning, and

"Adam? Would you take me to meet your parents sometime?"

"Sure. If you want to brave my mother, who thinks you're a bad woman. It won't be pleasant, though."

"Maybe I could change her mind."

"I doubt it. Well, actually, the two of you might get along very well just trading clichés. But, see, besides living in sin with me, you're also a *goy*. That's already two strikes against you."

"I still want to try. Oh, hey, listen, I saw a sign today in town, some place is looking for a musician. Right down on"

"Oh, it's probably some kind of holiday stuff. Or a wedding."

"No, it looked like a really hip place."

"Really hip places don't put up signs. And, by the way, the sugar was soaked when I got up because you didn't put the top on. The toothpaste is drying out. You even leave the door half open. . . ."

"I don't."

"You do. Why the hell can't you close things?"

"Because I'm stupid. Born that way. All the strikes were against. . . ."

"Goddamn it, that's not. . .look, how can you try to use exactly the phrase I used five minutes ago, as though you just thought of it?"

"I, I wasn't. . .it seemed to. . .I mean, I guess that's my way of understanding things. I mean, I know you said it, but, we're just. . .we're different, Adam. I think differently."

"The hell you do. You just don't think. I bet you've never had a real idea in your life. You're like a monkey."

"How do you know? Maybe I"

"I know. I know. I'm a human being and you're like some kind of cow or goat"

"Okay, stop it. I heard you. I'll try not to"

"Something is wrong with that, Jeannie, I mean, a goat is a goat, but"

"Please stop"

"A woman should be at least a little less stupid than"

"STOP," and her body hurled at him, scratching, he pins her against the wall, *let me go*, and struggling, holding her down

115

on the floor, *let me go*, screaming, *no*, then she's limp, crying, and he is

"Sorry. I'm sorry. Once it starts I can't. Jeannie. Please,"

"Let's go to bed," she sobs; and Adam wants to fight dragons; storm castles (*let her go, now. let her go*), do anything, to protect her from—

41 *Decrease*

> At the foot of the mountain, the lake:
> The image of DECREASE.
> Thus the superior man controls his anger
> And restrains his instincts.

how?

boom, bOOM.......

It's a crisp bright day: almost warm enough to lie in Jeannie's hammock, but he is too lazy to put it up. He sits on the deck, tries to play his guitar despite the noise, BOOM, they're pounding the old bridge into the stream. Dust, men and machines, BOOM, grit in his wine and a shadow of road through the trees now a school bus comes barrelling down round the bend and lurches to a stop, its wheel stuck in a shoulder. All the workmen converge on it. There are no children. Only the driver emerges—a stocky woman who leaves fairly soon; and the workmen leave, finally; then the whole next day, a Saturday, the bus sits, abandoned—a bright yellow hulk that beckons him.

Midafternoon. He succumbs. He climbs in and walks down the aisle, *it's so narrow*, and sits in a seat, so small it seems, *remember?* The driver seemed enormous: he had such authority then, *remember*, a seesaw, a sliding board, low hills, and robins at the country day school they'd hated so when they first moved to San Francisco. The bus started picking them up every morning in late September, the grass turned green,

"Now? How can it turn green now?"

"It's different here. It's the opposite from back East."
"That's *silly*. . . ." Becky had said

(*relative* . *relativity* . *relation* . .
    (blood   *relatio*
                   :   (tell / / *naming*
                  relationship
    Dad? Mother? Jake? Kay? Rebecca?)

"Was there any mail?"
"No. Are you going someplace? I just got here. . . ."
"I'll be back in a little while." Adam put on his coat. "Unless. . .do you want to come with me? I'm going to hear that'
guy. . . ."
"Oh, at that place? The Cave?"
"Yeah, he's really good. He makes me think of Miles a little—
the mood. Strange to say about someone playing the flute, and
he's not black. Still he gets that real lyric soul sound. . . ."
"I didn't know Miles Davis was a black man."
"You what?"
"I didn't."
"Jesus, what *do* you know? I'm not gonna take you out to the
Cave, look, Jeannie, I've got a chance to sit in with these people,
I really like them, I'm not going to"
"Okay. You don't have to take me anywhere. I'll be your
hidden mistress or something."
"Oh, that will make me feel really great, won't it."
"Well, I don't see what I can do that's right."
"You can't do anything. But why the hell not? Why can't
you?"
"I told you, I'm stupid. Brain damage."
"That's not funny," he snapped, and slammed out and drove,
and drove, the bright center-line studs glinting and Jeannie's
face, her eyes spaced too close, her head too narrow, so ferrety,
he thought, hungry, for what? Fog dampened the windshield,

moistened his face as he walked down the beach, the big waves buffeting, surface of silver lava, then a light rain. He stood for a few moments under the boardwalk, inhaling the dank smell. They used to piss under boardwalks when they were kids, in summer, coolness and that smell of wood mixed with sand, salt, urine, *remember?*

(*Becky* . . .

squatting: the small rolls of fat, pink, flopping over wet trunks; dark curls; and the pail she used to make castles with down where the sand turns mud, small wavelets were gurgling. The tide was receding, leaving a swathe of mud studded with things that glinted: pebbles, seaweed, a starfish, and long purple shells like the ones that maggie made into wind chimes long ago, some were missing now; some broken; but still they clattered lightly, as he stalked into the house again he saw them: tied to an Eastern twig, at the window.

"I'm glad you came back," Jeannie said. "I was worried."

"You should hope I'll stay away one of these times." He took off his shoes, settled onto the bed. Jeannie handed him a drink, as though he had never been gone. "Why do you want me so much, Jeannie?"

"Why? What do you mean, why?"

"I'm not a man, really. I'm like a doll you feed and massage and who spits at you. You never see anybody, and"

"I don't want to. I mean, I see people all day at work, that's enough. I've never had many friends, really."

"Why not?"

"I don't know. That's just—me. I was close with my family, but they're so far away and it's been so long since"

"You're lonely," he said, suddenly.

"No, I'm not. I don't need"

"You are. You are. You're so intimate with it you don't even know what it is anymore."

"You're wrong, love. I really don't want anybody but you." She smiled. "Besides, you turn me on."

"Why?"

"You just do. Why don't you lie down?" She crawled onto the bed beside him. "Come on—you're so much nicer when you're horizontal. . . ."

Firelight. Kerosene light. Soothed and tingling, the dark sweet tide rising now it suffuses the night breathes alive the walls swelling the bed is a raft in black waters that surge through his belly and thrust, inside her, swimming in luminous waves, inside, him, billowing, crashing, subsiding, then they doze; then they wake, slowly, delicate this time a smooth mosaic of feelings constantly shifting and flowing out, so easily, to the dark woman- ness of her, wet satin shell so welcoming, always, soft, lazy, now,

"Let's go across to the city," she says, "and play tourist. We could take pictures of each other."

"I left my camera"

"I have a Brownie,"

but. . .

me? riding cable cars, all that day in San Francisco they snapped each other's pictures, up and down hills, they drank Irish coffee at every bar on their way, she always kept up with him, always had to show her I.D. and always said, "But I'm twenty-eight," with the same small laugh of delighted surprise, but today even that pricked him only lightly. He put it away as they wandered through Golden Gate Park and lay on the grass, *snap*, Jeannie ensconced in a red bush; Jeannie under a tree; then Jeannie looking out at the ocean at sunset the sun breaks through for a moment there is a light so huge Adam wants to dive into it, suddenly he *is* it, and all the despair lifts: the color comes back in the world, though the light fades quickly, for now he knows it is there in the fog steaming up from the waves' surface, gulls sweeping over their heads, God, God. . . .

Something warm, nuzzling—Jeannie beside him, looking at him; and he turns away from her now he is filled with longing for those who would see this light as he does: for maggie, her wit, her understanding, she understood all of it: she and Rebecca: those he can't. . .touch.

9.

The snail moved up and down the side of the tank. Its track cut a
delicate scalloped swathe through green fuzzy algae. Its orifice
oozed open, closed, open—a means of locomotion; a mouth. It
started back up the diagonal now, sucking glass, and maggie
sucked, too, leaning in on her elbows close to the glow, her soft
lips puckered, pushed, pouted, in, out: mouthing air.

*

In New Mexico, in November, the hills are outlined in black:
creases, folds, merging silhouettes of trees etched into snow.
Horses munch shriveled rose hips along a barbed wire fence at
one edge of the orchard where I sit on a stone and watch a jet
stream white across blue, moving east; and blur, crisscrossing
occasional daubs of cloud.

Two horses lie down together. And I stand up; stamp my
cigarette out against hard, packed snow. My shoulders ache and
my ankles pound as I come out from under the trees to an open
field. Two thousand miles from the salt smell, I carry an ocean
inside me: backed up from my shoulders down through my
ankles, tense with the pressure of years hardly tapped, it ripples
now.

I crouch down. Crescents of cold burn into my knee caps.
The field glistens, all the way to the mountain, white, smooth,
sown with bursting diamonds and stained with the shapes of
fence poles, trees, the luminous bright blue shadows of afternoon.

I swivel my head. Horses, only horses; the face of the mountain, the steaming breath of my dog. I stretch my mouth and try to squeeze it out. I scream, as the shepherd dog flees, the horses scatter, I press snow on my face. I howl at the mountain, that mass of stone coated now but unyielding as always: contained; seductive; impersonal.

I give up. I get up, still aching. Back under the trees, my face drips, but it's just snow. The dog, so much like Cairo, follows me at a distance. The horses are ghosts. I climb through the barbed-wire fence and slide down to the darker shapes: shadows embroidered like lace on the icy road.

There were horses there, too.

On days when the car wouldn't start, or I was busy or mean, she'd walk a mile to the store for cigarettes. Narrower country. Cramped hills. The road ripples, and mist inhabits the branches that arch above her head as she wanders past the barn with its broken window; the gutted refrigerator sprawled in a ditch; the oak split with one thick horizontal bough like a chaise longue above the stream where she found that skull, last summer—it's nailed by the door, still. The road forks: part of it turns to dirt and veers uphill. Just beyond there's a small, fenced-in field where she stops and calls. The horses come to nuzzle.

A sorrel with a pale mane. A buckskin. A skinny white mare with ribs like knobs sticking out.

She said, "I have to learn to drive. It's stupid. I'm too dependent on you."

"Why don't you buy cartons of cigarettes, at least?"

"I don't know. That's true—I never cover myself. . . ."
The year slopes: dim light through pine/maple branches, reddening, blue-gold patches of sky. The sun blares into my eyes whenever I drive south in afternoon, and a soreness is creeping across one side of my throat. Cold, cold: the Snow Queen has speckled my windshield with tiny feathers of frost, as we turn onto Hollowbrook Road, the back seat loaded with groceries for tomorrow, Thanksgiving, a party, she said,

"Did you see a horse?"

"What? Where?"

"Running in front of the car. A black one. You. . . ."

"No. Did you really. . . ?"

"No, no, forget it. I just"

She sneezed, groped for the Kleenex. I gunned the car up the drive and stopped it and looked at her.

"You just what?"

"I don't know." She got out and stretched. Puffs of steam came out of her mouth. "I forgot. Look, it's clouding over. I bet it's going to snow."

Is it always summer in fairy tales? Except for the Snow Queen, of course: those wolves, swans, witches, those kings and step-mothers, all of those children fugitive or abandoned seem to wander through woods warm and lush with green leaves. . . .

I'm wrong, I know. I *know*. Little Tiny hid underground from winter, and barely escaped a marriage to Mr. Mole. The storks flew south. The year slopes, even in fairy tales, the earth tilts. The ice returns at a gallop or at a snail's pace. And every quest requires some time of silence: at risk of life, even; and even to our best-loved, a face impassive as the mountain's, rock chis-eled with snow.

She said, "What does 'silence' mean for you?"

"I'm not sure. It's not literal silence, of course."

On Thanksgiving morning, Rebecca woke up with little voice. Up most of the night squeezing yams through a sieve, mashing butter, brown sugar, and pineapple into the pulp, licking bowls and palms and fingers smearing yams into her mouth, did maggie eat, too? Or did she only reflect that orgy of tasting, yams, yams —delighting, encouraging, both of them so absorbed they never glanced through a window before they collapsed, in their clothes, their faces grimy with flecks of bright orange pulp and juice at four A.M.? Five?

It's ten now: pale glow through the heavy sheet of plastic we have stretched taut and stapled a semi-opaque wall across the windows next to the bed. Aching bones, burning throat—the body presents its bill. And the feast's not even begun, I thought, as I croaked at the heap of blankets across the room. I dragged myself up, let Cairo out, turned up the heat, then came back and shook maggie's shoulder.

A muttered protest. Bailey, curled into an armpit, stretched one paw. Rebecca-I shook again and maggie half opened her eyes, the lower part of her face writhing.

I am a torturer, suddenly, I am become the Gestapo. Rebecca-I, furious, stalked to the kitchen, set water to boil, and, revolted, stared at the counter where a big, dead, mutilated bird with a bulging breast bone was oozing watery blood.

Chop apples. Fry garlic. Soak bread crumbs.

I put some chestnuts into the oven to split. I took out some butter to soften. *Boil cranberries. Why??* Steam spewed out of the kettle spout. maggie came straggling in, said,

"I'm sorry. Can I do something?"

"Make coffee." It was an attempt at a snarl, but only a cracked whisper came out.

"Okay. I'm really sorry, hey. Did you look out the window?"

"No."

"Go look."

"They're due in an hour. And Jesse has to leave early. I promised I'd have dinner ready by three."

"Don't worry, they won't be here in an hour. They may not even get here. Go look."

Records shuffled behind me. Then Monteverdi, *The Vespers of 1610,* and she was beside me at the living-room window, one we'd left clear, with no plastic. Her face was radiant.

"It must have snowed all night. We didn't look. Hey, can you really not talk?"

I started to say something nasty. My throat rebelled. The music swelled, joyous, it shriveled the tendrils of spite inside me already wilting because of the wonderland, oh, a fairyland out

123

there: white, white tufts on the apple tree, white spraying down from the branches, the eaves. Cairo swam in the drive, a furry black dolphin floundering in and out of huge drifts. The phone rang.

"Hi. Uh-huh. No, it's maggie. Seventeen inches???"

"Who is it?"

"Susan. Well, try to get hold of Joel. Yeah, he has a VW, maybe he can make it. Okay, call back." She hung up. "You know, they can't tell our voices apart on the phone any more."

"I know." I could hardly whisper now. "What's going on?"

"They had seventeen inches in the city. We must have two feet here. She doesn't even have snow tires."

"She and Joel. . . ."

"I know. But they should be able to stand each other for sixty miles. Shouldn't they? They both knew the other was coming. Anyhow, Jesse will be in the car, and his girl friend. That should help."

I wrote on the telephone pad, with a green marker, "It's a small car."

maggie smiled. "Good idea. You shouldn't try to talk at all."

"I *can't* talk," I wrote.

"You don't need to. Have some coffee before you start cooking, okay? Jesse won't get to any concert tonight. They'll probably all stay over."

(*rrrringgg*

"Hello? No, it's maggie, hi. Yes, but you can today, Rebecca's lost hers. What? Yeah, we looked all over. It's probably under the snow."

"Ha ha ha HA," I scribbled in red.

"She didn't care for that. Yes, she's up—so to speak. Uh-huh. He says, do you have tonsillitis?"

"I had my tonsils out. When I was four."

"She says she had them out. Oh. He says they can grow back."

"Shit," I wrote in green, then changed to orange, "who's that, anyway?"

"Joel, of course. She said, 'shit, who's that anyway.' Yes, we

124

know. She's writing with magic markers. Green and orange so far."

"And red."

"And red. No, the shit's green." She giggled. "He says you should go back to bed, and we'll have Thanksgiving next week."

"NO!!!" I scrawled. "Is he afraid of a couple of feet of snow?"

"Are you afraid of the snow, she says. Yes, obstreperous, well, she always is. Purple. Uh-huh. Look, this is costing money, why don't you two continue it when you get here? Hey, did Susan get through to you? Good. Okay, we'll see you—whenever."

"When are they leaving?"

"Now. Jesse and what's-her-name were there already. They're going to pick up Susan. I'll cook the turkey."

"I want to," I croaked.

"Don't talk. Look, Joel's right. Why don't you go back to bed, and we'll do the whole thing around you? You can kind of hold court."

"I don't want to go to bed. I want to cook. I don't need a voice to cook," I wrote in three different colors, jammed the pad and the markers into my pocket, and started for the kitchen.

"You're really a drag when you're sick, you know? Have some coffee at least. I'm going to take a shower."

　　　rrrrrringggg

　　　"Eeeeeee..."

She picked up the phone. "Grand Central Station, good morning." Her voice changed. "*Hi.* Where are you?" I stopped and looked at her. "Adam," she told me, then seemed to disappear into the phone. "Yes. We have two feet of snow and a whole bunch of people coming. Joel and Susan and Jesse and Jesse's. . . . No, I guess you don't know him. Old friend of mine. Yes. Oh, and Rebecca's lost her voice. Laryngitis, I guess. No, she really can't talk. Well, why aren't you? But. . . . Really? *Really?* Okay. Well, you know. Don't worry about it. I miss you, too. Well, how can I? No, she really can't, but she can listen. I think you should. Here," she said, and held out the phone.

I am kneeling by a ledge, near some windows. A pot of ivy, a goldfish plant. Snow, snow. Madamina rubs her big belly against me. I push her away, and maggie's hands lift her out of my field of vision. I think I'd known. I still have the doodle I did those few minutes, in blue on top of my notes—a maze of dots forming leaves, flowers, then some distorted faces with eyes thrown here and there as I listened, not surprised. Yes, I'd known. For a moment, superimposed on this world of snow-laden oaks and maples, the heavy wood beams of the house, and the apple tree, itself a film over fields of blue shadows, I see a country where grass turns green in winter; roses and fuschias blooming, signs in Chinese, and the cable car clanking over a hill past a door on the corner of Jackson Street. . . .

Twelve stories up a big man carefully carries his paunch to a window. A woman's voice chatters away in another room on another phone,

> "Yes, our son is home. Yes, he's better. Well, but he's staying with a friend across in Marin. Oh, you know this generation they don't want to live with their parents. Yes, I agree but what can you do. No, I've never liked turkey. We're having a goose this year. . . .

Fog, water and steel. The man turns away from the window. A clatter. A hiss. The aroma of onions frying. He lowers his bulk to a sofa. He lights a cigar. He shuffles through newspapers scattered in heaps on a coffee table. He coughs. . . .

click

My father, I felt you beside me in these woods three thousand miles from you: hands on the camera, saw, fingers naked and blunt like yours, flushed pink in the heavy biting air of an eastern winter. Those Sundays we drove through Pennsylvania, New York, in search of country restaurants, there was always a time when you'd stop the beige and brown Packard; unload the tripod; set up the big, unwieldy machine you used to take pictures, *pictures*—the membrane between us a film, that moment, so thin I felt I could pierce it and talk to you, touch you, before one or both of us dies. But the sound of your voice is drowned in a whin-

126

ing buzz as the reel spins, unwinding, a washed-out print: *close-up* of your eyes not focused, pale blue, and *shift* to a fuming cigar tip, ash lengthening, one corner turning brown, black, and spreading, smoldering orange, steel, water that hisses to flame and ignites all the wood I've shored up against loneliness in New Mexico, New York; while in California my brother's car darts in and out of traffic glutting the four-lane highway that crosses a bridge painted orange. . . .

Three bridges. Three homes—or three umbilical cords? maggie's voice said, carefully, "How do you feel?"

"I expected it." For a moment I almost enjoyed the pain in my throat. "How are you?"

"Don't talk. I did too, I guess. No, that's bullshit. I didn't. But it makes sense." She lit a cigarette, coughed. "I wonder what he was doing in Mill Valley?"

"Probably has a girl friend. Who knows?"

"Hmm. That might be good."

"Yes, Auntie Marguerite."

"Well, but you know. . . . Do you think he's okay?"

"Jesus, what's okay? Am I okay? Are you?"

I stood up, clumsily, knocking against her leg. Madamina jumped down from her lap and sprawled, her head nestled on maggie's foot, her body stretched in a furry calico arc on the red rug. Her bulging middle rose, fell, rose. . . .

"I bet she'll give birth the minute we put the food on the table," maggie said.

"Right. I have to start that turkey."

"Rebecca, *don't talk.*"

I am mashing salt and basil into soft butter. I'm slopping fried bread, garlic, apples, into a hole. I'm hot. Water sloshes all over me. Then there is terry cloth, cool, green dacron against my skin, maggie's navy pants, Mexican earrings—these props.

"It smells incredible."

"Cairo, shut UP."

"You can't get out of your driveway, you know."

127

"Can I have a cup of coffee?"

A sign hangs over the threshold to the kitchen: *I must be alone for a while to make delicious food for all of us to eat—*maggie's style, bright, with curlicues. Rebecca is never so nice; would like, in fact, to spit at those bodies struggling out of galoshes, jackets, scarves, and spurting nonsensical sounds as they drip snow all over the rug, they violate her, space, that ought to be rinsed in silence today, today maggie speaks for both of us.

"Wait till you taste the yam pudding."

"You mean you have *two* pregnant cats?"

"We almost skidded right into the Croton reservoir"

"Christ, I only asked for a cup of coffee,"

Joel said, bitterly; that long face full of laughter changing now he exudes the sense of injustice done him: irate, stomps away from the kitchen; and Jesse's voice booms out, smoothing, in counterpoint to Susan's ironic tones and then soothing sounds that are, maggie is, here in the kitchen she dances around me, wearing a purple velvet shirt, a heavy silver chain with antique pendant and one big crimson stone—she's making coffee.

"Take it easy. They're friends. Remember?" she whispers, and dances out. I spoon drippings over the carcass. Heat spews out of the oven, parching my cheeks and forehead. In my skull, she's still dancing, whispering, *there must be a hole in the film*, then miming, an Italian of the Quattrocento? a juggler from Tudor England? Something—that makes me the scullery maid, I thought, the course, fat smelly one getting drunk on food, closed into this odorous sweatbox alone, and sweat trickling down from my armpits under the blouse already spotted red with spitting cranberry juice, and she is a sprite, and I, and she, and I, and

They're friends, I told myself; *they are*—blows punctuating the soreness encased in a bag of skin that is: Rebecca? maggie? *Are two of us even—necessary?*

Scrape, clatter—laughter, and coconut incense. Candles. They've taken the stereo off the table, opened it out to its full length, and kicked Cairo out, and the cats have vanished under the beds, because, it's a formal dinner at Manchester House, for Thanksgiving, he's not coming back. I knew.

"We need two more chairs"

"Were you really up all night?"

"Hey, watch the aquarium!"

"There are too fucking many animals in this house"

"Let me do that, lady,"

Jesse said, taking the heavy platter from maggie's hands; maggie reaches and takes more plates, bowls, glasses, from mine, and my stomach churning, the walls rippling, now the air is rippling, too, again, as it did that day in August an old man's face rippled in through the windows and asked me, *What are you doing, Rebecca?"*

"Don't trip over that cat!"

I stood surveying the table as they sat down. Four patrons, one usher, attending My Production. And on the screen, ladies and gentlemen, there is a big brown bird stuffed to bursting; an orange pudding; wine and greens and sauce I've made with real cranberries, not the smooth, bland jelly Bea used to plop out of the can and onto a silver dish. . . .

"That looks beautiful."

"Can we eat this much?"

"Hahaha HA"

There was always a fancy white tablecloth loaded with silver, silver and glass surrounding the duck, the goose—never turkey. My father would carve. Bea would pick at a wing as she watched us, hovering, somehow, without getting out of her chair. Adam would sit as Joel sits now, still sunk into his pique, reserved. . . .

He'd said, "We're two different people, Rebecca, separate. Yeah. Sure, it has to be all right. It's my life."

"Happy thanks-GIV-ing!"

"Rebecca, sit down."

"I want skin. Yes, skin. And the ass,"

Joel said; his sulk dissolving in instant, gleeful greed as he smelled the food. Jesse carved. His heavy, beautiful, black-haired girl friend, Grace, spooned stuffing out. maggie nibbled, making tiny, delightful sounds, and Susan ripped into a drumstick with coarse, carnivorous pleasure, her pointed teeth scraping it clean of meat, neat, precise, and then belching, loud, to Joel's delight, Joel, her enemy, up to his wrists in stuffing and pudding and sauce and covertly watching maggie.

"It's dry."

"Hey, Pass the wine. Yeah, pass the bottle."

"What's dry? It's perfect"

"The stuffing tastes strange, don't you think?"

"No."

Jesse stood up, stretched, twisted luxuriously and grinned, "Who wants more? Everybody?"

"Not me," maggie said.

"Sure you do." He ripped off a wing and tossed it at her; past Joel licking his plate, Grace drinking out of the gravy boat, and Susan, her face in the pudding, lapping it up like a. . . .

No. They're friends—these greasy, convivial faces; these voices joking, squealing, are doing what's proper on this our National Gluttony Day, and I, I invited them here, for gluttony? for nostalgia? One drowns the other, I guess, Rebecca thought; that must be why I, too, am swilling the food down my gullet, stuffing it into my craw with fingers turned slick as theirs, cheeks as greasy and stomach already aching, we all tear, gobble and gulp,

"The pudding's incredible"

"Cairo's been out too long"

"Don't talk"

"Well, there's a pound of butter in it"

"Put on a jacket, you fool,"

Susan shouts at my back; but already I'm out the door. With my little sac of revulsion tucked under my ribs, in the snow falling lightly now, and snow almost up to my thighs, I waded out to the railing. I pressed my palms down deliberately, I rested my weight on snow. Feather-flakes brushed my skin; soft, soothing the fever flush of the indoors, heat, wine, food. The air dissolves that bilious pocket of nausea as I breathed deep draughts of it in and tried to force them to carry my voice up and out,

"Cairo...Cairo...."

The sound plummeted into big drifts and sank. Silence, silence; nonresonant, clear space. This snow has soundproofed the world. It all glows. The tips of my ears are tingling, my eyes prickling, nostrils spouting steam, and my head feels fogged, but it knows that hulk a quarter-way up the drive must be Joel's Volkswagen; that asymmetrical pile below the deck is my car, and those shapes near the road are houses, mailboxes, trees, all glowing faintly—themselves and not themselves. I tried to call again,

"Cairo...come...."

The door opened behind me. Sound, someone. A jacket tossed on my shoulders, then, warmth, flesh beside me, and maggie said,

"I could barely hear that from the doorway."

She leaned across the railing. The long, wide sleeves of her shirt sprayed snow down. She yelled, "Cairo...COME," but her voice, too, is muffled, absorbed into silence like water in cotton wool. "Cairo...ooayyoooayy," she yodeled and something black, dog-shaped, came loping up the road.

It's Cairo, of course, my mind tells me; but I see a hole. A moving hole, cut into the fabric. A moving, flowing glimpse of the void that is real—an Unworld.

"I was doing it!" I whispered, furious. "He's my dog, too!"

"But you can't...."

"Don't try to take everything out of my hands!"

My cracked, piping voice sounded ludicrous; and this rage that must be fear, *fear? Grief? And why must I track down my feelings like a dog sniffing out...ludicrous*, Rebecca thought, savagely, *that's what's ludicrous*. maggie's big eyes watch, bewildered. Her hand reaches out. But I shuffle away from her, down the steps into the drifts, like a pillow, a life preserver, I hug my anger close.

The hole comes struggling up the hill towards me; to me: nothing. Grass, snow; green, white; summer, winter, it's all a stage set. Is this what maggie sees? what she feels?

She's still on the deck, in her vivid purple velvet. She coughs. She leans over the railing, her hair white-powdered, the pendant swinging. She's not Italian now, not medieval, but still an actress; or, no, a boy-actor playing a girl disguised as a royal page in the court of—Elizabeth, maybe. Snatched from the stage of the Globe for some cosmic joke she's been transported here: a live gem set into this timeless matte white space like time itself just a form of deception.

She knows.

"Come back, you idiot. You'll just make yourself sicker."

The hole is close to me now, too close to be anything but Cairo. He swims along beside me as I slide, hip deep, through the drifts, and finally fall to a stop, panting, braced against the small pine near the turtle pond. Ice, tufted needle fronds. Cairo rears strangely skinny with his bushy coat wetted down. I hug him. The life of him hums through his ribs. His tongue laps my mouth. The pine smell shoots up my nostrils, shivering-pungent, it clears my head, courses down through my muscles and veins and I feel buoyant. Somewhere the jacket fell off. My throat still burns; snow straggles down from my lashes, my hair, trickles under my blouse—but I'm not cold. I'm too happy. Everything, everything glows. This is fever, this lens imbuing the world with such radiance, I know, this is sickness. Yet I am filled with joy at my body's health. Even clambering up the hill, now, every step an effort, I feel a lightness: a strength that will carry me through the hells that wait just over the ridge of this week. . . .

A brown spot lies by the steps on a big white mound. Fake suede, fake fur: the jacket—a tawdry thing, alien here, but I wipe my face with it, wrap it around me to go back up to the house. On the deck I hesitate; shuddering, drawn, reluctant. A feast world glows through the glass, an eighteenth-century world this time, amber light, warmth. I think of country squires; of

132

huge hogs roasting on spits, apples stuck in their jaws, and hounds
bred to flush out foxes. I am cold now. Pressed against the inside
of the door, I see an intense white cat face: whiskers and nose
distorted, flattened out on the bottom pane. Tonta. Susan and
Jesse and Grace are clearing the table. Joel has lit a cigar and sits
like a king, enjoying his indolence, he surveys it all.

Yellow light, white light; carpets and pine. Their voices
bounce off wood through glass to me standing here outside, a
beggar, a robber, I think. Where is maggie? I open the door.
Tonta streaks out past me. Cairo knocks me aside and rushes in,
showering everybody with snow.

"Look out. . . ."

"Yaaaa-hoooo!"

"My God. Are you out of your mind?"

"Oh yes, oh absolutely,"

I said. I felt so good I was shocked by my tiny voice. "Oh, it's
beautiful. You should go out in it, really, all of you," I babbled,
but Susan was dragging me into the bathroom.

"Crazy. Totally crazy, you are insane," she kept repeating.

"Be careful—that's an abominable snowwoman," Jesse called.

Susan slammed the bathroom door. She peeled off my clothes,
like an angry mother, she rubbed me, furiously, with a big blue
towel.

"Look, I'm all pink," I whispered.

"Wonder of wonders."

She wrapped the towel around me and started to pummel my
hair with a smaller one.

"Ouch. Take it easy."

"Take it easy, indeed. A five-year-old has more sense."

"I love you, Susan."

"Shut up and sit down and wait here. I'll bring you some
clothes. Do you have any special preference?" she asked sardon-
ically.

"No thanks, Momma." I stuck out my tongue.

"Jesus Christ."

"Well, you said five years old. Hey, Susan, I feel wonderful."

133

"I hope so. It's going to cost you a week in bed."

I sat on the toilet, sweating, a little numb. My naked, chapped skin was beginning to smart, now. That and the dampness, the look of the shower curtain, even the little whimsical patterns crawling around the wall, took me back for a moment to summer: to sand, waves, boardwalk, the roses, a chestful of curly hair, and the bungalow where a dark, warm woman called mother cooked sumptuous meals.

(Where's maggie?

A medley of voices came spewing through the door: none hers. The patterns are cracks in plaster. Cracks, that's all.

"Dessert? are you kidding?"

"Can I give Cairo a turkey bone?"

"Shit. Can't a man relax a little after"

"Let's just put the pies on the table."

Susan came back with a nightgown, a flannel robe, and slippers.

"Where's maggie?"

"Making coffee. Here, put these on. You're going to bed."

"I am not going to bed."

"Did I say five? I must have meant three."

"Did you love Thanksgiving when you were a kid, Susan?"

"Yes. I liked Christmas better, though."

"We didn't have Christmas. We were Jews. That's strange, it was really different. We got to hang up one stocking on the mantlepiece, Christmas Eve—that's all. Thanksgiving was my favorite holiday."

"Did you also talk a lot when you wanted to avoid something? Like"

"I-am-not-going-to-bed."

"Oh shut up and put these on. You're going if we have to carry you in there and sit on you."

The door opened. maggie came in, glasses on, looking brisk.

"I've been wondering where you were," I said. "Susan keeps telling me to shut up."

"Well, you shouldn't talk, right?" She hoisted herself up onto

134

the sink and perched, her weight on her arms, shoulders hunched. "Look, they've all moved into the sunroom and made a fire. Grace even changed the bed sheets." She smiled. "Joel says you're doing this deliberately to get really sick and get attention. We're all ready for you, see? So get dressed and come on."

"Sounds," I wriggled into the nightgown, "like a lion's den."

"You're the fiercest lion around," she said, "even with laryngitis."

"Oh. Look, I'm sorry about that. I don't know why I got upset."

She nodded. "I only shouted because you can't talk."

"I know. I got crazy."

"Okay, well, I don't feel so great about it either, you know."

"So great about what?" Susan asked.

"Adam's not coming back," maggie told her.

"What? You're mumbling."

"Adam's staying in California," maggie enunciated. "He's getting back into music, he says."

"Whatever that means," I muttered.

"Good," Susan said.

She wrapped an orange towel around my hair. I sat down on the toilet top.

"Is that all you have to say about it?"

"What's there to say? He had to leave, didn't he?"

maggie slipped down from the sink. "Look, the coffee's made. It's my turn to disappear for a while. Okay?"

We looked at each other. Then Susan pushed my head forward to fasten the towel with a safety pin.

"Okay?" maggie asked again, her voice soft, urgent.

Susan said, "Sure."

The potbelly stove crackles. Apple pie, pumpkin pie, mincemeat pie sit on the table. Under it, Cairo chomps at a bone. Smoke. Body smells, breath smells. My bed is turned down, white sheets, a big red comforter spread on top, and just for this moment I'm happy for all the warmth; the laughter, the humanness that has come so seldom to my house.

I got into bed, amid a round of applause, I croaked,
"I feel like Louis XIV at his levee."

"I knew it," Joel chortled. "I told you. She's doing the whole damned thing to get attention." He farted and twinkled at me. "How about some pie, your highness? Wine? Coffee? What's your pleasure?"

"Everything," I whispered, "you beast," and a plate with three wedges of pie swooped down on my lap, and wine beside me, and coffee; then Joel curled himself into the armchair, lit another cigar, and looked out through the doorway across the other room, at maggie's closed door. The Roses leapt onto the bed, started nibbling a crust.

"Disgusting," Susan said.

"But I love her. I love you all."

"Uh-oh. That means you'll hate us all in five minutes."

"Sometimes," I said, "it's not so wonderful to be understood."

Cairo chomped.

"Which cats are yours and which are maggie's?" Grace asked me.

"The Roses and Madamina are maggie's." I'd found a spot in my throat from which, if I was careful, I could give almost normal voice to my words. "Bailey and Tonta are mine. But now of course it feels like they're all. . . ."

"The Roses is the white one?"

"Stop asking questions," Susan said. "She shouldn't talk."

"This is The Roses." I picked her up, then dropped her. She came back, intent on pie. I tossed her away again. "Would you think a Grande Dame like this could be such a pig?"

"That's what they're supposed to be like," Joel said. His eyes flickered, constantly, back to maggie's door.

Cairo chomped.

"She must have some Persian in her," Grace said.

"I suppose. maggie picked her up off the street. The short-haired white one that blinks is Tonta. She's a killer."

"She's yours, right?"

"Right." I peered at Grace's face through the thickening

smoke. Pale skin, fine features, black eyes, peasant body—Jesse's girl. Very helpful, she'd been. But, now: was she being ironic? or dumb?

"And Bailey's her brother," I yawned. "The orange one. He's the only cat doesn't know how to use the cat door. He's not here much, lately."

Cairo chomped. Joel looked at the door.

Grace yawned, and Susan watched me through narrowed eyes, smiling a little. I looked away from her. She had been right: she is, now—now I want them all, everyone, out of my house.

"There's one more, right?" Grace asked. "You don't mind if"

"That's okay. Yeah, Madamina—the very pregnant calico. She's friends with Cairo, takes walks with us. maggie found her last summer—maggie and my brother. Hey, does anyone else feel hot?"

"So it's maggie's cats that are pregnant, and by your cat. Right?"

"Probably. Do you find that deeply significant?"

"I, uh—what?"

"Hey, don't get nasty, babe," Joel said.

"Me? I'm not"

He raised one eyebrow at me, pursed his lips. "I hear Adam is staying out on the coast."

"Yes, he's. . . ."

"What?"

"I'm sorry, I can't talk any louder."

"That's okay," Jesse said. "Talk as low as you want. We can hear you."

"I think it's that Cairo's making so much noise," I whispered. Somehow I'd lost that special spot in my throat. "I feel like I have a lot of competition."

"It's pretty fuckin' loud," Joel yawned. "Sounds like something out of *Tom Jones*. You remember old Squire Western's place?"

"Yes, some of us took that course in college," Susan purred.

"Screw you."

"Let's put the dog out," Jesse said. "That seems easy enough."

Joel shook his head. "Not me, man. You can if you want to risk your hand. I'm not messing around with that dog."

"O valiance," Susan sneered. "Hey, Cairo." Cairo looked up, then went back to chomping. "Hey, Cairo, come on, baby. . . ." She squatted, whistled. He crawled out from under the table and sat up. She patted his head. He licked her hand, and her other hand surreptitiously drew out the bone. She stood up, rosy, triumphant. "Come on, boy. Let's go play in the snow," and led him out, holding the bone aloft.

"Nice work," Jesse said.

Joel snorted. "Quite a performance, you mean. We were talking about Grandes Dames?"

"Oh, Joel. . . ."

"Sorry, sorry." He belched, then looked at me hard. "There's something wrong with being afraid of your animals, babe," he said, seriously. "You know?"

"I'm not scared of him," I wheezed. "He's a sweet dog, really."

"Horse shit."

"I mean it. I mean, he's a shepherd, not a doberman. I can handle him."

"You shouldn't *have* to. . . oh, to hell with it. You know what I mean." He looked at the door again. "Where'd maggie go?"

"She's in her room. She wanted to be alone for a while."

"Yeah." He stood up, stretched his neat, muscular body, and looked at Jesse. "We better get going if you want to make that concert, man."

"Already?" I said. "You really think there will be a concert?"

"There better be." Jesse yawned. "We ought to go, anyhow. You're talking too much, lady. Besides, we're all falling asleep. That food was toooo good."

"It's not the food, it's the smoke," Susan said from the doorway. "You don't notice until you come in from the outside."

"I knew it was getting thick," Joel said.

"You don't know how thick."

"Yes I do."

"No, you don't. It's fantastic. And with that plastic up everywhere—that fire should go out, now."

"It almost has," Joel muttered, lacing his boots.

"We can't be in this room without a fire," I said. "Not when it goes below thirty-five or so. It's too cold even with plastic on the windows. The walls are like cardboard."

"Great," Jesse said. "We better move the bed into the other room."

"No, no, please. I'll just stay under the covers. Really. We'll fix the pipe tomorrow."

"That's not the point," Susan said. "You'll suffocate in here, now, cardboard walls or not. Why don't we set up your sleeping bag on a mattress in there? It might be a little hard, but"

"Yeah, that's it," Jesse said. "You stay there, miss, until"

But I'm out of bed already: watching them close up the table and move it back against the wall, and boots, and sweaters, the foam rubber mattress from upstairs and my bag stretched on top of it,

> "We should do this again at Christmas"
> "Say goodbye to maggie. . . ."
> "Well, it's stopped coming down at least"
> "Have you looked at your aquarium close lately?"

Joel asked me. I put my head next to his and stared through the glass. Plants undulated gently, and gold and red specks darted in and out among the leaves—as always.

"What do you mean?"

"The Siamese fighter's fins. You see?"

"They're kind of—ragged."

"They sure are. I'd get rid of that snail if I were you."

"You mean—would a snail. . . ?"

"Yup," Joel said with an impish grin. "A snail would."

*

In a terminal
stunned; in a bubble of time floating silent despite the whirl of
arrivals, departures, the echoes inside my bones tell me they are
hollow.

He's gone to the Snow Queen's palace.

He may come back; or I, or she, will go out to him where he
sits in the empty throne room. A sliver of devil's mirror stuck in
his eye, he tries to solve the jigsaw. Shards lie strewn around him.

There is an opening, barely glimpsed past the tangled, leafless
branches. But first, through a coil of green light, I know I must
follow the path of a snail; to a bleak spring.

> There were a clown and a witch. Now I take away,
> one.

> I have painted my nails red. My teeth crunch silver-
> ware. Swaddled in pink silk-and-velvet, maggie
> sucks egg.

When Passover falls on Good Friday, I'll write *division*. I'll
turn the book upside down. Then I'll begin again from the other
side.

10.

nothing . limp. not even anguish. sleep, plants incense at
my most vunable moments—'come hither'—gently
writhing her translucent form. sleep, traps me with
dreams that, awake, i cannot awake from; or takes them
back, like a jealous lover when i leave her. sleep, the
witch, seduces, i must come back and possibly she will
bestow oblivion on me—my dreams are my life—my
'waking' my amnesia—living a lie. why? who is
deceived? no deception. . . .

what would the sun think of all this?
was Cecchetti right about this venture?

*

The black-and-white cat across the road was named Mitty, but
we called him The Gypsy because he sulked about and looked
dashing and yowled a very juicy, full-throated yowl when he
came courting. Sometimes we'd find him out on the deck in the
morning; or hear a scream and Bailey wouldn't come home all
night. Then we'd search and find Bailey, usually, at Carrie
Woolf's; and she'd say,
     well, *her* cat, *her Mikey*,
  "got an infection from Mitty's claws, he's half wildcat, you

know, maggie, I mean Rebecca. They've got a cage for him, yes, a cage, with bars, outside, but of course they have to catch him to put him in there, and that's no picnic. Yes, even in winter. You just can't figure out why some people keep a pet at all, can you, maggie, I mean Rebecca, since that's the.way they treat 'em, but they won't give him up because Sandy's so attached to him. She's a nice girl, really, Sandy is, but Ron, that brother of hers, is strange if you ask me. He's just too quiet, and I can say it that's pretty close myself when I want to be. No, I don't think it would do any good to talk to Sylvia Brenner. She's very excitable. Just like her father. A regular clan of 'em over there, aren't they—and I don't envy Frank Brenner living right in his father-in-law's backyard, so to speak. Well, old Mr. Dodenheim's a firebrand, let me tell you, even at his age. All right, so, I won't let Bailey in any more. He's so pathetic, though, meowing away at the door, you know, it just breaks my heart. And so loving. Isn't it funny, him being the only one of your cats don't know about the cat door? It would make it all so much easier. . . . Well, you know, I think that's true, the female is more intelligent in a lot of species. Don't do to let the men know you think it, of course, but. . . . No, I'm just waiting around here for my Jehovah's Witness ladies. I can't seem to stop them coming now I started, and I'm sorry about the whole thing. No, they won't be here until three, maggie, I mean Rebecca, sorry. Oh, by the way, we noticed you're having trouble starting your car, you know we had a VW once and the same thing happened, and then we found out if we kept the wires dry it was fine. That's right, in the motor—just wrap 'em up in plastic whenever it rains, or a blanket, even, it works for cold weather, too. Just don't forget about it when you go to start the car. So, about Bailey—we'll try and see what happens. Sure. Now, you really don't have time for a cup of coffee?

*

142

rrringgg

"Yes, hello, Momma. Yes, it's me. Sure. Now take it easy. I know, but has anything. . . ? Okay, I'll come tomorrow. In the morning. She's sick, but I can get a ride to the station. The man down the drive, he goes to White Plains early. Laryngitis. She'll be okay. Look, is Poppa. . . . okay, no, NO, let me sleep, I mean let HIM sleep, for God's sake. I SAID I'll be there tomorrow. . . ."

"That was a nice one," Rebecca wheezed.

"Oh, shut up and go back to bed. It's nothing I didn't know already."

"Sorry."

"Go back to bed."

"I want to eat. Hey, Madamina's going upstairs. Do you think. . . ?"

"She's been up there about five times today."

"Well, she looks like she's going to burst soon. . . ."

> *Nov 27, Fri:* Madamina gives birth to four kittens under the eaves.
>
> *Nov 28, Sat:* maggie to city. B gone all night.
>
> *Nov 29, Sun:* Gypsy lurking. Pick maggie up at station, 1:20. Disrupture over snails. . . .

"But I love them," she said. "Look, I'll ask the next time I'm down there. I'll stop at a pet shop. Maybe it's something else."

"Why don't you ask Joel? He's in love with you, after all, he might change his mind."

"Oh, now. . . ."

"Well, it's true. You've done it again, see, you're irresistible."

"Thanks a lot. I'm almost sorry you've got your voice back."

rrringggg

"Yes, Momma. Sure, of course. Hi, Poppa, how do you feel? I'm fine. Sure. It's a beautiful day here, too. Tomorrow, okay? I'll be there in the morning. I miss you, too. Yeah. Go back to sleep now, okay? Okay? I love you."

143

"Is anything. . . ?"

"I don't think so. I can't really tell on the phone, but I think he just wants to see me. I'll check on the snails tomorrow. Okay?"

"Sure. I hope that fish has fins by the time you get back."

"Well, if you *see* them. . . ."

"I don't like to look at them close," I said. "They're disgusting."

> *Dec 3, Thurs:* maggie to city. a walk to the point, waded ankle deep snow on the trail no one uses it now. a narrow path leads out to the small, almost circular blob that was an island in summer. The birch still shakes out her curls, they cascade over ice, not water, and there is snow on them now,
>
> *Dec 5, Sat:* call from Joel. Gypsy. Make sign, hang sign, pick maggie up at station.

"So?" I said, "How is he?"

"Weaker. The morphine—the thing is, he has a tolerance for it now. They're afraid to give him any more, but the pain. . . .I had a fight with his doctor, the bastard. He won't prescribe any more. And since he's on Welfare. . . ."

She looked out the window. The car hummed, skidding a little, past the store, the big field, the small cemetery next to the road where a willow trails brilliant yellow branches, above the snow, then we turned onto Hollowbrook Road. *All this.* . . .

"What?" I said.

"Nothing." She lit a cigarette. "What doesn't help, you see, is my mother getting nuttier every week. And he's sensitive, even though he's vague. And also—it's kind of hard on me. Though I shouldn't complain."

"Why not? Look, do you really have to go down there so much? I mean, if he's sleeping most of the time. . . ."

"He's not sleeping. He's—I'm not sure where he is. He doesn't even know me, always. It's harder on her, she's living there. And he—he's the one that's. . . ."

"Oh, before I forget," I said as I turned the car into the drive,

144

"Joel called. He said to tell you that if you need someone to go up there with you to let him know."

"Oh. That's nice of him."

"Yeah."

Smoke. Getting out of the car with our big bags of groceries, over and over, the cold air turning blue, I watch smoke gusting out of the chimney next to the TV antenna perched on the Woolfs' roof; and barking from our house; and maggie climbing the steps, talking into the milk and lettuce and eggs,

"I told him, a long time ago, that if the pain gets too bad I'll get him something to"

"Watch out!" I yelled and she lurched, did a little dance, legs askew, then caught herself.

"Whew." She stood braced, the groceries wedged between her ribs and the railing. "It's icy."

"We need some sand for those steps," I said, "or rock salt. To, what? Oh, NO," I shrieked as a black-and-white haunch disappeared around a corner. "Goddamn it, there he is again."

"What????"

"The Gypsy."

We opened the door. Cairo exploded at us, a cyclone of fur. maggie dropped to her knees and hugged. him. "Hello, baby, hello." His tongue lapped her face. "Yow! Yes, I missed you, too. Be quiet, now. Yes. Shhhhh." She started to take off her boots; peered up at the sign I'd hung to a height just above our heads in the center of the room; smiled, stood up, smiled, more and more, as the black letters, scrawled on pale blue cardboard, formed words,

> THE WAY OUT IS VIA THE DOOR
> WHY IS IT THAT NO ONE WILL USE THIS METHOD?
> . . . . Confucius

"Oh, I love you." She threw herself into the chair by the window. "I love you. You do such beautiful things."

145

(*rrrringgg*

"NO."

"It might be somebody else," she said, and reached.

"I won't let you, damn it. You just got here."

(*rringg. . . . rrringg*

"It really might be somebody. . . . "

"I don't care."

"Rebecca, let go, please. . . . I *have* to. . . . "

(*rrrring*

Listen. *listen.* . . .

to sounds of the quiet time: dawn, and Charles' car warming up, and maggie moving around, getting ready to go to the city again, *again she's gone*, and it's pink where that hill dips down like the waist of a woman reclining. A quiet light, diffused through the plastic in the chilly sunroom, narcissus blooms, crisp, small flowers. The wood stove. The dog scrambling out and in, tracking snow. The Gypsy's loud yowls. A silent calico cat gliding up the steps down the steps into the kitchen and out and up, and now there's occasional peeping. The oil burner turning on, off, on. The hum, which is sometimes a burble or rasp, of the motor that runs the aquarium. . . .

Warm water bathes my hand. A delicate, subtly pink thing flicks at my wrist. I scrub my wad of steel wool over glass encrusted green—lacy slime, algae. Scavangers aren't enough to keep it off —not even "Egbert," that hideous glob of slick, gray muscle she loves, creeping over or under the pebbles; or the snails, crouched motionless now, attached to the lower left side of the tank as I scrub at the front, working upward, diagonally. The glass is almost opaque. Despite the shudder I feel in the presence of any nonmammalian life, I enjoy the gaps I am making: the light let into this world. Five slender, striped, red-and-blue bullets zigzag away from my arm. The angel fish flutters into a corner behind some plants. Then I notice.

She came in running. "What? What's the matter?"

"Look at that."

"What?"

A shuddery sickpit: cuteness, o yes, cleanliness. "Egbert," that ghastly living vacuum cleaner, and those two monsters oozing out of their shells to suck, chew, devour their way through a world of us, I mean uP

("You're infecting me, damn it."

"*What*????"

and down and across and so, now: that spine strewn on top of the water.

"Verbal slips."

"What?"

"That." I pointed. "That was the glass catfish."

"Oh, no."

"Oh, yes. Now, can we take back those fucking snails?"

"Are you sure the snails. . . ?"

"I thought you were going to ask."

"I forgot," she whispered.

"Do you want to make a long distance call?"

"It's Sunday. The stores. . . ."

"Well, I'm going to take them out of there. I'll return them to some store tomorrow. I asked Joel about them again, by the way, when he called. He said. . . ."

"They're really evil," she murmured, staring into the tank.

"What?"

"They're evil," she whispered loudly. "We shouldn't take them back anywhere. We should kill them."

"Okay," I said, and walked away from her. "Go ahead."

I sit down, turn away. Still I can see her reflection in the window. She dips the net through the water and lifts and turns it over a coffee can, one; and dip, lift, clatter, two. I can hear heavy, determined steps striding out to the back door, she opens and leaves it open, a draft? but no sound. How could there have been no sound?

She crushed them, I think, with a hammer, and threw them into the woods in the snow somewhere behind the unfinished doghouse and then came back to where I am still by a window

shivering even now that she's closed the door again. I stare out.
Hint of hill-shapes in fog. Small flakes eddy, sudden birds, the
dim red silhouette of the mailbox,

>*maggie...*

sat on the floor by my chair and punched my knee lightly. I
pulled my head around, looked at her face getting thinner and
thinner before my eyes, almost; the acne erupting all over her
skin; her hair limp; but still those big square eyes are beautiful,
and her mouth—smiled.

IV.
FREEZEUP

11.

There are too many crumpled pieces of paper around here. They fill the orange basket, litter the floor. I step on them. Don't want to make a fire, and something keeps me from putting them into the garbage; so they pile up like the bottles of No-Cal cherry, orange, grape soda I'll take in for recycling someday.

Someday—like, we'll fix the pipe someday; and study stars, Kant, physiology, someday; and tar the doghouse; and she will start drawing, and he will come walking up the drive, some, day, or, night, or I...*what, I? Rebecca thought; really? What?*

It came to me in the dark, as I slid into another romantic pulp fantasy trip to California, even before my eyes opened

> (behind the plastic it's gray, but always earlier than I
> think)

—it came to me: that I run these scenes inside my eyelids every morning to quick-obliterate the Dream; from which I wake before dawn with my hands already clenched, clenched in sleep?

Winter. Over the desk on a bulletin board full of photos, notes, dried leaves, there's a calendar—two months' highlights spelled out in succinct detail, *viz:*

> cat births / kill snails / cat disappears /
> kitten dies / b. disappears / fight / cat dies,

as though some mad attack had been mounted against the whole feline world, then

> fight / m. tries suicide / m. on sedation / j. dies,

and I don't want to go there. Don't want to, follow her into

151

that bleakness, where sickness became the norm and death was omnipresent, seductive; don't want; to hear that siren song, nor see with that special vision I coveted so before I learned it reveals the molecules of flesh dissolving, pink globs of decay suspended by tenuous threads to a pile of bones collapsing inwards, no; a worldful of maggots; a constant, slow-motion process of putrefaction, in Technicolor, no,

> *no, I don't want to be*

what those leaves remind me,

> *remind me, maggie,*

I, am; and the rumpled couch; the lantern; the sheet of asbestos taped to the plastic so neatly,

> *remind me*

configurations; materials; people drift into my lifestream, become its details—an intimate furniture, so familiar that I can walk through those rooms, in darkness, and hardly stumble; except for once or twice or a few times and something tears, or is crushed; or streams out, or trickles out, or I push it, *out, something*, and then a chill. Then a hollow, shivering dark—a need to be filled with some, whatever it is that will start the process again; and again; and again—

"That's life," Bea would say; with a sigh of what she calls "mature depression." Or, "You do what you got to do." But, what's that?

A cold, dull light in those photos—December light. Viewed from above, from outside the lower right door pane, Tonta's urgent white cat-face seems caught between two arms of an asymmetrical cross, or, bars. Beside it, a dark mass, wrapped around a branch. Then Cairo, sitting on snow, and my writing says, *Follow the Contour.* Down, counterclockwise: the skull. Madamina, dark, stiff on a small white island, floating, it seems on dead leaves. A log like a gnarled reclining Lazarus just beginning to wake and reach up. Then writing again, in blue: *Listen.*

(but I can't

listen. . . .

Boots crunch in hard snow. Boots squeak. Snow clatters down through the branches, bare except for a few tenacious oak leaves rattling above the cove, near the sagging boathouse—its faded sign like a title: NO TRESPASSING. Inside, a broken rowboat, prow askew, looks defiant.

A thin skin of ice is spreading over the reservoir. One. Then rain again; mud stuck to our boots, in Cairo's fur, his paws tracking mud across the red rug and out on deck there's a quiet dripping. Droplets hang from black, shining boughs along the trail, as we slog up, there is a new lake on top of the ice—that rigid shaft unmelted, wedged between liquid depths and a liquid surface like silk. Two. Then freezing again. Birch trunks, patches of pastel smudged on the sky by bleached sunlight turn wavery on the water slowly hardening: ice: on water: on ice; on the water —three strata, hard blankets protecting their warm, dark, shifting foundation.

Lie on your belly on some frozen body of water. Look down. You can see it—the whole physiognomy: veins that are streams, long wedges of frozen rivulets, dimples, cracks that were currents, and constellations of small, festive bubbles at different levels, trapped air; twigs; pebbles; each horizontal layer preserved distinct in its own rhythmic pattern.

The cold begins to penetrate jeans, gloves, sweater. Your knees and hands start burning; your pelvis; then your chest, and an ominous boom, but don't leave yet. Keep looking. Slowly the larger design will come into focus: the vertical one, with all its separate rhythms dancing in counterpoint to each other, parallel, perpendicular, some even joined by a piece of debris caught between them—a door between the dimensions, proclaiming not *is*, but *towards*; a chunk of space choreographed by frozen time.

But not yet. It's not hard enough, yet. Here, now, at another beginning, again and again beginning, we only circle it: walking around, around, the same periphery as in June or October; then, one day,

("What's that?"

"I don't know. It sounds like a bass organ."

"Not too likely. Here, let's get under this pine."

"Oh, it's lovely in here. It's like a tent."

Snow whirling around us, blown by the same cutting gusts that are swaying the, trees, are squeaking like cat cries, snow: crawls on the hard, gray surface, advancing, receding, advancing, while there is a noise like some giant moving glaciers; arranging a hunk of land here, a bridge there. . . .

("what's *that?*"

"It can't be an earthquake here—can it?"

"I don't think so. . . .")

Snow, snow, swarming, piling up on itself, a huge amoeba spinning designs with its own soft, powdery flesh, white on white, then a rumble; a growl, a crack, a crash like dynamite,

("Christ!"

"It comes from under the dam, I think. . . ."

"No, it's okay. It's only"

The voice of the lake: freezing.

＊

Dec 10, Thurs? Heavy snow. Bake bread. Gypsy. Search for snow plow, no luck, B. missing.

Dec 11, Fri: The Roses gives birth to six kittens, maggie's room, all black and white except one,

rrrrringgg. . .

"Yes, Momma. Well, we're snowed in. Has anything. . . ? Oh. I don't know, whenever we can get someone to plow us out. Well, we're trying. There's no way except by car. It's eleven miles, Momma. He doesn't go tomorrow, it's Sunday. Well, this is the country. Wait till Monday, or maybe Mrs. Goodman can help. I just did it last week, you can't have that much laundry. . . ."

Dec 12, Sat: plowed out. get: ice scraper, rock salt, milk, peach yogurt, nails, lettuce.

Dec 13, Sun: maggie to city. threw stones at Gypsy. Dinner with Wolves, ate a pound of steak and cake and quake, lake, stake, break, brake, wake, fake. . . .

Dec 11, 15, Mon-Tues: T. to city. Cairo chained out. get: pastels, construction paper, cheese, tape, ski gloves, 'Macrocosm,' putty, long underwear, teach, meet maggie/Mike's/Tues,

then the long ride. . .

away from steel and neon towards the older terrors: witches, spiders, the implications of black branches, *mother-darkness,* maggie thought; as the highway narrowed, the last lights receded behind them.

Rebecca said, "How's your father?"

"The same. There's nothing to say, let's not talk about it. For once, you know," she said, "I think we got everything."

"I'll come up there with you next week."

"Okay. If you really want to, it would be. . . good." She lit a cigarette. Rebecca opened the window a crack. maggie pulled her coat around her. "It's fuckin' cold. I hope Cairo's okay."

"Sure he is. He has that long, thick coat. The doghouse is some protection, anyhow, even without. . . ."

"Shit. That's what we didn't get. Tar."

"It wasn't on the list. We got everything on the list. We'll have to make a new one tomorrow."

"Why wait till tomorrow? Tonight, as soon as we get home."

"Well, if you feel that way, why don't you start writing now?"

"I don't have a pencil," she giggled.

"Here."

"Look OUT. . . ." The car veered away from the oncoming headlights, back into its own lane. "Jesus," she shuddered. "Whew. You know, Rebecca, that's the first time I've ever felt scared with you driving?"

"Sorry. Let's try not to laugh for a while, okay?"

"Oh, don't worry."

But we were laughing again by the time we came to the long, curving downhill slope and then the rise just before our turnoff, and all along Hollowbrook Road we were laughing, up the driveway, and up the steps in counterpoint to the barking that came from behind the house; it was always so good to get home. It was so good to be with her—an absolute value, I thought, as I moved towards the kitchen where she was feeding Cairo, I saw my reflection in the window: dark shirt, long dark hair, and the set of my shoulders, okay, I thought. He could have been right, that little Italian. Maybe. Is my life fated to women?

rrrrringgg

"Hello. *Hi*. No, it's maggie. Do you want to speak to. . . . Oh. Sure, I'd love to talk to you. Fine. She told me, that's really nice of you. I'm not sure—next Monday, I guess. Susan's. Well, I'll call you when I get in. Oh, we got rid of them, you were right. Hey, and thanks. . . ."

"Was that Joel?"

"Yeah, he says hello. He's really sweet, you know?"

"I know," I muttered; and started towards the bathroom and tripped on a pillow and stumbled and fell against the wall, screaming, "Fuck, FUCK. . . ."

"Hey. . . ."

"Do you have to leave everything lying around, goddamn it? So that I can't take a step without, Christ, banana peels, and bicycle wrenches, and"

"Huh? Did you say *bicycle wrenches? banana peels?*"

"Well, OBSTACLES. . . ."

"Are you serious?"

"YES. It's like walking down a garden path," I raved, "and you can't look at any flowers or the sky or trees because it's littered with JUNK. . . ."

"It's not exactly a garden path in here. Oh, fuck, you know. . . ." She curled up in the chair by the window. "And you put that pillow there, by the way."

156

"I DID NOT."

"Listen," maggie said carefully, "I just happen to have this thing about big men. Okay?"

"What thing?"

"I'm—drawn to them. I. . . ."

"Congratulations. What does that have to do with anything?"

"Are you kidding?"

"All right." I squatted, my back to the wall, beside the aquarium. "There's nothing like that between Joel and me. You know that. There's absolutely no reason why it should matter if you. . . ."

"But obviously it does." She lit a cigarette. 'And if you feel that way, then why not?"

"He likes pretty girls, that's why."

"Oh, come on."

"No, really. There's a certain physical type some men. . . . there just is. Like you. A certain kind of face, and very slim. . . ."

"You're skinny!"

"THAT DOESN'T MATTER."

"What?" she frowned. "Now I'm really getting confused."

"Okay, wait." I went to the kitchen, got an apple, a knife, came back, and settled onto the rug. "It's that men don't fall in love with me," I told her, and started to peel the apple. "Not any more. They like to be friends with me, but they're not attracted. At all."

"You mean you don't notice."

"NO, goddamn it." I tossed half the apple skin onto the rug. "I knew you'd try something like that. You're always trying to make it sound good. But it's not. Like you—you just walk out the door and trip over them."

"Huh?"

"You do. Like that man who plowed us out. Or the guys down at the lumberyard." The other half of the apple skin. "Or, or Carrie. . . ."

"*Carrie?* What does Carrie have to do with it?"

"Well, she never looks at me when she's talking. She looks at

157

you. And she calls me 'maggie' ninety percent of the time."

"You don't look at *her* when she talks," maggie said.

"Of course I do. At least I did until. . . ." I bit into the apple, ferociously. "She was my friend," I mumbled, "before you moved here."

"I wish you could hear yourself. You sound. . . ."

"I don't care. It's true. It's all the same thing. Carrie, Joel, the lumberyard"

"Rebecca"

"It's something you have and I don't. That's all. Everybody you meet responds to it. Everyone falls in love with you." I gulped another hunk of apple down, hardly chewed. "Even now, right now, you're so fucking holy," I said.

"Oh, yes, it's great. Like the twenty stores I can't go into, right? And the classes I had to stop. I don't get to be friends with men, you see, and I'd like to." She ground out her cigarette. "*I* envy *you*."

"Oh, bullshit."

"No. it's not. Can't you understand—there are all these people I can't see, really, and all these places I can't go, and the n . ."

"What?"

"No, I don't want to say that."

"*What?*"

"I don't want to say that," she repeated.

"Okay. I say that's all unimportant. It's the kind of inconvenience that's really funny and flattering, and there's not one serious thing"

"Okay, how about Dr. Cecchetti?"

"Cecchetti?"

"Yeah, well. I didn't tell you because I knew what you'd say. We've been having these—conversations, is all, when I go to get checked. About—realities. Consciousness. And, well, they seemed to transcend the doctor-patient thing," she said, "but this last time. . . ."

"Did you tell Ann?"

"No."

"Uh-huh." I finished my apple, tossed the core on the pile of skins, and stared down at my palms. "*Transcend*," I said, bitterly.

"Well, I thought so."

"What happened?"

"Nothing, really. Just talk. But, you know what he said to me last time? We got to this point, you see. . . ."

"What point?"

"Well, I don't know how to. . .it felt very, close. And he said, *You'll never be a happy woman, you know.* Unquote."

"Oh, great."

"It's just, after that, things got funny. It will be hard to go back. I mean, nothing happened, but it did. He. . .and I really need to go back, you know? I'm taking pills. Like, I really might have epilepsy. You see? That's the kind of thing. . . ."

"Yeah." I got another apple and sat down, heavily. "Still. At least you know you're attractive." I looked down, concentrating on keeping the skin intact.

"That doesn't matter."

"I don't believe it."

"It doesn't. It doesn't touch the deep stuff." She pulled herself up in the chair, wrapped her arms around her knees. "Can you listen a minute?" she said. "I mean, just, try to listen?"

"SHIT," I snarled as the peel broke three-quarters of the way to the end. "Okay, okay. I'm listening."

"Well, I know I do something, okay? I don't know exactly what, or when, but okay, people make me into this magic— thing."

"Right. Exactly. You are. . . ."

"Yes, but, *a thing*. It's not me. That's happened to you, I know you know what I mean. It's some kind of myth. And it always winds up with them wanting to suffocate me, like Richard, or, disappointed, like. . . ."

"Adam," I said quickly, and bit off a piece of apple.

"Yes. Adam."

She looked at me. I chewed hard. The walls said, *I, i, I, I, I,* and her eyes, *Rebecca,* but I won't say it. Cairo came whimpering in, shoved his big head under her hand and she stroked him, absently. *No. I refuse.* I got up and went to the kitchen again.

"You want an apple or something?"

"No. You're going to make yourself sick."

"Don't worry." I sprawled down and started to peel the apple, very carefully. "Besides, it's really over for me. I haven't had a period since last August. That's almost four months."

"And that doctor cracked up when you said menopause."

"Well, he could be wrong."

"He's not. Besides, even if by some weird chance it's true, it still doesn't mean. . . ."

"Okay, okay, let's drop that. None of it changes the fact that you're beautiful. That makes a difference to—people like Joel."

"Didn't you tell me Joel's never been with a woman, seriously, for more than two weeks?"

"Since I've known him. He may have. . .but, well, this has nothing to do with Joel, not really, anyway. I feel like if I looked different—like, if I could lose twenty pounds and get my nose fixed. . . ."

"Your nose, fixed???"

"Well, I mean, change my face. Aha! Did it!" I added a perfect spiral of yellow apple skin to my little pile and put half the apple in my mouth."

"You're crazy. You're really crazy. Rebecca, you're beautiful. . . ."

"I AM NOT," I shouted, reeling up to my knees. Bits of apple sprayed out of my mouth.

"YOU ARE."

"THAT MAKES ME FURIOUS WHEN YOU SAY THAT."

"WHY???"

"BECAUSE IT'S FAKE!!!"

"IT IS NOT."

"OH, SHIT," I snarled. The half-apple still lay in my palm. I

160

thought of throwing it. "I HATE you when you try to pretend. . . ."

She was staring at me. "I didn't know before," she said. "Not really."

"What now?"

"You're just as crazy as I am."

"Of course. I've been trying to tell you."

"Yes, but—you really are."

"Okay, I really am." I sat back down on my heels and considered the apple, already turning brown. "So, do I get a medal?"

"Look," she said. "I've always envied people like you, and Susan. You have a really individual kind of beauty. I've always felt kind of, you know, usual. There are hundreds like me."

"Oh, there are not," I said disgustedly. "I've never seen anybody who looks like you."

"Really?"

"Really. What infuriates me is that people like you can afford to be all abstract and noble about 'beauty,' but when you come down to it, most men like pretty, slim. . . ."

I finished the apple.

"Okay," maggie said, "look. Remember I told you I used to be fat? Before they took out my thyroid?"

"That's absurd. It should work the other way."

"I know. With most people it does, but there are exceptions, and I'm one. Now I'm thin. Then I was fat. I even remember looking down one day and not being able to see my feet." She stood up, put her feet together and stuck out a nonexistent stomach. I jammed the pile of apple peels into my mouth. She said, "Really. Couldn't see 'em." She mimed leaning over to peer across a mound, then fell back in her chair. "Ask Jesse."

"Okay, so?"

"Well, the point was—still, I was attractive."

"That's what I'm saying. Exactly. I could lose fifty pounds and have plastic surgery and still—it's like some magic cloak. I just don't have it."

I ground the wad of apple cores in my teeth. maggie frowned.

"But—aren't we going around in some kind of circle?"

"Maybe. I don't know. I've just always felt that some women know a secret they won't tell me. Like, you know, and you won't tell. That's why I hate you."

"I don't believe you hate me."

"Good." I started for the kitchen.

"Hey, please," she called, "don't eat any more apples. You'll really get sick."

"Guess what? There aren't any." I came back in with half a loaf of bread and butter and honey. "Want some? There won't be any of this left, either, I'll warn you now."

"No. You're going to hate yourself."

"I already do." I tore off a hunk of bread and buttered it. "Haven't you noticed?"

"How about Jesse?" she said suddenly. "He's attracted to you."

"He's living with Grace."

"That doesn't affect what we're talking about. Besides, you could have him. I can tell."

I spread another hunk of bread with honey. "Well, you said he liked you when you were fat. I guess he likes fat women."

"Of course. That must be it," she said ironically, and lit another cigarette. "Look, is there any way. . . ?"

"No."

She pulled herself up to a squat on the chair, her arms wrapped around her knees. "I feel like I'm caught in something and can't find any way out of it."

"That's exactly right. That's what I meant. There isn't one. It's true, that's why. TRUTH. FACT," I told her, rolling the rest of the bread up into a cylinder, dipping it into the honey, "besides: I bet Jesse would turn on to any white woman."

"Oh, now wait. That's ugly. That's really insulting. It's bad enough you denigrate yourself, but laying that stuff on Jesse. . . ."

"You see? I'm a slob. I'm NASTY," I spat at her, feeling my

mouth twist. "You don't like me either, not really. You're just now seeing it. Why don't we"

"I DO like you," she shouted, "I LOVE YOU, GODDAMN IT!"

"That's NOT what I WANT!"

"What DO you want, then?"

The sign sways. I feel my jaw drawn tight, eyes popping, my whole face mirroring hers, but her eyes brim, and mine are dry—as always. A dark, sweet aftertaste throbs in my mouth; honey; echoing in my veins, a thousand bees buzz, hieroglyphs I can't decipher although they are spun of my own tissue. . . .

I looked at the rug. I muttered, "I don't know. To be left alone, I guess."

The sign sways. The windows are misted.

Tonta comes in through the cat door and tries to climb on my lap. I push her away. I stare at the jar of honey, hardly seeing at first, but then the label comes into focus: a wise old Indian's head, feather bonnet, surrounded by words: *Pure. Raw. Golden. Indian Sage Honey.*

I drag on my socks and boots. The air seems thick, as I eat another two spoonfuls, the membranes in my mouth pucker. I stagger up. maggie coughs behind her door. I pull on a sweater, a parka, even that small motion an effort because I have gained fifty pounds in the past half hour; or more, a hundred, two hundred pounds of aching pouch called a stomach I'm carrying out the door, now, Cairo circling me, shrieking, I go down the steps with my two-ton legs pumping, down the drive and dogged-ly up the hill. My shoulders are stuffed with little lead slugs like they sew into curtains. My head is a pumpkin stuck on a dandelion stem. I want—*to cry, to cry, to cry. . . .enough.*

Ice rubble is piled up under the spillway. Tracks on the lake crisscross. I walk out onto the wall and a blast of wind hits me. The sun is casting long purple stripes on the snow banks. Good

163

cold on my face, *breathe*, the poison is draining out, slowly, *breathe*, and the weight, draining. *Poison, weight*—metaphors for me, but she can't move, sometimes. She sleeps, or she strangles. Her throat, her skin, her lungs get involved in what for me are—ideas.

I lay back on the wall; turned my face to the late sun setting, waning towards solstice. *Solstice. Indian Sage. Ideas*—these lurid dancers obscenely jerking their arms and legs, but the motions are abstract. The pigments my mammal's body portrays, changing red to yellow to green like a lizard's are abstract—a camouflage spun of emotional pus but finally words, only words, I spewed all over her, words containing that spectrum and yet the measure of this ugly creature, the sum of its four dimensions, flattens to gray.

There is no ice in California, now. Only fog and rain.

I close my eyes, try to absorb these last drops of sunlight before the ice closes down, as it has, already, on the rowboat, its prow still jutting inside the boathouse; the dead leaves caught in stratified pools on the path where I have knelt to look at their scalloped borders, so perfect; vaginal; then Cairo races down from a slope. . . .

     (crunch

        Listen:

to dusk in the woods: December. Black, slate blue and tawny grasses showing through the fresh white as it darkens, then it is night, *listen*—stars crackle sharp through the branches, the snow is snapping, the air piercing, pure, and the house with its windows lit up like a palace as I come up the hill the icicle-studded eaves glint, casting shadows. I hear maggie's voice: her height of rage, the most vicious words she could think of: "I LOVE YOU, GODDAMN IT."

The door to her room is closed. A pot of coffee sits on the stove, still warm; and a note on the counter:

Guess what? we did forget tape—that thick silver stuff!

The essense you radiate is predominatly quite good—Does

the woods help at least to convince you of that— The dividing line sense of self in that respect I d̶o̶ ̶n̶o̶t̶ ̶t̶h̶i̶n̶k̶ ̶c̶a̶n̶ be should heighten the contrast especially out there. That feeling, the true predominat one should never be forgotten. You are like the shapes and crevices of that log. Physically and psychically —Would it help to think of that sometimes when in the full t̶h̶r̶o̶n̶g̶ throws of disgust one dimensional feel. The experience with the log should be assimilated to other areas— It's just as fucking real. I know, I do, that is far more complicated. But it seems like such a loss t̶o̶ not to take t̶a̶ that fusion with you.

12.

"It's okay," she said. "I mean, it's not, it's awful, but. . . ."

"It's like a distortion of vision. As though a part of that glass were moved half an inch to the left, you know, but only a part, and it stayed transparent—so that all the proportions. . . ."

"Yes. I understand."

"*Do you?*"

"Sure. I get the crazies, remember? So you get the uglies. I just hadn't realized how bad. . . ."

"Yes. Look, not to change the subject, but—aren't those kittens making a lot of noise?"

"They are, aren't they. Are those the little ones?"

"Yes. They were before, too."

"Hm. The Roses went out this morning, early. I don't think she's come back yet. Anyway," she said, "when it starts to happen —the dislocation—is there anything I can. . . ."

"That's a long time to leave them," I said, "at one week old. Isn't it?"

"I guess so, yes. *Not to change the subject.*" She smiled. "She may have come back when we weren't looking."

"I'll check."

> (*rrrringgg*

"Yeah. Yeah hello Momma, what. Oh. Well, that can wait." Her voice rose to where I knelt upstairs, the flashlight illuminating a cardboard nest and six tiny red mouths stretched wide. "*It can.* And listen, do you realize all these calls are costing. . . ."

"SHE'S NOT HERE," I hollered.

> *Dec 18, Fri:* Search. Call vet. Get: eyedropper, cotton, Karo. Feed kittens. Search.
>
> *Dec 19, Sat:* Feed kittens. Put up sign at grocery. Search. Get: smaller eyedroppers, heating pad, milk, thermometer. Feed kittens. Search. Feed kittens. search. . . .

Dusk. The oil burner hums. I have just finished feeding the kittens with my finger. A voice cajoles me from inside my mind, *music?* but, *No,* I tell it, *not music. Not now.* I want to hear the pulse of motors and coils; wood, glass, orchestrated with kittens' peeping, then the door, and Cairo rushing in, and maggie kneeling to take off her boots, her parka, wiping her snow-flecked glasses,

"That smells great," she said. "What are you cooking?"

"Any sign?"

"She's dead. I know she's dead." She came into the kitchen, sat down on the three-step ladder, and lit a cigarette. I flicked the flame on under the coffee pot.

"All kinds of things could have happened," I mumbled. "She's a beautiful cat. Maybe somebody picked her up."

"Carrie says anybody would see pretty soon that she's nursing kittens, and bring her back."

"Maybe they wouldn't know where to bring her back *to.*"

"Well, okay. No one's seen her, anyhow. I asked all up and down the road, including the Brenners."

"What did they have to say?"

"*'Pretty hard to find a white cat in the snow, ho, ho, ho.'*" Stood up, stretched. "Whew. My face is still numb."

"You were out there a long time. Here." I handed her a cup of hot coffee. "It's fifteen, the radio said."

"I believe it. Oh, and I also mentioned The Gypsy hanging around. To the Brenners. They said they'd try to keep him in his cage." She sat down again, sipped, puffed, coughed. "I feel bad when I think about that, but."

"It's him or Bailey."

"I know. I told them. They're going to Florida, though, for the holidays, all except the old folks and that strange kid, Ron. So he'll be the one who does it." She coughed again. "He's really strange."

"That's what people say about us, I bet."

"No, but scary-strange. I was wondering if it was, you know, a fox or a person who. . . . I could really imagine that kid killing."

"*We don't know she's dead.*"

"I'm pretty sure." She coughed again, cleared her throat.

"We would have found her in the woods."

"Not necessarily." She sipped her coffee, choked, coughed, and coughed, dropped her cigarette, coughed, reeled up to the sink, "I can't stop," she gasped, gulping water, and little explosions of water sprayed out of her mouth. I pounded her back. Her ribs protruded through the nylon shirt. "My God." She staggered into the living room, then, "Hey, come look!" she called, and I ran out in time to see Madamina climbing the steps.

We crept up behind her and knelt in the doorway. She stuck her head in under the eaves, hissed and started back out, but I grabbed her and dropped her into the carton. Six black and white wormlets reached out to her, but she hurtled out again, spitting, she ran past us down the steps.

"Shit."

"We could try to put them in with the others."

"After that? Besides, the little ones would get crushed."

"Oh, well. We'll have to keep doing it ourselves. We better move them, I guess."

We made them a nest beneath the shelves in the bathroom, with all the paraphernalia—eyedroppers, cotton, bowl, Thermos— just above. The first days we fed them as much sweetened milk as they would take. We cheered when their mouths had learned to close on the plastic dropper and suck it, "More," we crooned, squeezing the rubber tip and milk squirted out all over them: dribbled out of their mouths and coated their faces, their paws, their whiskers all sticky with milk and our shirts encrusted, the whole place stank of old dried milk, but, "More," we warbled,

(more, you got room, kid, MORE. . . .

Above, to the right—cross-legged, she sits on the floor in her black silk dressing gown. A towel is draped over her shoulder. Kittens crawl all over her. She holds the biggest, who sucks away,

"Ach," she says in a strong Yiddish accent, but delicate, "doesn't it do your heart good to vatch him itt?"

"Now and then I remember where you came from."

"Ja. This is really ah feisty one. Ah, gorilla." She handed him over to me wedged next to her knees, against the wall. I dipped a wad of cotton in hot water and swabbed the kitten under his tail. A yellow trail oozed out,

"That's a boy!"

"He really does shit more than the others," she said. "And yells more. Now this one. . . ."

"It's funny about Madamina," I said. "I'm a little afraid of"

"Well, she has kids. But I don't think she'd really hurt these. You know, I think they're going to be all right."

"Yeah." I put the gorilla in the nest and started on the next one. "If they'd just shut up between feedings. They're not even hungry."

"Well, they miss Momma. There's nothing much we can do about that. We're too big to crawl in there with them."

"I'm worried about their bellies, too." I held up the kitten. "I mean, look at this."

"All infants have distended bellies." She examined the one she was feeding. "This one, too."

"Keep that one a minute," I said, "this one hasn't shit yet."

"Okay. It's really amazing, isn't it, all the things a mother does."

"Oh, isn't it just!"

"Well, you know what I mean. Ready? Two more to go. . . ."

On Sunday night we called the vet and learned we were killing them with overfeeding. *One dropperful, five times a day,* he said, *that's all,*

169

"Oh, look! His eyes are open! I told you he was precocious!"

"Cairo, GIT!"

(*rrrringggg*

"No, Momma. No, not today. Because we have to nurse six kittens is why. She can't, she has to work. Momma, damn it, I told you why. Not unless he's really...eeeEEEEE...."

"Eeeaaas-y."

"It's not her fault. It's not her fault. It's not...."

"It's really amazing," I thrilled, "all the things a mother does."

"Oh, fuck you."

"Sorry. Couldn't resist. Will you be all right with them alone for two days?"

"Of course." She lit a cigarette. "All this calling of hers is getting impossible. They'll turn off that phone if she can't pay, and then when something really happens...."

"The bill will get paid, don't worry. Look," I said, "would it make a difference if, I, went up and checked what's happening there?"

"That's quite an offer."

"It shouldn't be."

"Well, it is. Don't do it if it's not easy, okay? There isn't anything"

"Would it make you feel better?"

"Well—yes. But, not if there's any problem at all...."

*

the roses gone—six screaming kittens left behind—i
cannot seem to bear it—cannot bear anything—my mind
running filmstrips of animal traps—fox—car runover—
stolen but worse—cannot help feeling someone has hung
her has axed her to death—and everyone is suspect—

*

170

Dec 21-22, Mon-Tues: **R.** to city. Get: popcorn, cranberries, shells, tinsel, watercolors, stapler, *Messiah*, brandy, duck, wrapping paper, fish food, frame, silver tape, blue sweater for m, light switch, kerosene lamp, book for S, glass 6¼ x 8, teach, and

race rush rain chew through a red traffic light swinging Third Avenue, hardware; art supply, market; rain rain chilling boutique where a charming young, *no*, man, *no*, back to hardware, jump, jitter, *down, cowgirl,* veer lurch on the slick *keep your balance* the sidewalk is turning glazed, and the joy turning sour, and now, despite greens in a vase, and cocoa, Susan's tight, arrogant words drive me out to the street again, to the Lower East Side. . . .

A pale moon was climbing over the rooftops; blurred behind the storm it created dark, twisted shapes that seemed to loom at me through a fine mist. I stalked past windows lit up to display pots, beads, clothes, merreee, now headlights blared past the fruit stands on vivid, grimy First Avenue bustling, still, at eight turning ten, oh, clock,

merreee Christmassss. . . .

"Breathe deep," Joel said. "Thaaaat's it. Relax. In fact, let's go get a drink. You could use one."

"*I* could?"

"Yes. You."

We squeezed in the tiny, dim elevator creaking down with two girls in pea coats straining not to look at us looking at them, then out through the drafty hallway. The mist was turning white —feathery stuff that lay on the ice like down. We slid along Third Street, linked, passed the firehouse, sole oasis of light in this dark desert, then turned up Broadway and into a bar a few steps from the corner.

Brandy fumed up in my head. Smoke almost blinded me. Voices seemed to slap my eardrums. It was too sudden, this bombardment, and for a moment I was almost afraid. I mumbled, "Joel? Let's get,"

"Sure," he said and led me out again, and we walked uptown. The flakes fell thicker, festive now. The breath of the city seemed to sparkle, in a world soft and white. Joel said, "How 'bout Max's?"

"I got thrown out of there a couple months ago."

"Oh yeah?" He grinned his foxy grin. His beard and eyebrows were speckled white, his skin glowed, his dark eyes snapped under the white woollen cap. "What for?"

"It was either Cairo growling or maggie and me sitting under the bar. I'm not sure which."

"Sounds like both. Let's go on—I doubt you'll be recognized."

He held the door open for me, but I paused to peer at him: looking so warm that moment, so vital, I heard myself blurt,

"You really like her, don't you."

"Like who? maggie? Oh, yes." He smiled. "She's really lovely. She's like a little fawn."

He pushed me into the bar, gently. Smoke and brandy, again, packed bodies, music and voices again, but this time it's better. We sit near a window, looking out on the world of winter night through streaked glass. Groups form beside us and shift, dissolve, re-form, laughing, swirling like flakes that cascade behind my eyelids birds are circling water tanks in autumn, waves dissolving, re-forming. . . .

"Let's go," Joel's voice said, and then we were out again; in again; out, in out, the exquisite alternation of ice and brandy, the cold light outside and inside the warmth, the faces.

A man with a duffle bag was circling one bar, from table to table he spread his wares: and Joel took *Blonde on Blonde*, and I took Janis, and then we were squeaking back up in the antique elevator,

"You should do this more often, Rebecca."

"Yeah, I know, but, I have to teach tomorrow."

"You'll be okay. Come on, I'll give you the bed." He ushered me into the bedroom and left me there, but fifteen minutes later his face appeared, "uh, Rebecca?"

I opened one eye. "Mmmmm"

"Would you mind if, I, uh, came in there with you?"

Under the covers, on opposite sides of the big double bed, we snuggled, hugging our pillows, and giggled and shrieked as two wild wads of fur leapt in after him, somersaulting between us,

"That smell," I gasped.

"Yes," Joel said, "Clara does stink, some. You'll get used to it. It's better when she's not moving. *Quiet*," he barked. "*Quiet*, Clara. *Quiet*, Murdoch. There, that's better." He patted me, as the dogs subsided, he curled up, his back to me, sank down into the mattress, exuding warmth, breathing heavily, then he began to snore.

And snored. And snored, in counterpoint to the schnauzers' wheezing and snuffling, he snored and snorted, as dawn came up I couldn't catch my breath; couldn't sleep, not or hardly at all. At ten o'clock I finally left him, still snoring, and dragged myself out to a dreary, slushy day, five cups of coffee and fifty strangers wondering why the teacher was so bad tempered and then it was ten P.M., twelve hours later; the slush again frozen, and I in my car, already on my way out of town, when I remembered Susan's suggestion.

I stopped at the one open drugstore, then inched the car home, slowly, rigid with fear a gust of wind would blow me into a skid; down the winding part, up, the turnoff, the driveway, finally, then the steps,

She said, "You got it ALL!"

"I've been racing. How are the kids?"

"All alive. I'm a little worried about the runt. Coffee?"

"Tea." I started unpacking the bags. "Susan said it would be kinder to let them die. She says they'll all be stunted."

"Well, that may be true, but"

"I know. We had an ugly scene, and I wound up staying with Joel. *He* says we're playing out a symbolic drama."

"Has anyone else expressed an opinion?" She handed me a cup of tea. "Your students, maybe? My God," she squealed, "what is THAT?"

"A clock, of course. Before things got nasty, Susan told me we could put one in with the kittens to keep them quiet. They think it's their mother's heartbeat. Don't look at me like that, it's worth a try."

"*What a color!*"

"Well, it was ten o'clock. It's the best I could do."

"Oh, it's gorgeous," she said. "I've always loved magenta. And we won't have any trouble reading the numbers. Is that Mickey Mouse?"

"We don't have to look at it." I wound up the clock, wrapped a towel around it. "Except when we wind it. It only runs for two hours."

"Great." She watched me put the clock in with the kittens. They squealed, and I closed the door. "Is Susan still coming?"

"I think so. The afternoon of the twenty-fourth. That's Thursday."

"We'll have to get a tree tomorrow."

"*Listen. . . .*"

We tiptoed in. Six globs of fur lay cuddled around the clock, asleep.

"It worked!"

"Shhhhh"

"Come on out, let's close the door."

"I'm going up the walls," I whispered. "I wound up sleeping in Joel's bed. Very chaste, but I nearly choked."

"You could attack him," maggie said in a normal voice.

"Oh no. He runs."

"From everybody?"

"Every woman I've seen him get close to. Romantically close. . . ."

"Hmm. Well, you're a very attractive woman, whether you admit it or not, so even if nothing happens sexually. . . ."

"No, you're wrong. That may be true for someone like you, but"

"Listen, I don't see that *someone like me* versus *someone like you* bit, so don't see for me. All right? As I say, you're a very attractive woman and probably no attractive woman who's a match for him is exempt forever. That's just a hunch, but—well, I've been that way about men all my life, you know. A runner. If they really wanted me and were really possible, I'd get claustrophobia. Hives with Richard, or"

"You didn't do that with Adam."

"He wasn't a threat. He never really wanted me, I could tell. It was hard on my ego, but—getting back to Joel, it sounds to me like he's really turned on to you."

"Oh, the hell he is. He snored all night."

"Okay. Just don't be too shocked if something strange happens, that's all. Maybe I'm wrong. I hope so."

"I do too. Look, maggie, what I didn't do was, go to see your father."

"Oh. That's okay," she said, quickly. "I told you it was okay. I. . . . Great looking cheese."

"I'll go next week," I told her.

"Sure. If it works out. You know, you really don't have to."

13.

december 3
i fear sleep now—fear of waking up to the enivitable
same—fear of not waking—

*

maggie, do you remember
getting up in the chilly mornings; making a fire, quickly, in that
stove with its pipe still leaking smoke? the windows and walls
leaking cold, and the bathroom smelling of plaster, of milk and
kittens, of plumbing; and then the kitchen, maybe a crocus
blooming in a pot, and coffee—the sharp, moist smell of the
Eastern woods

> (outside, yes, Rebecca; and inside
> that house made of wood and card-
> board, everything was rotting. . . .

Above the creek, we found a small hemlock. You put an axe
blade to it—the boygirl, *an axe blade to it*, you said, determined,
knowledgeable in your glasses, your big black sweater—and cut
it down and we carried it up the drive. All five Wolves-in-a-row
stood laughing at us through their window; gesturing.
"What's the matter with them?"
"I think they're saying it's huge."

176

We hauled the tree up the steps and in through the glass doors and propped it against the windows. It took up most of the front room.

"It looked so small in the woods."

"I don't care," you said. "We hardly use this room. Oh, I want to sleep under it."

"It might fall."

"No. Well, maybe let's nail a few branches to the casements."

You got the ladder from under the pipe, and the hammer and nails, and climbed up. I leaned against the bottom rungs, looking out past bars of wood, needles, glass, at a gray and white sky.

(bars of blood. . . .

"Hold on, okay?" you said. "It feels really unsteady."

"Okay. I wonder what Adam's doing this Christmas."

"Hmm." The ladder shook. "Why? Did he like Christmas trees much?"

"No. I don't know why I thought of it. Hey, careful," I said, as you started to pound in a nail, and the ladder swayed.

"You're not letting go, are you?"

"No," I said, "don't worry,"

(but I almost

peeeeeep

and for just a moment, I thought I heard something scream. But no. It's only the heater grill

"Hmm." You reached for a far branch.

"No. I don't know why I thought of it." Then, "Hey, careful," I yelled, as the ladder swayed, and you squealed,

"You're not letting go, are you?"

No I told you I'm not letting go don't worry.

but I almost

(peep peep

and for just a moment. . . . . . .

but no: it's only—the heater grating on below us sitting on our identical big blue sleeping bags guaranteed to stay warm at

177

ten degrees stretched out on the red rug under the branches we are stringing popcorn; laughing; talking like any two normal, *normal*, but, what did we say?

I can't see you. I love you, but I can't see you. The moisture unvented, blinds me. A pressure wells up. Now, for the second consecutive day, I have left the flame on, and walked away from the stove, and come back to find: the pretty blue saucepan explosed to shards; then the white one—enamel melted, blackened and fused to the grate.

Charred milk has a stiff, gummy texture, and stinks.

The sun came out today, for the first time in almost a week. I look at the sign that says, follow the contour. *Follow*. Burn every pan in the house, and my throat burns, my back aches, and Adam's back in California, his spine twisting (*follow, around, around to*

       maggie...you taught me to blow eggs out through pinpoint holes and to paint their shells: bright, fantastical wings, beaks. White eggs on your palm. Red, yellow, and blue eggs stud the tree as we drink eggnog tonight *The Messiah* is playing, A Man of Sorrows; or is that my new hot record? got in another universe, which doesn't exist, with Joel, who doesn't exist, because there's only: the dog, the cats, the snow, the tree, and us, maggie. We talk. We laugh, yes, merreee, but now the crescendo is building. It's gaining momentum, maggie, the Hallelujah Chorus, or maybe *Take it—just another little piece of my heart*, maggie, maggie, the deaths, now now now now now its... Christmas Eve.

                  (*blue brown and white pinwheels*

"What?"
"What? Oh, I was only looking at the fabric on that pillow."
"That's African."
"Yes, I...know."

And Susan had brought many little gifts to set under the branches sweeping low and festive with the eggs suspended on threads; the wreaths of popcorn; the dark red cranberries nestled in green, lush, elegant as the tall, blonde woman is elegant, always, and awkward; kneeling, carefully placing little packets with tinsel, sprigs of weed and gold paper stars here and there,

"Oh, I love Christmas," she says.

Such long, strong lines in her face. But the blue eyes are naked as any child's, I-Rebecca thought: this is for her what Thanksgiving is for me.

"I glad you came, Susan."

She smiles, instantly warm. "You know, if you rub the smell of that cat's nest on the babies," she says, "she might think they're her own.

"She can't be that dumb."

"I think I've heard of it working. They go by smell a lot. Try."

"Mmmmmmm...mmm...m...mmmmm"

"mmmmmmmm...mmmm...."

(flames rising up into a waterfall)

"What?"

"What? Oh, sorry," maggie said. "Just mumbling."

"...so different here," Susan was saying, "from how mmmm Thanksgivmmmm"

(no. focus.

"Well, the table," Rebecca said. "And the tree."

"No, it's not that. It's mmm air, or something. I even felt it on the steps when mmmm. Before we came in." She shivered a little, and yawned. "I'mmmm awfully tired, somehow."

"mmmmm m then mmmm"

(say something. ...

"Kitten time," maggie said. "We could try to switch them now."

Susan yawned again. "If you don't mind, I won't stay for this. Who's sleeping where?"

"You can have any bed you want," Rebecca told her. "We've been sleeping out here."

"Okay. Guess mmmmm mmm."

179

(listen. listen. . . .

Susan said, "I don't know why I'm so tired."

(because

"What?"

(because it's started

"What? maggie. . . ?"

"What? Oh," maggie said, and blinked. "Sleep well."

"Mmmm." Susan got up. "Have a good time. I hope it works."

(Rebecca?

peeppeep

(rebecca-sane. don't burn. . . .

I can't remember, maggie,

how exactly it went. We must have carried the big kittens downstairs, the small ones up, and switched the rags. We must have, tossed Madamina in with them; watched as she tried to climb out, put her back, then, "oh, look," you whispered, clutching my shoulder, as she fell on her side and the kittens swarmed against her; attached their ravenous suction cups to her nipples. . . .

I've missed that.

"What?"

"I didn't say a word."

"I heard you."

"But"

"Yes, I know," maggie said, "but I heard you"

(rrringgg

No. That didn't happen.

"What?"

"That didn't happen, maggie. It's one o'clock in the morning, the phone doesn't always ring when the kittens are crying. Sometimes, just sometimes, one happens without the other."

"What are you talking about?"

"You thought the phone rang just now."

"*I* thought. . . ?" She stared. "Rebecca. . . ."

"Didn't you? Weren't you hallucinating?"

"N-no. . . I don't. . . think so. . . oh, NO," as Madamina dragged one of the big kittens out; she dropped him; picked him up by his neck, dragged him to the foot of the steps; and dropped him,

"Doesn't seem too efficient. I thought instinct"

"She still might get him upstairs if we don't stop her."

We carried him back to the nest. She followed, tried again, and again, then curled around them and closed her eyes. We tiptoed out.

"That's okay," she said. "Now: what are we going to do?"

"Now? To do? Are you kidding? I'm going to sleep."

"I mean presents. Susan. Did you see what she brought?"

"Oh. I'd managed to forget that."

"Well, I'm going to try to make something," maggie said.

Upstairs, in the room where the small kittens are, that was Adam's room, I am wrapping things in tissue. A fancy candle. A plant. A string of my own beads that I've never worn, that Susan will never, but that doesn't matter. The heater goes on. Its nagging, hoarse voice jabs my nerves. maggie sticks her head in the doorway.

"Got any wrapping paper?"

"No. There's some tissue in the top drawer."

"Maybe there's something here," she said, and crawled in under the eaves, peep, and dragged out two cartons, *but, this is MY room*. "Aha!" She held up a sheet of blue paper. "Do you want some?"

"No."

"Okay. There's more if you do." She went out. The cartons still squatted there in the middle of my, MY room. . . .

I started rummaging. Junk: some green ribbon; old newspaper; then, three contact sheets, photos of water and stone; and an 8 x 10 print of the devil-god. Glossy, black, he stands silhouetted—all his arms reaching up to a white sky. How could Adam have left that?

(Eons ago, in a notebook that's found its way under my hand now, just now that I squat and peer at those glossy limbs, a pale yellow slug oozes down the window. Something dark is inside it

181

(but that must be

Adam—speaking inside my head. Adam? watching the sway-ing horns of a slug in a California torrent, and merging with that page out of autumn when rain poured into the pans we'd set all over the house, a flood, the leaks widening, one dripping into the open bottle the doctor had given

maggie

said, "That's incredible!" Staring into the vial at a pink glob of what had been pills. She always leaves things open. The tooth-paste, for instance; the coffee jar; the bowl of sugar always there on the table under the rain trickling down, a big stain on the blue-and-white tablecloth. . . .

There is a stain on the bedspread where I sit now; and from a place on the rug, downstairs, a spot is spreading—dark red on the nubbly texture oozing under my bare foot near the phone

(*Rebecca*

said, "There must be holes in the roof."

The heater rasps on.

No, not holes, a voice tells her. The wood has to swell. In California, in winter, damp populated by slugs, my back hurts; but I am a woman, maggie. Or I am a man? Or I am caught in the Snow Queen's Palace, which I am I then? and you, maggie—what are you?

The big tree sparkles. The rug glows red, the aquarium green, not lethal now we have killed the snails. There's no rain. The slug is gone from the window. Behind a door, Susan is sleep-ing—I hope. It's icy Christmas Eve and the two blue piles of goose down look like two blue creatures as I come down the steps I hear cutting.

I look in her doorway: clouds of smoke, eggs, feathers, dry leaves, that O'Keeffe black iris, and maggie—it's all maggie: glasses, jeans held up by a cord to her frame getting more and more skeletal; scissors in hand, or knife, or razor in hand, she looks up and says,

"I hope Susan is sleeping."

I know she heard the phone an hour ago.

"What?"

"What? Oh," I said, "nothing. Do you have colored paper?"

"Some, over there. You'll have to cut it, though. It's in big sheets." peep peep. She coughed. "Where's Madamina?"

"Don't know. She wasn't upstairs."

"Not here, either," maggie yawned. "What time is it, anyway?"

"Three. Are you nearly done?"

"No."

I am cutting paper into odd shapes. Orange fish. Yellow heart, laid out on the bed, blue star—it's hard to see letters on that. The toilet flushes. The shapes look garish, and I crumple them, throw them on the floor.

Between three and seven A.M., there's a cutting edge to what moves. Electric light hurts. Noise, especially motor noise, seems a muffled assault on the layers of cottonwool that are this world's proper texture; and my own muscles, tuned up, but, simultaneously, tuned down, strain, swaddled painfully wide awake in a medium alien to me, but to maggie it's home.

I cut out a few gold rectangles; take my typewriter in my lap. A riddle for Maggie. I pull it out. Another sheet, a different spacing, now: a riddle for maggie. I start again, the keys clattering, counterpoint to the furnace now the refrigerator then in the noisy silence downstairs someone moving, peep, and running past me, clutching the clock in one hand, a cigarette in the other, "here," she says, and slips in under the eaves; and falls back, laughing, "Madamina's here! She must have been here all the time!" and, still holding the clock, runs out, past me on the bed where I have been trying to keep my body between her eyes and the paper shapes I've cut out to surprise her, but now I feel—rage.

It rises. It lifts me off the bed like a tide propelling me out of the room to the place where Adam used to stand looking down at us, in rage, but a different taste feel a ridge through my neck my shoulders like iron my jaw clenched gut churning bare soles thudding on wood as, I want to, BREAK her. I'm sorry. I'm sorry, SORRY, I want her to say, I BEG your PARDON. Tension aches around my, please, release me, I want her, to, PLEASE say PLEASE RELEASE ME. . . .

In maggie's room, leaning against a wall, my arms folded tight across my stomach, I wish for any place else in the house: the cool attic solitude; the landing; the rich red living room smelling of hemlock; the sunroom, where Susan is sleeping now. In this cluttered cubicle reeking with stale tobacco, I can't get my breath. A voice drones: *privacy, chaos. Respect*, I say, *order, say, night, blood, vampire, milk*, she is trying to talk I don't let her. It prickles my throat. Won't let her, *say the words*, will, *god damn you*, sinking my teeth in the gaps I knew, *self*, twisting, *love*, sucking it

"What's that?" as something clanked, out in the living room
      (sssssssss
"WHAT'S THAT?"

A black-and-white cat crouches under the tree: The Gypsy. He stares at Madamina, halfway up the staircase staring at him and hissing the high-pitched whine cats make when they want to kill. Sharp intake of breath, beside me, maggie's hand clamps on my wrist, but neither of us can move. We are spectators, watching a confrontation natural almost necessary to us in the midst of what has become a Walpurgisnacht soaked in milk—yet it seems hardly ludicrous.

A calico missile plummets down through the air, right paw swinging. The Gypsy scrambles under the tree and out, Madamina close at his heels, he runs around the room, tries to climb the aquarium table then finds the cat door and hurtles through its gray metal lips, out. . . .

Madamina sat down, licked each paw carefully. maggie lit a cigarette, said, "Well, now we know why Bailey won't come home. That cat has been leaving his smell in the house."

"I wonder. If she attacks him like that. . . ."

"But maybe it's just now tonight because her own kittens are down here. That was really fantastic. I should have had a mother like that," maggie said, as Madamina mounted the steps. "Now she's going to check on the others."

"Look," I mumbled. "I'm sorry. It's that you ran into my room without"

"Yes. I knew that."

"I wanted to surprise you. I was making a present for you. It's crazy, isn't it."

"Yes," she said, half smiling, then, "Oh, no! Look!"

At the top of the stairs, Madamina had reappeared and was hobbling down, a small, dark, raglike thing in her mouth.

"I feel like we've been here before."

"Yeah, but that was the other direction."

"I don't believe it. I just don't believe it." She started up.

"No." I grabbed her arm. "If we startle her. . . ."

"How many fucking steps are there, anyway?"

"Ten, or twelve. Ohhhh. . . ."

Step by step, down, she almost dropped it, got a grip, and, step, it seemed they would make it, then, two steps from the bottom, she let it fall. . . .

"It's dead," maggie choked, and covered her face. I turned on her, suddenly furious.

"How do you know? How the fuck do you know?"

"The way its head twisted. . . ."

I went and stooped beside the calico cat, who was nuzzling the motionless kitten, curiously. I took it away from her, carried it into the kitchen and laid it on the counter. It was breathing. maggie came in—sallow skin, huge eyes surveying a field of corpses—Auschwitz, something like that. I wanted to hit her. She quavered,

"It's dead, I know it is."

"IT IS NOT DEAD!!!"

"Really?"

"Really. It's breathing. Sorry to disappoint you," I spat. "If you can pull yourself together, go close the door upstairs, so she can't do this again."

"Then she won't be able to nurse them." She shook her head,

185

wonderingly. "I don't understand. I was so sure. . . ."

"You're always sure it's the worst. If someone gets a cold, you're sure they're going to die of pneumonia."

"But the way its head. . . ."

"You want it to die. You're in love with death," I ranted, and cut a piece of cake and crammed it into my mouth and glanced at the kitten. "Oh, look. Its eyes are open."

She came to stand next to me and ran a gentle, tentative finger over the black-and-white fur, down the throat, chest and belly. It gave a feeble peep. "I guess it's okay," she whispered, but doubtfully, and we looked at each other. Something softened in me, something I didn't want dissolved. Her eyes got larger, enormous, began to brim as they do so easily, too soft, I gripped the counter. The kitten peeped again. Tiny gleams of its eyes, mouth puckering, tiny sucking motions, and maggie warming my left side: the rasp of her breathing. . . .

"Poor baby," she murmured. "Maybe I could move the little ones down to my room. Then they'd all be on one floor, at least."

"Good." I looked at her briefly, then quickly away. I couldn't apologize this time. I cut another hunk of cake, "Do it, then," I said, harshly. "I'll take care of this one."

The sky was dull gray by the time she'd got all the kittens down and nested them in her closet. I fed the bruised one milk from my finger and ate a few more chunks of cake, quickly, surreptitiously,

"Is it still okay?" she said, coming in and leaning against the refrigerator.

"Caught," I mumbled, my mouth full.

"What?"

"Do you want to eat something? Like, breakfast?"

"Oh. No." She looked at the kitten, asleep on its back in my palm. "It seems all right, doesn't it."

"Uh-huh. It even took some milk. Are you finished?"

"They're moved, yeah." She sank down on the ladder. "I still want to stay up, a little longer. How are you?"

"Dead. No," I blurted, "I only meant. . . ."

"Don't worry." She gave me a tired smile. "I can still use it that way, too. Why don't you fall out?"

"I will. You should, too."

"I just want to finish one thing. Will I keep you up?"

"No, I can go upstairs."

"Good idea." She stroked the kitten. It opened its eyes a crack, but didn't move. "It seems awfully weak. You think we should put it in with the others?"

"Maybe not right away. I'll take it upstairs with me and close the door. maggie. . . ."

"Yeah. It's okay, don't worry." She touched my arm, lightly. "Merry Christmas, or something. I'll seeya. Go to bed, go on, go."

Under the warm, blue, nylon-covered down, on my back, in bed, with the kitten nestled in my armpit—the light grows, all around me. I must have slept a couple of hours; woke to sun and blue sky through frosted windows. I had turned on my side, and the baby animal lay in the crook of my arm, dead.

I lay with it quietly for a while, not grieving. Even the thought that I might have smothered it turning in my sleep didn't ruffle this morning's calm. The house was silent. No sound from the road. There was something clear in the air, an intimation of some translucence not yet truly come, but its fragrance was there to soothe me, even after I got up and carefully carried the kitten downstairs: past the door to the sunroom, still closed; past maggie, a motionless mound beneath the tree; to the bathroom.

Madamina lay curled with her own brood, under the shelves. She opened one eye to watch me rummage above her. I found an empty shoe box, wrapped the kitten in tissue and laid it inside. It had already stiffened a little.

I put on boots and a parka over my nightgown and tiptoed past maggie again to the back door. My face, in the mirror hanging over the window, seemed happy, almost. I waded out beyond the doghouse, up the slope a few yards through the woods to where there's an open space. With gloves and a trowel I cleared away some snow. The earth beneath it was soft—so soft it was

187

easy to dig a small grave. I put the shoe box in it and covered it over again: dirt and pine needles, dead leaves. Snow prickled in through my gloves, through my silly nightgown. I could feel my face, my hands chapping, then turning numb, but still I squatted there. For a moment, the small buried thing and I seemed alone in the world.

*

"I want to know where it is," she said,
                    where is it. tell me where it is.
"All right. Later," I said,
                    No.

14.

Christmas morning, the three of us sat beneath the tree. The Woolfs came, bringing a fancy bird feeder, drank some eggnog, and, after they left, Susan said,

"Shall we open *our* presents now?" in her best, gracious, tea-party mode, and anger welled up in me, suddenly, as it does these days. "Let's take turns," she said. "You start, Rebecca."

I forced the anger down, leaned under the tree, chose a small gold package tagged with a red star, *for Rebecca from Susan*, and unwrapped a tiny, wood Japanese spoon.

"Oh, that's love-ly," maggie said, and I echoed, "Lovely. Thank you, Susan," stiffly, and then we continued around,

for Susan from Rebecca: a spider plant in a round pot
for maggie from Susan: a brown and green scarf
for Rebecca from maggie: a rose petal framed in a locket
for Susan from Rebecca: a string of beads
for maggie from Susan: *The World of M. C. Escher*
for Rebecca from Susan: a sheaf of dried flowers
for Susan from maggie: a white spiral sea shell
for maggie from Rebecca: a scented blue candle
for Rebecca from Susan: five museum post cards
for Susan from maggie: a framed collage of dried leaves

"Well, I guess that's it for me," Susan said and leaned back, and watched us, awkwardly, we continued to open
for maggie from Susan: a packet of Wildlife stationery

189

for Rebecca from Susan: *The Annotated Alice*

for maggie from Susan: a bar of strawberry soap.

for Rebecca from maggie: two painted eggs

for maggie from Rebecca: a purple sweater

for Rebecca from maggie: an antique black iron pot

for maggie from Rebecca: a poem—three pages, typed on stiff yellow paper with loose-leaf holes punched and bright green ribbon holding it together. She started to read. Susan peered down over her shoulder, said,

"Is this one whole poem? Or should the separate pages be read as separate units?"

"Why don't you read it first," I snapped, "and see what it is, instead of trying to grab it in advance?"

"But I was only asking if. . . ."

"You won't understand it, anyway. It's very personal."

"Oh. I see," Susan said in a hurt, surprised voice, got up, and went into the sunroom.

maggie looked at me. "That felt bad."

"I know, but she always tries to control things."

"Not always. Sometimes. And this. . . ."

"She'll recover. Why don't you read that?"

"I feel like we ought to do something, like, go after her."

"No. She shouldn't be here," I said, "no one else should be here now but us."

"I know," maggie said.

the color of the animal

1. is seasonal

   is dull

(for example)   gray

          the riddle
          is
          name
          the
                season.
                        .

.   .   .   .

.

.   .   .   .   .   .

                               .

.   a riddle for maggie   .

.   .   .   .   .

But beware!
not all seasons are consecutive
the underside of the leaf
in spring
$\neq$
any part of its summerwhen
—
ever

2. a few constants
   sticks
   scales
   the aspect of the fox,
   the female forms   of trees

(urgently)   giving benediction
                    the sinister vibrating   branches
                    masculine.
                    the wall
                            looming

                                        bisecting the
cracks etched in   universe
   ice or ivy   perimeter

                    the animal
                        is not   (necessarily)
                            a   in all
                        solid   seasons

                         (name the)

192

3.   it limps always now.   .

                                        name

        but in certain   .
             lights
        it seems to grow
        a glittering silver skin   .   season

                        .   .

                    then
                    when

        the world   a form
          turns   falls
      (morning   between
        is also   the animal and
            a season   the light

                    or
                    it
                resumes
                the color of
    (gray,   .
    for example)   .   .

                    *

193

"I love it," she said.

"Can you guess the riddle? What beast it is?"

"Yes, but no. I can feel it, almost. Let me try again." She looked down. . . .

Bailey's head nuzzles mine. Tonta writhes next to maggie, who absent-mindedly strokes her head. *Peace*—a moment echoes here in this fear-filled way I've traveled, at midpoint, all my pores recall that warmth. I'm estranged from: *the human dimension*, maggie would say; in exile amid skulls and sunflowers, here in another cycle, still, I hear winter—a high, tense sound. I see winter, skies full of clouds like crushed velvet, the wind blowing, winter, in through the walls, and now a few flakes like moths lie daubed on the apples; on pears; on the ground where yellow leaves steam, ripe, delicious odors of Fall, fall, delectable rot that, honeycomb white, this snow will preserve; as it preserved the earth of a New York forest soft for my fingers that Christmas morning; soft for a corpse; then covered my footsteps, to keep that pilgrimage secret even from her.

She raised her head. "No, I can't get it. Tell me."

"I don't know myself."

"Oh, that's not fair," she cried, rearing up on her knees, and the warmth, but then Susan stood in the doorway: beautiful in her soft white sweater, queenly, wintry, she said to maggie,

"I'd like to speak to Rebecca alone."

"Wait," I said, "this is maggie's house, too. *We* should. . . ."

"No, it's okay," maggie said, and got up. "I'll do dinner."

"But"

"Well then," Susan said, "shall we go in the other room?"

Across the table—the room filled with smoke, the door closed, and there is a nasal, shrill voice I'd like to disown—we talked. And talked, wrenching, ugly, elliptical talk, helpless, finally both of us knew this was nothing talk could solve. We sat silently, then, a while. I looked at her clothes draped over maggie's bed made up differently, somehow; and something began to throb at the root of my skull.

194

"I'm going to get some aspirin," I said, and opened the door, and called maggie, and then we went through the motions of dinner. I finished first, as always; my left temple pounding, I sat back, narrowed my eyes, and just for a moment I saw us as though on old film. Murky, yellow, and soft, in that special light electric bulbs cast in daytime, I saw three women: each twisted inside herself, but each remarkable—so alone, so pinched and chilled and yet so entwined with the others, and that configuration contained a uniqueness, I thought; a beauty that seemed to derive from the very twists, the pain. . . .

I've learned better since then. Still, I can love us at moments with less arrogance—as we were, even as we are now.

maggie coughed. Susan clanked her silverware down. The rancor came burning back, and I looked down, at the tablecloth with its stain, our plates piled with bones and wilted leaves. My stomach lurched.

"Uh-oh," maggie said, "It's really coming down now. You might not get home tonight, Susan."

"Oh, but I have to. I have to work tomorrow. The train will be running, won't it?"

"Yes, but we have to drive to the station," I said, "that's the problem," and wrenched myself up, and Susan's reproachful eyes, and the air full of fumes from the stove and maggie's cigarette, made me queasier; sharpened the ache in my temple. I said, "I'll start the car," and left them to talk about, me, ME, I knew, my impossible, antisocial nature, my rotten, ugly, UGLY, I dropped three more aspirin down my throat. My head squeezed, pounded, bursting, I thought as I went through the long, laborious process of dressing for winter: the weight of flesh, leather, and wool, and such an effort, it seems, to move, when rage and greed have drained the animal. . . .

Wet flakes drove into my face as I made my way down to the car. I brushed a patina of snow from the windshield. My fingers were stiff in a moment, but my headache eased by the time I jammed the key in its slot the pain was almost gone. The motor whinnied. I turned the key again and again, then sat back and waited a while. In that small space, with a faint smell of gas, and white stuff piling up on the hood, I felt relieved and bruised. I hugged my hands in my crotch; watched the white lace veils swirling all around me. Dimly, I knew that my swings of mood were getting more extreme and more frequent. I was afraid—of myself, of maggie, for maggie. The cosmos had turned more lethal in these past months, very gradually; although it was no less beautiful now, I seemed less able to bear the sense that it was impersonal. Love me. Love me, God, universe, please, I thought, love the unloveable. Still, I felt half ironic. The fear was muffled, dim as the outline of hills or the sound of Cairo barking from up on the deck, muffled, dim, as the ache in my temples, still there, it might always be there, I thought. I tried the motor again, and again, and then stumbled back up and got Susan and packed her into the car. Cairo scrambled in with us.

We coasted silently down the drive over new snow. The engine coughed, finally roared as we slithered past the light flowing out of the Woolfs' big window and onto Hollowbrook Road. I saw someone plodding towards us. We slid to a stop. I rolled down the window. A pale boy-face looked at me; thin sullen mouth.

I said, "Ron, your cat's been coming into our house at nights through our cat door. Could you keep him at home?"

"My father don't like him coming in our house."

"I know, but your father told maggie he has a cage outside."

"Uh-huh."

"Well, could you keep him there at nights? Because our male cat is afraid to come home."

"I'll try," Ron said.

"Thanks."

"If I can catch him."

"It's just for at nights," I said.

"Uh-huh."

He moved away and I rolled up the window and we continued inching through dusk, white-flecked and sown with lights—trees, Santas, a reindeer, Merry Christm—— It was dark by the time we got to the station; the waiting room was locked and the train would be late, of course, so we huddled with two other faceless bundles of clothes on the platform under the eaves. The snow was falling straight down, now—dark white in the arcade lamplight. Susan's face looked purplish.

"You better go on home while you can," she said.

"Will you be all right here?"

"Of course. It's driving that's risky, not standing." She grinned a little. "That's just uncomfortable."

"Okay, then. Uh, Susan. . . ."

"Yeah. Don't try to say it, that's worse. Go on, I'll see you," she said, as I hesitated. Her eyes looked so tired, her face so lined and drained I wanted to touch her; but it would be a long time before I could do that, I knew. I turned and walked away from her, quickly, and drove out of town.

Cairo's ears obscured the rearview mirror. My head was beginning to pound again. Even the Christmas lights were hardly visible now. Something fell—black on black on black on the windshield, during that hour it took me to glide the ten miles home, and some unearthly smooth substance under the wheels. Not snow, I thought; not earth. My legs felt unsteady when I finally stopped the car and stepped out, almost rubbery: as though I'd been swimming.

Cairo walked up the steps with me, strangely quiet. Behind the glass doors *The Messiah* was playing again, and maggie sat on her sleeping bag under the tree, again; said,

"We got trouble."

"*More?*"

"I just called Mr. Dodenheim. You know, Mrs. Brenner's father that lives next door to them. I asked him to keep The Gypsy home."

"Uh-huh. I just met Ron on the road and did the same thing."

"You're kidding."

"Nope. On the way to the station. What did the old man say?"

"Well, that must be why—he got hysterical. He must be

really crazy. He started screaming that he hates all animals, any animal he finds near his house he's going to shoot, and on and on. . . ."

"That can't be serious."

"Well, I hope not," she said. "I don't know. I'm suddenly wondering where the animals are. Tonta's here, and Madamina, but Bailey went out."

"It's probably really okay. The worst is they may not do anything about catching The Gypsy. And since last night. . . ."

"How did things go with Susan?" she asked.

"Awful. She felt I'd completely excluded her. There's nothing much I could say. She's right."

"And so she proceeded to do exactly the same thing to me."

"Yeah, well—I think we just might not see her for a while. Or I mean, I won't. She doesn't seem angry at you. Let's not talk about it now," I said, "it's making my headache worse."

"Take some aspirin."

"I already did, about five of them. It's been going on all day."

"You're tired, that's the trouble."

"I know. How are you?" I asked, looking at her for the first time in hours, it seemed, since this morning when she-and-I had been separated. "Did you get any sleep today?"

"No. We always wind up dead tired on holidays, don't we."

"We're always up all night, that's why. Preparing. For visitors."

"Let's spend New Year's Eve alone, then," she said.

"I don't think we have any choice at this point. I've managed to alienate everybody."

"Oh, not really. But still, I don't think I can handle another holiday."

"Well, then let's try to ignore it. Have you checked that lump of yours recently, by the way?"

"Every day. Don't worry. Hey, listen," she said, as I started for the kitchen, "I really want to know where that kitten is buried."

"Sure. I'll show you. But it would be impossible to find it now," I said. "We can do it tomorrow."

*

"After breakfast, okay?"

*

"Well, I'm right in the middle of writing a letter."

*

"Just wait until this side is done."

*

"I think we ought to put up a sign about Bailey first."

*

"Oh, look, there's the snowplow."

*

"I'm calling the state cops. It's too much of a coincidence."

*

"Yeah, maggie, I know, but it's dark."

*

Mr. Dodenheim:

This is to inform you that your threat to shoot any animal found on your property and the coincidental disappearance of my tomcat the next day are on record with the state police. The police has informed me that your property rights do *not* include the right to kill animals who have "trespassed," and that if any more animals "disappear" an investigation will be made. In case you are not aware of it, the penalty for killing a cat is one year in prison and $1000 fine. Although prosecuting you will not bring back my animals, I will not hesitate to do so if you make it necessary. I hope very much that it will not be, since we, and hopefully you, do not enjoy living under such conditions.

Sincerely,

*

"Hello, Miss Stark? This is Frank Brenner, across the road from you. Yes. I want you to know that when my wife opened our garage door this morning, your white cat came running out. What? *What?* No, it was a short-haired one. No, I haven't And what's more, your dog has been coming over here and. . . . No, I don't want you to do anything like that, but don't. . . . Well, I saw the letter you wrote to my father-in-law, and I think it's outrageous. Yes, that's what I said. . . . Oh, my father-in-law didn't kill your cat. I don't know. All kinds of things can happen to animals. This is the country. You people come up from the city and. . . . Well, your dog comes over here, he chased my mother-in-law inside her house last summer and. . . . No, I told you, I don't. We let our animals run and you can, too, but don't call up and annoy people. What kind of crazy idea is that, a cat door, anyway? No, I told you, I don't, I wasn't raised to call up and write and BOTHER people. . . . Yes, I do. Now listen, young woman, we've had about as much as, now, GODDAMN IT, DON'T YOU INTERRUPT ME. . . ."

*

15.

18   *Work on What Has Been Spoiled* (Decay)

It furthers one to cross the great water.
Before the starting point, three days,
After the starting point, three days.

Roots grow out of a cliff above the stream in Mill Valley where Adam wades, jeans rolled over his knees, knobby knees and *huaraches*, splash, up, past rubble—pieces of broken piñata lie mixed with crushed stone from the old bridge, still crumpled under the new one: it forms small blockades. Roots dangle. Further on, the stream splits in two for an island: rust and green lichen etched on the stones, light rippling like water over his ankles, his feet turning numb, but when he climbs out, when he sits on the bank, the sun is warm.

He hates her most when he's missed her most. Today, for instance, this walk is suffused with that rare emotion, gratitude: the tension gone out of his body in less than three months he has been with her, yet she has helped him to crawling; stuttering; speaking, now, listening, breaking his bubble to let in the noise of, life again, music, love, he loves, he wants to give her anything she might want as she has given to him, so: he will be vicious tonight when she comes home.

Scene: brandy, firelight. Jeannie with gift-wrapped package, extended: says,

"Merry Christmas. I'm sorry it's late, but"

"You're always late," he grins, tearing the paper off; then, "Oh, baby, I can't wear this. It's so...bright."

"Why? It's perfect for under lights. It's patchwork."

"I can see it's patchwork, but"

"Oh, I'm so excited. How long is it since you've performed?"

"It was just before the accident. A year and a half, I guess, now. It seems longer. I really thought I wouldn't play again."

"You're healing," she says. "I knew."

"It's not the way I expected."

"Well, maybe healing isn't always what we expect it to be when we're ill. Maybe that's part of sickness—forgetting."

"God, you sound like a wise old sage at the end of a bad flick."

"Couldn't it be a good flick?"

"No." He raised his voice to falsetto. "'Maybe healing. . . .'"

"Oh, stop. I don't care how it sounds, it's true. I can't wait to hear how the show goes."

"You're coming, aren't you? You said you'd get that night off."

"Well...if you're sure you want...I mean, look, if you're ashamed of me, I don't want to"

"You know that?"

"Of course I know. You've always been ashamed of me. You're a snob. But I love you anyway."

"I don't know why. I'm full of poisons—ambition, pride. . . ."

"Oh, what a lot of names," she says. "I think you're proud of being *bad*, for some reason."

"What?"

"I said. . . ."

"No, no, I got it. You really told me something. Sometimes you're so damn smart, Jeannie, and the rest of the time...I just begin to relax with it, then you switch and sound like, like, Pollyanna, or Candide, or something."

"Oh, I loved Candide when I was in school. I identified with him."

"You knew it was a satire, didn't you?"

"Is it? No, I never knew that."

"*No I never knew that,*" he whines at her. "Here we are again. How do you do it?"

"Do what? I really—didn't."

"Jesus. You really are a wonder. You have a real talent, Jeannie, I bet you could manage to see Auschwitz saccharine sweet with a pink bow. I bet you could Candide your way right through the gas ovens."

"But I just said"

"It's all one-dimensional, that's it, like the world gets turned into some kind of idiotic cartoon, some simpleminded, super-sweet"

"But I just"

"You haven't had one real idea in your whole. . . ." But he stops. He's used that one before.

"Is it really such a sin to think that. . . ?"

"Yes. It's goddamn lazy. It's slovenly. It's an intellectual sin,"

(and her blouse is a sin; and her ears; and the way she moves, even grace can be caught and used in this rage as he goads her, today and every day, his head jabbering, *why are you aren't you you you you. . . .*

"I want to be what you want me to be," she'd said, later. "If you'd just tell me. . . ."

"Tell you, what?"

"How. . . ?"

He thought of strangling her, one night. Then of tearing her to pieces with his hands, literally—at the moment of. Then the guilt came, turning in on itself, to resentment, to anger, to guilt, and it's only in music he felt it loosen—his fingers moving of themselves, finally, taking off and becoming

"That was beautiful."

"Hey." Adam looked out the window. "I didn't know you were here."

"Just came by. I didn't want to stop you, so. . . . That was really nice. Where'd it come from?"

"Just came out."

"You ought to write it down. Listen, we're having supper at Don's before the gig on Saturday. Want to come?"

"On Saturday? Sure. . . ."

"Good. Six or seven, I guess. Bring the Mystery Lady, too."

"The Mystery Lady? Now where did that"

"Well, you know. We all know she's there, and Don caught a glimpse, he says, once, but"

"She's a physical therapist, works at a hospital in the city. Weird hours, you know. Shifts."

"Oh, uh-huh. I see."

"Yeah. You want to come in?"

"Sure, I'll visit a while. You think, you can get that thing you were doing back again?" he said,

Paul said: that's his name, Paul, a friend? Adam thought; but so good, just that casual tone; so good to hear men's voices, more and more, welcoming him to the world again, so easy— when need isn't so great that anything less than nurturing love seems a mockery. *Too much of that.* Still. . . .

      Forty-two last night a real cold snap here in the city, across the Bay it was

click

and her voice came drifting around a corner: "What's wrong?"

"You know I don't like to wake up with the radio going," he snarled; coughing; followed her voice around a corner and into the kitchen where she stood huddled against the stove in her white nylon uniform. "Damn it."

"I'm sorry. I thought you were"

"I was. I didn't get back from rehearsing until after three. And I can't sleep all day like you do. Shit, you know what happens if I don't get enough"

"Oh, love. . .I thought you wouldn't hear. Can I"

"No. And, by the way, I feel the need to explain to you very carefully that I can't stand seeing clothes on the floor like that because whenever they catch my eye, that is, my peripheral vision, there is a moment I think they're alive."

"But that's crazy."

"Okay, then, you're living with a madman. I never said"

"Oh, stop. I'll try to remember, all right?"

"Well—try hard. I mean, you do it with my clothes, too, you know, and I wind up with nothing to wear, like last night I"

"I'm *sorry*. I never heard you to care about clothes that way."

"Well, I do. Now that I've started," but he was stopped by a spate of coughing.

"Are you sick?" she said.

"No."

"That sounds"

"No, goddamn it, I'm playing Saturday night, I'm not going to get sick *now*."

"Oh, that's why you're acting so strange. You're nervous."

"Congratulations. You're so perceptive."

"Well, I didn't think of...listen, before I forget. I just had a nice long talk with your father. He says you should bring me to meet them."

"Why don't you go on over yourself? I'll give you a letter of introduction."

"Don't be mean."

"Well, you hit me with all this stuff before I've even washed my face. Christ." He swallowed to moisten his throat. "What were you doing talking to him, anyway?"

"Your father?"

"No, the milkman."

"What do you mean? There isn't any...."

"Oh fuck fuck, I should know by now the most blatant irony doesn't get through your....Yes," Adam said. "I meant my father."

"Well, he called. You were sleeping, I'm surprised the ring didn't wake you," she said, *was that irony?* "We introduced ourselves, and"

"I see. What time is it, anyhow?"

"Eleven. I said we might come over tomorrow for New Year's dinner, since I'm off. Your father said to come early and watch the Rose Bowl. I said you'd call when you got up. But since you're sick"

"I AM NOT SICK." He leaned across the sink and splashed water over his face, then poured some coffee. Jeannie sat down, watching: now, for a moment, she looked weary; fragile. Something softened inside him. "The Mystery Lady," he murmured.

"What?"

"Never mind. You really want to go over there? Even though I warned you?"

"YES. They wouldn't have invited me, if"

"Oh, you don't know my stepmother."

"We'll get along. Want to bet?"

"No. You probably will, damn it. Okay, I'll call them later," he said, and she leaped across the room to hug him, her face so radiant he couldn't stand to look at it; pushed it down against his shoulder. . . .

Standing there, holding her; feeling the life of her pulse against him, he thought of the night before—of music, that flexible structure, like bones? yet it seemed to delineate some clarity just on the edge of the audible: leading him on by a thread, unwinding, inexorably, it turned and twisted, playing through him as Jeannie's love seemed to play through her, now and constantly, changing, as hexagrams change from one to another, another,

51   *The Arousing*

Shock comes—oh, oh!
Laughing words—ha, ha!

. . .

Shock comes bringing danger.
A hundred thousand times
You lose your treasures
And must climb the nine hills.
Do not go in pursuit of them.
After seven days you will get them back again.

Wet wind blew spray on the windshield: watered gray sky, swooping gulls, then, halfway across the bridge, the fog came down. It surrounded them, chilling, as they walked across Jackson Street, inside the building, still Adam felt chilled, coughing, in the elevator,

"I think you really are sick," Jeannie said.

"You may be right. And tomorrow...hell, I'll play with double pneumonia if I have to,"

then his father was at the door. He took their coats, at his most expansive, *my how formal*, Adam thought, as Bea came out of the kitchen, fluttering,

> "Well I'm so glad you could finally"
> "Oh I've wanted so much to"
> "Really an awful day for"
> "What a beautiful shirt Adam I've never seen"
> "And would you care for some eggnog, young lady?"

his father said; beaming; genial—Walter Stark drinks maybe four times a year, and New Year's is one of them. He never starts this early, though.

"It's not even one o'clock, Dad."

"So? You want one, Adam?"

"Too sweet for me." He poured a shot of straight rum for himself, as Walter handed Jeannie a glass of eggnog with almost a flourish. She simpered. Adam got away, fast, before he could say, *no, don't*, but here there was just one other place to go.

It's steamy; fragrant; orderly, even now it has to be orderly, he thought, watching Bea kneeling above the open oven: wrapped in a flowered apron, so goddamn clean, her hair tucked under a scarf, her thin shoulder working, almost fragile it looked, the socket covered with pale green sequins that glittered like scales moving back and forth as she spooned drippings over a big, brown bird, she seemed...old, he realized: she's getting old. And his father, too, in an opposite, fleshy way—old. And Jeannie looked fragile-weary the day before in their kitchen, *what is this*

208

compassion bit, anyhow? asked that familiar, carping voice-in-his-head, but it seemed almost powerless, now.

"Turkey?" he said, looking over Bea's shoulder. "I thought you hated turkey."

"Well, I wouldn't say exactly hate. And since you weren't here for Thanksgiving I thought we might"

"You thought I didn't come because you don't make turkey?"

"Oh, don't be silly," she said, standing up and facing him: sharp gray bird-eyes glittering under her plucked, penciled lashes; her cheeks bright pink in the runnels that sweat had made through her makeup.

"You're blushing," he told her.

"I am not. I'm just flushed from the oven. Listen, why don't you go back in with your father and...what's her name?"

"Her name's Jeannie, and you know it."

"Well, I forgot for a second. Don't be so snappish. That's a bad cough," she said, as a fit took him. "Is she taking care of you?"

"I'm taking care of myself, Bea. I'm thirty-eight years old."

"I know how you take care of yourself. All right, all right," she twittered before he could get an answer out, "I'm just a mother. You're coughing all over the food though, go on, *out*," she said. "You know I can't cook with anyone else around."

He wandered back into the living room: huge, it seemed now he hadn't been here for a while. There was a gold pile rug where the dark-figured carpet used to be, under a lumpy blue sofa—not the sleek divan Jeannie sat on, shiny green-cushioned, its wooden legs and arms looking fake, though they were perfectly real. His father sat hunched in a sleek chair next to, *but that will always be the same*, picture window; through which they could see not a thing today the fog seemed thick as a wall.

Adam drew the curtain to hide it, sat down beside Jeannie.

"No kidding," Walter was saying, leaning forward, eyes alight. "Do you? I have three shelves full. Look them over, take any you want."

"I've never seen you reading a mystery," Adam said to her.

"Well, I've been too busy since you came. Before. . . ."

"Uh-huh," he tried to call after her as she walked away towards the bookshelf, but it was hard to raise his voice. She ignored him, whether she heard or not, she knelt in front of the books.

"You sound like a foghorn, son."

"I know. Don't start, Bea's put me through it already."

He grinned. "Well, how about a hot rum?"

"Wouldn't that be better after dinner?" Bea said from the doorway. Beads of sweat stood out on her forehead. "We're ready to eat now."

"Can I help?" Jeannie tinkled.

"No, dear, it's all ready. I'll just go and comb my hair. You can all come to the table now."

Walter put out his cigar and got up, stretching, big paunch protruding over his pants belt. Jeannie walked by Adam, Three books in her hands, as he stood by the sideboard pouring another shot, she asked Walter, "Can I borrow these? I promise I'll bring them back."

"Keep them! Maybe I'll come out there to Mill Valley some-time and take some from you."

"Oh, I'd love that," she gushed. He beamed, almost bowed. Adam downed his shot, thinking of Jeannie rushing out to buy mystery books for his father to borrow, and followed them into the dining room, where, on the fancy white tablecloth, crystal and porcelain seemed to surround the big turkey; a blob of cranberry sauce sat in a silver bowl near a dish of green peas; and there were even two bottles of wine. . . .

"That looks beautiful," Jeannie said.

"You sit there, dear, next to Walter, that's right," Bea said, and settled into a chair at the foot of the table. Walter stood, still beaming, wetting the carver, happy, *they're all too happy*, Adam thought, *a real family scene, no, don't*, but

"Happy Thanksgiving," he tried to crow. His voice broke in the middle. Bea blinked at him, reproachfully.

"Oh, you. . . ."
        "Now, my dear, do you like white or"
        "Pass the wine. I do think wine always"
        "Sit down, Adam, please"
        "Skin. Yes, skin. And a drumstick"
        "Well, your appetite seems healthy enough,"
Bea said; the apron gone, skimpy hair smoothed down.
"Quite presentable," she would say, still the memory of her
shoulder encased in what seems an elegant blouse now, but,
aged, then, in that vision, remained vivid; strange in the midst of
all this lavish food. Walter carved. Jeannie, flushed and smiling,
spooned stuffing out. Bea ladled cranberry sauce and peas onto
each plate, nodding, especially gracious to Jeannie, Jeannie, her,
enemy? nibbling daintily at a wing, she made tiny, delighted
sounds,
        "Oh, this is absolutely wonderful"
        "It's dry"
        "Will you listen to that rain?"
        "Dry? It's not dry at all, it's perfect"
        "Who wants more?"
Walter said, standing up. "Jeannie? You can eat more than
that, now what can I"
    "Oh, I couldn't possibly"
    "Sure you can," he said, ripping a wing off and tossing it onto
her plate. Gravy dripped on the tablecloth. Bea moaned.
    "Oh, Walter. . . ."
    "And what can I give you, Bea?" he said, his voice low and
dangerous. There is an edge Adam knows well, it's sharpening,
Bea's lips compressed in a straight slit, all of it so familiar that
only Jeannie, perched there in the middle and the unknowing
cause of it, this time, makes it seem—almost bizarre. He tried for
a moment to see what she might see as she looked from one to the
other; gave up; got up.
    "Another drink, anyone?"
    "Aren't you drinking wine, son? This is good stuff."
    "No, I don't feel like it. Jeannie, do you want a drink?"

"Well, I have...maybe after...with coffee, I mean, some brandy like we had at, might be nice, but,"

"Oh, dear," Bea said, "I'm afraid we don't have any brandy. We have rum and creme de menthe and Dubonnet and"

"It doesn't matter," Jeannie said quickly. "I only even thought of it because Adam said"

"I'll run down to the corner and get a bottle," he said, and fled: their voice following, high and amazed,

> "But aren't you going to finish"
> "Really I don't care please Adam come back"
> "Adam don't you dare go out there with that cough"
> "At least take an umbrella,"

His father called, but, already, he was out the door; plunging down, down, and out. . . .

The fog was so thick he could see barely two yards in front of him. Still, the cool air, even the dampness of it, felt good. He started down the hill towards Polk Street: towards little green and red signals that punctured the fog; promised substance. Doors materialized below them, and he walked in and out, and out, and down towards the Bay, feeling better despite his cough, his scratchy throat. Tendrils of mist crept over his face, but he wasn't cold. He was buoyant. It was fever, he knew, this flush of energy, it must be sickness. Yet for this moment, he was filled with joy at his body's health

(but—that's not my thought. . . .

He shook his head, violently; stopped for a moment. A cable car clanked by, its sound oddly muted yet amplified by the fog. All sounds seemed different—cars, buoys, music leaking out of a second-floor window he saw as a dull glow, Mozart, he thought; a piano sonata. Just for a moment, superimposed on this damp, gray, city-world, he saw a country where leaves turn red and gold, and fall, in winter, snow covers the ground, it is cold, and two women sit at a table, listening to Mozart. There is a paisley tablecloth; an overflowing ashtray; a wood stove, its pipe leaking constantly, smoke, smoke. . . .

A small cat emerged from gray nothingness, almost as though on cue, and twined itself round his legs, purring. Adam squatted to pet it. It climbed on his lap: its outer fur damp, but still warm, soft. He couldn't see its color. It looked gray, like everything in this fog. It started to knead his leg, humming. He removed a claw.

"Where do you come from?" he murmured. "Where do you live? Inside those windows?" It trilled softly. He lifted it so it could scramble onto the ledge and watched it ease in through a crack in the curtains—the glow more golden now he was close, and behind him a woman's voice, low, but very distinct, said,

"There must be a hole in the fog you can see through."

"*What?*" He turned sharply. "Who the hell said that? Who's here?" He turned once more. Nothing. No one. The coughing began again, as the music stopped, he heard laughter, almost in counterpoint to the wheezes and gasps coming out of him, uncontrollably, then,

"Look, she must have got out, get a towel, Joanne,"

> (*Go back, you damned fool; back to*
>   *Push me...*
>   *just a flick of the wrist*
>   *Let her go, Let her go, now*
>   *who? who? who? who?*

and another record began from behind the windows.

He leaned against the building, shaking; sweating. The music leapt, in somersaults. Vivaldi? he wondered briefly; but, he couldn't listen now. *Something is broken*, he kept thinking, *some, broken, glass? in my lungs? my mind? No: cure means separation*, the voice said, and this time he didn't even bother to look up. He knew he'd see no one. *Take that far enough*, he answered it-her, *and you're dead. . . .* then pressed his hands into his eyes, palms held out against a vision of arms falling off, and legs, and a throat ripped out of a torso, skin peeling away from the rib cage of flesh and the bladders of air and blood, cells, dividing, they, re-produced, molecules alive, *but you're dead dead dead*, then his will began to pull him together. Almost literally, he felt it:

213

encouraging this, supressing that, arranging the various psychic parts so that, finally, weak but sane, he could walk back. . . .

"LADIES AND GENTLEMEN, WELCOME TO THE 1971 ROSE BOWL," the radio blared as he entered the liquor store. The salesman sang a hello, then looked at him oddly: an ugly crack in his chipper exterior. Adam ignored him; found a bottle of Courvoisier, under bright fluorescent bulbs that turned his hands purple, he paid and got out, quickly; back to the damp street where shadows still ruled—people shadows; the shadows of buildings; and lights like great soft diamonds flowing, illuminating so little in this lovely, misty space disappearing now as he turned onto Jackson Street small patches of clear blue sky were showing through. From here he could see the top of the building: his parents' apartment, alight; shapes in front of the window. . . .

The door was ajar, as he'd left it. He paused, a moment, in the hall; watched Bea and Jeannie clearing the table. His father had moved to the living room and sat watching people in tee shirts move through the grandstand in sunny Pasadena. Voices seemed to bounce off the walls: merry, meaningless to him, a robber, he thought, a beggar, shivering now that he'd come indoors again he felt cold. He went in, tracking wet across the gold rug.

"Oh Adam where have you how could"
"You sure are drenched, kid"
"Are you out of your mind?" Bea screamed.
"Well, haven't I always been?"

"THE TEMPERATURE IS 70 DEGREES, A BEAUTIFUL DAY. THE GOODYEAR BLIMP CAN BE SEEN OVERHEAD IN A CLEAR BLUE SKY. JUST GETTING READY FOR KICK-OFF. . . ."

"Very funny. I hope you enjoy the joke when you're lying in bed with pneumonia."

"Oh, don't get dramatic, Bea."

"Who's dramatic? Look at yourself. Now you get into the bathroom, and"

"Bea."

"Get into a good hot shower, right now, and"

"Bea, you're not planning to come in here with me, are you?"

"Why not, I raised you. All right, just leave your clothes on the bathroom floor, then. I'll take care of them. Look what you've done to my rug, my lord, you're like a five-year-old. Go on. You'll have to wear some of your father's"

"...HAS WON THE TOSS AND HAS ELECTED TO RECEIVE"

"I can't wear Dad's clothes. He's"

"Well, you'll have to. There's no choice in the matter, is there. We'll tie them on you. Go on," she said and actually pushed him, "I'll put dry clothes in when you're behind the shower door. I won't be able to see you, all right? Since you've gotten so modest. . . . "

Hot water ran over his cold skin. Steam filled the glass stall. The door opened; closed. Words drifted through his head, no longer strong enough for sound, *but, she mothered you*. No. *But just because she wasn't the other one, must you*, no, he thought, leaning against the tile wall, inhaling the steam, hot, good, it opened spaces in his chest; opened need for, Kay? maggie? Rebecca? or the dark, laughing mother made all of warmth, of a moment, just a, child is a, moment of need so great he wanted to dissolve in, *yes, that one*—her features indistinct, dissolving, always in a fountain of blood and sand; blood and tile; blood and blacktop.

He shook his head; turned the water off. No. He stepped out of the stall and toweled himself dry, not panicking, *this time I know you*, and slid into the clothes Bea had left piled on the toilet top: pants four sizes too large; and a big blue shirt; and some twine he tied around his middle. The mirror was fogged. He slicked down his hair with a comb he found near the sink, the noise in his veins becoming static, he tried to concentrate on voices, real voices, he thought, seeping in through the door.

"That must be such very rewarding work"

"Yes, I'd really like to have the recipe for"

"NOW A PILEUP LADIES AND GENTLE-MEN"

"But it's such a nice shirt and so much work I hope it's not ruined,"

Bea said, then looked up; and they all saw him.

"What are you laughing at, huh?"

"Oh, you look wonderful," Jeannie giggled.

"Time for dessert," Walter said. "We've been waiting for you. How about some pie? This is terrific pie, let me tell you. Apple."

"What's the score?"

"None yet. They can't seem to move."

"I think you should stay here tonight, Adam," Bea said, starting to cut the pie. "Really. Your shoes will take forever to dry, and your father's are too small. And it's ridiculous, going out in the rain again. With your cough."

"Bea, it's not raining. It's"

"It doesn't matter, it's raw." Her voice clucked an end to it. She passed him a wedge of pie. He felt like throwing it back at her, but, that shoulder, and now, above it, her throat, criss-crossed with wrinkles, seemed to pulse in-out, in-out. His throat prickled.

"No, I want to go home," he said; but the words sounded harsher than he'd meant them to.

"Not before your hair dries," she said. "Besides, you were going to have a hot toddy, weren't you?"

"I'd forgotten that. Sure."

"I'll get it," Jeannie said, "all right? I can find it all."

"Well, son, and what are your plans?" his father said, as soon as she'd left the room.

"Plans?"

"Yes, what do you expect to do?" Bea chimed in, "about"

"Well? About what?"

"Well, uh. Everything. You can't have much insurance money left, can you? and"

"I have a little. I'm getting back into music, I told you. It takes a while to make connections. Tomorrow night is the first"

"Yes, but," Walter said, "that's not a really reliable source of a living, is it? And with two of you. . . ."

"What do you mean, two? Jeannie's an independent person. She gets a very good salary."

"But"

"What?" Adam croaked.

"Well, if you have children, she won't"

"Oh, Jesus Christ."

"Well, you might. In any case, you might as well have some security. Now, Bea and I were thinking that maybe you'd want to go back to school. In something related, like, oh, teaching music. . . ."

"Dad, I don't want to go back to school."

"I meant to say we could help you. Financially, I mean."

"No, thanks."

"Well, don't jump so quickly," Bea said. "Think it over a little."

"I don't need to. I'm not going back to school, it's absurd."

"Why?"

"Because, Dad, I'm a musician, that's what I do. I don't want to do anything 'related.' And I'm not planning to have children, either, damn it. I'm not even thinking of marrying"

"That's a beautiful little girl you got there," Walter said. "*Shiksah* or not. She really loves you, you know."

"Come on, Dad, don't play the wise old"

"Do you know how rare that is? You don't, do you? She deserves to have you make a living for her."

"Why don't you just leave that to Jeannie and me?"

"What?" Jeannie said, coming back with a cup.

"Oh, we're just talking about, uh, the future," Bea said.

"Did you have your brandy yet?" Adam asked Jeannie.

"No, I was waiting for you. I'll get it now. Anyone else?"

"I'll have some with you," Walter said. "In fact, let's move back to the living room. You can warm up next to the fireplace, and we can see what they're doing in Pasadena now."

"You never used to use that fireplace," Adam said, as they went in the living room, "did you?"

"Not so much. But now," Walter said, "watch." He put two eucalyptus logs on the grate then turned on a small gas jet that had been bent to feed directly into it. Flames licked the logs, igniting the bark. Walter looked at Adam, proud as a child showing off a new toy, and heaved himself up. "Ain't that cute? It takes a while to really get going, but we don't need to do a thing to it now. It just burns. The only problem is getting up after"

"If you'd just stay on a diet," Bea said tartly, "you might find out it's not"

"Yeah, yeah, I know. Tomorrow." He sank into his favorite chair. Jeannie gave him a glass of brandy. "Thank you, dear. Does she hold her liquor well?" he asked, winking. "Sometimes these little girls. . . ."

"She's not bad." He clicked the TV on.

"THE TEAMS ARE HEAD ON AT THE THIRTY YARD LINE. NEITHER TEAM SEEMS ABLE TO MOVE THE WALL. NO SCORE SO FAR. . . ."

"Now, Adam's sister," Walter said, and paused to sip, "Ah, that's good. Adam's sister, she can't take more than one or two shots, then she's out. And I mean, out cold. Have you heard from her recently, son?" Adam shook his head. "They're supposed to be having a heavy winter back there. I don't like to think of her alone out in the wilderness."

"It's not the wilderness, Dad, and Rebecca is very efficient. Besides, she's not alone," he said, watching his father carefully. "You should meet her roommate sometime. You'd like her."

"Adam," Bea said.

"Well, hasn't that grudge gone on long enough? Dad? Hasn't it?"

"Adam, that isn't something to discuss in front of"

"FOURTH DOWN AND SECONDS TO GO FOR A FIRST DOWN AT THE FIVE YARD LINE. . . ."

"I'll get you another toddy," Jeannie said quickly, and started to take Adam's cup. "Oh. You're not finished."

"Here." He gulped and gave her the cup. She almost ran out of the room.

"That was *very rude*, Adam."

"Oh, I don't know. Since you're both so determined to make her part of the family, she may as well know"

"What do you mean, *we're determined*," Bea started. Walter cut her off.

"Look, son, that's finished. You don't even know the whole story."

"I don't need to. I don't care what happened a hundred years ago. That old man is almost starving, Christ, and you want to give me money for *school*. . . ."

"I'm going to see what Jeannie is doing," Bea said, and stalked out of the kitchen. Walter lit his cigar again.

"THE BALL IS SNAPPED"

"That has nothing to do with it," he said. "And I think it's pretty poor taste for you to throw an offer like that back in my face as though"

"RUNNING, RUNNING, HE ELUDES HIS ATTACKER, SNAGS"

"Dad, he's dying. I don't care about taste. He's on Welfare, you know what that means? and his daughter is going crazy, his wife is crazy already, no one is really there for him and he's your BROTHER. . . ."

"TIGHT IN, HE TUCKS THE BALL UNDER HIS"

"Look, kid. Sometime you may have a little respect for other people's decisions, even though you don't know the reasons for them. And you may understand that there are other kinds of survival besides just physical"

"Are you saying you won't survive helping Jake?"

219

"I don't know." He puffed his cigar. "I put certain feelings behind me a long time ago. I won't stir them up again, no, you listen to me, by even thinking about it. I'm taking these few minutes to explain to you, and that's too long. By tomorrow it will be out of my mind, do you understand, I won't remember him, his name, his face, his wife, his drinking, his whole goddamn life won't exist for me"

"Dad"

"And don't talk pity to me. He didn't have any. Maybe he was smart, he was always the smart one. He knew pity's just as debilitating as killing rage, he was born knowing that kind of thing. I had to find out the hard way."

"Yes. I can understand that part," Adam said.

"What?"

"THE FIRST SCORE IN THIS VERY"

"I said I can understand that part. About pity."

"Well. Thanks for that much." Walter sighed. "I've got my reasons for letting what happened die. Believe me."

"*He*'s going to die, Dad, any minute."

"I don't care about that. I know it sounds callous, but he's a part of me, you know, and that has to die, and it won't. All I can do is keep him down, not give him any, any, food for"

"You sound like you're talking about possession, almost."

"It feels that way, sometimes. Oh, I know it's not. The whole thing is perfectly natural"

"In its unnatural way," Adam said.

"If you like." Walter smiled a small, bitter smile at the coffee table. "But, just this conversation, for instance, has brought it to life. If I started—like sending a check, okay, then it turns up in my accounts next month, and then"

"Write *me* a check. I'll take care of it."

"That's still a connection. I'd still know. And then he'd want more and more and. . . . Besides, I don't want to help him, haven't you understood that? I want"

"What? for him to suffer?"

They stared at each other. Then Walter looked away at the gas flame licking the logs; and Adam at the smooth glass face of the coffee table littered with magazines, and the ashtray full of cigar butts. Walter cleared his throat. Adam looked up. Goodyear tires were rolling around on the TV screen, fading into a man with white teeth and a beard of foam, shaving himself. Cigar smoke billowed. Adam coughed.

"Oh, is this hurting your throat?" Walter stubbed the cigar out.

"Thanks."

"You should have said something." He rubbed his eyes. His face seemed to sag from two rays of the lines surrounding his blue eyes, watery now below the pale forehead lengthening as his hair recedes, *he's old, old*. "Can we stop this now?" he said, finally. "Adam? Can you trust me a little? There's no way out—I know it. Besides, there's nothing I could do would make that much difference."

"Oh, of course it would."

"Do you think so? You're wrong."

"Look, I don't know how he feels about seeing you, but—well, how would you like to cough yourself to death in a ratty tenement, no proper nursing, and have to take the subway and wait in a long line whenever you need to see a doctor"

"All right"

"And they're Welfare doctors, you know, that means it's every week a different one, mostly, and mostly they think you're shit"

"All right, that's enough." He started to reach for the cigar against, then caught himself; put his hand on Adam's arm. "Let it be, kid," he said, softly. "Please. Believe me, sometimes you just got to sweep people out of your life like your mother sweeps out a closet. Or you wind up with a house fulla skeletons."

"FUMBLE AT THE THIRTY YARD"

"He's almost a skeleton now," Adam muttered.

"I SAID THAT'S ENOUGH," his father barked, letting go of

his arm and sitting straight up. His eyes bulged. Adam could see the light red tracery of the veins as rage clenched his own back and chest, and all tenderness seemed to dissolve,

"THE CROWD IS GOING WILD"

"Dad," he said, very quietly, "don't shout at me."

"Don't what? WHAT did you say?"

"I SAID DON'T SHOUT." He got up, clicked the TV off. "And stop calling me *kid*."

"Well, you're acting like one. You come here and, I don't know what gives you the idea that you can"

"WHAT? PRESUME to question your GODDAMN"

"NOW ADAM I WON'T STAND FOR"

"GRUDGE HOLDING, THAT'S ALL IT IS"

"YOU DON'T KNOW A THING ABOUT"

"THAT'S RIGHT, WHY NOT? WHY NOT?"

"You ought to be grateful to me for that," Walter said in a lower voice. "If you had a little respect"

"I'd like to. I'd like to think age has something to do with wisdom, you know. Not a lot of bullying, self-indulgent"

"DON'T CALL ME NAMES ADAM NOW YOU JUST PIPE DOWN AND LISTEN TO"

"NO. I won't listen while you're shouting, damn it," and walked out; through the dining room to the bathroom and closed the door.

He sat on the edge of the tub, heart hammering acid into his throat, burning, *bastard*, and gripping the doorknob, *can't shout at me like, he'd better*, knocking, *say,*

"Adam?" It was Bea's voice. "Adam, please." He unlocked the door, pulled it open. She stood in the hall, determined, hesitant. "You know, you've been in there quite a while. Your father"

"My father owes me an apology." It was almost a whisper.

"Oh, come on. You know better than to think that"

"I mean it."

"But what happened? What did he say?"

"It's not what he said. I won't let anybody shout at me like"

"Oh, Adam, really. We're too small a family to let that kind of thing"

"Look, where did you put my shoes and coat?"

"You're not serious. Why don't you just go back in?"

"Why won't he just come out? You know he won't. It takes two, how come I'm always the one that has to"

She sighed. "Two stubborn people," she muttered.

"Just let me have my shoes and my"

"All right. Your coat is in the closet in the living room. Your shoes are in the kitchen. They're still sopping."

"Thank you." He headed for the kitchen. She followed. He bent and pried on the cold sticky leather. Her voice jabbed his head.

"You realize you're biting off your nose to spite your"

"You realize it's not your affair," Adam snapped, then he looked at her tired face. "I'm sorry, Bea." He felt even more tender towards her now, somehow. "I just...I can't...."

"You two always, but I hoped that now you're grown up you could"

"Tell him. Tell him I'm grown up. No, forget it, look, where's Jeannie?"

"They're both in the living room. She thinks you're going to stay the night. So does he."

"Well," Adam said, "let's go break the big news."

A log had caught fire, finally, in the grate, but the gas flamed on. Jeannie sat on the couch. Walter, smoking again, was leaning across the coffee table towards her.

"The *I Ching*?" he said. "What's that?"

"Oh, you don't know?" Jeannie sounded delighted. "It's—oh, why don't we wait and show you. Next time we come, I'll bring it. Or...." She looked up, saw Adam approach with their coats. "Oh...aren't we staying here?"

"No." His voice sounded like gravel. "We're going home."

She opened her mouth, then closed it and stood up. He gave her the coat, not looking at his father, he started for the door.

Treble voices were saying goodbyes, but Walter said nothing; didn't accompany them, didn't say one word, then they were out in the street and home and still he hadn't, *why doesn't he*, every day Adam woke with it, *call, why don't you doesn't he don't you* in Bea's voice,

"We're too small a family. . .two stubborn people. . . ."

40   *Deliverance*

> Thunder and Rain set in:
> The image of DELIVERANCE.
> Thus the superior man pardons mistakes
> And forgives misdeeds.

"There," Jeannie said, as Adam closed the book, "it's really talking to you. Why don't you pick up the phone and just say"

"No."

"But, love"

"Just leave me alone goddamn it for a while," he snarled, and lay back down in bed and closed his eyes. Rain dripped down through the redwoods outside the window. He heard Jeannie's footsteps, approach, stop, her breathing, then footsteps receding then it was quiet except for the rain, rain, gray despair, rain, turning image behind his lids, soaking, *cure means*, pebbles and ice crystals, red leaves or black, *separation means*, cinders in front of a white haze where Becky fell, *reminds me of. . . .*

Some grooves slashed in the soul never heal; never heal.

V.
WHITE SECTIONS

16.

new year's day after lunch—

body caving, falling in. passed by a cast iron crock out of
which is growing a berry-like bush. no leaves but many
snarled branches with little brown-crimson berries touching it. when i turn to see it i recognize the potted bush
intimately and though i have not seen it before i become
within seconds so close to the bush in recognition that the
light around it changes gray brown crimson and me with it.
the intimacy is so great there is no difference between us.
in a flash its life becomes stronger than mine. i convulse
screaming one long sound and my arms are caught clutching the air. rigor mortis. i am dead. could not awake
immediately—felt like my body was dead and my mind
slowly dying too. if i could open an eye or something it
would change. only, i have taken it with me. it has taken
me with it. somewhere we have exchanged and are forming in our respective places—what? i do not know.

january 2
There is no usual ergo unusual
nothing unusual

                    I am not being driven invisible
                    hand leading by invisible thread
Out of one's mind—to go

227

Literally one of the more vital experiences
where   does one go?
                where has one been?
location?   importance of reflection in
                      continuous change)

space?   illusion   what do these words mean—
                          depend on what
         fantasy   from what reference point they are
                    being related, contrasted references
                    not (   ) able in essense

                  this is not limibo. this is. . . . .
                        directional
                            to
                        again don't like
                      where as word here

                  i am experience "going out of"
                  "my" "mind" don't "know" (where?) i've
     apparent   been or (where) "i'm" "going" all words
    "awareness"   needing quotes. can ramble off data but
    that exists   not essense. is it going"from-to?" not
                  unilateral direction

groceries
furnace, gas   constants? perceptions
not though people

no energy—drainage—not "mysterious" body is
      hibernating
will it live with me. no snese of what i hear is termed
              "sense of self"
don't want can't false to   but sense of "life" (not
talk talk talk facility of pre   commmnicable) exists—as
tending even without my   in all things
noticing is deteriorating
—not frightened by this

it's not that words have become meaningless (depend-
ing on what expects from them anyway) i don't want to
"know". i need to "experience without distance. not self,
but air.   but what really?

      (later)

the day is a mockery. the sun and blue sky are mockeries.
smiling, pushing the flesh around but it's stiff and black,
ice, creeping over the sky, 5: 30, 5, what's to stop the tide
from continuing: 4, 2, noon, 10, 9, until it's all dark?
and he, and i, then, no—i'm alive. i am, what my eyes
see, what my ears hear, literally. i. smile. froowwn.
cough. cough. when the aquarium looked like a butch-
er shop and i projected my body into the form of those
two snails entwined in each other, i felt absolutely
passionate. . . .

hum outside; cooking gas for the human—equation,
abrasion. barracudas of practicality, mouths, moths, a
caterpillar is squirming up that wall. now? it's winter,
you know, that's a crack, miss. yes, but i know you, this
is a cracked miss. a miss, crack, bullet whining black ice
cracking glaciers erupting but nothing melts. nothing is
soft. i-am in a process of being transformed to, what? red
ripping striated raw welts spreading across me like a new
landscape carved by, no. promised. black ice, then, will
that feel more natural? than this shape i was first assigned
to, how long will it—take, an ice pike, stab it, again,
make it bleed—and in sobs screams maybe the rock will
melt turn flesh again. the heart beat, black ice will tear
and those tears will glitter like minute crystals. . . . or will
it be squashed like a tick a stain on the snow and snow
crystals fall and bury it? fairy tales have all kinds of
endings.

     . . .

she. saying something. say, something. she flounces out
past print from faraway, beautiful, blue brown white
pinwheels. i am faraway, ugly. she yes matters but i can't
speak to her now. the wooden bowl full of nuts—the
bowl wooden of nuts, did you see it? the pinwheels hang
there, amused. stole a nut. am eating it. one less! i am a
bowl full of nuts, so why does she ask me questions? now
she stomps out front door and i am—am i? assimilate into
the walls type of apple. a leaf. a sniffing cat nose, just the
nose or perhaps the left nostril. . . .

what am i writing down/ WHO ARE YOU ASKING?
STOP SHOUTING. . . . they got me again, so. tricks all
the time, now you see us, now you don't. don't shout or
we'll steal blue brown pinwheels whisper. they will tell
i'm on ice skating over my own nervous sytem the blades
getting sharper now they've stuck bees in my ears. i'm
trying to practice necrophilia on my own body. get out of
it. out of what? body? no, it. get out, FIGHT! tell me
why. why. remember how to play make believe? pretend! can you at least pretend—WHAT PRETEND
WHAT—MAYBE I AM PRETENDING NOW! . . .
    "and so he sayeth, first ye shall discover thou assign-
ment and in the effort do or die"

                                —do = die you have not
begun—but most of all, be simple. what the hell does that
mean? where the fuck are those blue brown white
pinwheels?

january 3, sunday

i feel the presence of another dimension—no
words for it except that i am in its path—its winds
are already approaching enveloping my perceptions—the nature of the beast remains a mystery.

230

even its effects are not describable. not ominous. i
lie in the painless sunlight now like a seed. rest
like an embryo. the nature of it is preparing me.
although i do not know him her—beyond gender
—i am given to it. nothing seems contradictory
somehow, somewhere, the i is changing and so the
earth.

change not meant in the usual way......

*

"I just came up for a minute, I tried to phone, but it was busy
so long I—oh, I see. Is she sick? Oh, uh-huh. Oh, no, I don't want
to disturb you, well, one cup, if you're sure. . . ." She settled into
a chair, uneasily. "I just wanted to ask if you'd take me along on
one of your night walks some time. Why yes, I would, I truly
would. When I was a little girl my father would take me into the
woods in the mornings, at four or five o'clock he'd wake us up
and we'd tiptoe out and go deep in the woods and then he told me
to just sit and listen and watch. And I'd sit very still, you could
almost hear the air move, you know? And then the birds would
start to come and the animals. I'll never forget that. It was the
happiest time, I can't tell you, maggie, I mean Rebecca, all alone
there, him and me, and everyone else asleep and I saw so much
that otherwise I never would have knowed. The rest of my family
didn't care for that, like my family now don't, except for Charley,
he likes to see but he don't like to walk. Oh, my father was wonderful, he was a fine man. I've never knowed anyone like him
since. Looked a bit like Mr. Dodenheim, but nothing like as
fierce. Yes, I believe that old man could have killed Bailey. He
goes out in his truck at seven o'clock every morning, so you're not
likely to find no evidence if, but he's got a terrible temper, everyone knows. Even his wife is scared of him, after forty years married. And when I think of how I kept pushing that poor Bailey

231

away from my door, and that Gypsy coming at him, and Mr. D, I feel so bad. . . . " The mole on her chin quivered. "Well, I better be off now. All right, I will. Well, I haven't before because, well, your sign—oh, it doesn't mean visitors? Why, we was sure— Charley said, *Why, I wouldn't go up there again for nothing.* Well, my land, what's it mean, then? *'The way out is via the door.* . . .' Oh, uh-huh, uh-huh. Well. I'm surely glad I mentioned it."

*

Stillwhite. Winterscape. Contrast to bleak December, it's bright in January, even though death continued into the human, there was a whitening. Branches swayed under the weight of the new snow tripling their width. Seeds trickled down from the bird feeder Carrie had given us, broken streaks of yellow and red on the white deck, under clusters of phoebes and woodpeckers twittering, fluttering off when we came out to shovel, or just stand looking down at the road obscured in a mist of flakes every day now. . . .

Inside the boathouse, first surface frozen, I took my first steps on the lake. On New Year's Day I moved farther—my hands burning, cheeks, and nose numb, pulling down in a mask stiff as clay but that didn't matter. Nothing mattered in that expanse of ice, sky-speckled, as I slid past the island, a mound of white, where maggie nearly drowned, then back to the line of brown trunks, deepening, tracked on blue-white smudged on the bank. I climbed up and followed the path I had walked that day with her clothes in my arms, and I was afraid of Cairo. . . .

Gray birch is white in that light; white birch almost blinding.

The wall above the spillway was icy; a clutter of snow below. Three men were fishing through holes in the lake. I lay on the wall and watched them; cold seeping into my clothes, *don't let the chill begin*, I thought, and started home—pale colors, dusk by the time I got back to the house where Madamina still nurses the smaller brood; and maggie dozes under the sleeping bag; and Cairo crashes into the sunroom, scattering snow, as always, he runs to maggie, who moans and turns her back as—more and more often.

I shed my clothes. I settle into my bed beside the wall of windows covered with plastic. Tonta cuddles against me; or even Cairo's big, warm bulk. When he's dry I let him climb on my bed, later, now, then, oh there were days when the flakes fell big and we were all in bed as though on a ship; nestled snug in that white light filling the room, so still sometimes you could almost forget. . . maggie, coughing; the first orphaned kittens all growing up stunted, despite Madamina; Susan; Bailey; my brother's vivid absence, and then that central dread we hardly mentioned. . . .

"What?"

"What? Oh, uh, mmmm. . . ."

She slept more and more. And I woke at six and lay for hours in bed. I stared at the plastic, already torn; and got up exhausted.

Who cleaned the house? Who fed the animals, who paid the bills? The lamps stayed lit all day, I remember that, and the sage turned yellow; the fern got mealy bugs, spread to the calla lily, we threw them all out and hacked up the Christmas hemlock and burned it in the smoking stove, "we have to fix," and birds flew in. They nested under the eaves; then I found one lying half dead on the rug below the aquarium, Tonta crouching over it

(center, near petal)

she growled at a kitten.

Jan. 3, Sun: my calendar—spar in the ocean, these next weeks: to keep me afloat, or is it only a tool to guide sounding? What populations can I find living in this water? under its surface, hard frozen, tonight, there's only—Madamina, going out the cat door, she stopped in the middle, and those gray metal lips stayed open. It was cold and I pushed her, as she resisted, "No," maggie said, "don't," but still I kept pushing until

233

she was through. I opened the door, then, let her in, "No," maggie moans, and the little calico cat looks up at us: one eye welling crimson.

"No."

        maggie is crouched in a corner, and I am dialing; spitting at her, huddled, hands clutching her face, I am cooing words into the phone, I almost slap her, "*No*," then we're carrying Madamina down ice-slick steps. We had to pour boiling water over the windshields to thaw them. maggie ran up and down the steps with a kettle, and I sat trying the engine again, again,

"Do you think we could ask the Woolfs to borrow their car?"

"Oh, no!" I cried, suddenly.

"No?" she said, almost whimsical, almost delivered from horror that moment, but I had leapt from the car and opened the hood to: an engine clogged with rags of blue wool—shreds of blanket we'd wrapped around the wires to keep them dry, so twisted with coils we had to peel it off, our hands stiff, Madamina howling, then finally we were driving, the highway, a turnoff, lights, and a kind-looking man stood at the door of a long, low building.

"Put her up on the table," he said, "and hold her. Good. Now. . . ." He pulled back an eyelid. We expected to see—cut? raw? red? white? nothing? nothing? "Well, look at that," he smiled, as we all looked down at the brilliant emerald iris staring up at us.

"But"

"Don't worry," he said. "I know those things can look pretty frightening. Here, this stuff turns purple if there's any serious lesion." He poured something into her eye. She squinted. He lifted the lid again. The eye was still green. "No, she's fine. That's all right, I can go back and have my dessert now. Let's see, that's, with medication, I think, yes, seven dollars."

She said, "My father should have a doctor like him."

We ripped out the cat door that night, we threw the metal lips in the garbage. We burned the wood frame and nailed cardboard over the gap. The next day we got a pane and maggie put it in; and I watched her, thinking of how she had knelt there, smashing glass with a hammer to make that gap for, "*a cat door? what kind of crazy idea is that?*" the morning we had our first snow; and Adam left.

"You know, if we'd done this before, Bailey still might"

"No. We're not supposed to think like that."

It was that same week water started to leak from the fish tank. After she'd killed the snails, the glass got more and more thickly encrusted, neither of us bothered to clean it and often we both forgot to scatter food, so: we put the remaining fish (two neons; an angel; and Egbert) into a plastic bag full of water and took them to the pet shop. All of them had a fatal fungus the salesman said,

"See those black spots? You can leave them with me," he said, helpfully. "I'll take care of them. . . ."

Still, "i" felt calm: except that I ran out of milk or yeast, or dashed down the road obsessed with, one apple = two tangerines, or 1½ eggs = ½ cup cottage cheese, but, with peripheral vision, I did see the puppy.

It stood by the side of the road, on my right. I'd slowed down for a curve, I thought I was ready for anything, but it started to cross just before I reached it, swerved, felt it thud, the car veering, the dog screaming, SCREAMING, it limped away to the woods. I followed it: found it beside a fallen log, not far from the road, it lay huddled behind a screen of thorn bushes.

"Come here, puppy." It was all black, big dark eyes looking at me: a baby Cairo, but gentle. I whistled, "Come on, pup."

"What happened?" Two men and a woman were standing behind me. "Oh, a dog. No, never seen it before. We live up that driveway, that's the only house in half a mile. You better move your car, we nearly ran into you. You might ask at the store," said one of the men as they started back to their truck, then the woman said,

"Hell, ya can't even see any swerve marks."

I stood up. "YOU BITCH," I shouted.

"What?" Long horse-face, buck teeth, bleached blonde hair in curlers under a pink scarf; started for me. "YOU'RE A"

One of the men grabbed her sleeve. "Come on, Marge."

"You think I'm gonna let that whore. . . ."

"Ahhh, she's nuts. She's the one lives across from Frank Brenner you know, she's a. . . ."

"PERVERT," the woman screamed as they pulled her towards the truck. "Why don't you get out of here, you're corrupting the neighborhood, YOU SICK BASTARD. . . ."

I turned my back on her, knelt, as I heard the truck drive off, I held out my hand. "Come here, baby," I whispered. It made a move towards me, cowered back. I reached in, thorns scratching my hands, and picked it up. It lay trembling, violently, as I felt it over. A female, lightly built—just her front leg seemed hurt: torn, dripping onto the newspaper I put under her as we drove to the vet,

"Seven, eight months," he said. "Yes, looks like a sheep dog. I'll take some X-rays. How's your cat? Think they'll get along? *How* many? Sure, put a note on the bulletin board if you want, and I'll call you if"

"Oh," maggie said. "Ohmygod. Oh, look at the ears."

   (*what lives near me dies*)

but just a badly torn paw; and so we acquired Sossa.

*

Fog rose into the valley that afternoon, warm and whitish; then rain all that night; then, the following morning, a dawn of pink clouds. Where that hill dips, at eight A.M., the sun showed—a shadow of pipe on the wall, a shadow of shadow in glass, my round cheek, half-profile, alone at the table this and every morning my mind flies to: endless arrivals in San Francisco; the endless sequence of open arms, even incest is better than grinding loneliness now insomnia gives me fantasies gives me insomnia every morning I'm up before dawn. I put on Machaut or Bach (nothing wakes her); and, every morning, to tempt her, I bake muffins: and I will eat five, and she may nibble half or a quarter when she gets up, at ten, I shake her shoulder.

"N-no." Eleven. "Oh, let me, just a little more," eleven thirty, "oh, no, no, leave me aLONE. . . ."

That hurt too much.

　　　(*rrringgg*

"Hello?" Heavy breathing. "Hello?" Breathing. I hung up, but two minutes later it rang again. "Hello?" Breathing. "Listen, whoever you are, I'm going to call the police when I hang up, so if you don't want to get in a lot of trouble. . . ."

She raised her head. "What is it?"

"Something nasty. I bet it's one of those people I met on the road. The ones who think we're perverts. . . ."

　　　(*rrrringg*

"OH, no."

"It might be someone else," she said, but I stalked to the phone and shouted,

"LOOK YOU GODDAMNED SONOFABITCH. . . ."

"What's happened?" she said.

"It was Joel. He wants to borrow the car Monday. I said no because of the kittens. He sounded really miffed, but I'm going to stay at his place, anyhow."

"Um. You'll straighten it out," she muttered, and started to sink back into her pillows. I wanted to yank her out of there, wanted to scream, I wanted to

"Aren't you getting up? It's after noon."

"Mmm, i. . .i. . .need to sleep. . .a little. . . ."

Mud coats my boots. I walk, weighted, up past streaks of birch, past the cove, to the upper lake. Under the banks, flanks of ice move. Stones are islands. I hop to one, wobbling, I almost fall in the water but a lurch, then my foot finds driftwood.

Perched here: straddling wood and a stone, I pause for a moment to gather courage; breathe, then leap forward onto the shore of that big white continent, solidly frozen, still—the second day of fifty degrees, in any month, it's crazy to walk on the ice: around the point and under the bridge and across the lower lake, surface wavy with indentations the rain left; slowly; breathing easier now but keeping away from the center where there is a current...

The wall approached: an easy way to climb out; to lie and watch flotsam, imbedded just a few days ago, float. A finger of leaf points. A sinew of driftwood gapes. A pebbles shines, ir-rridescent, the kind maggie loves, she loved all things speckled, mottled leaves and stones and a snow-powdered slope, grainy-textured, and *dead*, I thought, as I walked down the hill, but....

This space is even more beautiful now, in false spring.

*

"sorry if i made you feel bad can't explain—just not too quick today or something—not shareable—please do not take offense at previous whatever happened—i'm a pris-oner today—so probably you should ignore me—bad effect on you possible—yes you remembered—the way is out the door!"

*

On *Monday, Jan. 11*, it was raining again, and colder. We put two calico kittens in a box and start-ed for New York City. Tiny paws scratched at card-board on maggie's lap for maybe half a mile, tiny voices screamed, then in the rearview mirror I saw Madamina.

I backed up, opened the door, and she jumped in. I turned the car quickly, maggie keeping her off my lap as she sniffed at the box of screaming kittens, then at the house we closed her in again.

"I'm late. We'll have to rush," I said, but then a quarter mile up the road, "Am I hallucinating? Is that?"

"Madamina, damn it, yes. There may be a window open."

I stopped again, but she shied away into the bushes.

"Oh, no. Ma-da-meeee-naaa. . . ."

A whisker appeared. An ear. She started forward, then scurried back in the bushes. We left the box near where she had disappeared and crouched behind the car. The box squealed, rocked. She came out, we crept towards her, but, again, she was too quick.

"Look, this could take all day. I have to get down there."

"Maybe we could outrun her," maggie said. "If she can't see us. . . ."

I gunned the car up to fifty. We jolted around the curves, into the ruts, then stopped at the highway. We looked back. No sign of her.

"Maybe it's okay?"

"It has to be. She'll go home," I said, turning onto the highway. "She has five other babies. And she can get back in if she got out."

Trucks passed us, splattering muddy water. The spray from oncoming cars almost blinded me. It was a nerve-wracking hour, as we sped into the city, a wait near the bridge and another because of a wreck, wrecked cars lay all along the edge of the East River Drive, wet, strained faces; and strained, and late, I finally let maggie off with one kitten on Second Avenue; drove uptown, late, late in New York City is quintessentially late, I must have taught that night; must have given away the other kitten; but I remember only speeding to Joel's, late, and the tight, cold look on his face when he opened the door. He was wearing a jacket.

"I waited to let you in, Rebecca. I'm staying at Karen's."

"That's the new girl? You like her?"

"Sure. She's nice." He pulled on his gloves. "The dogs are on

239

the roof. You could let them in and let them out again tomorrow morning. If you want to."

"Okay. Do you know when you'll be back? Like for breakfast?"

"No, I don't think so." He opened the door. "Can't tell what will happen. Just be sure to lock up when you leave."

"Joel?" He turned, his hand on the knob. "Are you angry?"

"Of course I'm angry. What did you expect?"

"You mean because of"

"Yeah, because of." His voice was flat and very precise. "How many favors have I asked you? There's lots of talk about friendship, but what I see finally is a power struggle. I knock myself out to accommodate you, and you won't take a step out of your way for me."

"That's not true. If it hadn't been for. . . . I don't know how"

"I know you don't. That's the point. That's what shows up the whole farce of our 'friendship.' All these games. I have better things to do, Rebecca, frankly, if that's all there is, I'd rather stop going through motions."

"But that's not all it is," I said. Everything wavered, spun around Joel's face, framed in the doorway, so loving it can be, but now he was closed to me. I tried to keep my voice steady. "I didn't know you needed the car so badly or I would have. . . . I'm really sorry. I love you, Joel," but his face remained tight.

"Sure, you love me. That's easy. You mean I'm useful to you, I turn you on, maybe, it's all taking, don't you see? No," he muttered, and turned away, "you don't. You can't."

He closed the door. I heard his steps in the hall, then silence—as silent as it can be up here in this little box ten stories above the city, with the big untidy aquarium, schnauzers, a view of the Empire State Building, and the bed I will sleep in alone tonight I feel everybody receding from me; including

(*Tuesday, Jan. 12*, still raining, a day of going
through motions, teaching, getting supplies, then rushing, always I was rushing towards

240

maggie. . . .

I met her sitting hunched in a bar; green babushka; the fake-
suede coat hung over her shoulders; the big black sketchbook she
always wrote in open in front of her. Over her shoulders, I saw,

"CECCHETTI DRO_P
_P_E
_D ME!!!!

Antonio. . . Tony. . .
sonofabitch

really hurt. Are you worth it? ahh_h
_h_{h.}
. . . . .

then a picture in ballpoint pen: a demon superimposed on two
heads, girls' eyes and mouths like flame-holes, swan-neck-bodies,
wild hair; then a ghost head, its mouth like a stylized vagina—all
of this is a kind of circle, superimposed on another demon-head,
but large, with four points like black flames. An outline of bowler
hat near the top was almost obliterated. The pen had torn the
page a few times scrawling eyes, chin, cheeks, a chest with suggestion of jacket but then the genitalia had horns; and eyes and a
nose: a death's head scrotum extended to forepaws where feet
might have been at the end of threads of legs, then next to it:

WHAT have i done?
(left a mark?)

I sat down beside her. "Hi."

"Um. So glad to see you. Like my pretty picture?"

"Lovely. He dropped you?"

"Dropped. End. Will not see me again. No more injections,
no more pills. He feels it would be a mistake for both of us,
hrrumpph."

"Uh-huh."

"Says he thinks I never had temporal lobe epilepsy. It was all
an experiment, as he told me, he said, at first, it was worth a try,
but now, and etc. Oh, you should have seen it. He was all ready

for me. He sat at his desk and sat me in front of it just like I'd never seen him before, with my hands folded," she mimed good-littlegirl in school, "right? while he gave his little prepared speech." She deepened her voice and stiffened. "You're a very intelligent girl," she intoned, with mock sincerity, "a very *pretty* girl...."

"Oh, Christ."

"It's his timing that really hurt. To do it now, just now, when...oh, he's not as perceptive as I thought he was."

"He may be perceptive, all right, but he's a bastard. To get you into this in the first place was so self-indulgent it makes me wonder what kinds of feelings, I mean, if he has any...."

"Yes. I think that's what it amounts to," she said. "Because of too much feeling, he had to reject.... Like, it was an act of professional, human self-preservation...."

"Professional human shit. You could sue him for malpractice."

"Well, look, I had something to do with it, too. And nothing happened, except—oh, I thought he was straight. And he lied. I know this decision was more recent than he was trying to make me believe."

"You're well out of it. Let's go home."

"Also—my own response—like, is it a need to—conquer? Is that the word?"

"The word is *bastard*."

"I meant me."

"I know, I don't care, you're in trouble, even if you try to seduce every man alive, that's part of the trouble." I got up. "He's supposed to be the doctor."

"But I felt sympathy with him," she said. "I really liked him. I don't feel—completed with him."

"That looks pretty completed." I pointed at her drawing.

"Yes, well, there's something about that." She frowned. "So —pedestrianly deranged. I've been sitting here waiting for half an hour, and I just started...I didn't intend to...."

"It's quite expressive."

"Yes." She smiled, slightly. "Obviously, I've been affected."

"How's your father?" I said as we walked out to Seventy-Fourth Street.

"Bad. I'm going to have to move down there—Thursday."

"*Thursday*? Day after tomorrow?"

"Or Friday. I have to. I'll help you with the pipe, first, and the kittens...the little ones should wait a week, but." She leaned against the car, looking up at the dull red clouds swirling, low, above the city. "I'm really sorry. It will be better for the animals, though. That I'm gone. What lives near me dies."

"Oh, stop that," I said, violently. "That's just—melodrama."

17.

Adam . . .

The rain is melting a frieze of icicles: crystal swords hanging outside the window, and purple crocuses I've forced into bloom and a daffodil. Last night we got home late and found Madamina gone. Fear the worst. Five kittens are left now Bailey is gone and one kitten dead and the snails smashed, who's next? maggie's father, I guess. She's going down there this week, getting near, I don't want to think, where are you? No word from you since our Thanksgiving phone call. maggie has odd ideas I deny but almost share, getting odd, too: last night I woke in darkness, felt a presence, almost burst with fear, but I dozed again. Then something cold touched my temple—just a dot, but I woke sharply.

What am I becoming?

Last weekend, I walked on the reservoir, though. I go up almost every day now. In the middle there it's like walking on sky, clouds of snow, when the sun comes out, so beautiful—I'm a sun person still, I told you, I was talking to you in my head all that day, do you remember? me? us? here? any of It?

There is nothing like that space out there; that silence.

244

maggie giving me the creeps.
and Madamina frozen outside on the porch
Rattling
stillness.

It's still before. Sunlight streaks on a group of small cows huddling, all at one side of the grove. Some fold themselves down on the ground like dogs. Some stand. Two horses stand with them— one black, one spotted. The cows bend their heads back, moo, deep belly-sounds. A curtain of gray is descending, before my eyes, thick veils of air, approach,
    (*approach. . . .*

An arrow of clear gold pierces the west; a brief window. The puppy scratches at the lower pane her claws have smeared muddy, whimpering, time: to let her spill out, round, fluffy, black on the yellowed grass and frolic around a heap of twigs, time: for fire against the touch of the wind rising, weeds rolling, trees leaning, wind shrieking birds swooping, stuttering,
    storm

The tarp on the woodpile flaps. Like outposts against the wildness, stakes holding up the barbed-wire sway. Now the cows' forms dissolve into gray stuff even less substantial then my words, dissolving, the wilderness churning, even the hope of substance fading, and I call time,
    time: for all creatures.

("Come in," I said to the man outside; but he can't understand. He jogs away into the field; disappears, as the cows disappeared, and the puppy, and. . . .

    There were horses there, too. . . .
and a puppy: larger, but female-black like this one. She yelped as Cairo tossed her over on the red rug. Wind gusted in through the bathroom door and beyond the nest of kittens screaming that

night we came back and found: a bulging black hole, splintered wood, and, scattered over the toilet, a pane in shards.

The kittens were all alive—five ravenous black-and-white dwarves orphaned now for the second time in a month. We could feed them from pans this time, they were older, and robust, though stunted. We nailed some cardboard over the hole. Rain dripped from the ceiling. The kittens screamed, we stroked them, they screamed,

"The clock," maggie said; hurtled upstairs and back with the big magenta monster, but, this time they won't take ticking wires for comfort. We closed the door on them, made a fire, in that cold room gray with smoke maggie coughed all night, and the cold spray of rain had turned sleet the next morning we walked a cold, wet, half mile calling, "Ma-da-meeeena. . . ."

Near the place where we'd left her two days before I noticed something; veered off slowly until I was sure what we both saw: a strip of calico,

"OH NO," maggie screamed, and fell on her knees on the wet concrete, leaves, mud. . . .

I held her sobbing until she looked up, touched the corpse, then lifted it: hard already, and soaked, but not banged up. We carried it down the road in silence. A car passed, spattering slush. She took it back of the house and placed it, carefully,

> *middle-right, edge:* stretched out on an island of snow the sun hadn't reached, leaves shored up all around her pelt seems the same dark color, but it was richer in life, more russet.
>
> *"maggie. . . ."*

squatted; took a few pictures, then handed me the camera.

> handed me. . .
> gave me. . .

How did I come to hate her?

That day in the small, warm world of the car, snow squishing against the windshield, I was alone, but the wipers scraped voices: Joel, Adam, Susan, the tires on slush rasped words, and the animals moaned; their images dripped; the old man I can't see or won't, but, I see him, withered, eaten in his lungs, I hear, maggie cough, I see her, she, spins out of time into a whirlpool where no color is, goes down, wants to go down, I lose my hold or is that her, her fingers loosening as I swim, not knowing now if she is on any shore or in the water pulling me down with her...

Death, I thought, deathness—hours afterwards: up and down hills, in and out of the lumberyard, market, all afternoon, and it was dusk by the time I slogged up the steps to the sound of Cairo baying, and found the corpse thrown into a box, like a piece of rubbish, under the snout by the front door.

I opened the door. The dog and puppy rushed out. I shooed them back in, light, rug, now the heater grates on, my nerves stretched to, kick the puppy, *no, say, some, thing,*

     "maggie. . . ."

wandering out of her room and helped put in the new pane; wood putty hardening, fingers encrusted, milk, the kittens, but, she speaks monosyllables, faraway, and my voice screams,

"DEATH IS NOT YOUR PRIVATE PROPERTY!"

"What?"

Then, as though we'd said nothing, she goes back into her room.

Yes, I know. But I can't get away from a feeling of fakery; of her melodramatizing at the times she seems most sincere; of necrophilia on a well-set stage. She comes out, falls onto her bed, pulls the sleeping bag over her.

"Want some dinner?"

"mmm-mnn"

"What?"

"nn-nnnn. . . ."

"Let's keep Tonta in after this."

She coughed, closed her eyes.

"We have to do something about the kittens."

She turned over.

". . . Cat flung in a box," I spat, and leaned to watch her face. I thought I saw her lips tremble. She coughed again, and I took my books and a blanket and moved upstairs to the room where I'd spent Christmas Eve; where Adam lived once.

*

(january 13

madamina so perfectly dead—so perfect

she lies there frozen stretched body long as though that were her form as though she were always reaching for that perfect form so untouchable, perfect, irreversable. . . . why is there such pain in seeing her exquisiteness?

i do not understand enough to relate to rebecca. nor do i wish to at this time.

it's too hard and i am very far away from it.

perhaps i did breach a unity but i thought she sensed i had to be alone with madamina. that it meant something else to me. so i was wrong—she did not sense it or if she did it is that precise fact that brought into play the hurt. the hurt i suspect is not just from this. rebecca is far too sensitive not to have understood. "Cat flung in a box." i knew what i was doing, but. so many associations for her. i was sorry for that. insensitive. but what came out of her mouth before i cannot plow through. there is where i cannot relate—for all its covering.

i seem to consistenly bring out entanglements for her. misplacements of feelings which are hers independently but also, i think i add to the problems just by the air i breathe—my motions of silence screaming in cement blocks and then quiet absolute because i must rest from screaming. . . .

i do not feel responsible for her frustrations. i merely feel that i add to them. she to mine. yes, energy has flashed but basically my feeling that i cannot live with people has been both supported and negated here. the support is becoming stronger.

*

"I want to know where it is," Rebecca said,
                    where is it. tell me where it is.
"All right. Later," maggie muttered,
                              No.

*

Reach, out of the bitterness, the, *recoil*, mid-January: a light coat of snow the next morning when I-Rebecca got up, the corpse gone, and now the curtain has lifted with all its creatures. But smoke rises out of the ground, bisecting the plain, it seems to approach us—a wall? bridge? tunnel?

She must have got up to bury Madamina; but when I spoke to her, she was already back in the sleeping bag, eyes closed.
"Want some breakfast?"
"Mmmmmnnnn"
"Where's Madamina?"
"Mmmm...mmm"
I drink my coffee a few feet away from the bed, I clatter dishes. She coughs. I stand by the glass doors, peeppeep from the bathroom, the puppy nudges my foot, I kick her. She whimpers. I want to kick her again, don't, walk outside to watch the wind clearing patches of blue now I'm very lucid, suddenly, I know....
There is no one who gives me anything. Even the ones I most want, that I "love," they give me nothing, or, not enough. And

249

they want something I can't give, like Adam, or just don't love me, like. . . .

What is the magic? the cloak she and other women have that I don't, is it just i'm not pretty? but—I could give men up, I thought, and not-care about sex—*if she could.*

That day she stayed in bed, a motionless lump of blue in the drafty room, no fire, Cairo beside her. There was a gash in the plastic stretched over the windows, we need tape, I said. She murmured. The puppy cowered under the table. Remember? that thick silver stuff, I told her, peep, and the kittens, I said. She half opened her eyes. It was your cat, I sneered, right? peep peep. She coughed. I called the pet shop, doesn't need kittens, but maybe the animal shelter, 5-5-6-1, "Hello,"

"*kills them*," I yelled at her.

Sometime after two o'clock I heard her going into the bathroom, then coming out, and dressing, as I looked down from the top of the steps, "the kittens," she said, "the market"; brisk, efficient, in those absurdly studious glasses, yet there was something remote about her: a quality very different from other times I'd felt her distant. I couldn't even be vicious now. I knew there was no way to reach her.

"Here, we can use this," she said; and we jammed the kittens into a box and carried it down the steps. The car lock was frozen. I poured boiling water over it

   (always carry hot water, and candles, and sand, yes, big-brother. Check the battery, yes sir, Mr. Stark in California, but where were you when the fish died? when Bailey, The Roses, and yesterday, where were you, and the snails, how long ago the deaths began to toll, 1, 2, 3, 4,
   reality testing. . . .

"That's a fire zone, Miss. You'll pay twenty-five dollars for leaving your car there. I'd park it if I were you."

And I drove around to a slot between white lines and walked through the parking lot swarming with mothers and children bundled in mittens, scarves, in the late sun slanting

Midwinter Special
            24-hour Service
      LETTUCE 39¢ a Head,
and pinned to the bulletin board a sign in purple: a maggie-scrawl:

* * * * * * * * *

part Persian kittens

* six weeks old *

free to good homes

* * * * * * * * *

She stood almost lost in the fake-suede coat, she was so small now; kittens crawling all over her. Children squealed,

"Oh, mother. . . ."

"Oh, mother, please'

"Six weeks, hmm?" A hearty, redhead with healthy red-headed brood. "They look awfully small."

"Well, they're really five. They lost their mother, though, so they're weaned already."

"Poor little things." She stroked one. "But they're healthy?"

"Oh yes."

"Please, please, mother. . . ."

"Allll right."

They walked away with two. People passed, some looking away, some smiling. My toes had gone numb. maggie shivered, beaming at everyone with that false, delectable radiance I had once loved.

(She'd said, "Are you disappointed?"

A thin little girl about twelve years old danced around us that whole afternoon: torn sweater, no coat, but her sallow skin was not even reddened, somehow, she seemed immune to the cutting wind. She pelted us with strident questions,

"How many cats do you have? Do you have any dogs? Do they get along? Why don't you keep them all? Do you like them? What do they eat? How come they're so little?"

"You shouldn't be out without a coat," I said, finally. "Where's your mother?"

"She works in the cleaners next door. I'm not cold I have a dog too he's a collie-shepherd." She jabbed at a kitten with her forefinger. "My mother hates cats, or I'd take one of yours."

"Let's wheel them around on a shopping cart for a while," maggie said, "and get warm."

"You go ahead. Take one, and I'll stay here with a couple."

"Okay, if that's what you want."

She went inside with the smallest kitten. The child disappeared, too. I stood alone with small claws piercing my coat, the sun setting, women, women and children and women passing me all these domestic presences,

"Please, Momma, please...."

"Oh, I don't know. Should I, Helen?"

She spoke with a German accent—a big, attractive woman, but deeply uncertain, I could tell in most parts of her life she played helpless. Her friend, American, also big, but fat, seemed happily cast in the opposite role.

"Well," she said, sternly, "do you want to take care of a cat?"

"Please, Momma, I'll take care of it."

"Would you really, dear? Oh, Helen, I just don't know."

"Mark my words, you'll be taking care of it, Bertha," her friend said. "You know children."

"Momma, I *swear*...."

"I think I better call my husband. Would you hold one?" she asked me. "I'll just be a minute."

"Sure, I'll keep one for you."

"I don't think you'll have much trouble," Helen said.

"Oh, thank you. I'll be right back."

It was darkening quickly, now. The store lights and head-lights came on. The child, like a troublesome gnat, was back again, with a coat on. "Aren't you tired? Where do you live? Where's the kittens' mother? How old are you?" A little old lady in fur stopped.

"Oh, how lo-o-ovely. So little. Is one a girl? Oh, good. And they're part Persian? What do you feed her?"

"This," maggie said, coming back with two cans of Figaro and her best smile. "We're giving a can away with each kitten."

"Why, how sweet. Well, I think I'll take her. Now, here's my phone number, and may I have yours? Just to let you know how...."

"We shouldn't have done that."

"Why not?" the little girl asked.

"Because she might call and pester," maggie told her, "Like you."

"Oh, well," I said, "it's probably okay. Where's the baby?"

"One of the checkers took her. You want me to hold that one?"

I gave her the kitten and put my hands in my pockets. The little girls' mother, looking tired, came out of her shop, locked the door, and they walked away across the parking lot.

"Now, what makes that child so obnoxious?" maggie said. "I'd expect to feel sympathy for her, but...."

In the glare of the artificial lights, the skin of her face seemed pinched, purplish. The kitten clung to her. Wind gusted up, the stars disappeared. maggie's glasses lay askew on her nose, were they cold, I wondered,

"maggie...."

She looked away that second; as though she hadn't heard. She'd been perfectly civil, even friendly at moments, since we'd been here, I thought, it could be a coincidence, I thought—we'll be glad to be rid of each other.

"Oh, you still have one!" The German woman was back, child in tow. "Oh, I'm so glad. My husband said...is it a boy? Now, what can I feed him? Oh, thank you. How can I carry him? Could I take that carton? Careful, Stephanie, let me do it. Oh, all right, but don't squeeze him, he's only a baby, careful...."

"Whew. Three hours, five kittens. Not bad," I said.

"No." She pulled down the sign and threw it into a trash can. "Let's go fix the pipe," she said. "I really have to leave tomorrow."

That night. . .we cleaned the stove pipe. We had to separate
lengths of it, empty them, then fit them back together and into
the stove and the hole in the wall above her bed. A draft blew in.
The ladder wobbled. Soot leaked on the furniture.

"What a mess. You look like a chimney sweep."

"Thanks, you're also. . .hey, watch it."

"Don't worry, it's safe. It just shakes."

"There really ought to be someone on a honky-tonk piano."

"Yes." She did a twirl and almost fell off the ladder. "See,"
she panted, "It's fine. I'm the one. . . ."

> (*You're not letting go, are you?*
> *No, I told you.* . . .

Cairo barked. Tonta fled. The puppy hid as maggie went to
the door and came back with Carrie Woolf, huffing from her
walk up the hill.

"Wheee-ooo. Windy," she said. "It's going to storm tomorrow."

She sat down gingerly on the edge of what had been my bed
and accepted a cup of coffee. Even though I had explained the
sign, I think she still didn't quite believe she was welcome. We
talked, we laughed, we laughed a lot that night, only stiffening
once, when the phone rang, *but, it's only,*

"Those babies," Carrie sputtered. "Can't get along without
me for even an hour. *Really,*" and bustled away, happy.

We stuffed the gaps. We swept. We put the ladder outside
and rubbed off the soot. Then we even had tea at the table, we
babbled easily on about pipes and joints and the weather before
maggie climbed in her bag and I went upstairs, and

She's going down there tomorrow.

I don't care what she feels; what she wants needs where she
hurts she is leaving, I don't care, I'm a bitch. It is possible I don't
care about anything or anyone. It is. Possible.

I want her to go. Want the freedom, no, want the physical
fact of what is figuratively true: isolation—really the possibility
of never seeing anybody at all.

I could take pictures and take walks and music books think love the puppy and Tonta and never see anybody again. Yes books and music are human, but at a distance—best self to best self.

Why not? Maybe once every few months, only as some kind of spree, at a bar, maybe. Not a pretense at anything else. I've done it with sex, why not with friendship? I could write letters, maybe, keep a check on sanity that way. And teach my classes?

No. No classes. No letters. No more pretending. Alone. I am, so why not really. Alone.

We hardly spoke the next morning, early, we drove to the station. I got out to wait on the platform with her. She said,

"You'll take care of Cairo?"

"Of course. Here it is, on time for a change."

We watched the two-car train come chugging around, its bell clanging. Clouds like a fish spine were etched, paler white in the white sky, above it, the riblets radiating over the tracks, the river, the mountain's hump ashen. She got up one step, then turned. Her face, surrounded by metal, people, looked the same ashen white as the mountain's hump—but in flesh so desolate I could hardly

Look. . . .

"Be careful," she said. "You're doing something, you know."

"Am I?"

"Yes."

(but I can't

putt-putter, around, the house,

think

she thought

I was disappointed, and yes, I was. I was in love with madness. Like Adam, like all of them. It ran its course, then—the magic wasn't what I had thought. I feel remote, cut off, yet, I know we are versions of one—insanity? at this moment,

255

*where maggie foundered, I know I, I-Rebecca, can
founder. . . .*

> (*No. Not that surface.*

> *Sure?*

After dinner I walked up the path with Cairo: the wind
blowing wild, clouds and legions of stars like those above Perry
Street, here, again, they're all double. I pass the old devil-god,
crowned with pin points of light, not ominous now. Venus pulses
low in the sky, so icy-deep, once before she pierced me, too; and
the good cold.

Around the lake, gleaming icebound expanse, I follow footsteps that might be hers: to that tree Adam loved, frozen tremor
above the place where I swam this summer. I thought about
vampires. Is that going way off? Trees creak like a cat, like
Bailey, might come home now she's gone, I thought, no more
stars, creak, but, *yes: it's way off*; the big dry flakes coming
down now the trees, *it's only trees*, blowing down on top of me,
who's to know I am gone? and how to survive immobilized in
snow this time lying in drifts. . . .

It's a desolate place—maggie's country. There is in the middle
of the path a stake. Did she put it there?

Striped maple buds a promise of life.
They don't don't don't don't wilt.

*

january 15
madamina. . .

. . .i do not understand enough. . .

i am not an artist. i lack that independent source of
energy which creates despite and in conjunction with
circumstances of changeabilities of mind. it takes some

element of religion to work. i have none. i have not
been. i think it about time to recognize this and because
of it, the treadmill, i want to die, every cell in my body
is longing to and this very loud silence is permeating
here. my depression has existed all my life. i belong to it.
i am it. this is not self-pity. it is telling and admitting a
truth that i have not been able to overcome or rather
reach the level of human condition in such a way as to be
anything else than what i have always been. i deceived
myself and others because of it. i do not wish to any
longer. i see no way out, nor do i think there is one.
i make one true wish, one that i do not have to magically
wait for. to disinherit my life.

18.

"Tickets, please, all tickets. . . . Miss, may I have your ticket, please. . . Miss, excuse me. . . thank you. Smoking compartment is right in, *there*, you are

(*steady*. . . .

white hair. white mustache. white sky wrinkling, maggie thought, white flesh fat yellow mangled like metal like not-alive but there's no sage F SAFE NO SAFE for flesh rubbish out-side: dismember, in-side: de-compose, called digestion, slowly, fast, sickles, no, it's a scythe he's supposed to but, those two horses are brown, and he isn't, he doesn't, even, know, she thought, all of them really REALLY don't know and it's only my, eyelids, sticks to prop them open to, witness, strapped down dare i miss a detail or, cut off my, thrown inside the arena, punish my, head in a vise i can't turn it to turn to the horses are gone are past *past* whinnying *hear* but a

SCREEEEEAAAMMMMMMMM

(*Croton-Harmon. . . Alllll change*. . . .

"Watch your step, *Miss*. . . ."

a gentle old. gentle, man. gentle snow soft seemly cover the, seam, where the gentle, horses, rotting in-side all all any, now, right now or, frozen rigid until so: how to delight, how to even bear, witness, the seeming of any thing?

people do.

yes, i know, but. . . is courage infectious? am i even—susceptible? *what lives near me dies*. . . .

"There's the New York train, Miss. The forward one. *You're* welcome."

(clankclank

the veins take a long time. an artery makes most sense, he said, if you really want to

("oh, i'm sorry")

do it. one branches out from the place inside the elbow they puncture for tests, runs down to each side of the wrist you can feel the outer one beating that should. cough. cough it up. or, the quickest of all is the neck: that one carries blood oxygen up to the brain would stop brain needs most oxygen, breathe, in, out, in, smoke, still i'm ritualistic. arms, wrists, the council table said, cough; bark, like Cairo, the dandy gambler the devil-god poor crazy beast he was friends with, madamina, was like a dog but, no more my business is sleepsleep endless sleep by unanimous, *cough, bitch, cough, vomit, off with her,*

yes. there's a nail stuck into my head put there by lightning it's attached to a wire thread they can turn, whenever, but now it's loose, now i'm falling through

(clinkclankclinkclank

where?

not susan's. not my parents' jesse? a helluva mess to clean up after, that's not fair. do i care, do i care? best is probably some-place public the station bathroom a bar and someone who never saw me before, best, as long as no one sensitive happens to

(Dobbs Ferry next...All tickets)

"Miss, your"

yessir. yes, yes, yellowhand

. . . .

but, simple. it's all simple ≠ easy; now where have i heard that? simpl-y, too bad but some one or two or three will have to, all right: it's not much worse than the stink that's behind me, maggie thought, sniffing—the odor of icing, grease, perfume, *don't turn.* nausea. there are a woman and two little boys settling into their seats, stale perfume, White Shoulders? and doughnuts,

259

most absolutely sickening doughnuts they put in their mouths and chew and then, no, let's change perspective

(she told her-self: sitting opposite her own skull-face nodding slightly on its thread,

now . . . there is the doughnut, *and* there is the hole. and there is the other side of the hole that's still the continuous surface of dough, *nut*, and then there's the edge on the other side of the, still continuous, surface of, see the Infinite via Thomas' Baked Goods serving the WHOLE of Manhattan, Brooklyn, the Bronx, Queens,

(125th strect. . . New York Citeeeee. . . .
screeech)

ARE WE COMING INTO DARKNESS?

NO, WE AREN'T. WE AREN'T COMING INTO DARKNESS. ("What's the matter, Davy? You've been on this train before. It's just we're coming into the big station."

"But, I thought we were coming into"
"we *aren't*. . . ."

(Graaand CENtral. . . Grand Central Staaation

"See, Chrissy's not afraid, and he's littler than you are. Now you be a brave boy like"

"Chrissy,

ARE YOU AFRAID?

"BUT I TOLD YOU. WE AREN'T COMING INTO
"I KNOW. I KNOW WE AREN'T COMING INTO DARKNESS, BUT, WHAT I *WANT* TO KNOW IS: *ARE . YOU . AFRAID?*

(screeeeecchhh. . . .

"Be careful, *Miss*"

station change   this is a
                                                    station change

                      hey.
                                    the Lexington's this way.

260

no baby,

    that's times
    square

                     times square what?

    what?

           what?

               said, it can't be times
                 square

   why?

          because we're at grand central!

am i going ar o
          u
            n
             d LADIES.......
       i
         n .
   a
             straight a-head .

                       no
                          no

("oh, sorry, MISS"

                 it's this

                   way.

   which way?
          here.
   where?
          here. come right down.
  where? why?
        "HERE!
           (crackle)
don't ask me why goddamn it you called me and I am telling you
get yourself on a subway and get down here right away don't stop
just get here NOW"
        ann said:

COUNCIL TABLE BULLSHIT

okay (whisper) tell me why not.

WHY YES? LIFE'S ITS OWN VALUE. YOU'RE
JUST SCARED AND HIGH ON STARVATION. . . .

can't stand food sicken

WHAT? TALK SO THAT I CAN HEAR YOU

can't stand it's too painful why wait
it happens anyway i'm not really human
i'm alien

THAT'S A COPOUT. YOU'RE AS HUMAN AS I
AM. A VERY SELF-FLATTERING COPOUT

no. really. okay human but have to see
that always disintegrating can't stand
seeing waiting for

ARE YOU SITTING THERE SAYING YOU DON'T
HAVE THE GUTS TO LIVE?

i don't *want* to

YOU DON'T HAVE THE GUTS

that's a psychological trick you're
trying to

WHAT?

you're trying to make me angry, i, know,
that's a trick to make me fight

GODDAMN IT EVEN IN YOUR STATE YOU NOTICE
IF I USE PSYCHOLOGICAL TRICKS

*   *   *   *   *   *

262

* * * * * *

(*rrringgg*

"Yes, Rebecca, I was just about to call you. No, she came
down yesterday. You found what? Really? That was a letter she
wrote you, then. No, she didn't. She doesn't want to, really. She
made me a promise she wouldn't do any cutting, but she's in very
bad shape. No, she can be reached, but she's doing a lot of hallucinating. She has been for months, of course, but it's worse now
her father is. . . . Yes. I gave her some pills, and I've made an
arrangement to get her sedative shots starting Monday. She'll
have to go to a doctor for them, no, don't worry, not Cecchetti.
What can I tell you, it's any day. That doctor of his is a sonofabitch, though. He should be in the hospital. Well, that's Welfare.
I'm trying to. . . . No, as long as they're both alive I can't stop her
going up there, she has to go through it. At Jesse's. Yeah, he's okay
for now, he'll feed her at least, but. Well, there's one hospital I
would have liked, but I can't get her in there, and any other place
would be. . . . Yes, I think you could if you want to make the com-
mitment. The shots will help, but she'll be doped all the time for
as long as. . . . No, she can't take it straight. Well, she was doing
fine until this with her father. Yes. I thought her moving up to
the country with you was a definite move towards health, despite. . . . No, there's no reason you should come down before
Monday. I can imagine. It must be beautiful there, it's so ugly
here, you know, snow in the city. What's with your brother, by
the way? Uh-huh. No, she's talked about him in sessions, of
course, but. Don't worry, she'll be all right until, yes, I'll let you
know. We'll be in touch, then"

(*touch, then.* . . .

"I envy the cats," she'd said. "You know—touching."

Webs. . . hang over the bulletin board: stretched, wavering,
black on the photo of Tonta crouching above a chipmunk, they
come together and *touch*: the animal. Gather it in, where the

263

strands meet—that circle, there, in the center, that ring from which they radiate outward, spokes charged with life and life caught there, fresh and beating, the prey, the *predator, touch*: the dogs curled around each other; the chipmunk with Tonta; the cow's rib jutting through snow and the hoof Sossa brought, neatly severed, the fur still on, *touch*: that creature-thirst for warmth, the fluid curve of a shoulder that's healthy, drink it, and my own flesh breathing, pounding, secreting, but, here alone—there's a reeking old age smell.

    Touch that?

"Cancers live on their own terms. They happen to interfere with the human, the cells are alien to ours, that's all, you know, and they thought they'd caught it when they took out one lung. You can do very well on one lung once you're used to it. She felt fine for a while, and then they found out it had spread all through her. She probably died of something else, it's impossible to really know because cancer hits so many organs once it's metastasized. Well, they sort of surround the healthy cells and kill them. Choke them, I guess, or, eat. . . . At the end she wasn't a person any more," he said. "She just wasn't a person."

    maggie. . . .

today I saw death's reflection to the east, in a pale purple sky: the mountain all grainy black, wind sweeping white dunes, a desert, in this cold room at twilight I start a fire. I put on water to heat and watch sparks outside the window one light fades: through icicles hanging like scythes, hooks, horns, or plunging like birds, and beyond them the chestnut horse: black tail swishing, his back powdered white, he flows past the barbed-wire fence and the skulls, the west gold, the sound of the kettle a dull crescendo counterpoint to a woodpecker drilling taptap on the roof and smoke now mist obscuring the windows pushes me back to:

    Second Avenue: wet-cold: fever heat beating at cracked grimy walls, pipes knocking, that sour reek bubbling his in-sides choking, flesh, shuddering now the aliens are feeding on charming Jake Starski

. . . .
Touch him.
(*rrringgg*

"A black dress well it's necessary" (Susan said) "no, she's at Jesse's, but, no, his girl friend's not there you know okay I'll take care of it. Well of course do you really I know but the old man may go any minute."
(*rrrringg*

"I don't want to bother you, oh no" (the little old lady said) "nothing's wrong I just love her to pieces but could you tell me the day she was born? So we can celebrate every month. December 11, Sagittarius, how nice. I've always been sentimental," she said, "about birthdays."
(*rrrringg*

Dial, 212. Dial, 415. Dial 1, dial 0, 2, 3, in California it's six in New York it's nine, oh, clock, swwingg, seven, time winding, eight, ten and eleven,

No answer.
"Pain," he said, "lots of pain. All the vital functions, you see, it's a gang of nonfunctional cells. That's the sense in which they're alien. . . ."

(*painpainpainpainpain. . . .*

Where is he?"

The animals shift; yawn. Small, high sounds are coming out of the animal can't, can't cry, can't, laughter is human, can't see the keys for horror stretching the mouth, *pain*, called, *no answer*. No one in the back-door mirror, no two, no, pity reflecting the crow's-feet and jowls hanging down, then a phone, a red rug and beyond that's a visual echo: sheets hanging over a mirror that's past; or future. Wood. Sand, water, and roses grow out of his chest, red, piercing the glass, in-side, *pain*, exquisite, shattering —what?
No answer.
(*rrringgg*

Dial again. Dial. Dial, but: silence; the heater, the clock, and taptap the refrigerator, but no-thing human. A gibbous moon shines through mist. Call, time and weather, says 12, 0, 3, winding, swwingg, clearing, colder and colder on tape, the mechanical voice,

but, where is she?

"Yes. Certainly, ma'am. *I'm* sorry you're having trouble."

(rrringg. . . brrringg

But, somewhere past numbers; past hours—these phantoms, my twelve enchanted brothers wound up to endlessly tick and peep and clank and tap and ring, somewhere in this mountain of sound, I know there's a way: to speak. To hear.

The animal shifts; yawns; dials once more, *no answer*, and crawls upstairs, under blankets the animal shivers, wanting and chilled, wanting, simmering female accused by a moon-yellow egg blasting seeds through the glass and odors of apple and rose and corruption, my own hand pushing yet holding her,

swwingg

(push me, back again

don't. . .let it start. don't don't let the wanting start don't don't tell Rebecca.

*

Can you look at it now? Just, straight on?
You pushed her out—then and later. or,
"Let me see," said The Man Outside, "what was it?
You were deficient in—compassion, wasn't it?"

*

There is a tempo of months—a blur; then of weeks, moving quickly, though some clear images happen. Then there's the tempo of days; of hours; slower and slower until they are still shots.

Slow horses graze in the field this cold morning the flies are slow, but still the machine will jerk sometimes, or race, in a moment of jagged, nervous, New York, for instance: that Monday. . . .

I couldn't get plowed out, spent two hours shoveling snow, rolled the car down the hill, armpits aching, and drove, with the puppy next to me, down to Jesse's on Seventy-Seventh and Third Avenue.

This was the first time I'd been there—a low, dark, sprawling apartment. maggie had gone to the doctor, Jesse told me, right nearby. Yeah, he'd gotten some food down her, just a little and that was hard. Want some coffee? Pie? Any minute, he thought, it's touch and go but really a heavy scene down there. That old woman is nuts, freaks maggie out more than her father dying right now she's getting some kind of sedative shot Ann says will last a week, he said, pouring water into the Chemex pot, carefully, Susan's with her. I'll take her downtown later, here you are, it's apple. Homemade. We're trying to get him into a hospital, but he's on Welfare, so, you know. Or do you? Yeah, it's great pie. No, Grace made it before she left. Upstate with her parents, he said, for a while, and put a tentative hand on my waist; very delicate unmistakeable question I moved away from, not, now, sure, he said; leave the puppy. We'll probably be here when you

> (finished work, parking the car, cold but left my coat in the back seat and ran, ran, to get back: at nine thirty-five, found, the key hidden; and a note inside,

> *We're downtown. Don't come now, there's no place to sleep and two is plenty. It's risky at night around here all the scum rises up to the surface. Feel free to raid the fridge, play music, make yourself at home like they say and we'll seeya tomorrow. love, J.*

There were no books. The walls were covered with photographs, of children, of city scenes, of Grace: her face strong, vivid. A trumpet was propped in one corner, and sleek electronic equipment everywhere. Back of a door I found the darkroom:

long, narrow, smelling of chemicals. Water was running over some prints in a tray. *I like this*, I thought; avoiding Grace's intense black eyes, *I like him*. I went to the kitchen, tore into a ham, bread, finished the pie, *she looks like Kay a little*, then forced myself out to walk the puppy, coatless, but the car was too far it was icy, running,

       running

in only a heavy sweater and vest, why? pulled at the end of a leash down Seventy-Eighth Street, wind cutting, there's nothing can cut like a New York wind, *and alone.* . . .

       the pipes knock.

There was something involving roses: cutting red roses. Stop it, I thought, cut it out, the night's just begun. I rolled over and drifted off again, then a voice came, immediately, it seemed, very clear and crisp,

       YOU CAN'T TAKE PICTURES OF GAPING HOLES
       it said,

and started to laugh: a tinkling laughter like bells like ringing, ringing. . . .

The puppy's snout lay on the pillow beside me. I picked up the phone. "Um?"

    "hi."

       (husky voice whispered; what did I say, or did
       I just breathe and

    "yes."

       (hear her, dragging her cigarette across the wires
       buried under the streets at the other end of the line,

    "are you okay?"

       (asked, and I asked

    "Am, *I*. . .?"

       (sitting, holding a black thing with holes called
       receiver, I stare at, dusty and moistened with
       This is the end of the

stored-up years gushing out through my eyes, burn, relief pouring now from some cave beyond tears, out through the channel tears opened, sounds: fall in the, cross-one-word and the rest don't matter, maggie, only the voice: we still don't know if it's yours or mine,

hold on—don't do anything now. It's the hardest, time, to sleep now it's dark but already getting light, I love you. Now is the coldest hour, then dawn, I promise. I love you, remember, hold on, believe me, remember, this is the middle of the night.

. . . . .

"R-rebecca? this stuff makes me fuzzy, i heard, yes. come. . . when you can. . . ."

But: the car hood was up, when I reached it. The right-hand vent had been pushed in. My coat and gloves were gone.
"low last night was minus four at Kennedy Airport, it's seven degrees now at 9:15 this is WABC AND here's the Lovin' Spoonfuls with"
racing, station to gas station, *no, you'll have to*, auto supply, *no not today* but I don't have a *that will cost you* but *we'll have to order it*. coat. *What? hell, no*, but there's a man dying, a girl going mad and this is the coldest snap of the *colder, they say, tonight*, and I left a dog out, sixty miles, *you could call the state cops, you know*. But he bites. I have to, I know, *guess some guy really needed a coat*, buy, gloves at Macy's or updownaround, but a man is, teach, *I am you are* and drive, "here's the number-one tune for this week, New York!" *He is*, down to, finally, race past the mailboxes bottles the bums on the steps, at
10 P.M., Jan. 19, Tuesday. . . .

It's taken me years to reach this room; this presence—her sallow face, the pale wisps of hair stuck into her eyes, she's emaciated and doped, her arms held stiff to her sides now her voice is a whisper, "come in. are you hungry? come into the"

Jesse is gone. Tante Bella has got into bed with, the old man sits under a heap of blankets, propped up shrunk to almost nothing but two dark brown eyes in the skeletal face, deep-faraway staring, rigid, staring at "maggie. . . ."

his two skinny hands held out in front of him, shaking, cold inside
his bones he tries, to, shift, all his motions like spurts, of pain,

"m-maggie. . . ."

helps him up, around, into his slippers; the withered feet; and
walks him across the room, her shoulders under the weight, bent,
bow of her spine made me think of that curve of land near the
place she almost drowned, help, him, into the bathroom, wait.
Pain. "All the vital functions," *pain*, traveling down the spine
like, glass in the kidneys, cracking, each breath each motion each
second, tinkling, an icicle falls; crashing; *pain*, wrenching, *pain*,
and out again slowly, the white hair the dirty pajamas with nothing inside but bones and need and terror, she helps him, back to
the bed,

("Well, morphine would make him hallucinate most of the
time. And he probably couldn't focus on things too well. Oh, like
eating. They probably gave him morphine.")

but not enough: never enough for, months, for weeks now
the hours are melting a pool where there's no sharp hot cold muffled but pain, only,

painpainpainpainpain

He folds himself down, in one of those spurts of movement,
beside, the old woman moves over and mumbles something,

"Sure," maggie said, and went to the kitchen and came back,
slowly, holding a bowl but still her sticks of arms pressed into her
sides, she bent over him; brought the spoonfuls of soup to his
mouth, slowly, dribbling, can't, can't

"poppa"

quietly; wiped his chin. He quavered something. She put the
bowl away and lifted him down and under the blankets, next to
her mother, mad and bright-eyed beside him. Now only his
thatch of white hair, one hand and those rigid eyes, show, fixed
straight up, staring at

"come on into the kitchen."

There is a pot on the stove; a phone; a light bulb hanging, harsh, in this decrepit place, so hot yet the cold is a presence: it presses in on the windows, the walls, and maggie's voice is strange, vague—but still, it is one I can share with her.

". . . trying to get him in a hospital. can't find a doctor to help so far. he's a bastard, you wouldn't believe. . . but you have to go home now," she said. "Cairo could freeze. i'll be okay, really, this stuff dulls things. Go on. It's after midnight,"

and she smiled; and I left her there.

I drove, the vent gaping, over glass roads, I alternated hands, one steering, the other between my legs, all the way home, I saw the horn of her spine like that mountain's crest; and the purple sky, the snow on the ledges of that grim green-walled room where the old woman sits in bed with him, *all the way*; and her smile when I left her followed me up the road the drive to the dog

(chained out by that box of wood she'd built but it never got tarred; it never got any insulation at all, and he spent days there, howling; ice-pebbles stuck all over his fur. . . .

He rampaged in the house, hysterical. I crouched with him on the red rug. I hugged him. Wind came through the walls. The frieze of icicles hung down in moonlight like inverted witches' hats. We crawled in her sleeping bag and huddled, half-awake, until the morning.

"Mourning," she said, much later; dull-voiced, gestures spurting, "morning, mourning. Is it the same root, I wonder."

(*rrrringgg*

"tried to take him off it was so cold, but I was afraid and then he bit Charley. . . .No, Charley says he forgives him because he was very excited and didn't mean it. No, just barely broke the skin. It surely is cold—eight below last night. We got three pipes froze. Well, I guess we should be thankful we got any water at all, some folks don't. How are things? Is maggie? Are you going back down? Uh-huh. Yes, you call him. Won't that be good if he

271

can come, now. These are times you really need your family. . . ."

7 PM eastern standard

          rrringg

                    "emergency. . . .

no, there's no one on call who takes Welfare cases. We're full
up, anyhow, so is most of the city, in this weather, why did you
wait so long to"

          rrringg

                    "emergency. . . .

yes. Well there's Doctor Peters may be in the house, he sometimes takes, oh, no, sorry, he's out of town. The doctor covering. . . . No, I couldn't. If you leave your name and number, I'll"

          rrringg

                    11 PM eastern

                    "supervisor's desk. . . .

no, I don't think. . . no, there isn't a bed in the house. Sorry, I
can't hear you. What? Oh. Well, you could try"

          rrringg

                    "emergency room. . . .

the supervisor? You mean the supervising nurse? Doctor? There's
no. . . well, the doctor on call won't. . . . What? Oh, wait a minute, I think there may be. . . just hold on, dear, all right?"

          buzzz

"Easy now. Cold as hell out there probably he"

          "please don't jolt him"

"We're doing the best we can, MISS," the man said, "these
steps are. . . hey, watch out for that. . . Christ, JESUS. . . ."

*cold streets poppa stabbing red lights ice but warm inside
i'm here and the motor the bumping, siren, beginning to
whine mounting, easy, Miss, speeding howling now undulat-
ing a*

          SCCCREEEAAAAMMMM. . . . .

                              *

6: 12 A.M. thurs jan 21

*

but—if you get up close to that gray and black grainy stuff it
turns green. it's fir and pine and hemlock. to see it, though,
you have to get up on the mountain. you have to get close.
i think i've got that close to a sky, a few times.
perhaps if i could get close enough to a stone, i could
see its life.

19.

"Well, it's kind of hard to....Do you really think it would make a...? Okay, okay, then, I'll see what I can do. Yeah, I said, I'll check it out and get back to you...oh, say, Wednesday...."

("Just one more time before, I gotta go, baby. Sure, I'll be back in a week, like I said. Suresuresuresure,"

Adam said

it's the Cali-forni-a, *feel*-ing, a splinter of glass in his palm: won't come out. *Dial*, numbers that won't make letters that won't, can't, stop, dial again,

"Yes? Certainly, sir. *I'm* sorry you're having trouble."

*

"He's really coming?"

"Uh-huh. Tomorrow night."

"And I'm like this.... Oh, it doesn't matter." Her words slurred. "I think...I'll lie down a while."

She left the room, walking uncertainly. Jesse drew his finger across his throat and whispered,

"The old man. This morning. She doesn't know. Ann wants to tell her tomorrow she has an appointment. I thought tonight we could maybe take her out to a movie."

We went to a slick film, a shiny theater, and maggie so dazed in the midst of all that noise there's a long sequence showing an old man dying. It didn't matter. I think it hardly even mattered Friday what words were said behind a door as I waited with Jesse and Susan. Then a buxom, gray-haired woman came out, and maggie, slowly; uncertainly; smiled at each of us.

*

There is a table, not a coffin, in this room with its heavy furniture: still, polished wood, with cake, and bread and cold cuts on it. Jesse is cooking something. Tanta Bella eats and mumbles and seems the same as she did that night, but she's dressed now. Not in black. Only Susan wears black. maggie sits in a corner, her clothes as nondescript as her skin has turned, grayish, arms on the sides of an overstuffed chair, a bubble of foam at one side of her mouth, staring straight ahead, vacant. She falters whenever she has to speak, when she has to get up she moves slowly, her upper arms against her sides, very stiff, and her hands held out: palms down, the fingers spread, as though she's not sure of the ground.

"What's the matter?" Her mother leaned towards me. "Is something wrong?" the phrases staccato, and something avid in her face; said, "What's the matter with maggie?"

"Well—her father, of course," I stuttered.

"Oh. Oh, I see. Is that it?"

The small eyes darted away to Jesse, who put a turkey on the table,

some cole slaw? salami? delicious! just have a danish
(he said. she said. we said,
and all will be well. just a little. you got to eat
something kid more you got room more MORE
Is that *my* voice?

"No, don't. Please."

"but to see him," she mumbled, "just one more time. . . ."

"You won't see him. You'll see a wax doll. I swear, you won't see your father," I said, my voice rising,

"but. . . i left him there and. . . it's like i don't even know it happened. i didn't see him after, i lost him. . . ."

(*rrringgg*

"You'll really lose him if you go. What they do is grotesque. Makeup. Rouge. I don't know what else, but it's awful, maggie, I know what I'm saying. I was only a kid, but"

"That was Adam," Susan announced, "caught an earlier plane. He's at East Side Terminal now. I told him to just come over."

"I'm glad he thought of calling here."

"Yes. Since he went to the point of changing his plans," Susan said, "it would be too bad if he missed the party," and turned, before I could answer, and started talking to Bella.

There is a north window, light, but no sun touches the glass embroidered with flowers of frost through which I see him turn the corner; approach along the pavement barred with shadows bending in to the street he crosses, looks up, his eyes sharpening now he sees me, smiles, and I'm running out through the hall down the steps to the street door, opening, eyes and mouth and everything softening. . . .

Bright pastel-patchwork, a shirt of many colors against my cheek; the light jacket, open, a hand on my back, pressing; odor of cold and leather. An overnight case rests against my leg and his skin, fresh, only a little abrasive, cools mine.

"Feels like years," I said.

"Doesn't it? I can only stay a few days. This job. . . .'

"Yes. Aren't you cold?"

"Yeah, I kinda forgot. I brought a big sweater, though."

"Look, before we go in—so I can speak to Susan before—did you talk to Dad?"

"Oh, I talked to him, all right. Nothing."

"*Nothing*? I can't believe he"

"Yes, you can. You know what he's like," Adam said. "He killed Jake off thirty years ago. Why should he bury him now?"

"Okay. All right. I guess we'll have to let Susan help."

"We had a real bad one about it," he said, as we mounted the steps. "It's still not right. And besides that—well, I'm living, well, with this woman, in Mill Valley. It started out like just a sex thing, not really important, but"

"Living together isn't important? Sex isn't important?"

"Oh, hell, you know. It seemed one-dimensional. Before she met me she thought music was musical comedy. Now they've met her, and both of them have the idea. . . . Well, that's for later."

He opened the door; and Susan greeted him coolly, and Jesse shook hands and filled a plate for him, got him a glass of wine, but, he seemed to ignore Tante Bella; and, maggie. How could he not see maggie, crumpled there in her corner, the bubble still poised at the side of her mouth, but something spurting alive behind her eyes looking up at him now he waved to her; put down his plate and went to hug her, but, casually—as though he'd seen her last night; and moved away, downed his wine, got more, and started talking music with Jesse.

Susan was emptying ashtrays. Bella was trying to talk to me. maggie, eyes gone dull again, looked like a haggard rag doll someone forgot; and,

"What are you doing, Rebecca?"

turned my head, quickly, involuntarily, "What?"

"What? Hey, are you all right?" Susan said, coldly

. . . .

"Okay," Ann said on the phone. "Your brother has made it pretty clear he's not taking any interference in this new life of his for nobody. Right? You just be sure to stick around, then bring her in Monday to see me and get her shot. When is he leaving? Good. All you have to do is get through this weekend, then, and you're home free. Yes, I think so. You're sane enough, and she's doped enough, and he's selfish enough, to. . . . Yes. Absolutely. I want her out of the city while her father is being buried."

*

277

my father is dead. i am living. he lies in the earth pos-
sessed cold no human touch. it should be is still painful
but why don't i feel pain? I'm numb. feel nothing. can
hardly see the letters i write on this page. they say i live
yes i can imitate the motions.

*

The dogs raced out of Carrie's as we turned into the drive.
She must have seen us coming. They tumbled by the swing,
    "Nice puppy," Adam said. "She looks like a baby Cairo. Is
that the one...? What happened to the aquarium? Oh, you've
been sleeping upstairs? Well, while I'm here could I"
    "Sure. I'll move down where I was. How's your back these
days?"
    "Not terrible. I find regular exercise helps," Adam said, and
went out to chop wood. I replaced a cracked windowpane, maggie slept, mostly, and smoked, and looked at her candle. She ate a
mouthful of food three times a day at the table the three of us
echoed summer and autumn,
    "You ever see those wild dogs?"
    "Not since autumn. maggie met them once."
    "Oh yeah? What did they look like? maggie?"
    "uh, i" and stumbled into the couch, and abruptly sat down,
"don't...remember...."
    "Where are your glasses, baby?"
    "my...don't know. haven't seen"
    "I was thinking about you one day, you know? lying out in a
hammock, with a friend who wears thick glasses, like you should.
Lots of leaves and sunlight coming through them. I tried on her
glasses, and it looked like I'd slid inside an impressionist painting.
Big globs of light. Soft, really beautiful. Couldn't identify anything, just dark contours inside the lights or enclosing them.
Soft. It was all so soft. My friend said that's how she sees without
them."

"oh. yes i suppose. . .i think it's a little different"

"Uh-huh. I liked it. Hard to deal with practical stuff that way, but it would be fun to move in and out of it."

"Yes. I think. . .i need to sleep a little"

Kids skate on the lake. Men fish, this Sunday it's misty and warmer, but not much. We trudge around, around,

"Cézanne?" he said. "Utrillo?"

"I know what you mean. Something—whited."

"Yeah, that's it. I always used to sit on this stone. You sit out at the cove, don't you?"

"Sometimes. More on the wall. The cove is for summer."

"Summer," he said. "It's hard to imagine it here. I never again want to live in a place this cold. Get away, Cairo."

"Adam—what's going on?"

"What do you mean?"

"You seem, like, like a bad-tempered stranger. You've almost ignored maggie, and"

"And you?"

"No, I don't feel ignored. I feel like a distant acquaintance you're being very polite to."

"Well, you might be feeling some distance because I'm so deep into music again. And I'm tired. For weeks I've been working at nights, rehearsing, I'm not used to this daytime schedule. And there's the time change, of course. You know, there are really exciting things going on in music right now. It's going to change this culture, I mean the whole quality of our lives. . . ."

"I think Jesse said something like that a while back."

"Sure, he knows. He's part of it. So am I—and I guess I can't get very involved in anything else right now." He stood up. "Let's go back. I'm cold."

"Okay. Look, I wanted to ask you about the camera. . . ."

"You been taking pictures a lot?"

"A lot. Ice and trees and you know the barn up the road with the broken windows? I've taken two rolls just of that. I'd hoped"

"Sure, use it then. I won't. I wish I had time to help you set up a darkroom. It would be so simple. Maybe Jesse"

"I'll ask him. It's hard to imagine him maggie's ex-lover, isn't it?"

"Sure is. What the hell's happened to her? She looks awful. She's like a zombie or something. She was so...pretty," Adam said as he plodded along behind me, his eyes on the ground; and I stopped short, next to a big stone carved "Dave Morgan, N.J., 1960," I turned to face him and he nearly bumped into me.

"ARE YOU KIDDING?"

"No. I'm not. Don't look at me like that, I said I'm not."

      (rringg ringgg

"She's really a very good woman," he told Rebecca—

      and, maggie slept.

      (but, if you get up close enough to

      *

      (New York Airports Keep Left

"Well, I'm sorry I couldn't help more."

"Really."

"What's gonna happen with Bella, by the way?"

"The other people in the house will care of her. You know, they all take care of each other."

"Well, when I see you next you may be a photographer."

"I don't think so. I just want to take some pictures."

"Well, Jesse will help you with it. He's a nice guy."

"Yes. He is."

      (La Guardia Keep Right. Kennedy Straight A——

"I hope you get into darkroom work. It's good to work with your hands."

"Yes. Produce, produce. Feel no evil."

"That sounds like Dad, not me. That's one reason why he's so down on what I'm doing. I didn't even tell you about that. Well, it's too late now. But I just meant manual stuff can keep you from getting morbid.

"*Morbid*???"

"Watch the road. Cars still give me nightmares."

"Look, what... are you? What has happened to you out there? Like, why did you even come, you're like a piece of ice."

"Watch the road."

"My *God*"

"I came to help. And, incidentally, to get some things I left, and to see you. But yes, something's changed. I think I've finally... turned to the light, Rebecca; to the sun. I know you wrote you think you're a sun person. *Still*, you said. But I don't think you ever were one. And now you're sunk into something so dark you've forgotten what light is. You *and* maggie."

"Well, if you think that, why don't you deign to show us?"

"Believe it or not, I tried. I came with a lot of good energy that I wanted to give to... the situation. But you don't want it. You seem to be welded together, the two of you, in this thing you're doing. But nothing, *nothing*," he said, "is going to get me into it. I've had enough."

(United TWA Delta National Next Right

"Enough of what?"

"*Death. Insanity*. Wallowing in it. That stuff leads only one place and I came pretty close. As you know. Now I'm steering clear of it. That was the choice I made when I left—I didn't know it then, but I do now. I was saying, *not me*. No matter how much I cared for her, or for you, *not me*: I won't let you pull me down into your darkness."

*

A highway traces the coastline all around Brooklyn. It's hard to remember there's ocean so near New York. It's hard to feel grief on a beautiful, freak-spring day. I think I can't bear the hope of another spring, I thought, heading back towards Manhattan;

and, near the entrance to the tunnel, wondered:
Could someone's initials give a stone cancer?

*

Then there's the man who died laughing. Said, he started to laugh uncontrollably at his mother's funeral. Couldn't stop. They had to take him away, had to go to the hospital. It was something to do with the nerve cells in his brain, a deterioration, made him laugh. He died two months later.

*

30   *The Clinging*

> That which is bright rises twice:
> The image of fire.
> . . . .
> Six in the fith place means:
> Tears in floods, sighing and lamenting.
> Good fortune.

Sunlight glittered in splotches across the wing as Adam's plane descended over the Bay, bumped down, and then he emerged to: warm air, foggy but clearing now as they drove across the Bridge, and into the valley, he saw buds—tiny, pink and white on the fruit trees. The house seemed tiny and neat, the redwoods huge, Jeannie nervous.

"Oh, love, before I forget," she said, "some guy who leads a group in the city called, wants to talk to you."

"What group? What's the guy's name?"

"I don't remember. I have the number, though."

"Damn it, Jeannie...."

"I'm sorry. You know how I am with names."

"Yeah, unfortunately I do. Christ, it's neat in here. Did you clean up the house for me?"

"Sure." She smiled. "I spoke to your father the other day, too. You know, I think if you'd just"

"If you'd just keep your nose out of this, Jeannie"

"But I only meant that"

"In fact, why don't you just move over there with them? Then you can be one big happy"

"Oh, Adam"

"Well, don't hit me with all this stuff right away. I have to adjust to being here. And I'm sick of my goddamn family. Goddamn that rooster. . . ."

"Was it that bad?"

"Yeah. Bad." He sat down. "You don't know what winter is, do you. I mean, this place can be damp and nasty and give you bronchitis half the year, but it's not really winter—you know?"

"I guess not. I've never left California. I'd like to"

"Look, please don't get into your social-polite crap, okay? 'I'd like to.' 'That's just incredible.' 'I didn't know that. . . .'"

"I'm not. I wasn't doing that, Adam, I really would"

"No, you wouldn't. It's bleak. It's dismal and gray and frozen solid, you know, it's rigid, including the people, but they don't know it. They think they have real deep feelings, they pat themselves on the back for it all the time, but really they're wallowing in a very tepid stew. They're frozen into these attitudes—grief, pain, they, titillate themselves but, like ice, or stone, there are all these stony colors there, it's *dark*—they're locked into some kind of stony embrace with darkness. Death. I was, too. I thought it was very profound, like they do. They think it's beautiful, *real*, that's what they'd say, *it's real*, all that sorrow and woe, the whole damned culture, they really don't know. . . ."

"Adam? How would a back rub feel?"

"What? Aren't you listening? My *God*, I'm trying to tell you something that really means something to me, and you"

"I heard you. I understand, really I do."

"You cut me off in the middle of, look, I'm trying to understand something difficult, something that's very important to"

"Okay, I'm sorry. Go ahead."

"No, it's gone now. Why can't you listen for once, why the"

"I'm really sorry."

She put a hand on his knee; took off her glasses and looked at him, all contrition, the luminous blue of those eyes already softening him, but still, why couldn't she listen? just listen, he wanted to shout at her, listen, LISTEN to me. . . .

"Why don't you lie down?" she said. "Here, let's take your shirt off," gently, "That's it, love," and kneaded his neck and shoulder blades, strong hands penetrating to pain in the back of his head, knifing into his temples and sharp down his leg,

"You're so tight. I've never felt you so tight. Breathe deep," as she probed down into his muscles he felt it start; near the base of his spine, where the tears were trapped in all those secret recesses, but moving up, slowly, now through his back, *breathe into it*, pushing them out of his shoulders, neck, eyes spilling, wrenching it out in a long salt flood and with it the corpse of a self that must have died long ago,

"'After the first death,'" he mumbled.

"What?"

"Nothing. Line from a poem. I guess I'm through."

"Here's some more Kleenex," she said. "I'll be right back."

Cool hand on his cheek, lifted. Tissues littered the floor. Adam turned on his back, and air seemed to course through his muscles but there was still a knot in his chest. And still his head ached with, "if you'd just," "too stubborn," *no*, he thought, sitting up, abruptly. The knot felt rigid, a marble of pain, but, *I can't; I won't*, though, *soon he, too, will be, dying, and he's your FATHER*. . . .

"Want some of this?" Jeannie knelt beside him and put a cup near his nose. "It's Irish coffee. I got it special for welcome home, but it didn't seem right before."

"No. I never cry you know really"

"Oh, stop. Why can't men cry without being ashamed of it, ever?"

"Lousy upbringing. You know, I guess I really needed that."

"Whenever you're nasty, you do," she said, and crawled in next to him, and pulled up the covers. They sat sipping the strong, hot liquid through cold whipped cream, the window darkening, rain now again but the warmth of,

"I made it. Jeannie, I made it back. . . ."

"Shhhh. Quiet. Just sleep tonight," she murmured; but skin so smooth he didn't want to sleep; didn't want to stop the *feeling* —emotion and touch combined, he thought, that delight, welling up and flowing, into her, into him, sweet as it never had been, and her blueblueblue iris, huge black pupil reflecting his face,

Are you Circe? bewitching men into animals here on her island, the magical powers her flesh held so strong he no longer cared; cared only for skin rippling hollows filled with blue shadow and swelling, dunes, as he touched her turning, *so purely wanton, Jeannie*, so wantonly pure, again, *touch*, his joy in her joy in, giving his greater? Christ stopped on the seventh note of that scale. There's no difference, he finally understood in his marrow this giving is taking is pleasure mounting up through his abdomen vibrating inside his brain now everything shimmering melting the difference between them dissolving there's no, between, only, one, and: one who loves is not lonely.

*

A man goes jogging along a road in the sun. A plane comes down from the east, but not across water. It lands, but the airport is small, and there's no fog. It's a red, white, and blue day, lazy and warm, but still January: at 3 P.M., mountain, time. . . .

Smoky cat on a woodpile. The trees had white hair this morning. On the porch, Sossa licks one paw: ripped flesh lined with pebbles of crystalized blood melting now in the sun turning house beams to round, brown witch-faces. Long white hair hangs, framing them, icicles, weeping inside, elongate, crinkling, blue and water and through them I see the gnawed hoof.

Flies lie on their backs. askew, against the glass they have delicate rainbow wings. Flies' corpses litter the rug. Taptap on the roof this whole long day the Chinese guy in that book has followed me, showing his photos: *refinement*, he said, *of torture. The art of*. They'd cut out someone's genitals. Where there was some-thing fleshly a splotch then blood pouring out then a hole now another book told a hole where some face had, heads had, rolled down the steps in a film and then in my dream the top sliced off, oh godgod—just that bare equation: common to all vital

(pulse=flesh=pain=am) is, pain, I will, *will* to am-not
but, then—

I couldn't follow you, love; so how could you talk to me? couldn't lose my self so deep in the veins' blue pulsing the beat draining life out of, what me could I have planted then on what firm shore for: all of us? needed some death, dead-aliveness or numbness, at least, built in, to stand on or cling to life—in water last August; or dirt, so soft that Christmas morning; and and now, 6 P.M. eastern, three pacific, or four mountain, time, time, ice frames wood's density sliced through by sun but still the bone remains rigid; past tiny spinning lights in that field, the out-line. . . .

White sparkles, and bronze—afternoon-light. Wild wheat thrusts up through the snow, and blue smudges holes in a white moon almost full, rising opposite, almost exactly in line with the sun. 5 P.M., mountain. Clouds flame, slate-blue footsteps, my own, blue shadow walking beside me clearly but, only the top of the carcass shows. All the rest of the bones are scattered under the snow turning pink, every particle distinct, changing, mauve, changing, blue, blue granular, then a purple tinge suddenly, high up. . . .

Yes, I know. We are fragments. I know—we'll melt back to the whole hole face scrotum no-thing, and all, all we've never left—all of the masks of the Night Mare whinnying up on her rock with the purple sky and her blue eyes laughing, the blood dripping staining her white teeth, yes, even she; even we, will dissolve and become

. . . .

But, I couldn't follow you; shouldn't even have tried. That's a path one can't choose. I know that now it has chosen me, as then, as long before, it had chosen you.

VI.
RESERVOIR

20.

The term metamorphosis describes a miraculous transformation in most insects: for example, the change of the plodding caterpillar into the winged moth. But to dwell on this change may lead one to miss the real nature of the overall development of the insect. The moth is not a magic creation of the caterpillar. The magic newcomer is rather the caterpillar itself, which, almost waywardly, has managed to interject its form between those of eggs and adult. Two transformations occur: first the ancestral pattern deep in each egg gives way to the odd caterpillar, then the caterpillar recedes and the ancestral form asserts itself in the moth.

*

in dark red February
there were three moons, a mist
and a dead star

•

rim of a world
an edge to time
the bank is a dark wave, rearing up from its
cradle, bier, hollow groin, with a crest of frozen foam
she walks
in a blind land

maggie

is sick with the cold white light of a forest around her.
stars like splinters of ice above the wall, or, under its
shadow, *see*, twigs like hieroglyphs scraggled all over the
slopes; words; alien, but comprehensible, almost. she. . . .
        dribbles a little into the snow; thinking, *sleep*,
thinking *no, promised*, thinking, as Cairo nudged her,

> space is time frozen.
> people are processes.
> what will happen when spring comes?

*

Look at that picture, *that* one—above the skull, a pin stabbed
through it, the paper curling already brownish and slightly out of
focus, look: at maggie bent over a sketchbook, her elbows
propped on the page, head in hands, she sits at the side of her
bed. She had tried to draw Jesse, who lay there next to her, I can
see one shoe; a leg; half an arm across her back and the hand on
her shoulder. A hoop of earring lies fallen on her cheek, so incon-
gruous now her body is slumped in a shape of despair—she had
found her facility gone; the lines awkward, light and tentative,
as her writing turned light, and tentative, smaller and smaller,
until it could hardly be read, yes: deciphered and read,
    i feel like i'm trying to form water with my bare hands.
    Whitish gloom like a wall lies just outside the doors where
strips of wood make crosses on all those panes I had to replace,
again and again, Tonta sits, a prisoner looking out, *picture*,
Tonta—the high white hump of her back, lone, wistful, intrepid
—beside a jacket slung on a chair; a dusty curtain; a dusty rug,
no, that layer of dust couldn't show in the photo, but it was
there: powdered weariness burning the eyes, in the nostrils, a
suffocating dejection in, winter, stale air fills the dusty, drafty
hothouse where maggie. . .slept.

292

Jesse came, with his trumpet, camera, coffee, grinder, and Chemex pot; so we drank New Orleans brand straight after dinner and *café au lait* with breakfast and second breakfast, big, lush meals maggie hardly tasted. Jesse set up a primitive darkroom for me in the bathroom, and posed, and posed for maggie when she woke up; big, ebullient, Jesse went tromping around in the snow, packed into a bright blue parka, red scarf, and his sleek brown skin, laughing richly; or he'd play scales or little improvisations; or cook, or talk in his deep mellow voice, live eyes and all that warmth, by Saturday, afternoon of the fourth day, I couldn't stand it. I took my sleeping bag and went to the reservoir.

Snow was spilling over the wall, a sheen like silk, at twilight, the patterns etched in the cracks stand out. The path is a glittering crust; the lake white on white turning yellowish near the bank there's a patch of ice like green glass and one star reflected, Venus, I think; and Jupiter, almost exactly in line with her, higher up. Sossa flounders behind me; now she warms my leg as I sit and look at the woman-contour of hills from Adam's stone, *no, my stone. I re-claim . . .*

what's reclaimable. Not enough. Not nearly. Under Sirius, throbbing blue-white needles of light, I climbed back up.

Cold seeped in through the plastic I'd used for groundcloth. I slept, woke, slept and woke, later, shivering. Clouds like smoke gray oval, *a devil moon*; and so cold I stuffed Sossa into the bag with me, wedged Cairo's big head against my neck and again slept; fitfully; then at dawn, exhausted, I started back.

It was just a moment, near the beech grove: the dogs ahead, but neither barked, so I only saw him coming around the bend at the instant he took the rifle from his shoulder and pointed it, first at Cairo, then at Sossa. I screamed, *"don't you dare point that gun."* He froze: snarled something; pushed past me.

"It's the kid from across the road," I told Jesse. "They're a real clan over there. We had trouble with them about a cat, and since then"

"You better not let the dogs run loose," he said.

293

"You mean walk them every day? Like in the city?"
"Unless you want to take the chance."

I stare at my glass. Sun sparkles through burgundy—cold red, heraldic. There is an earthen dish of beef and mushrooms, Jesse has put on the table, coarse bread, sweet butter, white cheese we are eating with gusto while maggie, between us, takes a mouthful; smokes; gnaws her nails, smokes, then when there's nothing left but one pile of butts and two pools of congealed fat, she picks up the dishes, one by one, or, two, and one, hunched over them, arms at her sides, slowly, slowly, she carries them into the kitchen.

"Let her," Jesse said. "She ought to move around some. When Grace was crazy, it was good when she did stuff like that."

"Grace was crazy?"

"Oh yes. Is, crazy, in fact, but fairly lucid right now. She swings in and out of it."

"You seem to have a tendency. . . ."

"Yeah. It's been noticed. But," he poured more wine for both of us, "you're not."

It's warm; Sunday; snow dripping down and the sound of water. I feel tired, bruised from my night on the ground. We all go to stay at Seventy-Seventh Street tomorrow Grace will be back, but, "No, I. . . ."

"Okay. I might come up next weekend again, with Grace, and bring you some trays and bottles. How's that? Meantime, you do your homework. Hey, how 'bout some coffee, lady?" as maggie stumbled back, and looked up, vaguely, and mumbled. "What?" Jesse said.

"said, i think i need to sleep a little. . . ."

*

294

ann—i want my spirit back!
(february 4)

i want i need desperately in order to live, since i made the
choise, my spirit. my drive to live not just vegetate as i
have been for years. i remember my spirit. it lived. it
threw things, destroyed, but it was always awake to
create. if this cannot return i have not returned. i want to
live fully. burst again. see color again. laugh. hang from
trees. be mystified again. i want to drink wine again
and feel its warmth. is it possible to—regain energy? feel
people again. wonder. i am experiencing an emotional
lobotomy. cannot feel my father's death. or have i felt it
already / before the actuality. what is it i feel missing?
and paranoia—everyone is suspect. cannot control
though i know better. they have created a franken stein
and are now trying to make it work. an experiment i am.
even if i cut myself to prove there is blood. so what. they
could have dyed the embalming fluid. i always thought i
was missing an ingredient. what if i'm right. are my
thoughts being programmed? and my suspicions are
escapes which are a freak of the experiment.

can they hear me?

*

There was a regular back-and-forth routine developed: Monday,
leave dogs chained out, deliver maggie to Jesse who takes her to
Ann and then to her shot while Rebecca teaches and everyone
sleeps at Seventh-Seventh Street; Tuesday, teach again shot pick
maggie up and drive home. Cook. Walk. Pictures. Darkroom. Et
cetera

. . .

At the beginning, she drew—most faces and bodies, but so
inept an unwilling child might have done them; or skulls, or skeletons, organs hanging behind the ribs here and there a vein or a

tear duct. Later, patchwork faces, and beasts sometimes whimsical, sometimes crudely devilish. Later still, shapes like protozoans, lots of them: large, small, spinning greenyellowbluepurple cilia out of a central bright eye in spirals. And notes. And later... nothing.

"*i cannot penetrate the page,*" she wrote.

She tried to do chores, at first, she would taste all the soups and stews I made, one mouthful, watch me finish, then clear the table, slowly, a sleepwalker, rigid, the arms at her sides, hands held out in front of her, wearing that huge, black dressing gown, tattered, her face grayish-yellow, she would bend over the sink; wash one dish; then another; and then, an, other; and then, like the SS guard I'd begun to feel like I was, overseeing forced labor, I shouted,

"STOP IT!!!!"

She looked at me, dully startled. The bubble of foam at the side of her mouth dribbled down, slowly, glistening, then renewed itself.

No chores after that. No dishes. Still, there were tacit rules to which she conformed, *viz*: maggie will sit at the table twice a day. maggie will not fall asleep with a cigarette, or cut herself while Rebecca is out on a walk or locked in the darkroom filling with chemicals, now, amid funnels, graduates, with the acid smell of the hypo pervading and stumbling around in the dark,

"rebecca? c-could i use the toilet?"

"Wait. I just have to finish. . . ."

but, sometimes I took so long she would go outdoors—cold, in February, but it's hell getting film on the reel when you have no knack, you can ruin your negatives; so, "just a minute," again and again, and then there were long translucent strips hanging up in the shower; and then it is two or three or five A.M., and, energized, now, I-Rebecca, have fallen in love with, the night is, a space to wander; through woods, on the lawn, near the sculpture I made in a different life, or swinging over the creek, high, wide-awake to the savor of wind, of world, yes, despite the hell of it—

night is beautiful to me now; and would not be, had it not
been for her.

*

(february 6)

empty page for emptiness

*

Grace and Jesse arrived that next Saturday morning; and Jesse
and I walked up to the bridge that afternoon, leaning over the
railing, he told me about the time Grace killed a kitten. Said, *she
had to kill*—the words, dropped lightly, with hardly a pause,
seemed to cling to the concrete surface beneath our feet; so I felt
their echo as Jesse continued to tell about how he'd known she
was too far gone to go out, and so he had got a kitten for her.

"Then it turned different," he said, looking towards the
point. "It got—playful. With the kitten, and, each, other. It was
so much fun it seemed for a while like maybe she wouldn't, have
to."

A shaggy tree hangs, suspended, it seems, below the bridge
near the spot where we hopped from stone to stone to wood and

onto the ice, and across the lower lake, where men were fishing through ice, said, *she strangled it*; slowly; avoiding the central current and hardly speaking, now, up to the wall, but the stones spoke—not quite words. We stood there a while, our fingers numb and blue beginning to streak the banks, before we climbed out.

It was almost dark when we got back and found the sunroom cold and dark and Grace and maggie asleep in maggie's bed together. They'd opened the sleeping bag into a blanket for both of them. Cairo rushed in, someone moaned, and two heads turned as one as I snapped on a lamp, four eyelids opened, looked at us, narrowed, then closed again, and the heads—one black, one copper—fell back on the pillow together.

They got up for dinner. Jesse and Grace slept in my bedroom.

"It doesn't bother me, really," he said the next day, "at all," as he posed for me—I must have thirty-five shots of Jesse, nude, that day, and one of maggie in the sunroom drawing Grace, who lies on her side: black slacks, black sweater, black hair and the dogs' prone black shapes. An ashtray is perched on the edge of a chair. The pipe cuts across one top corner. Behind the Japanese lantern, there's a dark square: a painting maggie did years ago, black and mauve in a shape like clouds, a vagina, or,

"A mouth around which the world turns," she'd said.

"*What?*"

"It's not original. Some surrealist said it."

"That's chilling."

"Kind of. Somehow I just had an impulse to look at it."

"I meant the phrase."

"I know." She sits in a straight-back chair near the bed, at an angle that highlights her spine. You can see each vertebra sticking out of the humped back, all the way to her neck; and that strange little hoop stuck into her earlobe,

"*oh, where has form gone?*" she wrote, "*to a place from which it will not return?*"

Grace came to me just before they left. "Listen. Does this woman Ann know what she's doing?"

"I hope so."

"So do I," Grace said. "Because to me she looks catatonic."

*

The larva is a creature with no wings and a single goal: consuming food. If we watch the activity of any caterpillar, it is soon obvious that its major business is eating—in fact, the caterpillar might well assert it lives only to eat. Everything else it does, except for habits connected with its transformation, is subservient to this activity. It is a glutton, and its whole structure proclaims it.

The species has thus acquired a twofold mode of existence because of which it has the advantage of two environments during its lifetime. One is appropriate to the functions of the young, the other to the adult. The young insect may develop forms suitable to its own needs, but always eventually it must return to the structure of the adult.

*

And so, is this what you're like, madness? Dreary? Endless? like this sad month, every day seems, 8, 10, 14 of February, endless, but—there is a timelessness to it; an apathy,

"Life saving," Ann said, "on the most literal level."

"Is it? Really? *Really?*" I said.

"Oh, yes."

. . . . .

Giant shapes rise out of the valley floor—transparent creatures of smoke, they squat astride an unmarked equator, under a sickle moon imbedded in blue, the spotted horse and the black one leap up; seem to kiss; as I knock on Carrie's door, the orange of leafless bushes lining the road looks richer; deeper.

"We got a great idea for a job for her," Carrie said, and looked at Charlene, who laughed. "But, maybe I shouldn't"

"Oh, go on, Ma, tell her."

"Yes. Tell me."

"Well. . .in Central Park, you know." She raised both arms, held them out in maggie's posture. "Pushing, baby carriages?"

Still, Charley fed the dogs when we went to the city. Charles pushed the car when it balked; and Carrie was *there*—until

"The end of the month, I guess," she said. "Maybe sooner."

"But why?"

"Oh, that bastard is raising the rent. You ask me, it's to make us leave. We never did get along with him. And, well, we haven't paid this or last month yet. Charles can't hardly make any sales at all, and even with Charlene's husband kickin' in some, turns out he's not so bad, you know?" and smiled at her daughter, "It costs too much to live hereabouts. It's a bad time, I guess, maggie, I mean Rebecca, you want some coffee, don't you? Maybe Florida. Charles' brother said he might want to. . . ."

"The end of the month is only two weeks."

"I know. It'll be next weekend or the one after. Oh, well." She poured coffee, sat down, and pushed a big red heart full of chocolates across the table. "Have some of Charlene's Valentine candy, why don't you. She don't need it."

"Neither do you, Ma. The way you've been at 'em."

"And neither do I," I said, but I took one.

Carrie laughed. "Don't think none of us do—except maggie. Now, why don't you bring her down, and we'll feed her up a little?"

"She won't eat."

"Well, we could try. Do her good to get out of there, anyways. Oh, I know, she wants to stay in that cocoon of hers, but maybe you ought to, you know, tug a little. . . ."

She smiles. the hairs on her mole quiver. I take another candy, gnash at it, throw on my coat, and run out. . . .

The horses have moved to the other side of the field. There are three now—a white one has joined the others, a beautiful mare I'd never seen before that Valentine's Day with maggie, shivering down the drive in early dusk. I grip her elbow to steady her—bones, only bones she seems hardly strong enough to support her coat. The snow curves around us, blue hollows darkening, outside the big room, the fire, the presences—Carrie, Charlene, the baby, now Charley home from playing across the road with the Brenner girls, and then Charles comes lumbering in, shouts a few hearty phrases, and turns on the news,

San Andreas fault. . .earthquake. . .evacuating. . .
northern California coast according to. . .tidal flooding. . . .
"My God, you're shaking like a leaf, girl."
"n-no, it's. . .home i need to. . . ."
"You come on closer in to the fire. I'll get you a blanket. Now, what on earth"

(-quake, tidal, flooding

"It's that *he's* out there, maybe," Carrie said. "Is that it? Adam? I'm sure he's all right."
"Why, sure," Charles said, his small hooded eyes fixed on maggie, "it's only the little places had trouble. And even there. . . ."
"Why don't I just get you some nice, hot tea?"
"no, please. . .thank you. . .i. . . ."
"Oh, now that's too bad. We was hoping you'd stay for dinner this once. You sure you couldn't, now? maggie?"
"No. no. thank you, please, thank you," and all the way home, shaking, all night, *please,* and all morning, shuddering, *thank you,* suddenly, then I see—she's mimicking California: that golden calf quaking forlorn with all its fifes and fiddledrums falling to fire; to salt; to the sea, and, drowned, and left me alone with her out on this cold peninsula,

("Are you okay?"
"Yes. no. i can't. . .breathe. . . ."

and I grasp her shoulders, trying to pierce the film that dulls her eyes and reach through to their life with my own, life-energy sending her warmth and words to combine into solid ground; or a line. . . .

Her face clears, suddenly. "Yes, that's right. i was always scared of earthquakes. tidal. . .i'm scared of the wall, a little. did i tell you?"

"You may have. You just looked so much like it, I had a hunch"

"It was a good one," she said: the shuddering gone, but her gestures still spurt like Jake's did—she's mimicking him like she did the earthquake—a ritual prayer, her spurts of words, of steps, a mime of debility, in terror that the shock of her eighty-five pounds might set off a hidden bomb....

"It's all right. It's night. Remember?" (Fifteen minutes a day, reaching in to her, floundering there in those waters.) "It's all right," I tell her. "It will come back. I promise. It all will come back together. It's always there. You can't lose it, you just lose sight of it...."

Touch...her soft, pocked cheek. The eternal bubble of foam dribbles, *touch*, her fingers yellowed, chewed, and the sour smell as she moves to strike a match; puff; cough in spurts, and whisper,

"Yes, but how long?"

"Soon, baby. Hold on. A little longer."

*

When the larva is large enough, it stops eating. At the pupal stage, maggot, grub, caterpillar, all these worm-like forms, revert to their ancestral appearance. The word 'pupa' comes from the Latin 'doll' and many insect pupae resemble an infant wrapped in swaddling clothes. They are helpless creatures, not eating, unable to move except by wriggling their bodies. Although most pupae look dead, like mummies, profound changes are taking place under their surfaces. At some points during the breakup of old forms and the creation of new, the pupa's contents can be mainly liquid. At this time, the ancient insect form will be reconstituted.

*

no humor—no possibility of.
                    (february 16)

that ingredient—where? what? never mind must make
do. can't. maybe next time around. where? here again?
don't know where is, here again? sleep black liquid to
float in promise oblivion never quite

                    way out? way in? up? down?
                    is it directional?

                    who is writing?

                            *

"Well, but." I paused. The phone crackled. "Ann, if something happens while you're not here. . . ."
"You'll call me. There's a number I'll give you."
"In Mexico?"
"Of course. They have phones there, too. But don't worry, it's
only for two weeks, after all. Just bring her down for her shot as
usual, and I'm sure you can handle things very well. . . ."

Snow, again: a thick white-gray world—there are no deep,
glossy blacks in this photo. It's badly developed. Even the dogs
are grayed as they make their way through the blast I stumble
beside them, fighting the air; fighting lethargy, heavy as weights
just under my skin, and a hand holds the base of my skull and
clenches. I don't like this picture. I know its name. Tell the photographer. Ask whatever bastard made and titled this print
'reality' why the hell I ought to accept it. . . .
     One crow flies over the field, heading north. Down the road,
cows huddle around a broken-down shack, has, a wide, glassless
window frame through which the only brown one is looking at
me: ears sticking out of the gawky head, strangely alone inside
while the others, all black with black eye rings on flat-white
faces, lie out in the blizzard, together.

It isn't the beautiful, dry snow we had. It's messy. Wood and cartons stick up through it, like an abandoned lot, now, alone, with no human sounds, as though my house has repelled every creature that's tried to approach, as I have repelled every man that approaches me, I thought: I must be mourning, my— brother?

(*rrringgg*

"Hello, maggie? Oh, oh, Rebecca? Yes, I.... Oh, she can't Why? Oh. No, I'm fine, it's just been a long time since.... What? Oh, yes, my friends. But. Is something wrong with...? Oh, really? No. I just thought she could maybe help with some laundry, but.... Yes. How are you? Oh, you have to go? Now? Yes, all right, but. Oh. Yes, yes, you tell her to call"

"maggie? are you awake?"

"mmmm nnn"

"That was your mother. She"

"mmn oh no no"

Still, she got up for meals. She walked Cairo. She walked to the store with me, one day, she wrote out plans for shelves, and she even talked about dance classes once—a semilucid moment, absurd, she could hardly coordinate her hand and a pencil: the lines she made jagged, heavy,

my drawings look frankensteinian

[she wrote, february 19]

form—i cannot see it any more. cannot draw it. my pen can hardly carry my handwriting much less form. if i am an artist that title in its least of meanings where am i now in terms of a lifetime. i am so terribly lost. gone away having deserted my only source of life. it will make me fight hard to see that light again. price one pays for desertions. even my dog seems bored. are you bored, cairo? or do i make you into a mirror? must admit the medication changes day by day—from this point all i can

304

see doing is drawing on the other side of the page—i've
got nothing else.

The plastic is opaque, now; diffusing a dull white light that holds
her, a mound of blue, sinking deeper each day deeper into the
pillowing, fuzzy waters of sleep; the year sloping up; I cooked; I
whispered to her; with the dogs I walked around the lake, hard,
soft, crust, slush, then back to

"maggie? do you want. . .?"

"wha? oh please oh no. . . ."

So, is this what you're like, madness? Sealed in a bubble
secreted of fear and grief hardening, semiparalyzed. . . .

Little monotone screams spurt out when she's startled. I read
to her, poems, play great swathes of music like stained glass
breaking that dingy whiteness, Bach; Mozart—masses, not *Don
Giovanni*. The telephone rings now and then, Jesse, Susan, the
motors make noise and the dogs and Tonta but mostly what happened was silence: hardly grazed by

"maggie? you want an egg?"

"n-no. not to eat. maybe i could just. . .hold one?"

"Okay. How about I boil it, just in case?"

"oh no please thank"

"Okay, okay. You don't have to keep saying that."

"oh. th-thank. . . ."

She smells stale; hasn't changed her clothes, hasn't washed
for, how long? Her breath is sour, the acne erupting all over her
face and foam dribbles constantly, now, *please*. must, *thank you*,
somehow propitiate this *please* dragon, this, *please*, demon,
thank you, this SS guard going wild with, *please*,

"You don't have to do that I'm not a stranger I'm ME," I
scream; and maggie murmurs,

"thank you. . .?"

How much of this is starvation? How much is dope? I can't
remember the names of those chemicals circulating in her, aug-
mented each week, Ann told me once, but, she can't even give the
injection; sends maggie to a doctor, and

do they know what they're doing?

I thought, then, someone could really *know*. Walter Stark, for instance, or some smart doctor, some grownup—I knew I wasn't one of those. They *knew*, and I was guessing, muddling, my fears thrusting out in sharp points at the dogs or transmuted to private ecstasies late at nights on the path, or sagging to spasms of self-disgust, ugly visions of fat hanging down from a cow-body led to a program to take weight off me while putting it on maggie, with notes, computations in calories, protein, etc., and globs of chewing gum I would leave in books, under chairs, stuck to sheets,

"I don't mind if you sleep with Jesse," Grace said. "I mean it. I really don't."

"*Don't!*" maggie almost shouted that night; sitting up, her eyes wide, enunciation perfectly clear, as lucid that moment as when I'd first met her, how many lives ago. "Don't take the chance. She means it now, but later—listen, believe me. She's homicidal. I *know*."

She...*knew·* and fell back and slept and an hour later,

"maggie?"

"yes, oh please...."

I could have killed her. There was one moment I realized that—*on the most literal level.*

White powder blows over the wall. The trees are clogged with snow, snow on branches on stones like shreds of shroud tonight so alien I almost panic, but something else is driving me, up and around, the path a swollen rim I follow, soft butter-cream texture to it, under the

capuchin moon

-set; waxing; near the lake, I heard the hoarse screams of a dying animal rip through the seams of the night. Black branches stretched around me, the black sky; the crackling, crusty stars. I knelt in snow, afraid: reaching to feel what fear had made her mad. The dogs, tame shadows, following, I ran through woods

306

up steps through doors I switched the lights on, shook her, whispered, shouted, gripped, her, eyelids closed then opened, cringing, closed. . . .

I begged her to come back. I pleaded. An old woman's face lay toppled by the rim of the cocoon, it sent me screaming, rage of lovelessness, hers, mine, the dog was moaning, her face gray, and colder . after that. . . . "lentils—fiber boats," she wrote beside one group of strangle little shapes, then

"1st contest—Paul Klee
the feet
pinnacle in feet = zenith
future contest—other contestants have entered
the winner was judged to have
feet of Klee"

21.

Wings signalize the appearance of the adult insect. The adult only is able to fly. The adult only propagates the species. Some adult moths have no mouths; most adult moths do not eat.

*

Early morning. Groggy—again I've been up all night making prints in my big new darkroom. Last week I pushed maggie's drawing table into a corner, wedged her tools in the closet, built shelves and a work space and taped black paper over the windows. Still, it's not really light-tight, so dawn always stops me.

I make some tea and bring it in to the table, near maggie, lying inert, at six; at seven, the plastic turning gold, at seven-thirty, at nine, at ten she's just as inert, *muffin? no. coffee? y-yes....*

She drags herself up and sits at the table, limp, as I eat my muffin, she will sip coffee; slowly; she hasn't smoked for a week, but every day she's more listless, and now her face holds a question; and I say, "All right. I'll walk them both."

It's icy: I shiver along the path, almost up to the reservoir before I see something not right in the way the dogs roll around, too much, and snap, so different I walk home quickly and drive with Sossa to the vet, and he says, and then I say,

"But she can't be. She's too young."

"Well, I might have guessed a bit off," he said. "She must be nine-ten months now. Very delicate animal, small-boned." He let her go. She scrambled off the table and cowered, all ruffled, her eyes reproachful. "High strung, too, hmm? How does she get on with your cat? It was you, wasn't it, brought in a cat one Saturday night? Quite a while ago. Cut her eye on a door. . . ."

"Yes. She's dead. She got run over."

"Oh. Sorry to hear that." He turned and fiddled with some bottles. "Well, in any case, you shouldn't mate her now. Sometimes they aren't fully developed their first heat."

"There's a male dog living with us."

"Oh. Well, that will be difficult, yes." He turned back to face me. "The cycle takes about seventeen days. She'll only be fertile a few days in the middle but you can't tell when, exactly. You'll just have to keep them separate, somehow."

> *Let me tell you that the absurd is only too*
> *necessary on this earth.*
>   Nietzche
>   (taped to the bathroom mirror)

"Now, that's one I can understand," Carrie said when they came to say goodbye—Charles, Carrie, Charley, Charlene, her husband, the baby, Charles' brother, his wife, three kids, two cats, and a dog, all in two cars bound for the Florida Keys,

"No fuel bills," Charles said. "No heavy clothes. And cheap —hell, I hear you can pitch a tent and live off the fishing, practically."

"No, we don't have time to stop," Carrie said. "I wish we did, but, you know, they're waitin' on us. Well, my land, will you look at that dog. I believe he wants to come with us. Him and Charley. . . ."

"And I'd like my Ouija board," Charlene said. "Do you still have it?"

"Sure." I pulled the board out and gave it to the blonde girl.

"How is maggie?" Carrie said. "These past days we've been so busy what with packing I haven't had time"

309

"Not much different. I think she'd like to say goodbye, though. Let me call her."

"Oh, she don't have to"

"No, really. Wait."

I went in the sunroom, closing the door behind me, I shook the blue mound. I whispered, shook again, and she struggled up; came out, dribbling, and mumbled goodbye to each of them, then stumbled back. I walked out on the deck with them. Carrie lingered a moment, as the others clattered down.

"I'll really miss you, Carrie," I said.

"I know, hon. I'll miss you, too. I truly will." She hesitated, then put her hand on my arm shyly. "I just hope maggie can pull herself out of this soon. For the sakes of both of you."

That day, Sossa moved upstairs. I would lock Cairo in the sunroom when I brought her down across the rug, and lock her in my bedroom when I wasn't watching. He couldn't manage the steps, so I let her lie on the landing and look down at him whining and howling—he may have howled all through the two or three days a week we chained him out, no Sossa to warm him, now, she came with me to the city.

"Oh, it's so. . .obvious," Grace said. We all stared at Sossa's vulva, swollen bigger and redder each hour, it seemed, and set off by the fluffy black haunches, sweetly obscene.

"You sure can't miss it," Jesse said. "Come on, Rebecca. I'll go along while you walk her; help you chase all those *guys* away."

So I would walk in the gutter, holding Sossa, while Jesse shouted and threw things—none of the dogs on Seventy-Seventh Street missed the perfume she sprayed; and none of the dogs on Hollowbrook Road missed it. More came, and more, awaiting the damsel, who would emerge at the end of the leash I held in one hand, a fist full of stones in the other kept them a few yards back; but still some followed us up to the reservoir and back and then lay outside the door, Cairo pawing the glass that kept them away from that tantalizing aroma he lived with five days a week, getting crazier: tried to scramble upstairs, fell and lay there moaning. Sossa whimpered plaintively to him from her balcony,

"Romeo, Romeo, wherefore," maggie mumbled en route to the bathroom: such a rare flash that I almost dropped my watering can, almost screamed, *Humor*! but, a few minutes later, she'd sunk back back to vacancy.

"You have a dog to walk, remember?"

"oh, r-rebec—could. . .?"

"No. It's freezing out there. I won't take four walks today."

"But couldn't we just let"

"What? Let him break my arm if I take them both and try to keep him away from her? Or let the Brenners shoot him?"

She puts on her boots, her jacket, so slowly, and stumbles out, to the clamor of shrieking dogs, then, I have to watch, a zombie dragged at the end of the leash down the drive behind Cairo, she disappears in the dull white glow; then re-emerges, still dragged by a cord she holds that massive, black, moving hole I saw on Thanksgiving, the Unworld, I thought, that's: substance.

There were times I thought she might let him pull her into a fight; or fall and get dragged, or lose the leash and lie down in the snow or just wander away. Still, it was a week before I gave in: "He's your dog," I'd say. And, wherever I went, even down to the corner store, I took Sossa-Juliet with me.

"Haven't seen Mrs. Woolf for a while," said the grocery lady.

"Oh, they've left. They moved out last week."

"They've *what*?"

"They've moved. Is anything wrong?" But she didn't answer.

A few days later, a strange car came. All the suitors set up a howl, as I walked out, they ran down the steps, surrounding the car. I looked over the railing. A man rolled his window down halfway, called out, "Charles Woolf?" then, looking unhappy, drove away.

Another man came the next day, and another, and more, all from stores or companies, all of them harried by the pack leaping up at their cars. Some got out defiantly; some shouted up from half-opened windows; and finally one young man from Montgomery Ward told me they'd left unpaid bills all over the county.

"In Massachusetts, too, that's where they lived last. And probably other places before that. It seems like their way of life," he said, disgustedly. "But I could lose my job for it. I'm the sucker decided to give them credit." He aimed a kick at a yellow hound. "If you happen to hear from them, tell them I'd like them to call me. Not that they will. Mr. Wagner, in credit. Okay?"

It's muddy. Even one step off the deck is muddy. Boots on, boots off, mud in the house, in the car, and I no longer walk, except at nights. I drive. I squirm, in this flesh unwilling to, *wake up*, I pace and putter and dream escapes, *too soon*, but all my bones feel weary. I walk both dogs now: each on a short lead held to opposite sides of me. Once in the morning I drag us all out, and once near dusk. I put them in, then, come back to watch sunset: shadows subtler this month mountains merge with a sky blue-silvered, a moondusk color over the eastern peaks while red fills the west—such a radiance that I gasp when I turn, the cold wind filling my eyes. Lower down, yellow deepens to orange, the bands of red descend, then it's blue all round, a cold slate blue, and those curving dunes even more like a woman's flesh, unbearably lovely this moment just before it darkens.

It's now I breathe again: Venus setting as Sirius rises opposite, I will go in. I'll cook. We'll play out the dinner ritual, both of us hating it now, as maggie fades back in her blue cocoon, I will go to the darkroom; or out. . . .

It's so different, the night world. The sounds. The light. The way my skin feels, and my own shape approaching me through the windows or in that small mirror hanging over the back door. I can't see out; must either immerse myself there or continue the journey inside a space sealed by blackness—except for the moon. All those weeks, I went from my trays of images, always becoming, into the kitchen, and back, as the sounds of winter turned into the sounds of spring, I watched the moon change; the snow-to-thaw moonscapes gleaming, all that month, I thought of how she had loved this time: the night, a word
(*come on out. . . .*

Rebecca thought· am I becoming maggie?

*

february 22

there is nothing in life that interests me any longer. all
things seem foreign as though i were in another country
and don't speak or understand the customs or i'm too
weak of mind to try.

*

That Monday morning, the car wouldn't start. I pushed, as maggie huddled on the deck, pushed, it rolled down the drive, but
still it won't start; and phone calls, the gas station, waiting, late
finally then we were driving to Jesse's, late; to the doctor, late,
"well she'll get her shot tomorrow"; and, late, to school, teaching, late, then getting back I found: Grace holding maggie, rock-
ing her,
　　"i can't...breathe," her hands icy; eyes alive; panicky.
　　"Jesse's out somewhere," Grace said. "This started a couple of
hours ago. I didn't know her doctor's name. Goldstein? Gold. . . ."
　　"Goldfarb." I leafed through the phone book. "Here," and
dialed. The voice of an answering service clicked on.
　　"Yes, just a moment." clickclickclick. "Yes, Dr. Goldfarb's. . . .
No, the office will be open at ten tomor——no, I can't. Well, is it
a real emergency? Well, I'll have him call you as soon as"
　　"Please would you"
　　　　(choking, her head bobbing up down up down
　　"But," Grace said, "what do you think is the"
　　　　　　(*breathe*...two palms pressing cold spots, *in*, my head
　　　　　　is the, *breathe*, matter, *out*, elbows wedged in the floor
　　　　　　breathe, out-of, dust changing the shape smell of

313

(rrringg

alarm

"Hot drinks," a cold, stiff voice said. "And walk her. Yes, just walk her around until she calms down a little. What? No, I don't think it's dangerous. Just...what?" The stiff voice stiffens. "No. Bring her over at ten forty-five tomorrow."

(breathe....

"maggie. Hold my hands. Hold on. You have to get up."
"oh no please i"
"*Yes.*"

*(no—*hands stretch spinning my head *breathe, in,* faster a shirt sleeve spin fast *breathe out in* but that woman is really a

zoom

"Here," Grace said. "Tea. Careful."

(witch. *breathe. out.* a wolf. *breathe, in*-to, a ginger-bread house bulging *out* light slicing *in breathe* and *out* jamming time *in out* in gaping

zoom

zoom

zoom

zoom

SNAP

❋

Snow covered the road, on that silent drive back home. The house was cold. The skin on the sunroom windows sagged, wrinkled and dusty but glowing white around maggie: she crawled in her sleeping bag, right away, but her eyes stayed half open,

"maggie?"

no. thank you. please. thank you. please please
"Where are you? Come back, maggie"

now no now no focus in-to, no, jagged weight makes the bed sag jagged sounds cold hand sharp the effort of "maggie please just"

don't tell. don't tell her about the proprietors.

"What?"

"they're, i mean, we, i, called" and blurred. Sharper voice cutting through.

"*What?*"

"we're all laying in bunks. in sleeping bags."

"Lying."

"what?"

"No, sorry. mmmm mm Please."

"Well—inmates, kind of. in sleeping bags. and this little old Jewish couple, like gnomes, take care of. . . .they're the proprietors."

(stop. don't. tell. what? patterns make, sound? carves in air healing, can? shapeless? can air bleed? no too cold too

"But what do they do? What happens?"

much. can't. stand. haven't shape air hasn't skin to cut

"maggie?"

"yyyes. they're. . .very kind. firm. know what's best for us. we have to ask their permission to go out of bunks to, yes, bathroom, too. sometimes it's granted and sometimes not. sometimes granted and then they take it back later. depends. what's best

(sinking back to the wrinkled skin of the, *you're an old bag*; but warm; sweet; blue-veined sleep

"What? maggie? *maggie?*"

"i mmplea nneed to"

then, "I," am standing near the glass door, snow dripping, high squeaky birds, calling, I'm dialing numbers, 2, 1, 2, one hollow spot in my chest, twinging, incredulity, *rrringg*, sinking into my belly, and even humor, but—is she going very, *very* far off?

"Hello, yeah?"

"Hello, Jesse? Can you talk?"

"What? Rebecca? What's happening?"

"Well, look, I'm, I'm worried. It's...she says she has these...proprietors. Little old Jewish people, she says, taking care of a bunch of inmates."

"What?"

"Yeah. She really believes it. She told me. She's one of a bunch of people lying in sleeping bags in bunks, and"

"Jesus."

"Yes. They need permission from the proprietors to get out. It's all for their own good, she says."

"Hey, you know, that's kind of witty," Jesse said, "when you think of the circumstances."

"Yeah, I guess so, but"

"She's kind of put herself into a nursing home. Really a pretty good one, sounds a lot more human than most. Even the sleeping bags and the little old people—what did you call them? Proprietors?"

"Yes, but Jesse"

"When does that shrink of hers get back? You know, I wasn't going to say anything, but, if she treats psychotic patients, she really should"

"Any day now. It's been almost two weeks. There's a number in Mexico I could call."

"Well, maybe wait a day. She just came out of that panic, that might be why. I could maybe come up, if you'd like some moral support—not tomorrow, but, say, Friday?"

"Oh, Jesse, could you?"

"Sure. I'll take the train and drive back down with you on Monday."

"Great. That would really help...a lot."

*

The growth of insects is characterized by a series of abrupt increases in size. Between them, there are long periods when

316

increase cannot occur because of the insect's hard external skeleton. These static periods end with sudden surges of growth that leave the creature squeezed wrinkled inside its armor coat. Then comes the molt. A completely new skeleton forms under the old outer layer. Then, splitting the old shell from head to thorax, the insect emerges. The captive growth can now expand into real increase in size for the new skeleton.

*

"i can't get rid of the feeling there must be four points or four lines in a triangle.
(february 26)

*

The little train chugged round the bend, that Friday, at 4 P.M., on time, and Jesse stepped off, put his horn and suitcase on the platform, "Hey," and lifted me in a bear hug. Relieved, but not quite comfortable in his arms, I leaned back to look at him.

"Well, you look like you're surviving," he said.

"Yes, it seems okay now. I'm still glad you're here."

And I meant it: laughing, all the way to the house, but, as soon as we went inside, it all went wrong. Wrong light. Wrong music, too loud, those arpeggios, whimsies that so amused me before grated now we were three painful solitudes moving around each other; now and then touching, sometimes, violently, or gently, but, most of the time—not at all.

"How can she sleep when you're playing the trumpet, forgodsake? She needs. . . ."

"She needs to wake up, if you ask me. Okay," he said, "but, shit, it's so different here from last time. It's like living in a glass case. I'm scared to move, like I might break a wall or something."

"Yes, well, you might."

'Maybe then it ought to be broken."

317

"Not now."

"When?" He moved closer. I shuddered. "My God," he said.

"I'm sorry. I'm really sorry. I don't know why...."

"You know what? You're going to have to get out."

"You mean leave maggie?"

"I mean get out of this place, the dogs, maggie, all of it."

"You didn't leave Grace when"

"No, but. That's different. We're not sixty miles from the nearest friend with no transportation except a car that won't start half the time. We don't have two lovesick dogs around whining and mooning, not to mention that crew on your porch. *And we're not both women....*"

"What does that have to do with it? Can't there be love between two women, for God's sake?"

"Sure."

"Thanks a lot."

"Look, I'm serious. There's a thing between you two that's both more and less than...." He shook his head. "Look, I'm really trying to.... Okay, I'll say it. You're neither one of you really lesbians. That's why."

"Why what? I was talking about *love.*"

"I know," Jesse said, as I got up to answer the phone. "I heard you."

"Hello? Oh, hi, Dad, how.... I'm fine. No, she's still sick. Oh, please don't start, we're doing fine and.... Yes, I know it's been a while, and yes she needs longer. No, I don't think I could now. I remember. Yes, thank you, I know I'm getting up there. Okay, sure. Hi, Bea. No, and look. I don't want to discuss it. Bea, I'll hang up, if.... I don't care. Well, Adam is not an objective observer, you know. He can say what he wants, just don't accept his opinion as gospel. Who? Well, what's she like? How can I, I've never met her. Oh, really? No, I can't come out now. *I can't....*"

"Sounds like parents," Jesse said.

"Yes. Sunday call hour."

"What they want? It sounded heavy."

"Oh, they want to talk about Adam's girl friend, who they've apparently fallen in love with, and want to get me away from maggie. They call this a trip to San Francisco for my birthday. That's all."

"Is that their price?"

"What? maggie for trip? No, but"

"Yeah. Well, basically, I agree with them. When's your birthday?"

"Two weeks from tomorrow. Thirty-six."

"Wow. Never woulda known. Listen, by the way, I was looking around in your darkroom. A friend of mine has this magazine, and he needs some animal shots. So I thought I'd take some of those prints down to show him, if that's okay with you."

"If it's *okay*? Sure. You really think they're good enough?"

"You just have to spot them. I'll show you tomorrow." He stretched, then grinned. "You ready to go to bed now? I mean, since I gave you all this information. . . ."

"Oh, Jesse"

"Okay, okay. I'm only mildly bitter. I'd settle for some of that good beef we had yesterday, is there any left?"

"Yes. In fact, let's have dinner. You get maggie up, and I'll get the food," I said, and fled to the kitchen, and slapped the meat on a plate, "*a lovely, sunny girl,*" olives, tomatoes, "*you really should meet,*" and silverware, "*think he's going to,*" napkins, "*marry,*" and Cairo's long snout sniffling, *leave me aLONE,* but: carried it out to where Jesse and maggie sat, waiting, silently, at the table.

"Sure will be good to get home tomorrow," Jesse said. "You spend enough time in a place like this you begin to grow *mold.* Want some wine? maggie?"

"no, i. . .thank you. . . ."

"She can't drink wine, what the hell, with that medication?"

"Oh yeah? Well, how should I know? You want some?"

"No. Get away, Cairo."

"Hey, you finished already?"

"No," I said, tartly. "I just want to go to the bathroom. If I can get there. Cairo, get the hell out of my way," I snapped,

319

But he almost tripped me: drawn by the blood flowing down between my thighs for the first time in months, that special shift in my belly, but, now? when the touch of a man, his breath, his proximity, even, makes my flesh shudder? when Adam, Adam will. . . .

Yet, so, again: I become woman.

maggie was back in her bag when I came out. Bessie Smith was belting it out on the stereo. Jesse sat with his feet on the table. I wanted to hit him; I wanted, but, *no, no,* and balling my fist up, I punched Cairo.

"Get away, goddamn it. . . ."

"He sure is after you," Jesse said. "You got your period?"

"How could you tell." I shoved the obtrusive nostrils away from my crotch again. "It will be really great to walk them tonight. I don't suppose you'd care to?"

"Oh, no, thanks. You go ahead. Have a *ball.*"

(moon of locusts

white, oval, rising over the hill there's a reddish cloud: a sweet before-rain smell this warm night the trees creak, counterpoint to the water rushing, the mud mixed with snow squishing under my boots as Cairo tugs and barks and Sossa pulls, too, and I pull at them, stumbling, and almost fall, heat tonight, everywhere, violence, and now I imagine a fight to the blood between Cairo and me: getting down, finally, down to the dirt, the kill. . . .

The path slopes. The wall's shadow cuts out the moon for a moment—only a moment, until we walk up around to the top of the dam. Snowbreakers still foam along concrete. The red cloud has moved. The dipper emerges, suddenly, standing on end near the tree tops—a giant question mark. Inside it, slowly, inexorably, a speck of light is moving from star to star.

22.

GYPSY MOTHS MAY ATTACK CALIFORNIA

A threatened attack by gypsy moths, small insects with a voracious hunger for all kinds of trees, seemed alarmingly close here, said state agricultural officials on Tuesday. The moths are travelling to California with innocent vacationers from the East. They have destroyed millions of acres of forests on the East Coast, officials said.

The moths are arriving in California with mounting frequency. Some were discovered beneath a truck Monday in Mendocino. Many have reached Russian River in the wheels of trailers. The insects' eggs have a velvety, tan webbing. The moths are insatiable during the caterpillar stage, i.e., throughout the summer. The caterpillars devour forest, shade, fruit and ornamental trees. One caterpillar will eat approximately one square foot of foliage every day. . . .

East Bay Chronicle

*

64 *Before Completion*

Success.
But if the little fox, after nearly completing the crossing,
Gets his tail in the water,
There is nothing that would further.

"No peeking, please," the little Thai nurse said. She put a
vase of long-stemmed American Beauty roses next to

(wake up, Mr. Stark. You have to. . . .
"What time is it?"

"Noon. There's coffee made." She smiled at him, briefly, then returned to the book she was reading.

"What's that you've got? One of my father's mysteries?"

"Oh, no, I gave them back. I borrowed this from the hospital. It's interesting," she said. "There's one part. . .let me find. . . ."

"Well, what's it about?"

"The trophoblast. Did you know it's the only tissue besides malignant tissue that invades another?"

"What? What the hell is the trophoblast? *What are you reading?*"

"It makes the placenta. What feeds the baby in the womb."

"Jeannie."

"Listen, it's fascinating"

"No, damn it, NO. You think we're ready for a child? Even supposing, I mean, do you think we're that stable?"

"Listen. 'The trophoblast is. . .somewhat like a tissue graft, but it is remarkable that this graft is not rejected. Ordinarily, if an attempt is made to"

"Jeannie. . . ."

"I'm not sure yet. I've only missed one period."

"Good, then we can do something about it."

"What?"

"You'll have an abortion, of course."

"I will not."

"What?"

"I'd leave you first. I'd go away and have the baby and never see you again."

"My God—you really would."

"For that, yes. Yes."

"Now, look. I'm just beginning to hear again, really hear, and my fingers. . . .If I have to get some kind of steady job"

"You won't have to."

"How could I not? You couldn't work for a year or two, or four, goddamn it, the thing is expensive itself, and most of my accident money is gone. How the hell could we have a kid, not to mention raise it"

"Well, for one thing, I'd get unemployment."

"That's peanuts."

"It's something. And my family might help, and your father said"

"What? You talked about this to *my father?*"

"No, of course not. We were just talking about the future, you know, casually, the other day when I stopped by to return"

"He's turned on to you, the old lecher."

"Oh, don't be silly. Look, we'll have to finish this later. I have to go. I'm late to work."

"Work? You're going to work?"

"Of course. It's one o'clock."

"Shit, you must have done this on purpose—bringing it up just before you have to leave. You can't leave. Call them up, say you're sick."

"I can't, not now. I'm sorry. I didn't do it on purpose, I really didn't, I'm really sorry," she said, and grabbed her purse and coat and rushed out to the car and he followed her, calling,

"Don't be late coming home, at least. For once in your life. This isn't a joke, you know."

She turned and looked at him: her coat thrown over her shoulders, straighter, somehow, she radiated a dignity he'd never seen in her.

"Oh, *I* know," she said, finally; got in the car and drove off.

He didn't want to go back in that house with its jabbering walls, *not now*, Adam thought. He started to walk. That idiot rooster crowed, shrill, echoing, down the road, *not ever*: to be what he'd seen, those sad giants weighted to slow death, cells drying out, almost visibly. . . .

The white line curved. A small path entered the woods, and he followed it. Only a few yards in, a dead porcupine lay across

323

the path, soggy, covered with needles. It was so apt to his mood he could hardly believe it was there. He walked around it, continued up the path, climbing, studded with stones and mushrooms. At the crest there was one spot from which he could see through the narrow valley and out to a blue haze of ocean.

He'd never been here before. He stood a while, looking down, hardly conscious at first of the words that were leaking out of some pocket of memory, from a class? a book? one paragraph coming to consciousness, now,

> *"The individual has to procreate only because death is part of its scheme of life. The individual has to die only because procreation is part of its scheme"*

like an incantation: the rhythm retaining a thought that had meant nothing to him at twenty, but now it resonated with: *how can we, she, we*; and his father's leathery cheek sagging over an obdurate jaw, still set, refusing forgiveness; and Bea's red-taloned fingers wrinkling the years and years holding onto that grudge,

> *let it go*

>> *cure means*
> *"why the hell did you marry"*
> *let her go, let it go. let go,*

and he started down again; running, almost, off the path, cutting through woods until, panting, he came out to a different part of the road.

A car sped by, spattering dust. Pebbles got in his shoes, cut his feet, burning, all the way back to the house he didn't want to enter, the *Chronicle* laying by the door, and the mail, so ordinary, still it seemed that: Hansel suspected that Gretel is really a witch and has always, *cut it out*, he thought, and slid down to the creek.

He took off his shoes and put his feet in the water. Roots dangled everywhere, dripping. Roots crawled like tentacles over the ground, coiled like knuckles, like in the fairy tales this place had always made him think about, ovens; suspicions; Becky devouring whatever it was she saw and would never tell except, *roses*, she'd said, and *a ladybug* flying home to her *babies*,

Oh, he could see it—they'd have to be married. Then Bea and Walter as grandparents they would come and coo on Sundays his blue-eyed Witchwife would read out of her magic book to them, *Work on What Has Been Spoiled, Inner Truth; The Cauldron*; and even massages after dinner she'd knead his father's glutted flesh as Adam wished she were here to knead his, breathe. *Breathe*, she would tell them, follow the bridge of breathe, *birth* —*Breath—death*, she'd drawn that for him once, glowing, Jeannie—her systems, so pat, *breathe into the pain*, so one-dimensional, but, the witch needs to: nurture; ought to have *babies, babies, babies*, ought to: *leave me?*

"Why don't you marry the girl already?" Bea had said.

"You want me to marry a *goy?*"

"Oh, now really, what do you think, since you're living with her anyway. Now if you and your father would just"

"Look, I won't crawl. He'll have to make it possible"

"Well, he can't make the first move, you know that. He's too old to change now. You're both so *unforgiving*," she'd said, her voice breaking. "You were so concerned for your uncle, but he...he loves you, don't you realize that? Does he have to be mortally ill"

"Is this what you called about, Bea? Because if he is"

"No. I called to talk to Jeannie. A friend of ours needs a doctor and I thought"

"Useful to have a daughter-in-law who works in a hospital, hmm?"

"Well, why not? That's not the point, and you know it. Your father and I both happen to like her—*very much*."

"You would."

"Why? Is that a drawback?"

Why—is that a drawback? *Why is that a drawback?* Draw back, back out of the trap, *let me out*, Adam said to the daddy-longlegs running around upside-down on the rock as he pulled his feet out of the stream. They were numb now. He hobbled back up to the house. Two letters lay on the *Chronicle*, and a card, a picture of rocks and on the other side,

*"Let me know when you're ready to start talking.
Walter Stark"*
Is that all he can manage?

He crumpled the card and threw it in a puddle, and then the
rage was gone, completely, leaving a blank space. *For him it's a
lot.* He carried the *Chronicle* into the house, ripped a few pages
out, and knelt to build a fire. The wood smouldered. Adam started to crumple another page, but a headline blared at him, "GYP-
SY MOTH...," and he tore the column out, laughing a little.
Cure means, walking away from that, too, he poured a drink,
returned to the hearth and tried again with smaller kindling, *forgiveness means*, something quieter, sadder than he'd thought:
separation. The wood ignited. *My sister, my enemy—so we re-
main together*. He put a larger log on, watching the flames as he
knelt there he sipped his brandy, the house like a drum for the
rain, playing riffs all around him, *but*, he thought, *now what?*
A baby?

(cold coins on his palm on the floor, throw,
two and two and three and two and

40 *Deliverance*

Nine in the fourth place means:
Deliver yourself from your great toe.
Then the companion comes,
And him you can trust.

*

Every animal alive forms three layers at the beginning of its
development. Every layer, in every species, becomes the same
kind of organ. The ectoderm is basis for man's skin, the scales
of the fish and the feathers of the bird.

"i want to eat something that rhymes with i"

(march 8)

. . .

"Hello, Rebecca? It's Ann. Great, great, I really needed a vacation. How is she? Okay, could you . . . fine. Two o'clock. I'm going to take her off the shots, not today but next week. We'll see
what happens. Uh-huh. Well, I'll call him, but that makes me
want to do it even more. It may have been shock, she was unpre-
pared. Look, whenever she starts to feel again it will have to be
painful. We just got to watch. . . . What? Proprietors? Hmm. . . .
Okay. I'll talk to her about it when she comes."

*

Ice pelts at the glass. Then rain. Then hail—crows swirl up as the
small, white pebbles swirl down. Then rain again: wearing away
at the ice on the lake there are patterns now. Only a narrow
white band leads out from Adam's stone to a huge white continent, moving slowly towards the spillway. Water foams over
the wall; runs through transparent, delicate ice-islands, smaller
and smaller, then disappearing in, sunlight, finally, scattering
pebbles of joy near the wall where there's a flush of pussy willows
in bloom. . . .

I break some off: to bring this lilt of happiness back with me,
I run, all the way through the woods, my boots printing mud on
the rug, I toss the stalks of soft gray buds on the mound that is
maggie. I shout,

"It's spring!"

and she cringes, and mumbles, "ohpleaseno"

But she's off the dope. It's March 20, Saturday. Six days.

I tear down some weather-stripping; throw open the windows. I shake her, pull at her, no, she says, no, drag her, no, r-rebec, through the room, please, why, and push her, out the door. . . .

Orange crocuses line the steps as I lead her down to the lawn —it's brown, now: not quite decent, this moment between the seasons, disheveled, the winter's wreckage exposed. I sit down near my old sculpture, maggie huddled next to me: cowering from the wind, her spine curled, she shivers against a rock, dull, caught in the core of winter, still she cringes from spring as if from a blizzard; and that round bone of earth her only refuge.

I turn away from her, try to lose myself in the smell of earth; of witch hazel. Far off, I hear a trill; then a string of live beads in the sky, approaches: unraveling, raveling, closer, now, the sound harsher, one strand loose, they bend with every current, amid the clouds like seals, whales, oh, a rollicking sea-full of creatures up there, and, like those birds, I feel my restlessness—feel the equinox coming, *tomorrow*, *spring*, as I lead her back up the steps, and she crawls into bed, immediately; and I go to the phone, and dial,

"Hello? Oh, hi," Jesse said. "I been meaning to call you, Rebecca. Yeah, he liked them, wants to use two. Oh, and he's interested in your broken-window shots, too, I told him about, so. . . .No, he'll call you. Mackenzie, his name is, Richard. Oh yeah? Yeah, small world. Well, I'll tell you. Grace has gone off medication, she's okay, but, well, she's not sleeping, and soon I think she'll start having dreams awake, mostly nightmares. No, she thinks it won't happen this time, but it's happened enough times before that I. . . .No, this week is okay, but try to make other plans after that. Oh, no. I wouldn't want them together alone now, and, well, I might have my hands full. No, this week she's fine, like you've seen her. It's just when she's been off the pills a while. . . .Well, I don't blame her. I mean, like, who wants to spend their whole blessed life on downs?"

I sat there a moment, not thinking: letting the sounds of

spring wash over me through the open windows; then, dialed again,

"Yeah-hello?" Ann said. "Sure, Rebecca. What? Well, I think she's doing very well. Oh, that was a ploy to get her through the fear of surfacing, also me gone, very clever of her, and you handled it fine. Well, of course it takes a while for the drug to wear off. You do? No, don't feel guilty. I understand. You got to take care of yourself. It might even help her get on her feet. Look, can you hang in there another couple of weeks? Maybe we'll find someone else who. . . .Sure. Sure. Okay, we'll get her ready, and then you can take off."

It's colder now. Dogs circle, tripping me as I walk down the drive, feeling numb, but, "Get away," I snarl. There is one envelope, postmarked Mill Valley, in the mailbox. I open it, by the road, find, a newspaper clipping, "GYPSY MOTH. . . ." Cairo nudges my hand, "Go away," and he veers off, comes back, "IN-VASION," nudging, "THREATENED," not even a signature, whimpering, "go aWAY,"

("*Hey, you got your period?*"

barking, now, up the steps, down the steps, up

("*He loves Adam, and, well*"

"*Okay, you're right. I'm scared off*"

"*Well, slug him*"

"*I don't WANT to*"

SNAP

a dull shock my knuckles his teeth bone bruised bone, inside, now, the broom jabbing red froth, dripping, jab, swinging, SNAP, and he rolls on his side and lifts one leg, exposing a soft, gray, quivering belly. . . .

Sossa huddles in a corner, shivering. Tonta is under the bed. A terrified girl-face watches from near the wall

(*Did that wake you up, finally?*

she is; or I, I am, moaning, am crawling away from this desire, for violence, so voluptuous, I can't

stand up

dare

touch. . .

329

(rrrringg

"Hello? Hello? Rebecca? Where are you? What? Rebecca? Are you still on the line?"

said Joel. . . .

"Thirty-six, hey? Three years ahead of me. It's nice to know you're up there and still alive, I tell you, Rebecca, you give me hope. Really. Have some more"

lemon chicken, or duck, but, with plenty of msg, because there's a band of pressure around my forehead and I think of electro-cution or -shock, as Joel holds me up we are dancing to country-western/rock—or, was that another year? another death, *no, it's birth,* day, this frenzy that drives me in spirals around a hot little box, *breathe, remember?* Something squeezes my chest. Tears are spurting, oh, no, not again: not now, that vision, torn necks on these sweating, churning bodies, their heads toppling, rags of blue veins, I thought I was through with

(but someone died, somebody

(thank you please thank you please

"Hey, are you okay? Rebecca?"

"What? Oh, sorry, yeah. Let's sit down a while."

"Sure. That stuff really hits you, doesn't it." He peered at me in the smoky light. "You look really peaked, babe. Why don't we just go home."

"Okay. I think some air. . . .It's also, you know, I am getting older, Joel, and maybe. . . ."

"Oh, God. Look, I bet if you get away from all that up there, you won't have any more trouble. Steady, now."

"Whew. Air feels good. It's just kind of shocking after"

"Let's get that cab." He whistled. "Look," he said, as we climbed in, "do you think you could work it to spend some more time away? Like, a week in the city? You could stay at my place. . . ."

"Not until maggie is steadier. She's just come off sedation, and she'll need someone. I've already asked Ann if. . .maybe. . . . Oh, hell, okay, you're right. I really have to get out."

"I know."

He linked his arm in mine, and I leaned back, watching the streets slide by, too quickly. I didn't want to lose this moment amid the traffic lights clicking, gray ghost-buildings, steaming manholes, at almost-dawn, a cindery smell takes me back to autumn: to Riker's, Washington Square, and the car in front of a red door. . . .

The cab stopped. Joel searched for his key. As I leaned on a trash can, sirens howled. In the narrow channel of sky above my head I could see two streams of thin cloud, V-shapes, moving across a field of dim stars, not rainbow-colored; not double. A sickle moon rose through the haze.

"Joel, look at the moon. It's orange."

He glanced up briefly. "Yeah, must be the poison we send up does it. There's nothing like moonrise over Sixth Street." He guided me past two men crumpled in the hall and into the elevator. "I see maggie's mother now and then," he said. "Said she never hears from maggie."

"No, maggie can't talk to her."

"Clara! Murdoch! Stop that, now, down, DOWN," as two furry missiles leaped at us. "Here, you sit down. I'll get you— some brandy?"

"Fine. How does she look? I mean, healthwise."

"Who, the old lady? Pretty good. She's a tough one."

"I guess so. Tougher than maggie." I looked out the window. Birds were circling above the chimneys, in grimy dawn light. Joel came back with two glasses. "Thanks. Oh, it's good to be here, Joel."

"Yeah, be it ever so smelly. . . . maggie is pretty tough, you know. Don't fool yourself. She's a strong girl."

"Maybe. I don't know."

"I do. What do you hear from Adam, by the way? Speaking of."

"Nothing. Not since he was here. He sent me a clipping about the gypsy moths. I guess it was him—there was no message, not even a name." I bent to take off my shoes. My head whirled. "Oh, God. What's the matter with me? I had one drink. . . ."

"Maybe you just need a rest," Joel said. He opened a closet door, pulled a clean, stained shirt from the pile of clothes that fell out. "Here, you can wear this if you want. Go on, take the bed. I'll be fine out here with Clara and Murdoch. I don't think you need this brandy, do you."

"No." I went into the bedroom, slipped out of my clothes and into the shirt, then sank onto the dirty, friendly sheets. "Joel?"

"Um?" His face came around the door. "Did you say something, babe?"

"Yes, I, uh...about coming down...."

"Just let me know. A little ahead, if you can—I'm seeing a girl pretty regularly, now, so"

"Oh. Are you sure it's okay, then?"

"I offered. Didn't I?"

"Well, I...I'll have to stay up there another two weeks or so, but then...then, I think...I'd like to."

23.

if we could throw a sop to the dog of time
we could sneak around him

*

*I'd almost reached shore when I heard her cough. She was far
back, about midway between the two points of a crescent of land
that reached into the lake: suspended, her eyes intent on the
water a couple of inches below her face. . . .*
     "Are you okay?"

*

    The path to the island is under water again; and I can tell
by the way the twigs have fallen that no one has been here for
very long, maybe not since I waded through deep snow and saw
the tree bowed into the shape of a girl shaking out long curls,
                   under water; now
it's as though I'd never been anything but alone, as though you
were never here, not even the day I heard you cough behind me
choking *I can't breathe* words spurting going down
                  I turn

in warm blue water and you catch my ankle, heavy,
heavier, wet clothes drag me down I thrash I panic
my chest bursting Cairo screams I push him I kick
him away kick you

Hell
is where no feeling is.

(*there were a clown and a witch*
now I take away

. . . . .
neither I nor you
were here to see April. You're sane again, and I am close to sane,
although I live immersed in soft gray fog-stuff. One moment a
thread of it fell away, and for that second, just before the fabric
knit itself, I caught a glimpse of the cold night, the colored
sparks of stars, leaping, electric, the fresh, stinging smell of
oh, an incredible universe; and reeled, as you reeled,
far out in the sun of this world, where flesh crumbles.
I didn't know,
Moth, as you lay there, that you could grow wings again. I
lost hope, pursued imaginary monsters, ghosts of stars, knots in
the lines I threw from my shore to your whirlpool, no: from my
whirlpool to yours.
How could I not know what would untangle them?

She still seems doped. She sleeps.

Restless, scattered, restless, here upstairs where I've moved
with my tea bags, hot plate, even a chamber pot—yes, I know
this is madness. A hand clamps my head, squeezing, in-side,
something is pressing so hard it might burst through my eyes,
out-side, then it's dark. I sit and make lists. I eat. I pace, dry-
mouthed, and mostly: avoid the animate—dogs cat maggie her
pocked skin the bubble the smell of her helplessness pricking my
rage, her need my desire become a shudder at presence so visibly

334

absent, she breathes; excretes; coughs; eats a little: so—vulnerable?

Cruelty. Greed. Those two modes of despair, once unleashed, so quickly become one another.

Still, I come down to feed her; to print or to go outdoors. The air has turned warm, now. A handsome young couple are moving in where the Woolfs used to live. A few stubborn suitors still lie on the deck, but, "Sure, let her run," the vet said. "The smell will linger a while, but it's safe."

"Sossa? Sossa?" She hesitates on her landing, then clatters down to where Cairo waits, madly excited, he rushes to sniff her hindquarters, and she...sits. She sits when a suitor gets close, in the drive, on the lawn, where I bring maggie everyday these last weeks of March I force her, in spite of, constantly,

"r-r-rebecca? could we go back...?"

"No."

I close my eyes; try to stretch my five feet six inches in an arc with the curve of the earth. Sunlight beats on my lids, a moving mosaic of, bones intertwined with just enough space to show their separateness. White. No blood. No life to connect them, just, bones. I probe my own rib cage, down to the place where all the soft organs are, for just a moment, before I take her back in, then, feeling a lethargy almost like illness, I push myself back out. . . .

Tonta ambles by me, her belly bulging: pregnant, no doubt, by The Gypsy. Redwings chirp and whirr. Flies buzz, and wasps, adding still more texture to the orchestra constantly tuning up, now, the whole wet creaturely world is whistling, whinnying, dripping, even the trees moo and meow this morning; and on the lake that band of ice near the stone is dissolving, the crystalline ice-shapes more intricate, perfect, just for a moment, then continents melt to water. . . .

A still, blue eye steams vapor into the air, in New Mexico: hot springs I've bathed in all winter, but now a finger of cold rakes my chest. The rocks have faces: a delicate green cast over them, rough, as I climb, and a fragrance. Someone screams near the bank, no? Oh? There's a free, loose feel to my muscles, as I walk away from the sound, climb a barbed-wire fence and follow a gully, noting stray bones, hoof prints, scattered small green mounds.

Am I the only one here? Will I always be the only one here with the sage, rocks, purple cactus, the mountains, and cow turds?

I call Sossa; call and call, but she doesn't come. I'm far from the cliff now, far from the bank, far from people. A hawk circles over my head, its fin cutting the air like a shark's. The wind blows, waves of pain brushing my face and dark clouds puffing like smoke from some celestial fire, they open and close blue eyes of warmth, like the springs, but, it's too cold to bathe now: the river will hold them till summer.

A tinkling sound: Sossa leaps by in pursuit of a lamb. I shout, she disappears, then shoots back in view with two sheep in front of her. She chases everything—goats, cows, rabbits—and kills the smaller ones; munches their torsos, legs, innards, skulls. . . .

In spring they emerge, the dead animals. Hoop of a rib cage. Jaw like a paw. Spine split in two near my house now the cow's carcass I saw last fall has emerged from under its snow blanket: hide still attached to the neck and forelegs. A dog lies, intact, by the creek, full-lilting with melted snow, they come, out of their coffins of ice, now, out of its frozen dance, time emerges in all its varied, magnificent color.

I squat down close to the bank; I click my shutter: *click*, water moving quickly, *click*, trees, faces, rocks in the purple eye of the lens, *click*, bones and giant cranes in this semidesert where I have come to understand moisture, *click*: even the gaping holes in a skull or a pelvis, in the pasture it's easy to choose a perspective: to join the carcass out on its island of sage and dry mud, angle in on it, circle it, under a cloud like that mouth in maggie's painting, but flaming orange, *here*, I carry a .38 loaded for men, not dogs, but *there*—

I wanted a zoom lens.

Pollen clouds the air; and a green smell. March billows, almost bursts with the roar of new waters. Lichen here, too, cast their delicate patterns on rocks across from the cove where I lie now staring over the lake at water rushing over the spillway, and suddenly see a dark spot: stark on white, ribs, slowly coming to focus, then, wedged on the ice, on its back, its throat gashed open—there's a dead deer.

Swallows dive, and sparrows, in pulsating predawn blue. After last night's rain, there's a reddish glow in the woods, as I walk away from that deer's carcass, everything is budding. Coiled fiddleheads huddle, a circle of little green men, or dragons. The gold-red freckled skin of a young tree makes my mouth water. Tiny leaves pucker, furred and flecked with dew, so fresh I can hardly believe this morning's clarity; sweetness; a texture as tender as a man's genitals nestled lightly against my thigh, just beginning to quiver, between my legs, I feel softness, throbbing; rippling; unfolding in waves, sex, everywhere; everywhere.

*

march 29
and so i am back with you. i think. after a long hard night
which i am still passing through, not sure of the source
of light at the other end if there is one, the drawings i
stopped, why? lost faith in everything except sleep—
that's one thing you can be sure of. symbolic suicide.
stopped smoking.

*

Trapped on the continent of ice, the deer moved as the thaw moved: towards the spillway. Its gutted bulge of ribs gaped at the sky. The wind clattered, slammed doors, all that spring, as I drove back and forth from the city and pulled down plastic and carried out deck chairs and burned the doghouse plank by plank, in a torrent of air, the deer crumbled; falling away in hunks, prey to claws, knives, weather. Only a patchwork of fur and bone remained by late April, when I started staying home—the fur still clinging to haunches spread wide, the throat and ribs bare, a spearhead it seemed, on its wedge of ice as it hurtled over the wall in a rush of white water.

I found one foreleg near the cove, the following week; red pods splitting open to leaflets, Tonta gave birth to one kitten in May, then a hoof and a piece of hide as lilacs bloomed the trees' skeletons disappearing behind a wall of green surrounding the deck and screening the windows, in June there were just a few splinters of bone; a few tufts of fur on the path near the boat house where

    maggie...

stumbled: the first time she came back here after that Sunday, her third night alone, when Susan drove up to get her and most of her things and called animal shelters, one after the other, until a man said, no, they didn't kill, and yes, he would open his door long enough to take

    "Cairo? You gave him away?"
    "I had to...."

She squats, her back braced against a log: naked, wet hair glistening, near the water stained pink where we swam just now —very close to shore. It is June 21, and late as the sun slides down behind that torso of hills. Specks of strawberry glint beneath the maidenly birch, last year's egg cases rotting to dust in her hollows. Smoke. Stars in the water....

    "I couldn't be here alone," she said, "so I couldn't be here. And he couldn't stay at Susan's. I called and called you"
    "I should have been keeping in touch. But"
    "Yes. I understand."
    I stood up, abruptly. *"Do you?"*

"Ye-e-es. . . ."

                  (yes, Rebecca. It must have been
August; or January; or June night after swimming, the water
turning slate blue as we walk, around, past the boathouse, the
spillway, and down through the woods where worms dangle,
against, past the devil-god, then as we cross the creek the scent of
roses is sudden, overwhelming,

               swwwingg

                   (push me back. . . .
     She has to come out now. Jake is waiting
        Your mother did that
        You're infecting me

                 What?

     becky open the

                    maggie

   becky, *becky is*

            running
            running
the trees gaping slope turning black, cinders flaking, under
her feet on the drive, up the steps, then a house with glass doors,

"You took down the snout," maggie said, "and the little
mirror."

"Yes. But not the sign."

"So I see." She rummaged in the refrigerator. "You know, I'm
hungry again? I think I've gained twenty pounds. My teacher
said something about it the other night. . . ."

"That's absurd. You look wonderful."

"Not for mime. He said, 'You know, we don't need chubbies
here,' and then cracked up. Do you think I'm crazy, Rebecca? I
mean, starting this at my age?"

"Your age? Twenty-six?"

"Well, that's old for body stuff. But I can't paint—I'm afraid
to. Especially now I'll be living alone for the first time since"

"Oh, I think it's fine." I hoisted one of the cartons full of her
things we had packed that morning to move her into her new

apartment, on the Upper West Side, "No, sit. Eat your sandwich. I'm just working off nervous energy."

"But you're right. We should take off soon. I'll get the other"

"Take your time, it's not that late." I braced the box on the table, as she got the door for me. "What happened to that lump on your throat, by the way?"

"It's gone. It really was benign," she said, and followed me out. "And now it's just five years this month since my thyroid operation."

"So you're in the clear."

"Yes, well. . . as clear as you get."

"That's pretty clear, isn't it?" I called from halfway down the steps; and her voices drifted after me,

"No. I don't. . . think so. . . ."

(*ticktockticktock*

nine P.M., eastern, standard, *time*,

ARE YOU AFRAID?

BUT I TOLD YOU. WE AREN'T COMING INTO
YES I KNOW. I KNOW WE AREN'T COMING INTO
DARKNESS,

BUT WHAT I *WANT* TO KNOW IS: ARE . YOU .
AFRAID?

Poppa? *Poppa?*

Cracked green walls heave. Roaches scuttle. The Mickey Mouse clock is laughing, ticktock, pinwheels spinning and moths are circling a bulb blinking off and on, the bubble of foam dribbling, thick liquid oozing out of, his, sphincter won't work; throat and stomach won't, nothing, no part of him works and his skin torn by, only a touch, Poppa, touch is too rough, but his breath is sweet like a flower; spaced out in rhythmic gasps, pumping, air, in-to, out-of, the lungs almost gone, mouth puckering now his iron-claw grip on life is relaxing; releasing

"What happened that day?" Rebecca said, coming back up. "You never told me. You said you wanted to stay alone, so"

340

"I must have thought I could. You know, I can't remember much, Rebecca. I think I must have spent most of that time in bed."

"But what happened to make you call Susan?"

"Did I call Susan?"

"Didn't you? I thought...or did she call you?"

"I, i...suppose. All I remember is putting Cairo in the shelter, that's very clear. It was horrible, like a jail, bars.... Susan must have persuaded me. And a few days later I called and the man there yelled at me. Is that possible? Would he...? He said Cairo hadn't eaten since he'd been there...."

"Do you remember you came to Joel's right after?"

"No. Just about Cairo, nothing else. Maybe Ann set it all up."

"But I was in touch with Ann. She would have...listen, I need to"

(dial, 212, dial, 0,

"No, I can't remember," Ann said. "I know we discussed it in the office....Well, maybe we talked about it after the fact. Susan? I may have, I'm not sure...."

(and dial again,

"No, I don't remember," Susan said, "exactly. maggie called and said she'd like to stay with me, and I was pleased, but I.... No, she was calm, much calmer than before. Well, I must have had some notice, because I was thinking about it at work, I remember that, but what day....No, I would have managed with Cairo. She didn't have to give him up. That must have been her idea...."

(and again,

"What?" Joel said. "Well, I just remember when she called. No, she'd already been in the city a day or two. But you—you looked like you might disappear right into the phone. It made me shudder...."

(*ticktock*

"*Why doesn't anybody remember?*"

"It's strange, isn't it," maggie said. "I must have talked to

Ann before I talked to Susan, that's why I was calm. But I don't think I. . . maybe I called Ann and she called Susan and"

"Aren't we going to find out?"

(what happened? tell me what happened.

"I don't see how. It's awful, almost as though I wasn't really. . . here. . . ."

(no. let me go

ten, eleven

rrrinnggg

"emergency"

rrrringgg

"supervisor"

buzzz

twelve, ONE. . . .

leaning close to him; and he whispered,

"I forgive you."

There are snails in the garden. A fly is dragging its shadow up the wall. Pollen lies on a hollyhock leaf below the redwoods, apples blossom on a bone-littered mesa, and, near a reservoir, curves of flesh slowly swell,

click

"Hello?"

"r-rebecca? where have you. . .*been?"*

"Jesus," Joel said, "you looked like you might disappear right into the"

(ladybugladybugladybug

Something is pulling down at the corners of my mouth. Some thing is clamping my forehead, I'm moving, bewildered, an urge to laugh but a wave slides me downward; tightens; releases a roaring, red light raining seed, raining feather, mud, almost a joy but the membranes are bursting, slow down; can't stop, STOP, the wind spasms eating away at the edge, push, a pressure of blood smashes walls and wings crash out of silk strands, slap of

cold, light, and vibrating-still: on this stem, this shell, this ocean
wave or, white walls and my mouth puckered, sucking the air,
in, out, I wail,
    touch

. . . .
throw once, twice, thrice
(and mount to heaven as though on six dragons)

the clouds pass, and the rain does its work
and all individual beings flow into their forms

:

D
I
V
I
S
I
O
N

24.

june 17

first day alone. feel a bit of panic.
morning. i just had breakfast.